THE THINGS YOU FIND IN ROCKPOOLS

GREGG DUNNETT

Pole Hill Press

For my Family

A SHORT NOTE FROM THE AUTHOR

This book is set on the fictional Lornea Island located somewhere off the east coast of the United States of America. It doesn't actually exist, but a rough map follows this note.

As the story is set in America and the characters are American, the story is written in American English.

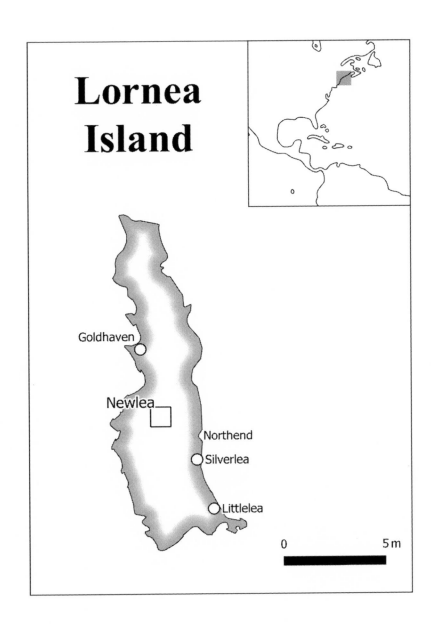

Lornea
Island

Goldhaven

Newlea

Northend

Silverlea

Littlelea

0   5 m

THE THINGS YOU FIND IN ROCKPOOLS

1

I see the body from my bedroom window. It's lying halfway up the beach, stranded there by the overnight tide. There's nothing else breaking the sweep of pale, silvery sand, and there's no mistaking *what* it is, even from this distance. It's funny, I've always known I would find something like this one day, living here. You see it all the time on the TV news, bodies wash up just like this. And now I've found one.

I grab my binoculars. They're big ones, they magnify ten times and it's hard to hold them steady. So, even though I press them up hard against the windowpane, all I really see is jerky snatches of skin, a ghostly white patch of belly, and a bright red color where a wound cuts into her back. Definitely a 'her'. I can see that. A female, young, lying dead in a puddle of blood and seawater in the middle of the beach. My beach.

I'm suddenly conscious of my breaths, visible as little clouds in the coldness of my bedroom. Could I be imagining this? Maybe I'm asleep and this is a dream? But the rest of the room looks real. My closet's open, I see my school uniform hanging inside. The posters on my wall look right, the periodic table, my 'Fishes of the Sea' chart with all the Latin names. I look closely at this, they wouldn't be right if I was dreaming because they're hard to remember. I look at the Striped Bass - *Moronesax-atilis*. I can't be dreaming.

I take another ten-times-magnified look. This time I notice the gulls. Some are wheeling above the body, others are standing on it, like it's a new rock that's appeared overnight. Then I see they're not just standing, they're bending over, pecking. Tearing at bits of flesh. I see one wiggling its beak right down in the eye. I drop the binoculars and think.

I should tell Dad. I know I should. But something makes me hesitate. Dad's been weird recently. He gets mad about nothing at all. And with something like this, there's going to be police and journalists, and Dad hates those people. If I tell him he might insist we have nothing to do with it. He might even say we're not going out this morning, and then I wouldn't get a chance to examine it. And how often do I get a chance like this? For someone like me this is an amazing opportunity. I mean it's sad too of course, but there's no point being too sentimental about these things. Mostly it's an amazing opportunity.

So I feel a bit bad about it, but right away I know I'm not gonna tell Dad.

I'm Billy, by the way. I'm eleven-years-old, but I'm a bit more interesting than most eleven-year-olds. Or at least, I am judging by the others that go to my school. I'm pretty sure you'd agree if you met them.

Luckily though, it's Saturday today, so there isn't any school. We have a pretty set routine for the weekends. First thing, Dad always goes surfing. He goes early in the morning because it gets busier later and he doesn't like going with other people. I always go with him, but I never actually surf. That would mean going in the water, and I don't go in the water. I don't just sit in the truck waiting for him, though. That would be boring. I've always got lots of projects going on. Like my treehouse project, for instance. I built it last year, from stuff Dad had left over from work. It's in the woods behind the dunes, although you'll never find it because I painted the walls in a camouflage pattern. It took ages too. I found out you can't actually buy camouflage paint, which makes sense when you think about it - all the separate colors would get mixed up in the can. But anyway that was last year's project. I've got other projects now. Better ones.

But obviously today I'm not thinking about my projects at all. Today there's a body on the beach. I decide to get Dad up and out of the house as fast as I can. That way I can be the first to the body. I can be the one who discovers it.

Dad usually gets up after me. He comes downstairs and makes himself a coffee. If it's not raining or too windy he always drinks it outside. He stands in our little yard on the clifftop and looks out over the beach to decide where he's going to surf that day. If there's a big swell, we go to our end of the beach, near the cliff, because the waves there are smaller and less powerful. But if there isn't much swell, we go to Silverlea, the town in the middle of the bay. It's more open to the ocean there. Obviously, if there are no waves at all, or if the wind is too strong, then we don't go surfing at all. But that's generally bad news because it means he'll be moody the whole day.

It's just me and Dad who live in our house. I don't have any brothers or sisters. Or a mom, not anymore. And Dad won't let me have pets, not after what happened with the seagull chicks. So it's just us. And we've lived here, perched up in our clifftop cottage, for just about as long as I can remember.

But this morning I make the coffee. And I make it in a really noisy way to wake Dad up, banging the cupboards shut, rattling through the cutlery to get a spoon. I need him to hurry if I'm going to be the one to discover the body, you see.

We have one of those silver stove-top coffee makers that screw together with the coffee in the middle. I'm not sure how much to put in, but I know Dad likes it strong, so I fill it right up. It doesn't take long before it's hissing and frothing away, and the room smells thick with coffee. I get a cup for Dad and bang the cupboard door shut again. Then I hear Dad going to the bathroom upstairs, the long trickle he always does. When it finally dies out I shout upstairs.

"Coffee Dad."

Then I go outside for another look. It's still lying there, no one else has discovered it. But I realize there's another problem. It's the waves. This morning they're small. That means Dad will want to drive to Silverlea where the waves are bigger. Normally this wouldn't bother me, because my projects are kind of spread out so it doesn't matter where Dad wants to go. But the body is here, at *our* end of the beach. If we go to Silverlea I'll have to walk all the way back, and there's a danger someone else will discover it while that's happening. I don't want that. I want to be the one that discovers it.

So when Dad comes outside to join me, coffee in one hand, I'm already thinking of a way to solve the problem. I look at him cautiously. He got in late last night and I think he was drinking too because he looks a bit rough.

"What's with all the noise this morning Billy?" Dad rubs his eyes. "I thought you were being murdered or something." He laughs and takes a sip.

"Jesus Christ. This is rocket fuel," Dad says, and I frown because I'm not sure if that's good or bad.

Dad puts the cup on the front wall. Then he yawns and stretches his arms over his head. He's only wearing a T-shirt and jeans, which pull apart so I can see all the muscles of his stomach. He's still brown from the summer, even this late in the year. He isn't wearing any shoes either, though the grass is wet from dew. Dad doesn't really notice the cold.

We stand in silence for a moment. Looking out at the view. Just in front of our wall is the old cliff path. It was closed a while ago because it got too dangerous, but I still know a way down. Beyond the path, there's just a big drop to the beach, all seven miles of it, stretching past the town of Silverlea, right up to Northend. To the right you can see the woods. To the left it's just ocean all the way. It's a pretty amazing view from our yard, really.

"Looks OK, huh?" Dad says, picking up his coffee again.

He means the waves look OK. You can see everything from up here, but Dad only notices the waves. That's why I think my plan will work. I wait a few moments before speaking; I let him watch what's happening below us. Watch the waves roll in.

The waves you see when you go to the beach aren't always the exact same size. They come in groups, or sets. So one minute, it might look like the waves are really big, but then, a few minutes later, they might be much smaller. Right now, while I'm letting Dad watch, it's pretty big. Actually I'm lucky, it's probably the biggest set of waves I've seen the whole morning. Perfect for my plan.

"It looks pretty big," I say as casually as I can. "It looks small at the moment, but it looked real big just before you came out. I reckon Littlelea."

If Dad had watched for as long as I had, it would be obvious I'm lying. It's obvious it's going to be better for surfing further along the beach at Silverlea, where it's less sheltered. But Littlelea is where the body is, so I need him to decide to surf there this morning. And to do that, I just have to convince him the waves are bigger than they really are.

Dad doesn't reply right away. We stand there together, looking out over the ocean. The body is visible enough if only he were looking for it, but he's not looking at the beach. His eyes are scanning the horizon, watching where the approaching swells begin to steepen into real waves. He waits, sipping at his coffee. And he's patient. As the minutes pass, the waves that had been unloading pass through, and it goes nearly flat. I do my best to look surprised.

"Looks a little small to me," Dad says finally, a funny note to his voice. "You feeling alright this morning Billy?" He turns to me, and for a moment, I'm worried he's going to get into one of his weird moods. But he's kinda smiling.

"Come on, we'll go into town. We can get breakfast after."

Town is what we call Silverlea. So we're going to drive two miles north, past the body, and then I'll have to run all the way back here to Littlelea to get to it. Obviously I'm disappointed. But getting breakfast afterwards is a consolation, because of where we get it. And I'll never change his mind now, so I might as well make the best of it.

Dad drains his coffee, winces and gives me a look.

"Leaving in five," he says then walks inside to get dressed properly. I follow, and in the kitchen I hurriedly shut down my computer. I grab my binoculars, a new notepad and my camera, and stuff it into my backpack. Dad walks past me as I'm putting my walking shoes on and he tells me to hurry up. As I step outside Dad swings his wetsuit into the open back of his pickup truck. It lands with a wet *thwack* on the ribbed metal base. His board's already in there; it pretty much stays there the whole time. I hesitate. When he's in a good mood he lets me ride in the back, even though it's technically illegal. But when he's mad I have to ride up front. I take a risk and climb in the back with the board, not making eye contact. He doesn't say anything at first, just pulls open the door to the cab, then before he gets in he says: "You see any police you keep your head down, OK?"

THEN HE GETS IN, and moments later, the engine roars to life and the truck judders. The smell of un-burnt gas fills the air. We bump down our lane to the main road, then Dad starts off down the hill, driving fast, using the whole road to smooth out the corners.

You can't see much of the beach from the road, just glimpses through the trees. Then once you cross the river you're quite low and the dunes block it out. But it's only a ten-minute drive and we don't see any other cars. I take that as a good sign.

We come into town the back way, crunching to a halt at the front of the parking lot by the beach. The Sunrise Café is right here, that's where we'll have breakfast, but it isn't open yet.

Even so, we're not the first car here. There are four other vehicles; I recognize two of them as Dad's surfer friends. I guess the others are probably people walking their dogs. I hope they've walked north, up toward Northend and not south down to Littelea, toward where the body is. You probably can't see the body from here, so I'm hopeful, but I won't know until I get down on the beach.

"Be back here at ten," Dad says. Years ago, he used to try and make me come surfing with him. But not anymore. He understands that I don't go in the water now.

"Sure," I say. "I'll see you later." I leave him as he sits on the flatbed of the truck to pull on his wetsuit. He doesn't bother to cover himself with a towel when no one's around.

I walk fast down the little path to the beach. It's easy at first because there's a wooden boardwalk, but then it runs out, and my feet sink into the soft sand. Then finally, I get to the stones. There's a strip of them, big flat stones the size of dinner plates. When I get there, I stop and pull my binoculars out of my bag. Even before I've gotten them focused, I can see something's wrong.

There are people on the beach. Right by where the body is. This far away, I can't see who, or what they're doing, but it's obvious they're standing right by it.

I feel a flood of disappointment. It's the dog walkers. Why couldn't they walk the other way? *I* saw the body first, over an hour ago now, and I wanted to be the first to get there. Now I don't even know if I'll get to see it at all. I expect the Coast Guard will be there soon. Or the police. They're all over the town these days.

I STAND THERE FOR A WHILE, feeling the disappointment wash over me, but it doesn't last long. After all, whoever turns up, they can't exactly move the body, it's a bit big for that. I suppose they might try and cordon it off, but there's no sign of that either. At least not yet. If I get a move on, I might still be able to examine it. I just need to get there fast.

So I set off again, walking just below the high tide mark. That's the best place to walk because the sand there is always hard and flat. Plus, sometimes, you find things washed up from the tide, which is a bonus. But today I'm not looking down. I keep my eyes focused ahead, trying to make out details as I get closer. Then, when I'm about halfway there, I see a police car driving slowly down the beach toward where the body lies. I puff my cheeks and sigh.

I know what you're thinking, it's not really normal for an eleven-year-old to want to examine a dead body washed up on the beach. But like I said, I'm not like most eleven-year-olds. I mean, probably, some of the kids at school would want to take a selfie with it or something stupid. But I don't want to do anything like that. I'm interested because I want to study it. Like a proper scientist.

If you know about Silverlea, if you've been on vacation here or something, you might wonder too at a police car turning up so fast, and so early in the morning. But that's just the way things are at the moment. This fall they're everywhere. It's all because of that girl. The one in the news. And if you consider it's not just on the local island news but the *real* news, next to stories about the President and earthquakes and stuff, you can imagine what it must be like here. The whole island is obsessed with it. How could a teenage girl just disappear like that *here*? It doesn't seem possible.

I met her, the girl who went missing: Olivia Curran. I might as well tell you now, since even walking fast it's going to take me a while to get there. She was staying in one of the cottages that Dad manages. She was here on vacation with her family, her mom and dad and her brother. They were staying in the Seafield Cottages. They're the expensive, beachfront ones, with views of the ocean from the bedrooms. Actually, they're just along from the lot where we parked this morning.

I wasn't supposed to meet her. I was just in the cottage next door when they arrived. I was fixing the Wi-Fi after the guests the week before had complained about it dropping out a lot. That's another thing I do, I configure the Wi-Fi for all the vacation cottages that Dad manages. Mr. Matthews, Dad's boss, he knows I'm really good with computers, so he lets me do it.

Anyway, I'd just finished fixing the problem as they were arriving. They had a Jeep or SUV or something and it was loaded up with bikes on the back and a roof box. I didn't talk to them, of course. All the Seafield cottages are self-catering, and when guests arrive, they get the door key from a metal box with a combination lock bolted to the wall. So I just ignored them like normal. But then I decided to get a snack from the cottage storeroom. There's a little stone shed in the yard of the cottages where we keep the spare linen and towels for the changeovers, and there's little packets of cookies, too, for the welcome packs we put in. So there I was, carrying my laptop in front of me, going out to the storeroom to get some cookies. That's when she must have seen me. Because when I came out, still with my laptop open, this girl came walking up to me from the cottage.

"Excuse me," she said, looking a little unsure. "Are you staying next door or something? We've just arrived and we can't get the Wi-Fi to work."

I didn't say anything. I couldn't, I had a cookie in my mouth.

"It's just I saw your computer. I wondered if you'd maybe figured it out." She had blond hair that was tied behind her head in a ponytail, but a few strands had escaped, and she had to brush them away from her eyes.

"Hey don't worry about it, forget I asked." She said and she started to turn away. I pulled the cookie from my mouth.

"I live here. I don't need to stay here. But I do configure the Wi-Fi for all the cottages that Mr. Matthews owns."

She turned back, she looked me up and down a bit dubiously. "Oh. OK. Well that's kinda handy I guess. Since, er, it doesn't *seem* to work." She trailed off and smiled. She had quite a pretty smile.

"It does work. I've just fixed it," I told her.

"Oh... Well, erm, I just tried and actually it kinda doesn't."

"Have you put the password in?" I asked her. Lots of tourists are quite stupid so we have to put instructions about everything in Welcome Folders - even things like how to work the electric stove. "It's in the Welcome Folder which is on the..."

"Yeah. I found that. It connects OK, but then it keeps dropping out."

I was annoyed at this because I'd had the same problem earlier, but I thought I'd fixed it.

"Have you changed any of the settings?" I asked, a bit hopeful.

"*No.* 'Course not." She gave me a funny look. "We've only just got here."

I frowned. If only I hadn't gone to get a cookie, she wouldn't have caught me. I thought about going into cottage two and trying to connect from there, but I thought the girl would probably try to come with me. And it would be quicker if I could connect to their router with a cable.

"I'll have to come in. I need to plug into the router. Is that alright?" Part of me hoped she'd say no, but she didn't. The girl - I didn't know her name was Olivia then - swung her arm out and around like she was doing theatre or something.

"Be my guest."

She did have a very pretty smile actually.

THE ROUTER in cottage number one is on the sideboard next to the kitchen table. I could see right away the LED was flashing orange, when it should have been glowing steady green. It's all open plan, in the Seaview cottages, and the girl's dad was there too. He was putting groceries away in the fridge.

"Hello there!" he said to me as I walked in, but I didn't have to say anything because the girl answered for me. "It's alright, he's just here to fix the Wi-Fi."

I put my laptop down on the table and poked in my bag for the network cable.

The dad put more stuff away, but I could tell he wanted to say something. Eventually, he did.

"You're very young to be fixing computers," he said. He had the kind of voice adults use when they're being patronizing to kids. I turned slightly away and didn't answer.

"You know, it doesn't matter if you can't get it working," he went on. "We'll be on the beach most of the time anyway, won't we, Livvie?"

"Duh. Yes, it does matter," the girl cut in. "It might not for you, but this place was advertised as having Wi-Fi. What if you got here and there wasn't a bathroom, but it was advertised as having a bathroom? You wouldn't like that, would you?"

"It's alright," I said. I didn't want to hear them arguing. "It does this sometimes, but if I reboot from the admin panel, it solves the problem." I sounded more confident than I was, though, because I wasn't sure why it kept breaking like that.

"Well, I'll be very impressed if you're right. And Olivia will be very grateful." He paused, and I hoped he might go away, but he kept on filling the fridge.

"So you're the *Silverlea computer expert*?" He said it like he was pretending it was a real job title or something. "You hear that Will?" He spoke louder, trying to attract the attention of a boy, about fourteen, who was at the other end of the living room, fiddling with the TV. The dad turned back to me. "We can hardly get William out of bed in the mornings, let alone working a responsible job!" The dad laughed and I took the opportunity to ignore him.

I GOT the admin panel up on my screen, and I could see I was right, one of the settings had got corrupted. It was an easy fix but I still didn't know why it kept happening. I fixed it and made a mental note to google the problem later. Then I rebooted the router. I wanted to leave right away, but I knew I should wait until it came back on, just to make sure it was working now.

"So, what is there for young people to do around here?" the dad asked me, still with his 'friendly' voice.

I don't like it when tourists ask me questions like this. Like I said, I'm a little different, so it's hard for me to know what they like doing. This one time, a tourist asked me, and I started telling them about my project counting the eggs of greater black-backed gulls on the cliffs. They looked at me like I was crazy. I tried to tell them they're the biggest gulls in the world, with a wingspan the size of an eagle's, but I could see from their face they just thought I was weird. So I wasn't ever going to tell Mr. Curran about my crab project. But I had a moment of inspiration. I thought about some of the posters I'd seen around town.

"There's the Surf Lifesaving Club Disco next Saturday," I said. "It's the end-of-summer one."

"Ah. The Surf Lifesaving *Club Disco*," he said, like that was just the sort of event he was expecting to happen in a small town. "You see, Livvie, I told you there would be things to do."

She rolled her eyes, but she turned to me too.

"Do you need to get tickets?" she asked, sounding surprisingly interested.

"I don't know." I knew *I* didn't have to, I'm a local. But I had no idea about tourists. I was saved from answering, though, because just then the router's green light came on.

"You can check it now," I said to the girl. She already had her phone in her hand. She'd had it there the whole time, like she couldn't wait to get it connected. And now, she poked at the screen for a few moments.

"Hey, it works," she said, not looking up. For a minute, she continued, typing something into the screen with her thumbs. Then she looked up suddenly.

"Here you go. Silverlea Surf Lifesaving Club End-of-Summer Disco. Tickets available in advance or at the door."

Then she looked at me with a proper big smile on her face. "That's pretty cool, thanks." She really *was* pretty when she smiled.

I told all this to the police, apart from her being pretty of course, I kept that to myself. Even so I was worried it might have got me in trouble. After all, if she hadn't gone to the disco that night, then she couldn't have disappeared *from* the disco. But the detective who took my statement didn't seem to think it was important. She said Olivia would probably have heard about it anyway, from all the posters up in town and everything. But then, she wasn't a very good detective. She can't have been, since she didn't notice when I lied to her.

But I guess that explains why I've felt kind of involved in the whole Olivia Curran thing somehow. Right from the very beginning.

I'm PRETTY CLOSE NOW to the group on the beach. It's grown just in the time it's taken me to walk here. There's now a police car *and* a Coast Guard truck parked up either side of the body. And this close, the wounds look pretty shocking: they go right through the skin, and you can see the layer of fat. I walk closer, to get a better look at the wounds. I want to see how she might have died.

"Hey Billy," a voice calls out, and someone steps in front of me, trying to cut me off.

2

"Hi Dan," I say, not enthusiastically because I don't much like Daniel Hodges. He works as a lifeguard. He knows Dad quite well because they go surfing together, but I don't think even he likes him much. The reason I don't like him is because he acts like he owns the beach, like now, where he's trying to stop me getting to the body.

"I'm not sure you should see this, Billy. It's pretty grim."

"Is it dead?" I ask, and I'm immediately annoyed at myself. It's totally obvious it's dead, but sometimes, things come out of my mouth that I didn't mean to say.

"Yeah, it's definitely dead, Billy." He says, smirking.

I try to peer around him, and I'm close enough now to hear the other conversations going on. A man I don't know is talking to the police officer.

"Do you know what species it is?" he asks. He sounds like a tourist. There aren't many here in the winter, but you still get some.

"We're not sure. We've got an expert from the mainland coming," the policeman replies. He's wearing his uniform. Police uniforms always look so strange in real life. Really impractical. "They might be able to tell us."

I interrupt at once, glad for a chance to step around Dan.

"It's a minke," I say.

The policeman starts saying something about waiting for the expert, but the tourist turns to me.

"How do you know?"

"You can tell by the distance between the dorsal fin and the blowhole, and how upright the dorsal fin is. It's a female. A young one too."

"Yeah, well," the policeman says. "Like I say, we'll see."

"Minke whales usually only occur in the northern hemisphere, but you do get dwarf minke whales in the Southern Ocean and around Antarctica. But this isn't a dwarf one because they have different markings, so this is a just normal one," I go on. I was fairly sure about my identification when I first saw it, and up close, there's no doubt at all.

Dan moves back now to let me look at the body more clearly. Just behind its head is a large open wound cutting into the flesh. It's dark red near the skin, but deeper in the color is brighter. It's sitting in a depression in the sand, filled up with a mixture of seawater and blood. It's pretty small for a whale, not much longer than the Coast Guard truck.

"What do you think happened to it?" the tourist asks. "Do you think it was a shark?" He sounds thrilled by this, in his mainland accent. That's how I know he's a tourist, his accent. Plus tourists are always going on about sharks.

I look closely at the wound. "No. We don't usually get sharks around here big enough to take on a whale, even a baby one. And it doesn't look like a bite mark, more like a propeller injury. Probably it got separated from its mother when it surfaced near a ship."

"You seem to know a lot about whales," the man tells me.

"I know a lot about all the animals on Lornea Island," I tell him. "I'm going to be a marine biologist when I'm older. I'm already doing experiments." I'm suddenly feeling confident, so I ask the policeman, "What time is the whale expert coming?"

I'm hoping I might be able to stay long enough to meet him or her. They might be interested in my hermit crab study. Unless they're just whale experts. Sometimes, you get scientists specializing in just one species, or one genus. Others are more general. So they might be interested, or they might not be. It just depends.

"The guy's coming on the ferry now. He should be here around lunchtime," the policeman tells me, and I check my watch. I have to be back at Dad's truck at ten. I can wait for a little while, but not that long.

3

I stay for as long as I can, and the policeman lets me take photographs of the whale, but then I have to go. I jog back, my bag thumping against my back. I'm looking to see if Dad is still in the water. He'll be annoyed if I'm late. But I should be OK. The waves are still good, so it's more likely that he'll be in longer than he said.

As it turns out, I get back to the truck just after him. He's got the door open and music playing into the parking lot, and he's drying his hair with a towel, his wetsuit peeled down off his chest. He's smiling and whistling, so I guess the surf worked for his mood.

"There's a dead whale on the beach," I say to him. "Down by Littlelea. It's a minke whale."

"Alright, Billy, how are you?" Dad says; he's being sarcastic, telling me I didn't say hello. "Have you had a nice time?"

"Hello, Dad," I reply, starting again. "Yes I have, thank you. There's a dead whale on the beach."

"So you say." His smile's gone already. "I wondered what was going on. I saw the police cars on the beach." He doesn't say anything else, but a look comes over his face. He doesn't like the police much. He never has.

"It's a female. A really young one too," I go on.

"You want to get some breakfast?" Dad asks, ignoring what I say. Dad's not that interested in wildlife. He goes to work, and he likes surfing, and that's pretty much it. But I don't mind too much. If he hadn't said anything, I was going to remind him about going to the café. I'm almost always hungry, and even if I'm not, I always want to go to the Sunrise Café.

The café is open now. It's actually the upstairs part of the Surf Life-saving Club, and from up there, you get a really good view of the ocean. When Dad's changed, we climb up the wooden steps and sit by the window where we always sit. There are photos on the walls of people surfing on days when the waves are really big. Dad's in a couple of them, although you can hardly see who it is because his body's so small against the wave. The photos are all for sale, so that sometimes, tourists buy a photo of Dad and put it on their walls at home, like he's a famous person. You'd think he wouldn't like that, but he doesn't seem to mind. I don't notice them today, though. I get my camera out of my bag, ready to show off my whale photos.

"Hey guys, what can I get you?" I stop what I'm doing when I hear Emily's voice. She comes over to us with her little notepad and pencil. She smiles at me, and I can smell her perfume. Like warm flowers. Emily works at the Sunrise Café, but she's not just a waitress. She's only there to earn money while she does her doctorate. She's studying marine biology. She's a real scientist. I like Emily. I like her a lot.

"You can get me a full breakfast," Dad says, rubbing his stomach. "And coffee."

"Good surf this morning, Mr. Wheatley?" She smiles at him, but not for long; she's only being polite. Then she turns to me.

"And Billy. You having your usual?" That's a white roll with two sausages in it and lots of ketchup.

"Yes, please, Emily."

"And *coffee*?" she asks. She doesn't wink, but she gives me a secret look. I once asked for a coffee, I kind of wanted to impress her, and then I didn't like it. She realized and went and got me a hot chocolate instead. So now she always says it like this.

"Yes please. Have you seen the whale? It's a minke, a baby one."

"I've heard about it," she says. "Haven't had a chance to see it yet, though."

"I've got some photos. They're sending a whale expert from the mainland. He's going to be here this afternoon. Maybe Dad could drive us all down later on? Once Emily finishes her shift?" I look at Dad hopefully. It's a long shot, but you might as well try when he's in a good mood.

"Sorry, Billy. I've got to work. Window frames to paint."

Sometimes, I don't get adults. What's the rush? It's almost winter. There aren't any bookings for that cottage until next year. Surely he could paint when there isn't a whale expert in town?

Emily senses my disappointment and tries to make it easier. "I've got a few things to do here too, I'm afraid." She glances at Dad, like she's trying to communicate something.

"Dan'll be there, though, Mr. Wheatley. If you wanted someone to keep an eye on Billy, I mean?" Her face is bright and open. Optimistic.

You remember Dan Hodges, the lifeguard? Well, there was something I didn't tell you about him. He's sort of dating Emily. I guess that might be a little bit why I don't like him much. It's not serious, though. She's only with him because there's no one better around here. I'm sure when she's finished studying, she'll marry a famous scientist, not some stupid lifeguard. Maybe she'll even marry me when I'm a famous scientist. We can do research together.

Dad thinks for a moment. "OK. You can go down there if you like, Billy. See this whale guy, and then run on home from there?"

I'm disappointed that Emily can't go with me, but not that surprised. And I'm not too unhappy since it's a lot better than helping Dad to paint. He makes me do the sanding bit, which isn't as fun as painting.

"Just don't get cut off by the tide will you? You know when high water is?"

"I can look it up if you want," Emily says, pulling out her cellphone. She's got an app that tells her the tide times. I don't need an app. I've lived by the beach so long I've got a sense for the tides.

I turn back to Emily, who's smiling because she likes helping me out.

"It's alright." I say. "I've got some photographs of the whale. Do you want to see them?"

"Sure. But hold on. I'll get your order first."

Me and Dad both watch her walk back to the kitchen. She's wearing black pants and you can see the outline of her butt. When I turn to Dad, he's still watching.

"THERE WAS a tourist there who thought it might have been killed by a shark," I say when she comes back with the drinks. "But I told him we don't get that type of shark here. I reckon it was hit by a ship or something."

Emily laughs at the idea of it being a shark. Clear, fresh notes that ring around the room, and make people turn towards us. That's what I really like about Emily. She knows the sharks we get here are too small to attack a whale. She knows almost everything about the wildlife of Lornea Island, even though she's not a proper local. Emily's like me and Dad – she lives here now, but she wasn't born here. She used to come for vacations and stay with her grandma, until she died, and now Emily lives here all the time. Maybe that's another reason I like her. We're both not proper locals, but we know more than they do about the important things.

"It could be the sonar from the submarines that confused it. I read about that," I say. "How it makes them muddled up. Then it could have surfaced too close to a ship and got hit by the propeller."

She thinks about this for a moment.

"Yeah, it could be," she says. "Maybe they don't need that whale expert after all. You've got it pretty figured out."

I'm a little bit proud at this. Then the kitchen guy calls her name because our food is ready.

Dad's not watching this time as she walks away. Instead, he reaches for a newspaper that someone's left on the table. It's the *Island Times*. I once saw they printed a photograph of a dead dolphin that washed up at Northend. The woman who found it was in the shot too. That's why I wanted to be the one to find the whale, because I could have gotten in the paper. Although, thinking about it, the *Island Times* has gone a little crazy recently over the whole Olivia Curran thing, so maybe they won't bother putting in a picture this time. The headline in this week's paper is about Olivia again. It reads:

Olivia - Three Months and Still No Sign

I don't think that's a very good headline, since it sort of tells you they don't have anything new to say. They might as well say, "No news today!" But that's the kind of thing they've been printing every week. *Olivia -*

could she still be on the island? Olivia Case: Police believe she drowned. Olivia mystery: Police search continues. Dad opens the paper and quickly skims the first three pages, which is all Olivia stuff. I flick through my photos on the back of my camera. Zooming in and out. Then Emily comes back, this time with our food.

"Here you go." She puts Dad's down and then mine. There's tons of ketchup in there, and the butter is spread thick and melting where the sausages are touching it. She sees Dad has the paper open.

"Anything new?" she asks.

He looks up at her, surprised, then shakes his head. "No. I don't know why the police don't just accept she drowned." Dad always says this. He thinks Olivia Curran decided to go swimming that night and got into trouble.

"I guess her parents are still hoping she'll turn up alive," Emily says. "It must be awful for them, not knowing. I just wish someone would find out what happened to her."

You get a lot of this kind of conversation around here these days. It's like people have gotten kind of obsessed with the Olivia Curran case. I don't really know why. It's not the first time a tourist has drowned. Everyone knows the water's dangerous, that's why there's a surf life-saving club here. But when people drown normally, you get the body washed up a day or so later, and that didn't happen with Olivia, so no one knows for sure.

People don't normally talk about Olivia Curran to *me*, though. It's like a conversation that only adults are allowed to have. When they turn to me, they pretend it hasn't happened. Whatever it was that did happen. I know why: it's because everyone *really* thinks she got abducted and murdered. Or maybe she's not even dead yet, and she's being kept in a cellar somewhere, and raped every night. But Emily's different. She treats me like an adult. So I'm not that surprised when she turns to me and says, "Maybe you should turn your investigative powers to the Olivia Curran case, Billy? After all, you've solved the mystery of the dead whale in about five minutes." She smiles, to make clear she's kind of joking.

Dad reaches for the ketchup and gives her a look. Like he doesn't think this a very good idea.

"Don't get him started. He's got enough on counting his eagle eggs." He tries to roll his eyes at her, but she looks away and smiles at me. She knows about the great black-backed gulls; I told her all about them. I told Dad, too, but he still gets it wrong.

She leaves us with our food because she has to serve other people. I take a big bite of sausage and bun, so that the grease drips onto my plate. I know it's only a throwaway remark that she's made, but already I'm starting to think about it. Maybe I *should* turn my investigative powers onto the Olivia Curran case. The thought of it has kind of floored me. After all, look at the paper. The police don't seem to be getting anywhere, and I know from personal experience how incompetent they are. Maybe I can be the one to solve the mystery? I think about what the *Island Times* headline would say: *Local boy solves Olivia mystery!*

That would be even better than getting my picture in the paper with a dead whale.

And after all. No one knows this beach like I do.

4

After breakfast, Dad goes off to do his painting, and I run back down the beach to the whale. By now, the tide is much higher, almost up to where the little group is standing, still surrounding the carcass. As I get close, I can see a second police car is there now. I hope it's brought the whale expert.

But when I get there, I'm disappointed. It's not the expert. It's Mr. Matthews. He's Dad's boss; he owns all the cottages that Dad runs, plus the big hotel on the other side of town. I don't like him much, but Dad always defends him. I reckon he makes a fortune even though Dad does all the work. He drives a really big car; you usually see it parked at the golf club. It's not here today. I guess he didn't want to drive it on the beach and get it sandy.

Mr. Matthews is talking with another policeman. He's older than the first one, and suddenly I realize I recognize him. Whenever there's a statement about Olivia Curran on TV he's always there. I think he's pretty important. I know it's him because he's got a funny mustache that only covers the lower part of his top lip, like there's a caterpillar resting there. And because he's black, and there's hardly any black people on the whole island. He's stroking his mustache now, as he talks to Mr. Matthews.

Another policeman joins them. It's the one I talked to earlier. He starts telling them that he thinks it's a minke whale, and how it was probably killed by a ship's propeller. Then Mr. Matthews pulls the senior police officer over to one side, which is where I'm standing. Mr. Matthews gives me a sort of smile of recognition because he knows I do the Wi-Fi stuff, but he doesn't say anything to me.

"Larry," he says to the police chief. "We're already getting a lot of negative coverage with all that's happening over this girl. I don't want to add to that with a..." He glances over at the whale. "With a *corpse* rotting on the beach." He says this last bit really quietly, but I've got good hearing. The important policeman is still stroking his mustache, like he's considering what Mr. Matthews is saying.

"I understand, Jim. Really, I do. We've got someone from the university coming on the ferry now. As soon as they're done, we'll see to getting it moved."

Mr. Matthews sighs and looks around the beach. There are about ten tourists hanging around the whale now, watching what's going on. Some of them are taking photos. And there's another five or six people walking down the beach from the town.

"I'm not sure you do Larry. Look, the tide'll be covering it in a half hour, anyway. How about I arrange for a boat? We can tow it out, get rid of it quickly and cleanly. Before the press get here. The town doesn't need pictures full of blood."

Again, I can hear all this, but I can't believe it. I want to interrupt and tell them the expert will want to do tests, to perform an autopsy. But I know I can't interrupt Mr. Matthews and the important police man. Dad could lose his job. I could get arrested.

"Come on, Larry. The goddamn tide's gonna wash it down in front of the town if we don't. It's going to look even worse. You can say it's a public health hazard. No one's gonna argue with you."

THE POLICEMAN STANDS THERE for a moment. He's still stroking his mustache.

"You can get a boat here in time?"

"Sure."

The policeman makes a decision.

"OK. If you can get it moved, then do it. It'll be easier to tow out from here. Swell's bigger in town. We'll use that as the justification if anyone complains."

"Good man, Larry," Mr. Matthews says. "Good man." He pats him on the back, and he pulls out his cellphone and starts dialing right away.

I'm horrified, but there's nothing I can do, except hope the whale expert can get here before they tow the whale away. I don't know for sure, but maybe they can overrule the police chief. Like the shark expert does in that movie *Jaws*. But then, *Jaws* isn't a very realistic movie, especially the part where the shark tries to eat the whole boat. That would never happen; they might bite on a boat to see what it is, but when they found out it wasn't food, they'd go and eat a seal or something. I think this as Mr. Matthews wanders a little way away and talks on his cellphone for a while. Then he comes back and talks quietly to the inspector.

"All set. Kevin'll be here in forty minutes." Then he shakes his head and says something else, but this time, I think he's just talking to himself.

"Christ alive. First that girl and now this. We'll be lucky if anyone comes here next season."

After that, the other two policemen go to the trunk of the police car and come back with two shovels. They start digging a hole on each side of the whale's tail. Lots of people think whale's tails are called flukes, but they're actually made up of two flukes, one on each side. The right word for the whole tail is just *tail*, like I said. I go and stand as close as I dare, and try to push the sand back into the hole with my feet, but they get annoyed and tell me I have to stand back, so there's nothing else I can do after that. After all, they *are* the police. Instead, I just check my watch and frown a lot. It takes about forty minutes to get here from Goldhaven, where the ferry gets in, but I don't know which ferry the whale expert is on. I just hope he or she hurries up.

I'm thinking so hard about this, I don't notice that the policemen have already got a rope under both flukes. They wrap it around twice and knot it. Annoyingly, they do it well. By the time they've finished, the water is really close, and a fishing boat is waiting just outside where the waves are breaking. Like I told you, the waves aren't very big down this end of the beach today. As I watch, the men on the boat trail a buoy attached to a line from the stern, and it doesn't take long before it gets washed ashore and the policemen can collect it. Then they tie it to the line they've already got secured around the whale's tail. And then we all wait.

About fifteen minutes later, the tide has come in enough that there's water all around the whale, and it's sticking up out of the waves like a rock. The boat tries to pull it a couple of times, but before it's actually afloat, and they've got no chance. But they keep trying, with lots of shouting, and then, ten minutes later, the whale suddenly moves. For a half second, I make the mistake of thinking that it was never dead at all, but then I realize, it's just floating now, and the boat slowly begins to pull it out backward into deeper water. A wave breaks over it, and it disappears for a moment. When it emerges again, it looks shiny and clean, and then it rolls over so we see the white underside. And slowly it gets pulled out to sea.

A half hour later, you can hardly see it: the boat is pulling it out around the headland. I don't know where they'll dump it; away from the island, I guess. I watch until the boat goes out of sight behind the rocks and then turn away, still feeling angry about what's happened. As I do, I see a man standing on the dunes by the parking lot. I don't know him, but from the way he's dressed, the backpack he's carrying and the funny round glasses he's wearing, I reckon he's probably the whale expert.

5

Dad isn't home when I get in, so I light the log-burner and start to make dinner. Usually, I'd put the TV on while I'm cooking, but today, I don't. I'm too busy thinking.

I'm really angry about what happened with the whale. Not just because I didn't get to meet the whale expert, or tell him about my hermit crab study, but because I know the police did the wrong thing. If they'd waited until the expert got there, he could have measured the wounds, and taken samples and all sorts of things that would have been useful to science. But now, they can't. They threw away the biggest piece of evidence they had.

I can't help but link this with how the police have failed to find out what happened to Olivia Curran. That detective who interviewed me practically ignored my information about how Olivia heard about the Surf Lifesaving Club Disco. If they make those kinds of mistakes, what else have they overlooked? Then I think of Emily and the way her face gets all worried when she talks about the girl. I know why. It's because she's worried that whatever happened to Olivia Curran might happen to her too. So maybe I *should* investigate the case? Maybe I could solve it where the police haven't? After all, Dad's always saying the police are useless and corrupt.

In a funny way, I think me being a child might help too. Look at the way Mr. Matthews and the policeman were talking on the beach today - they moved away from all the other adults because they didn't want to be heard, but they hardly noticed *I* was there. And lots of people around the town treat me like that, like I'm sort of invisible. So perhaps it's not such a crazy idea for me to try and find out what happened? After all, I do all my projects, and I'm really good at those.

On the other hand, I am really busy already, what with my project and also school and things.

I don't know. I change my mind lots while I'm cooking. I make spaghetti bolognese because me and Dad both like that.

But then, when Dad comes home, he says he's tired, and he's in another one of his strange moods. I guess he must have done too much painting. The first thing he does when he gets in is open a beer. Then he takes his dinner without a word and sits down in front of the TV. Sometimes I'll watch TV with him, but tonight I'm still kind of annoyed with everything, and I'm thinking a lot, so I eat in the kitchen. Then I go to my room. I've got homework to do, but I don't get my books out. Instead, I open a new Word document on my computer and start typing everything I can remember about the Olivia Curran case. This is what I write:

DATE OF MYSTERY: August 26
    Location: Silverlea Surf Lifesaving Club (End-of-Summer Disco)
    Summary:
Olivia Curran was a sixteen-year-old girl staying for two weeks in number one Seafield cottages in Silverlea along with her brother (14), and parents (ages not known, but fairly old). Halfway through her stay, she attended the Silverlea Surf Lifesaving Club Disco, which is approx. fifty yards along the beach from the cottage. Her parents claim she did not return to the cottage that night or the next morning.

On Sunday, August 27, a police search was begun using officers from the island and then later from the mainland too. There were lots of police cars (I counted seven all parked together at one point). Some of the police had dogs, and there was a helicopter that landed on the beach. Lots of local people from the town helped to search too, but not Dad (and not me either). No one was able to find any trace of Olivia.

On Monday, August 28 (which was still vacation, so no one had to go to school), the search kept going but got even bigger. There were lots of police now, and Coast Guard launches in the bay with their little boats and divers. And a second helicopter that hovered around the town the whole day. The story was in all the newspapers too. It was the front page story in some of them. Some of the national ones, I mean, not just *The Island Times*.

On Tuesday, August 29, the search kept going. In the morning, the woman police officer came to our house to speak to Dad because the family was staying in our cottage, but Dad said he'd not even met them. This is when I volunteered my information about how Olivia found out about the disco. In the afternoon, Dad and I watched from the yard as all the police searched through the dunes for clues. They were still going after it got dark; you could see the flashlights waving around in the darkness.

I START to write the entry for Wednesday, but realize I don't have much more to say, except that the search carried on and no one found anything. And I could say that for every day since it happened.

I decide the most important part is probably the night she went missing. So I go on the Internet and go to the *Eastern Daily News* website. A couple of weeks after Olivia disappeared, they printed a timeline detailing her last known movements. I copy and paste it into my document too:

Timeline

Saturday 20:30 - Olivia arrives at the Silverlea Surf Lifesaving Club End-of-Summer Disco with her mother, father, and brother. She immediately joins another group of female teenagers whom she met and befriended in the previous week.

Saturday 21:00 - Olivia and friends eat from the BBQ, and the group are observed drinking and laughing.

Saturday 22:00 - Olivia and friends are among the first to begin dancing and continue doing so for around an hour, staying toward the front of the hall. Olivia seems relaxed and appears to be enjoying the party.

Saturday 22:37 - Olivia's family leave the party to return to their rental cottage, less than one hundred yards from the hall. Olivia's mother speaks to her daughter and tells her that she must be back with the family by midnight, which she promises to do. This is the last sighting of Olivia by a family member.

Saturday 23:00 - Olivia and her group of friends go outside the hall, but stay within the confines of the party, chatting and drinking further.

Between the hours of 23:00 and 01:00, there are various unconfirmed sightings of Olivia, both on the beach and within the hall.

Sunday 01:15 - The party winds down. Many of the guests have left by this point. Those remaining are young people and teenagers, and many are heavily intoxicated.

Sunday 01:30 - The disco officially ends, the hall is closed and the doors are locked. A group of young people remain outside for some time. Many then proceed to a party held at 45 Princes Street, in an apartment rented by members of the Silverlea Surf Lifesaving Club. There are conflicting reports as to whether Olivia attended this after-party.

Sunday 04:00 - The impromptu event at 45 Princes Street winds down, with most partygoers either returning to their homes or vacation accommodation, or sleeping over in the Princes Street apartment.

Sunday 08:00 - Susan Curran discovers her daughter Olivia did not return to the cottage but at this point assumes she has slept elsewhere. The family does not call the police until nearly midday.

Sunday 11:45 - Joseph Curran contacts Silverlea police station to report that his daughter Olivia Curran is missing.

IT'S LATE NOW. I read back everything I've written, and I'm not sure. I decide that Emily's idea for me to investigate the Olivia Curran case is a little crazy after all. Plus, I'm pretty tired. I click the 'x' to close the file, and the computer asks if I want to save it. I almost say no, but at the last moment change my mind. I think for a moment, then I make a new folder called "Limpet shells" and save it in there. I've noticed that not many people are interested in limpet shells, so if my computer is ever hacked, they're less likely to look in a folder with a name like that. Then I password-protect the file like I do for all my stuff, because you can never be too careful.

Then I get into my pajamas and go to sleep.

6

Dad wakes up later than normal on Sunday. We go to Silverlea again because the waves are still small. When he's gone into the water, I think about going to find out if the whale has washed up somewhere. But I couldn't see it anywhere from the clifftop earlier, so I don't think there's much point. Maybe it's sunk. Instead, I decide to do some work on my hermit crab project. So I walk up the beach to Northend.

Northend is a strange place. Years and years ago, they used to mine silver from the headland up there. It's how the town got its name: Silverlea. It was proper silver too, real nuggets that they dug out there. There were tunnels running through the cliffs, right down to the beach in some places. But then, one day, there was a really big storm, and the waves brought down the cliff. Almost all of the mine collapsed. It was a big deal and loads of the miners died. But it was a long time ago, so it doesn't really matter anymore. The point is, all the silver nuggets they'd been mining and all the nuggets they had stored up, ready to ship out to the mainland, they all fell onto the beach too. And they got hidden there, in the sand and between crevices in the rocks up there.

And now you're still supposed to be able to find silver nuggets, in the rockpools and buried in the sand up at Northend.

When I was little, me and Dad would spend hours and hours up at Northend, me with my little bucket and net and him with his sleeves rolled up and his shirt open, and we'd search in those rockpools, hoping to find our nugget of silver. I'd shout out to Dad every time I found something, and he'd come over to see. And it wouldn't be silver; it would be the tab from a soda can, or the foil-inside of a potato-chip bag, but he'd still smile and tell me I had to keep on looking and one day we'd find some. I loved searching for silver so much I'd refuse to leave, and later Dad would have to carry me back while I slept on his shoulders because I was so tired.

We never did find any silver, not a single bit. And these days, we don't look anymore. I guess I got too old. These days, Dad's got more into his surfing, and obviously, I can't do that because of the going-in-the-water thing. I still see the tourists, though, in the summer. With their special "Silverlea Silver Nugget" buckets and their "nugget nets," which are really just the normal kid's fishing nets on cane sticks that you get everywhere but a bit more expensive. The tourists never find anything either. I'm pretty sure all the silver has gone.

But that doesn't mean there isn't anything interesting up at Northend. It's perfect for my project.

It's about a half-hour walk along the sand to Northend, and the exercise means I'm warm by the time I get close. I can see the tide is still dropping, which is good, but I'm frowning again, this time because I'm not sure if it's low enough. I need the tide to drop right down so I can get around the headland. There's another little beach round there, which is where I'm going. Dad used to call it the 'secret beach' although it isn't really secret; it's just hard to get to, and some people say it's dangerous. There's a sign warning people. I go past it now. It says:

Danger!
Do not pass this point
On Rising Tide!

When I was a kid, I didn't used to like going past this sign. I was always scared we would get cut off and drown. Dad would tell me it was OK as long as you kept an eye out on the water, but even so, we almost got caught out a few times. He liked going past the sign, partly because he thought we had a better chance of finding silver in the pools around the headland because not many tourists would go round there. And partly because that's just what Dad's like.

These days I'm much more confident though. I know you get about an hour or so at low tide before the water cuts you off, so it's not really that dangerous, as long as you keep track of time. I'm pretty sure today's low tide is at eleven, but I'm not totally sure because I was still thinking about the whale when I looked. I'll just have to be careful, that's all.

When I get to the headland, there's just enough beach to walk round without having to scramble on the rocks. And when I'm round, the whole of the main Silverlea beach is out of sight, blocked by the rocks I've just passed. It's a funny little beach, this one. There's no other way to get here, no path down the cliff. You can't even see it from the clifftop above. That's why it's dangerous if you get cut off here. At high tide, there is no beach, and the cliff is too steep and unstable to scramble up.

Today I can't see anyone else on the secret beach, so I know I'm completely alone. And since there was no one walking the beach behind me, I know mine will be the only footprints on the sand here in this tide.

But I don't have long. I walk a little faster, over the hard, wet sand toward the end of the second beach. Toward the entrance of the hidden pools.

I found the hidden pools with Dad, years ago. We thought they were just caves at first, but later, Emily told me they were actually part of the mines. They're the old tunnels and chambers that had been dug at beach level all those years ago. Only now, they fill up and empty out with the sea every time the tide goes up and down. Hardly anyone knows about them though; there's just a tiny little entrance where you have to duck under a ledge of rock, and then you're inside. You have to take your shoes off, though, because it's wet inside. It's dark too.

I have a long look at the sea before I go in. I think the tides are neaps, when it doesn't go out that far. It's a bit risky, really. Especially since when I get into my projects, I sometimes lose track of time. I think about it, biting my fingernails as I do so. I decide I'll just have a quick look.

I dig around in my backpack for my special flashlight. Flick it on, then duck under the rock into the darkness. I won't stay long. I'll just see how many I can find.

7

I step through the cold, still water, my jeans rolled up to just under my
knees. I keep my head down so I don't bang it where the rock ceiling
is low. After that there's a high section where a rock has fallen out of the
ceiling, and then another low part. I can't see much, there's no beam of
visible light from my flashlight, but that doesn't mean it's broken. And
when I get into the cave proper I shine it around. A few blobs of color
glow back at me from the darkness. Then something reddish scuttles
across the floor. The only sound is the slow drip, drip, drip of falling
water droplets..

I should probably explain about my hermit crab project, and why I
have to come up here to do it.

It all started with Emily. For her university course, she's studying
jellyfish, a special venomous type that lives off the coast of South
America (well, warmer waters anyway, they kind of live wherever they
float to, since they're jellyfish). Anyway. She went for six whole weeks on
a research ship last year to study them. Most little fish get killed when
the jellyfish catch them in their tentacles. They get dissolved and eaten,
but some special fish can swim around in the tentacles all they like
without getting hurt. Emily says they have a special antidote in their
blood. That's what she's studying. She's going again, soon, on the same
ship, the *Marianne Dupont*. It's French. Or Canadian. Or something, I'm

not sure. Anyway, I was a little jealous, and a little sad that she was going for so long. But obviously, I couldn't go because I've got school, and besides, it would be really expensive. But then Emily told me about some other research that her friend was doing at her university. And the cool thing was, the scientist doing it wanted volunteers.

It's all to do with hermit crabs. Their territorial range and population density. You see, no one really knows much about that because no one's done any research into it. At least, not until Dr. Ribald decided to study it. That's her name - the scientist, Emily's friend. Dr. Susan Ribald. She wanted people who live near rocky coastlines anywhere in the world to monitor their beach and record the numbers and distribution of hermit crabs. Obviously, it can't just be any people, though; it has to be professional, scientific people. And Emily suggested that *I* could do it because I'm very scientifically-minded. So that's what I'm doing. I'm doing Dr. Ribald's experiment.

There's lots of us around the world doing it, or at least there were. I think a lot of them have stopped now. The idea originally was we put a spot of paint on the shells of all the hermit crabs we could find in one particular rockpool on one low tide, and then count how many we can find in the same pool on the next low tide, and try and see how far the other ones have gotten. Well, I tried that, but it was really hard because I couldn't find any of the crabs again the next time I went to count them.

That's when I had my idea. The hidden pools up at Northend are inside a cave where it's *dark*. I already knew there were hermit crabs inside because I'd seen them before when I went in with dad. They'd freaked me out as a kid, the way they scuttled around in the dark.

So my idea was to get some ultraviolet paint; the stuff that glows in the dark, and one of those scanner machines they use in stores to test if the bills people are paying with are fake or not. So then, I just had to paint the crabs' shells with the glow-in-the-dark paint, and I'd be able to find them easily when I needed to see where they'd gone.

I told Emily about it, and she helped me write to Dr. Ribald, and *she* wrote back that it was a "really interesting idea" and asked me to report back on how it went, so I went on the Internet to buy all the stuff. I was too young to buy the scanner thing, but I found you can buy ultraviolet flashlights which look just like normal flashlights until you turn them on and think nothing's happened. And there's lots of different colors of the special paint.

That was earlier this year. Now, things have moved on. Inside the rockpool caves at Northend, I've now got over two hundred different hermit crabs. Some of them glow blue in the dark, some yellow, some green, and some red. And because they can't get out, I can find tons of them every time I go in there.

I shine my flashlight around today. A few crabs glow back at me, but not as many as usual. Dr. Ribald will be interested in that. I start to count them, and when I've done that, I'll put them all back in the correct pools. All the orange crabs in the rockpool with the orange rock, all the blue ones in the pool with the blue rock, and so on.

So that's what my hermit crab project is all about. I did tell you it was serious scientific research. And actually, because it's so important, I've decided I'm not going to investigate the Olivia Curran mystery after all. It would get in the way of my scientific work, and I'm sure Dr. Ribald would be disappointed by that. She says I've got an "unusually persistent approach"..

An hour later, I've counted thirty-two crabs. Twelve are red ones, there's ten orange, eight are yellow, and the other two are blue (the blue ones are always the hardest to find because the blue paint doesn't glow very brightly). That's *a lot* down from the last time I came to look. I'm tempted to go a little deeper into the caves to look there, but I don't like going too deep. It's like you can feel the weight of the whole cliff above pushing down on you when you go too far into the cliffs.

And then, with a rush of panic, I remember the tide.

While I was counting, I had to stop and roll my jeans higher, well above my knees, because the water in the caves was rising, but I was so busy wondering where all my crabs were that I didn't stop to think about why. Now I know, it means the tide is pushing in. Outside, the water will already be at the entrance of the cave, and there won't be much beach left. I quickly grab my bag from the ledge where I left it and go toward the exit. When I get there, the water is up above my knees, the surge of the waves pushing in. I can't see the ocean - I can't see anything much, just the dim glow of the light through the water. I've never left it this late before, and for a moment I hesitate, wishing there was another way out, or that I could stay in here and wait until the tide drops again. But I know I can't do that. The caves get filled right to the roof; I know that because there are barnacles growing on the actual ceiling.

So I don't have a choice. My backpack is waterproof, but only when I fold the top over on itself lots of times. I take off my jeans and put them in the bag, so I've only got my underwear on. There's no one around, but I'd feel silly taking them off too. I can feel my hands shaking as I do it. I know I've got to move quickly. Then I look at the exit, a narrow kink in the rock with water sluicing through it. If I time it wrong, I'll try and wade through just as a big wave pushes in, but I can't see the ocean; I've got no way of timing it. I just wait until it looks like the water is draining back out, and I go for it.

If you were claustrophobic, you wouldn't like the cave entrance. It's really narrow. I stumble at one point on a rock hidden under the water, but the walls are too close for me to fall. Instead, I just bang my arm on the rock. But I'm OK. Moments later, I'm out -back into the world with its high, gray sky and the cliffs around me. I'm shocked how little beach there is left. I'm going to have to run to get back around the headland, or I'll be stranded on the beach here. I'm lucky the waves aren't too big today.

I have to wade around the headland, but I'm just in time. Less than ten minutes later, I'm safely back past the sign saying:

Danger!
Do not pass this point
On Rising Tide!

I get dressed again, but I leave my shoes off and walk the rest of the way back on the wet sand, letting the ends of the waves tickle my toes.

8

Something happened today to change my mind. I wouldn't want you to think I'm indecisive, but I *am* going to investigate what happened to Olivia Curran.

It's Monday today, so I had school. When I was younger, I went to Silverlea Elementary School, but last year, I started at Lornea Island High School. That's in Newlea, the capital of the island. It's twenty minutes away by car, or half an hour on the school bus. I catch it a way down our lane, and there's another girl who waits for it in the same place. Her name is Jody. Even though she's a year older than me we're kind of friends. Sometimes we talk while we're waiting for the bus, and while it drives down to Silverlea. She always stops talking then, though, because other kids get on the bus in Silverlea, and she doesn't want to be seen talking with me. It's OK though. I understand. It's not exactly cool to be seen talking with me.

But I'm getting a little ahead of myself. It's because I'm excited. Because I've got a *lead*.

This morning, waiting for the bus, Jody wasn't talking to me; she was busy on her cellphone. When the bus came, I sat at the front, and she walked to the back. I got out my book like normal; I'm reading a new textbook called *Marine Biology: Function, Ecology, Biodiversity* by Jeffery S. Levinton. They didn't have it in the school library, but I kept asking, and

Mrs. Smith, the librarian, eventually ordered it for me, I think because she recognizes that it's important to nurture young talent. It's pretty hard to read, actually, but it's got lots of pictures too. Anyway. The point is I wasn't thinking about Olivia Curran while I was reading, or at least I didn't *think* I was thinking about her, but somehow I wasn't really reading the book either. Instead, my mind was kind of pondering things. Like, if Olivia Curran was kidnapped, or murdered, then who was most likely to have done it? And I was kind of running through all the possible suspects, and then from the back of the bus, some of the bigger boys suddenly started shouting, *"Pedo! Peeeeedo!"* and then laughing at each other about how funny they were.

I didn't really pay much attention at the time, but later on, when I got to school, that's when I realized the significance.

Mostly, I don't like school. I'm not interested in sport, or music, or any of the things that the other kids talk about. I don't know about the football players and singers they're always discussing. I don't mind the actual lessons, especially science, and some of the teachers are OK, but often, there aren't any teachers around, like in breaks and lunchtime. And when that happens, some of the kids sometimes give me a hard time.

That's what happened today, at lunchtime. I was going to the school library to read, but some older boys blocked my way in the corridor. They started by flicking my bag off my shoulder and asking what was in it. There actually wasn't much except *Marine Biology: Function, Ecology, Biodiversity*, but I didn't want to show that to them because, frankly, that's just the kind of thing that gets you into trouble with boys like that. And then one of them started calling me names. Again, that's not that unusual, they call me a loser and a loner quite a bit which I don't even mind too much since I don't want to hang out with them anyway. But today, the one who was on the bus this morning, he called me something else.

"Billy, you're such a fucking pedo, you know that?" It was Jared Carter. He lives in Silverlea. He's two years above me in school, and he's really stupid. I saw his English workbook once: a teacher was marking it while taking my class, and I finished my work early. I tried to read his work, and honestly, he's basically illiterate. It's shocking, really.

"He's a what?" One of Jared's friends started laughing at him, a tall boy with dark hair. I didn't know his name.

"A pedo." Jared said, sounding a bit unsure of himself now. He meant 'pedophile' by the way.

"How can *he* be a pedo? He's a kid. He's maybe a pedo's. . . I dunno, *bitch* or something. But *he* can't be a pedo, can he?"

"Why not?"

The tall boy suddenly slapped Jared around the head. He did it pretty hard. I took the opportunity to move a little way down the corridor.

"Hey! What you do that for?" Jared shouted. He sounded hurt.

"Because you're a fucking idiot, that's why. You don't even know what a 'pedo' is, do you?"

"Yeah I do."

"What then?"

And that's when it hit me. Just when Jared clammed up. You see, when he said it on the bus this morning it wasn't because he knew what it meant – he's too stupid for that. It was just because he saw the guy with the limp. And all the Silverlea boys shout that when they see him. It's like a Pavlovian response with them. Now I usually try to ignore the boys from Silverlea whenever possible, so I'd never paid much attention before. But then I hadn't been thinking about possible murderers or kidnappers before.

The way the guy limps does make him look a bit creepy too. I guess I'd always assumed that's the reason the Silverlea boys pick on him. But now, I needed to be sure.

"Hey, Jared," I said, hoping this wouldn't get me into trouble. "Why do you always say that guy with the limp is a pedo anyway?"

All the boys stopped and stared at me, like they didn't know I could actually speak.

"You know, the guy with the bad leg. You were shouting it at him on the bus this morning."

"The fuck you say? Pedo-boy?" the tall one said, turning on me again.

I'd started talking without really thinking about it. I wasn't sure now it was such a good idea.

"I just wondered why you all call him that," I said, my voice cracking a little.

"'Cause he fuckin' is. That's why," Jared answered, happy to be back on firm ground. He began advancing toward me.

"Yeah, but... Why, though?" I said, backing up a little more.

For a moment, I thought Jared was going to hit me, but the tall boy interrupted.

"He got done. My old man said. On the mainland, he got caught doing it with a schoolgirl." I filed this piece of information away for future reference, and since everyone was looking at the tall boy now, I took the opportunity to ask for more.

"Did he kill her?" I asked hopefully.

"No. You know, he just, fucked her. Or something. I dunno. Raped her, I think."

I was disappointed by this, but then, I guess if he'd killed her, he wouldn't have been allowed onto the island in the first place. He'd be in prison already.

"Do you know his name?" I asked. If I got that, I reasoned, I could google him and find out everything else I'd need to know. I could wrap the whole thing up tonight. But he didn't seem to know.

"No I fucking don't. Weird-boy," the tall boy said now, and he took a step closer too. So now there was him *and* Jared, looking like they were going to hit me. In my experience bullies don't usually like to *actually* hit you, because then they might get into trouble. But if there's others watching them, then sometimes, they will, because they don't know any other way to finish a conversation.

"Are you going to fuck off, or am I going to have to fucking slap you?" Jared asked.

I decided I'd probably got as much information as I was going to get from Jared and his friends, so I shouldered my backpack and chose the first option.

Unlike Jared and his friends, I'm not a total imbecile. They think this guy is a pedophile because they've combined two pieces of information: he walks with a weird limp, and they've heard a rumor about his raping history. But I've now got three pieces of information. Because I know something else about him. Something that's directly relevant to Olivia Curran. I know *he was there the night she went missing.* I know this because I was there too, and I saw him, hiding in the darkness.

* * *

So that's what made me finally decide I was going to investigate. All those thoughts I was sort-of-having about who might be a likely suspect, and suddenly I had one. A real suspect. A suspect who really might have kidnapped Olivia Curran. But I could be the one who helped to get her rescued. So I didn't really have a choice. And it was easy to get started. Because of Jody.

I'm on the bus right now. On the way home from school. I'm waiting until all the Silverlea kids get dropped off, and it's just me and Jody left. I'm going to talk to her because I know she knows who the pedo guy is. Well, her dad does, anyway. I've seen them coming out of church together. Me and Dad often end up coming back from the beach at about the same time their service finished. And I see Jody and her mom, all dressed up, and sometimes I see Jody's dad too, talking to the pedo guy, with his weird limp.

Eventually, the bus gets into Silverlea, and the last kids get off so that it's just me and Jody left. We're the last stop, so I make my way to the back of the bus where Jody's sitting.

"Hey Jody," I say, real casually.

She looks up from her cellphone for a moment.

"Oh... Hey Billy."

But then she looks right back down at the screen again. While I was waiting for this moment, it seemed like it would be easy. Now that I'm actually about to ask her, it's a little harder. But I don't have long before our stop. She glances up again.

"Can I help you?"

Even though she doesn't really mean that I decide to go for it.

"I was just wondering something," I begin. "You know that guy, the one with the funny leg who lives down in Silverlea?"

She frowns at me.

"You know the one. He's always fishing late at night. Your dad knows him. I've seen them at church together."

"Mr. Foster?" She screws up her face.

"Is that his name?"

"I guess. Why?"

"Do you know his first name?"

"No. Why?"

"No reason," I say. Then I go on. "Do you know much about him?"

"Like what? What's with all the questions?"

I've already decided not to tell Jody that I'm investigating the disappearance of Olivia Curran, because we're not *that* close as friends. So now I don't know how to answer her.

"I just wondered."

"Why?"

"No reason."

She scowls at me now for a long time. Finally she shakes her head.

"You are one weird kid, Billy Wheatley."

I think hard for a moment, wondering if I could try a different approach. But then I decide against it. Like I said, Jody sometimes forgets that we're friends. I don't care. I've got what I need. I've got his name. *Mr. Foster.*

9

I need to back up a little. I need to tell you how come I saw Mr. Foster on the beach that night. Like I said, I was there too.

I'm not really into parties or discos or things like that, but Dad likes them, so sometimes, I have to go along too. And as they go, the Surf Life-saving Club disco is quite good because there's always a barbecue and I like barbecued food. I like that it marks the end of the summer too. Afterwards the town starts to empty out, and I get my beach back. Almost the whole town goes along, locals and tourists, and somehow the two groups mix like they don't in the middle of summer, when everyone's worrying about making money.

The afternoon of the disco, Dad had to drop off some speakers. We drove down to the club with them in the back of the truck. It was a hot day, so the beach was busy and there was nowhere to park. Dad had to leave the truck in the space you're meant to leave so that ambulances can get onto the beach in case there's an emergency. Dad normally doesn't worry much where he parks, but he's got a thing about ambulance spaces. So I got left in the truck with the keys in case we had to move, while he carried the speakers in, one after the other.

But it was late in the summer by then, and people were already leaving the beach, so it wasn't long before a proper space became available. So I decided to park the truck myself.

I'm not really allowed to drive, but I know how to do it. Dad taught me last winter in the parking lot down at Littlelea, when there was hardly anyone around. I was good at it too, except for when I scraped the paintwork. It was just a little bit and it wasn't my fault, because the post was too low, but Dad got real mad anyway.

This time, I was careful. I backed the truck slowly out from where Dad had left it. And then, when I was about to move forward into the space, this van swept past me and went into the space instead.

Maybe the other driver didn't realize I was going into that space; after all, it did take me a couple of minutes to back up, and I might not have been that straight on it. But still, it was annoying and it made me notice the driver. It was the weird guy, the one with the limp. I remember feeling angry at him, and then feeling kind of guilty about that because Dad says I shouldn't judge other people on how they look. But thanks to this guy I had to wait in the middle of the parking lot, until another space came available. So I just watched him, while he opened the back of the van and started taking his fishing gear out.

That's how I knew it had to be him later on. Lurking in the darkness.

"Hey, shift up," Dad said. He'd unloaded the speakers by now. "I'll put the truck on the beach. Locals' parking only, hey?" He gave me a grin. He likes to feel that the laws are only for the tourists.

I shifted over to the passenger seat, and Dad drove us down the little path over the soft sand and the stones until we were on the hard part of the beach. It's really good for driving on, but you're not supposed to do it. Only if there's an emergency, like if a whale body gets washed up, then the police and Coast Guard can drive down to it. Or if you're Dad and there's nowhere else to park. Anyway. Dad drove along the beach a bit, so no one could see his truck easily from the parking lot, and the ticket guy wouldn't give him a fine.

Then we walked back to the hall. I remember how busy it was inside. There were people putting up banners and decorations, packing cans of beer inside ice buckets and moving tables out of the way. I was given a job right away. I had to take the surfboards and the wet-suit rack out around the back, which took me quite a while because the wetsuits are heavy and they smell bad when people pee in them. When I finished doing that, and washing my hands, Dad was fanning the big barbecue with two paper plates, one in each hand, and Emily was laughing at him because he was going red in the face. Dad had a beer open on the table in front of him, so I knew then we'd be there for a long time.

It quickly went from busy to crowded, and by sunset, the band started playing. I got another job. The price for the disco included a burger or a hotdog and one drink – a can of beer or one plastic cup of wine for adults, Pepsi or Fanta for anyone who was under twenty-one. My job was to give out either a burger bun or a hotdog roll. Mrs. Roberts, who normally works in the store, stood next to me, giving out the drinks because I'm too young to deal with alcohol. Beyond her, Dad was cooking the meat, and Emily was helping him and giving people sauces. The barbecue couldn't keep up with all the people, though, so there was a line forming. That was the second time I actually spoke to Olivia Curran.

She was there with her family, but she wasn't *with* her family, if you know what I mean. Although they were right next to each other, they were in separate groups - the mom and dad and the brother were all together, and then Olivia had made friends by then with some other girls, and they were hanging out together a little way behind, like she didn't want to be seen with her parents.

When the dad came past, he remembered me, and he said something about how I seemed to have all the important jobs in town, I don't exactly remember what. But it reminded me I hadn't looked up that Wi-Fi problem on the Internet.

Olivia looked quite different, all dressed up for the party. She was wearing makeup, and her hair was pinned up. I almost didn't recognize her until she smiled. And then I remembered that.

At first she was busy talking with the other girls. They were all giggling and glancing over at the lifeguards. They were drinking beer and pretending not to look back, but really they were. Olivia didn't say anything to me when she handed over her ticket, but then she recognized me, and she did a little double take.

"Oh, hello," she said. That's when she smiled. "They make you do everything around here, don't they?"

I nodded. "Sometimes. Do you want a burger or a hotdog?"

"What's best?"

"The burger's bigger if you're hungry."

"Hotdog, please." She held out her plate, and I tonged a roll onto it.

"Thanks," she said.

And then her attention was back with her friends and the lifeguards. I told all this to the police officer too - the detective woman I told you about - but she didn't think that was 'significant' either. I already told you though. She wasn't a very good detective.

A WHILE LATER, the line for food calmed down, so I got to eat. I had two burgers covered with ketchup and then a hotdog, too, which made me feel a little sick. It was dark by then, and the music was really loud. Inside the hall, people were starting to dance, and lots of the adults were getting drunk. Emily tried to get me to dance at one point, but I don't really like dancing, and eventually, I was yawning so much that I went to find Dad and tell him I wanted to go home.

But Dad was outside. He was chatting to his surfer buddies, and he didn't want to go yet because he was enjoying himself. Eventually, he agreed to take me, but then we couldn't go because he'd lent his jacket to someone who was cold, and now he didn't know where they were, and he still had the truck keys in it. I told him I could go and sleep in the back of the truck; I didn't mind. I often sleep in there when Dad wants a night out, but Dad said it would be too cold that night. But just then Jody and her mom walked by. They were going home too, and Jody's mom said to Dad that she could drop me off too. Dad thought this was great, because he'd be able to stay and drink more beer. But he said he'd be back in half an hour or so.

So I left with Jody and her mom. I think back now to when we went outside. I remember how quiet it was out there. I mean, you could still hear the party, but now the music sounded really far away, rather than pounding in your ears. And it felt empty too. Somehow you got the sense that everyone was at that party, the whole town was there. But then, just as I was getting into Jody's mom's car, I noticed this light on the beach – the only one. And I saw who it was – it was the weird guy with the limp. It looked like he was fixing bait to a hook, and when he'd finished he turned the light off and he disappeared into the darkness. But that's not the weird part. What's weird is this: Mr. Foster was just about the only person in the whole town who didn't go to the party. Even *I* went to the party. But this weird guy with his weird limp, the guy with the history of raping girls, he *didn't* go. But he was still *there*. He was there on his own, fishing from the darkness of the beach, or maybe just *pretending* to fish but actually just watching as people came and went. And choosing who he was going to take. And I'm the only one who knows about him.

10

I t's Tuesday evening now, and my head hurts a little. That's because I've been thinking a lot. I've been trying to remember more about that night, and I've been wondering what to do about it. And in the end I came to this important decision:

Even though I know Mr. Foster was on the beach that night, and even though I know about his raping background, I don't think it's enough to go to the police. Not yet. I need more evidence. And even though I don't really know how the police get evidence, I've got quite a good idea from what I've seen in movies. And what I've seen is, it's not too different from how scientists go about getting their evidence. And like I've already told you, I'm a pretty good scientist. So all I have to do is gather some evidence that proves Mr. Foster did it.

There's also a bit of me that doesn't want to tell the police just yet. Because if I do tell them about Mr. Foster being a pedophile, *and* being there on the beach, they'll probably just take over. They'll say I can't be involved because I'm only eleven. And then I'd miss out, and I've barely even gotten started yet. Or - and you have to remember what happened with the whale - they might miss something else, and then Olivia might never be found. So, between all that, I've got plenty of good reasons for my decision.

My homework sits ignored in my bag while I think over my options. I haven't even updated my crabs project with the data I got over the weekend, and Dr. Ribald won't be impressed if there's data missing – Emily told me once she's got a real temper on her. But instead of either of those, I open my secret Limpet file, and then a separate window on the Wikipedia page of the Olivia Curran case. After a little reading, I add the following information to my file:

THEORIES on what happened to Olivia Curran

1. Accident

Some people believe it is most likely that Olivia left the party at some point in the evening to go swimming. The water is at its warmest in late August, and it's common for people to swim in the evenings, especially if they have been drinking alcohol. Apparently, some people saw Olivia drinking alcohol that evening. The theory is that she might have swum out too far and been caught in a current, or even eaten by a shark (this would explain why her body was never found). Or she might just have not been a very good swimmer, and maybe forgot this with the alcohol.

However, there are problems with this theory. The first is that no one went swimming with Olivia, or can even remember her telling them she was going swimming (again, maybe they forgot because of the alcohol?). Secondly, the police didn't find a little pile of clothes like people usually leave on the beach when they go swimming. So maybe she went swimming with her clothes on (the alcohol again?) Third, her body hasn't been found, and the currents here tend to wash things onto the beach at Silverlea, not take them away from it. Like the whale body.

Overall, I don't think this is the most likely scenario, but I'm not able to totally discount it yet, so I think it's important to add it to my file. Then I add notes about the second theory.

2. Suicide

One of the newspapers covering the story said Olivia had a boyfriend who split up with her earlier in the summer (at her home, not here in Silverlea). It said Olivia might have been depressed and decided to kill herself. She could have done so by swimming out into the bay. And this might explain the lack of clothes on the beach (if you were swimming out to drown yourself, maybe you wouldn't worry about keeping your clothes dry?).

However. Olivia's parents then released a statement saying they were very angry with the newspaper, and that Olivia hadn't broken up with her boyfriend and had been looking forward to returning home and seeing him again. Also, just like the first theory - what happened to her body if this is what happened?

I'm not very impressed by this theory either. She didn't look very depressed when I saw her, not once I got the Wi-Fi working anyway, or at the disco. I carry on.

3. Murder/Abduction

The final theory is that someone abducted her.

Most of the evidence suggests this is what happened, and teenage girls quite often do get abducted. It explains why she disappeared without any warning and why no body was found. But the problem with this theory, at least according to Wikipedia, is that there are no obvious suspects. And the very public location of where Olivia went missing, and the poor illumination on the beach and in the parking lot, mean a very wide range of potential suspects.

WIKIPEDIA GOES on to say that the investigation is the biggest ever carried out on Lornea Island, but that so far, it hasn't found Olivia Curran, or even produced any credible leads. I stop reading and think back to that night. I try to remember what Mr. Foster looked like, the expression on his face when I saw him, lit up by his fishing lantern. He wasn't that far down the beach, now that I think about it. Not as far as he should have been if he really was fishing. And I remember how, when he'd finished baiting his hook, or whatever he was doing - *or maybe when he saw me looking* - he turned off his light, and you couldn't see him at all. He was just hiding there in the darkness. But he would still have been able to see me. He'd have been able to see everyone. If Olivia had slipped out of the hall, he would have seen her in the outside lights. He'd have been able to sneak right up close to her. And with his fishing knife he'd have been able to grab her and... I stop visualizing it. I feel sort of cold thinking about it.

A little bit half-heartedly I decide to google the name "Mr. Foster". I don't have much expectation of success though, it's quite a common name. It comes back saying:

"About 3,240,000 results (0.67 seconds)."

I try again, adding "Silverlea" to the search, but it doesn't help much. Then I try "Lornea Island" and I get a bit excited because there's a *James* Foster who runs a care home in Newlea, but then when I follow some links I find a picture and see he's not the right Mr. Foster.

I search for an hour, but I know I'm getting nowhere. If Mr. Foster has kidnapped Olivia Curran, then she'll be hidden in his basement, or chopped up in his freezer. Not up on the Internet ready for me to find.

No. If I'm going to find the proof I need to go to the police, then I need to be a little more inventive in finding out about Mr. Foster.

11

Silverlea isn't very big, and even with the extra police around, it's not very busy at this time of year. Even so, I don't know where Mr. Foster lives, and I can't exactly go down every street until I find his van. I *could* ask Jody's dad, since he knows Mr. Foster, but that's difficult because I've never actually spoken to Jody's dad before, and he's bound to ask why I want to know. If I tell him I suspect Mr. Foster of kidnapping and maybe murdering Olivia Curran, he'll want to go the police, and then I'll have exactly the same problem as before. I need to have more evidence before I tell anyone.

But I've got a plan. I know Mr. Foster likes night fishing. Not just from the night Olivia went missing either. I know because I often see him doing it. Or more accurately, on the weekends when Dad goes surfing, Mr. Foster is often there, too, limping around his van, packing up. He finishes his night fishing trips just as we get to the beach.

So, if I know I'm likely to see him at the beach, then I can follow him. I can use my bike. It's a mountain bike. Dad bought it for me, and one for himself, too, although his has got twenty-one gears and mine only has fifteen. When he bought them, the idea was we would go on rides together, but after the first ride we did Dad decided he didn't like it because he thought people drive too fast on the narrow lanes around here. We haven't used them much since then. But we've got a little outhouse and they're still in there. I just need to oil the chain and mine'll be ready.

It's a simple plan, I know, but that just means there's less to go wrong. I've already checked my bike over, and it's loaded into Dad's truck, ready for the morning. When Dad goes surfing tomorrow, I'm going to follow Mr. Foster home and find out where he lives.

12

Saturday didn't work out so well. Dad didn't even want to go to the beach because it was windy and blowing onshore, which messes the waves up, and because he was out late the night before. But in the end, I convinced him, and we went down to Littlelea where it was a little more sheltered.

Then Mr. Foster's van wasn't in the parking lot. Dad decided to go surf anyway now that he was there, so while he got changed, I wheeled my bike down onto the beach and then pedaled along the hard sand by the water's edge, all the way until I got to Silverlea. It was hard work, and I was worried that even if Mr. Foster had been fishing from Silverlea, he might have already gone by the time I got there. And when I did get there, all hot and sweaty, the Silverlea parking lot was empty too. I cycled around the town a little because you never know, but I didn't find him. Then I had to cycle back along the beach to meet Dad. He was mad because he'd been waiting for me, and I was exhausted from the whole thing.

But that was Saturday. Today is Sunday, and the day is going better. There wasn't much wind this morning, so Dad was happy to go surfing. We drove straight to Silverlea, so I didn't have to cycle anywhere, and guess whose van I saw as we pulled into the parking lot?

That's right. Mr. Foster's.

But now I've got to move fast. I can see Mr. Foster too. He's limping back up the beach, a fishing box slung over one arm, his bundle of rods in the other.

Dad parks the truck at the front of the parking lot, close to Mr. Foster's van. Dad's decided the surf is "going off" this morning, so he's already out there in his head, thinking about the waves he's going to catch. So he doesn't notice how I'm focused on watching Mr. Foster. I watch as he puts down his fishing rods to get his keys. As he pulls open the battered van's back door.

"Look at that, Billy boy," Dad says. He's standing, looking at the sea. I glance over at it; a set of waves are lining up, and there's hardly any wind, so the surface of the water is all glassy and silvery.

"I'll be a couple of hours," Dad tells me, but I hardly hear. "It's perfect out there." He laughs as the waves start to break, peeling smoothly across the beach.

"You know you should stick around and watch for a while this morning. Instead of running off like you normally do."

"OK," I say. Obviously, I don't have time for Dad right now. I just need him to get going so I can follow Mr. Foster when he drives away. I've already got my bike ready, and I'm taking deep breaths, trying to fill my lungs with air. It's occurred to me that Mr. Foster might not live in the actual town of Silverlea itself. If that's the case, I'll have to pedal really hard to keep up with him.

"It'll be a good show. You can go up to the café. Watch from there. Get yourself a drink. Tell Emily I'll come in later and settle up, OK?"

Of course, I *could* use Dad's truck. He hides the keys in the suspension spring of the driver's wheel. But obviously, I don't have a license. You *are* allowed to drive in emergencies, though. I wonder if this counts as an emergency? Thinking about it, I'd probably be quicker on my bike anyway.

"Billy?" Dad interrupts me, shaking his head. "Did you hear me? I said go up to the café if you get bored." A troubled look passes over his face. "Jesus, kid, what's got into you these days? You're so caught up in your crazy projects. What is it today, anyway?"

It's so rare that Dad asks what I'm doing that I'm totally unprepared for this. Now is hardly the time for a detailed explanation of my crab project. Mr. Foster has already loaded his fishing gear, and he's shuffling his way around to the driver's door. He gets in; I can hear the door slam shut.

"Nothing much."

Dad doesn't say anything for a moment, but I can feel him looking at me.

"You know, it's about time you got in the water, Billy. We could surf together. Wouldn't you like that?" Dad says.

Not now, Dad, I think to myself. I can't believe he's trying this on me now. Just to get rid of him, I say:

"OK. But you should go now. The waves are real good, you said so yourself. You don't want to miss it." I don't mean it; there's no way I'm going in the water. But Mr. Foster is about to drive away. I'll say anything to shut Dad up.

But still Dad doesn't move. He's watching me. "OK," he says slowly. "Well, maybe I can give you a lesson? Would you like that?"

The exhaust pipe on Mr. Foster's van shakes as the engine fires up. The tires start to move with a crunch.

"OK, Dad, but I'll see you later."

To my relief, Dad seems content with that for now. He reaches down and picks up his board.

"Go to the café, yeah? If you get cold." He looks down the beach at the surf. Another wave is feathering, rising up from the surface of the ocean like a smooth hill of glass, about to pitch forward. Dad whistles.

"Check that out. We'll have you riding those in no time."

I can see he's gone, in his head, I mean. He can't help himself; he loves it when the waves are smooth like this, so I don't even have to reply to him. He turns and is soon jogging light-footed down the beach, towards the ocean. And it's just in time, too, because Mr. Foster's van starts backing out of its space, and then the gearbox crunches as he changes into first.

My feet press on the pedals and I reach the parking lot exit just as the van crunches past me on the gravel. I put my head down and push the gears as hard as I can.

13

The van turns north out of the parking lot, along the seafront road. But immediately, I start falling behind. Then it turns inland again, up Claymore Street, which is where most of the stores are in Silverlea. It makes the turn almost before I'm even on the seafront road. It's so much faster than me. I didn't expect this problem.

What's worse, Claymore Street is slightly uphill. I haven't gone more than a minute before the van is almost out of sight. I'm pedalling as fast as I can, standing up out of the seat, breathing hard already; I can't get enough oxygen in to keep this up for long. I start to panic I'm going to lose him right away.

Then I get some luck. There's a set of lights on Claymore Street where it crosses Alberton Avenue, and Mr. Foster's van gets caught there. He sits there for a minute while I pedal up the hill behind him as fast as I can, standing on the pedals still and swinging the bike side to side underneath me. Out of the corner of my eye, I watch the light. It stays red, and I get close to him. But not for long. The light turns orange and then green, and then he's off again, straight on, still up Claymore Street. I get a blast of smoke in my face as he pulls away.

But then I have a big stroke of luck. While the lights were against him, another car pulled in front of him, and it's someone really old because they're driving real slow. It's only a few moments before Mr.

Foster catches them up, but he doesn't overtake, I guess because he doesn't want to draw attention to himself. It's still faster than I can cycle, but at least they're not disappearing into the distance in front of me. For about three minutes, we go on like this, me still pedalling as fast as I can, and Mr. Foster's van and the old person pulling away, but not too much. Even so I know I can't do this much longer. If the old person turns off. Or if Mr. Foster keeps going out of town, where the road is long and straight and easy to overtake on, I've got no hope of catching him.

I put my head down and really go for it. But even so I feel my legs slowing, and I've got nothing left to give. There's a bend up ahead, and after that, we'll be out of town. I'm going to lose him. I'm probably going to die from cycling too hard, and even so I'm going to lose him. But then the blinker on Mr. Foster's van comes on. He's turning off the main road.

I don't know the name of the road he turns onto, and I don't get there until a full minute later. And when I do, I have to stop. I drop my bike and hold onto a lamppost with both hands. Then I collapse to my knees, on the verge. I feel like I'm going to throw up. It's like when you have to do running races at school; the four hundred meters is the worst. Sometimes, kids actually do throw up doing that one.

Finally, I recover enough to look up again. I'm on a small road that I don't know. There's no stores, it's just houses and I can't see the van anywhere. I think I've probably lost him.

When I recover a little more, I get back on my bike and keep going. I don't know where exactly, but I figure I might as well look around. Silverlea isn't big and behind the houses here it opens right out into fields, so maybe I can still find him. The houses at the back of town here are kind of small, not the type that get rented easily to tourists, and I think quite a few of them aren't lived in at all. It certainly looks that way.

The road Mr. Foster turned into branches out into several different minor streets. I take one at random and cycle all the way to the end, hoping to see the van parked somewhere, but I don't see it, so I return to the main road. Then I take a second one, with the same result. I think this is hopeless; I might as well go back. I could go to the café and get a hot chocolate. I could update Emily on my project. But there's one more street, so I might as well keep looking. I cycle down it slowly, checking out the driveways. Most are empty, and where there are cars they're pretty old. There's a bend up ahead, and I almost decide to turn around before reaching it, but figure I should check there too. And there it is: Mr. Foster's van.

I almost can't believe it. My heart's still going hard from the exercise, and now something else as well. Nerves I guess. I stop by a tree and wait, watching. The van is parked on the driveway of a single-story house, right at the end of the street. It looks run-down, and it's kind of tucked away. Behind it, there's a stack of big trees, like a little forest.

There's a fishing boat on a trailer in the front yard, an old, open-style one. The lights in the house are all off. Overall, it looks really suspicious. Exactly the kind of place you'd expect a pedophile murderer would live.

Standing there, I get a creepy feeling, like spiders crawling on my skin. It's worse because I know Mr. Foster is inside right now. He might be watching me, like he did with Olivia that night at the beach. He might be sneaking out of the back door right now, with his fishing knife ready. I mean, if he *did* take her, then surely he would be careful now? He'd be looking out for anything strange. Anything that suggested someone was onto him? It occurs to me now that this is a *really* quiet street. I haven't seen anyone since I turned off Claymore Street. There's no neighbors out in their yards, hardly any cars on the driveways. He could be sneaking toward me right now, in the cover of those trees. I start to feel really scared. I want to jump on my bike and just get out of here. I nearly do, but I stop myself. I need to get evidence to take to the police. It is scary, but I'll just have to be careful. That's all.

I take a deep breath. I lay my bike down on the grass verge and move closer, keeping myself behind the trunk of another tree just on the edge of his property. I can see into the trees now, and I'm sure he's not there. I'm close to his van now. Close enough to hear the engine ticking as it cools down.

I risk another look at the house, scanning for signs of life. This close up, I can see it better. There are two windows in the front. The bigger one has got the drapes drawn, which means I can't see in. The smaller window is the kitchen, and there's no drapes. I can see a section of countertop, an electric kettle, and one of those wooden trees of mugs. One of the mugs has got fish painted on it. It's too dark to see further into the room. The lights are still off.

I look for any signs there might be a cellar. Pretty much all murderers use cellars, and if Olivia is still alive, this is where she'll be. But I don't know how you tell if a house has a cellar or not. I mean, it's not like there's any windows, because they'd be underground. I decide there probably is one – I just can't see it.

I slide back behind my tree and think for a moment. I've made good progress: I know where Mr. Foster lives, and therefore I probably know Olivia's location, whether she's alive or dead. This is good. But I know I need more. If I go to the police now, they still won't believe me. I'm just a kid, they won't realize I'm really a scientist. Even if I could get them to listen to me, they might believe me just a little bit and send one officer to ask him some questions, and then *they'd* probably get kidnapped and be kept in the cellar or killed too. So it's definitely too early for the police. I need to do what I came here for. I need to do a stakeout of Mr. Foster's house.

You see stakeouts in movies all the time. The people doing them always get to eat takeout, or donuts. Usually, they argue a little, or have a heart-to-heart so you learn their back story. But it always works. They always see something important. So I know a stakeout is the right thing to do. But obviously, I can't just sit on the street eating donuts and watching Mr. Foster's house. But don't worry, like I told you earlier. I did a lot of thinking the other night.

I have another look at the front yard. I notice the boat again. It's an open boat, quite small, like the ones that people use to fish in estuaries, not the open sea. The stern is facing the house, and since the front yard isn't that big, the bow is almost buried in the hedge. It's got a faded blue cover tied over the top, with gaps between the ties where the wind has worked it loose. From the look of the rusted trailer, and the weeds growing up all around, it doesn't look like it's been used in a while. And winter is coming on and people only use that kind of boat in the summer. So Mr. Foster isn't likely to take it out any time soon. That makes it perfect for what I need. I lock my bike to a post so I don't have to worry about that, then I sneak back towards Mr. Foster's house. When I'm right in front, kind of hidden from view by the boat, I run across to it and lift the cover.

My heart is pumping when I get there. I have to stand on the trailer because it's higher than I thought. And the cover isn't as loose as I'd hoped. For a second, I think I can't get in, but I'm already committed, sticking my head and shoulders inside the boat, my feet in the hedge.

The smell hits me at once, mold and decay. I suddenly start panicking. The idea hits me that I'm going to land right on top of Olivia's decomposing body. I frantically wriggle backward to get out, and drop down back onto the grass, breathing hard and in full view of the windows. I kind of half-hide under the boat, and I try to control my breathing. I tell myself to calm down.

It's just a boat smell. It's just fish guts and stagnant seawater. All boats smell like that when they get old or aren't looked after. I glance around at Mr. Foster's windows and around at the neighbor's houses too. I'm lucky. Still no one seems to have noticed anything, but I'm totally exposed, sitting under Mr. Foster's boat. If I don't move, someone is going to see me any second. So I take a deep breath and go again. I climb back onto the trailer and slide under the cover a second time. This time, I'm calmer, and I pull myself inside using the seat. I slither into the boat; my backpack gets stuck for a moment, but then it frees, and my body slides into the bottom of the boat with a bump.

It rocks at first, but then settles. It really does stink in here. It's so bad it's hard to breathe. It takes a few moments for my eyes to adjust to the darkness, but when they do, I'm relieved to see there's no body, just slimy wooden floorboards, and that I'm lying in half an inch of dirty water. I try and lift myself out of it, but I can feel the water soaking through my knees. I ignore this, slip my arms out of my backpack and retrieve my camera. Then I work my way to the back of the boat where I can best observe the house. There's a kind of cutout for the engine where most of the light in the boat is coming from. Through the hole, I can see the front of the house perfectly. With my heart still pumping, I settle down to see what's going to happen next. And it's not long before I spot something interesting.

14

_____

It really does look suspicious, his house. There are pieces of render missing from the walls, and the paint is peeling off the window frames. And looking now, I can see that one of the windowpanes is actually cracked. And they're really dirty. The drapes behind are dirty, too, and faded, with a big yellow stain on the ones covering the big window. And now that I think about it, why does he have the drapes closed when it's daytime? It's very obvious now that Mr. Foster has things to hide. I decide I should just get set up, then get out of here. I don't really know how dangerous this is. And I'm pretty uncomfortable in here.

But then the kitchen light comes on. I freeze. I can see further into the room now, and a man walks through the doorway, comes into the room. It's Mr. Foster. I know it's him because of the limp.

I try to get lower, so he can't see me. But that makes the whole boat move again, rocking on its trailer. If he looks out of the window now he'll definitely notice. But I'm lucky – when I dare to look again, I can see him, still in the kitchen. He doesn't seem to have noticed anything. Then he walks out of the kitchen. Before I've even managed to take a photograph. I'm annoyed at myself. What if I don't see him again?

But a moment later, a strip of light appears between the drapes in the other window, and they start to open. Now I can see it's a living room. It's quite big, but strangely empty – the only things in it are an armchair, pulled close to a gas fire, and a big TV. And it's dirty. Strewn across the floor are pizza boxes and beer cans; an ashtray is overflowing with cigarette ends. And there, limping around the room with a black garbage bag, is Mr. Foster. I can't figure out what he's doing at first, but then I realize. He's tidying up. He's collecting the beer cans and crushing them before adding them to the bag. I feel a rush of excitement. I'm right, I know I am. This is *exactly* how you'd expect a murderer to live. Alone, in a dirty, creepy house. And what's he doing now?

He's trying to destroy evidence.

I make double sure the flash is switched off on my camera, and then, very carefully, I take several photographs, trying to catch Mr. Foster's face. I get a couple of good ones. When he leaves the room, I review them on the camera, waiting to see which room he'll appear in next.

But then there's a disaster. The front door suddenly bursts open and before I have a chance to duck down I see Mr. Foster standing right there, just a few feet away. I almost cry out in panic as he comes straight towards me. All I can do is drop down into the belly of the boat, feeling the water soaking up my leg. He must have seen me through the window, or maybe he saw the boat move. I think about screaming for help. But I don't know if his neighbors will hear me. It's not the kind of area where you can rely on neighbors anyway. I hold my camera like a rock in my hand. It's my only hope. When he peels back the cover, I'll hit him with it and then jump out and run as fast as I can. I have a flash-thought of what it might be like in his dungeon-cellar, chained up next to Olivia. Even though I don't have much time, I still feel scared.

Then I hear him *right beside the boat*. There's a noise - I can't place it at first, but then I realize, it's whistling. Mr. Foster is whistling a tune as he comes to get me. I try to make myself breathe quietly, and I adjust my grip on the camera, getting ready to lash out with it. I wait. Each second lasts forever. But instead of the cover being peeled suddenly back, instead of his hairy hands reaching down to grab me, the whistling stops, and there's a new noise, a kind of metallic banging and then a crashing sound. And then quiet. For sometime, all I can hear is my breathing, short, fast breaths that sound incredibly loud. Is he still there? I don't know. Then I hear the front door shutting again.

I know it's probably a trap. I don't make a single move. I wait in the bottom of the boat, but the seconds tick by, then the minutes, and I wonder why Mr. Foster doesn't do something to catch me. Any second, I expect to see his face in the gap between the boat's side and its cover. But then something else happens instead. I hear the van's engine roar to life. I change position to look outside again, and I'm just in time to see Mr. Foster behind the wheel, backing out of the drive. He's not looking at me. I watch him turn in the street and drive off down the road.

What the hell is going on? I stick my head out from under the boat's cover, and immediately, I'm relieved to breathe air that doesn't smell of dead fish. I look around the yard, to where the noises came from, and I find one answer at least. I didn't notice when I climbed in the boat, but there's a metal bin in the corner of the yard. I put two and two together with the black bag I saw Mr. Foster with before. He was putting the trash out.

Putting the evidence in the trash.

I climb completely out of the boat now and go to look. I cautiously lift the bin's lid. The black bag is there; it smells of stale cigarettes. I gently push the bag open. All I can see are beer cans and cardboard pizza boxes. I don't know what they mean, but I grab my camera and take photographs anyway.

NEXT THOUGH I'M UNCOMFORTABLE. I know I've suddenly got an opportunity to actually rescue Olivia. Mr. Foster has gone, I don't know for how long he's gone, since he's left the lights on, but I know he's driven away. So if I can break into the house I might be able to find her and help her escape. But the thought of it is really scary. What if he comes back while I'm inside? Perhaps he *did* see me, and this is all part of his trap? I'm paralyzed with indecision for a moment. But I pull myself together for a second time. I'll hear the van coming down the street if he comes back. I've *got* to try and rescue Olivia. I have to be brave. Slowly, I approach the front door.

Up close to it, I can feel eyes on my back. I can almost sense someone right behind me. It's like when you're little and you're sure a monster is under your bed, but you're all alone, and you're too afraid to look. I spin around, ready to confront whoever's there. But there's no one. I'm alone in the street. The windows of Mr. Foster's neighbors are blank and empty. I watch for a long while, but nothing moves, apart from the wind swaying the branches of the trees.

I turn back to the door and gently push against it. It doesn't move. I turn the handle and push a bit harder, but still it resists. I put more weight behind it, but it's obvious now it's locked. I feel a puff of relief and wonder if I've tried hard enough. But I go to the kitchen window next, running my fingers around the frame to try and pull it open. It's too cold this time of year for people to have the windows open, but maybe he hasn't locked it shut. But it looks like he has, or more likely, he just never opens it. I think for a minute about breaking the glass and forcing my way in, but I decide against it. I know he's a pedophile and probably a murderer, but it's still wrong to go around breaking people's windows.

I move instead to try the living room window. But it's no good there either; it's locked shut too. I inspect the cracked pane. It looks like it cracked when someone tried to pull it shut, and the frame is still sticking out. I could get my penknife and prize it open. Maybe I could get in. But then I think of something. I'll only hear Mr. Foster's van if he comes back in it. What if he's parked around the corner, and even now he's sneaking silently back to catch me? I go really cold, thinking of this. And that's when I notice something, in the corner of the room.

15

It's on the floor behind the door. Maybe a little bit hidden, but definitely looking totally out of place in Mr. Foster's weird, run-down house. It's a pink backpack. I recognize the brand, some of the girls at school have the same one, it has a big red heart logo on the front. Now what would Mr. Foster be doing with a girl's pink backpack like that?

For a while I'm just frozen to the spot, staring at it. I don't know what it means – the bag being there – but I get a bad feeling from it, like a foreboding. It's like my mind is reaching out into darkness to understand the implications. But I can't grasp them. Only that it's bad. Real bad.

And there's another thing. Up to now this all felt just a little bit like a game. Or one of my scientific experiments. Important, obviously, but maybe not something totally real. But that's changed now. Looking at that pink bag, so out of place, I know this is real. And I know that Mr. Foster really could be back at any moment. He really could be sneaking back to catch me. A fully grown man, twice my size, and with no neighbors to see when he drags me inside. I just want to get away from here. Right now. As fast as I can.

So I don't try to get inside anymore. Instead, I get on with what I came here to do. You see, I never planned on staking the house out myself. I always knew I'd only have a couple of hours at best, and the chances of seeing something in that time isn't very high. I need to watch for much longer. But that's not a problem. I've got technology for that.

I was hoping there'd be a tree or bush, but the inside of the boat is much better. It's hidden from view, but close enough to the house so the lens will capture anything that goes on. It's even sheltered from the rain, which is good. I mean, obviously, the camera is waterproof, but sometimes, rain gets on the lens and makes it hard to see anything.

I use a couple of clamps to fix it to the back of the boat, so that it's facing the house. I'm using my latest and best camera. It's a Denver WCT-3004 Wildlife Camera. It's motion-activated, and when I bought it, it had 258 reviews on the Internet of four or five stars. There were a few one-star reviews, too, but they were mostly from people who couldn't figure out how to set it up correctly. They didn't worry me at all because I'm good at setting these cameras up now. I've had lots of experience. It was expensive, though. I spent most of the money I earned from setting up the Wi-Fi networks. But it was worth it for one thing. The Denver WCT-3004 has *infrared night vision*. That means that even if Mr. Foster sneaks out in the middle of the night, I'll still see him.

When I'm happy that it's all set up to record and the clamps holding it are tight, I back slowly away, making sure I've left nothing that will give away what I've done. Then I walk back to where I've left my bike. I look around carefully while I do, in case Mr. Foster is hiding somewhere, but I don't see him. I feel a lot better when I've cycled away. I feel good, actually. At least someone is doing something constructive to find poor Olivia Curran. And I get that familiar feeling that always comes when I set up a camera. I can never wait to see what I'll catch.

16

Feeling good doesn't last long.

"Billy, where the *hell* have you been?"

Dad's mad. I'm barely halfway across the parking lot before he's shouting at me.

"I've been waiting a half hour for you. I looked in the café and everywhere."

I squeeze my brakes and see right away what's happened. It's the wind: it's changed direction. It was blowing offshore this morning, which was good for the waves, but it's swung around. Now it's onshore, which surfers don't like because it ruins the waves. Behind Dad, standing with his hands on his hips, I can see the smooth, pretty lines of swells from earlier have been replaced with messy white-capped chop.

"I told you not to go far. I *told you* that. Now, get your goddamn bike in the back, and let's get going."

I open my mouth to tell him all about Mr. Foster and his creepy house, and how I'm going to catch him for abducting her, or murdering her, or whatever he's done. But the words don't come out. Instead, I let Dad grab my bike and watch while he throws it into the back of the truck so it scrapes the paintwork. He'd be so mad if I did that. Then he climbs into the cab and revs the engine too loud until I get in beside him. I don't try to get in the back. I'm not allowed to ride there when he's in a bad mood.

"Jesus, boy." He carries on as soon as I shut the door. "What did I do so wrong with you?" He shakes his head, "You know Craig's son James?" He asks, and I don't get a chance to say I do, "he goes surfing with Craig every weekend? Even when it's big, he gives it a try. He *tries*. But you? I can't get you anywhere near the water." Dad shakes his head again. "Where did I go so wrong?"

It's not really a fair comparison. James is *two years* older than me, and he's really sporty. He's even on the school football team. And anyway, Dad's got lots of friends to go surfing with, so why is it so important *I* have to do it with him? I buckle my seatbelt in silence and wait for the storm to pass.

"Where do you go anyway?" Dad says a few minutes later, as we're driving out through town. "We come to the beach every weekend, and you're always busy. Where do you go? What do you do?" We come to a rest at the traffic light that caught Mr. Foster earlier.

"Come on, Billy, tell me."

This time, he really does seem to want an answer. I calculate quickly. He's still in too bad a mood to risk telling him the truth.

"I told you before," I say. "I'm doing a study on the territorial habits of hermit crabs," I begin, but he cuts me off.

"Oh Christ. You're still doing that? Jesus. You're not a kid anymore, Billy. You can't just..." He lifts both hands from the steering wheel, but then stops. He puffs his cheeks out and holds his face in his hands.

"Shit. *Shit. Shit. Shit.*" He surprises me by punching the steering wheel. The light turns green, but we don't move. Then there's a horn behind us. Dad winds down the window really angrily, then leans out.

"You wanna fuck off buddy?" he shouts at the car behind. But then he starts going anyway. I'm too scared to look behind in case the other driver is going to get out to have a fight, but then I do look, just as the other car makes a turn. Then Dad and me both sit in silence for a while, him driving slowly, me pretending to look out of the window.

A few minutes later, when we're out of Silverlea, Dad pulls over onto the verge. The road around us here is deserted. For a long while, Dad doesn't say anything. He just sits there, staring out of the windshield.

"Billy, I'm sorry," Dad says eventually. His tone is changed now. He's much calmer. He sounds weary.

"I didn't mean to lose it like that." He sighs and stops talking again. There's just the sound of the engine rumbling away in front of us.

"I just worry sometimes. You know, Billy?" Suddenly, he's talking again. "I worry that it's just the two of us and that... That maybe I'm not such a great dad. I worry about you hanging out on your own all the time." He looks across at me and waits until I look back at him. "I don't even know if it's safe. Since that girl went missing."

I don't answer. I don't even move. I'm too surprised at him suddenly bringing that up.

"You know what I mean? I know it's hard, being here, just the two of us. But we have to stick together. We have to make it work."

I don't answer.

"I'm gonna make it up to you. OK, Billy?"

He looks at me, and I still don't say anything. I'm not even looking at him.

"Billy!"

I turn to look at him. But still I don't say anything.

As I watch, Dad opens and closes his mouth a few times, like he's trying to figure out what to say next. Eventually, some words come out.

"Listen buddy, I saw Pete out in the water today. You know Big Pete? Runs the surf store over in Newlea? We got chatting when the wind came in. How about we head over there this afternoon? We could pick you out a board. Your own surfboard? Get you set up. You'd like that, wouldn't you?"

The best thing to do when Dad's like this is to go along with whatever he comes up with. But I wasn't expecting that.

17

I guess I should tell you about Mom. Now that we're getting to know each other a little better. I mean, I should tell you what I *know* about Mom, which isn't that much because I was very young when it all happened, and Dad doesn't like talking about it. I mean *really* doesn't like talking about it.

I don't much like talking about it either, to be honest, but maybe you've been wondering why she's not here with Dad and me in the house.

Mom worked as a nurse in a hospital. Not here, not on Lornea Island; we lived on the mainland then, a long way away, I don't even know where since Dad gets all weird when I ask him. But the way Dad tells it is like this: One evening, she was driving home from work. She was on her own in the car, and it was raining real hard. It was so late, there was hardly anyone else on the freeway. And probably, she was tired, too, because she'd been working, saving people's lives. Up ahead of her, a tractor-trailer truck jackknifed. The truck was carrying one of those steel-sided shipping containers, and somehow it ended up sideways across the road. The driver didn't have time to do anything. All his lights had gone out, and it was on an unlit part of the road. It was just there. This steel box blocking the whole freeway. Just bad luck. Mom's was the first car to get there. Dad told me once it would have been over quick for her. But I sometimes wonder about that. Sometimes, when Dad's driving me to Newlea, I spot a tree or a building on the side of the road, and I count how many seconds we take to reach it, and I imagine what it must have been like for Mom. When she hit the brakes and nothing happened, except the car skidding forwards on the wet road. I wonder if she knew. And how that felt.

So I don't know what happened. Sometimes, I think Dad isn't telling me everything. I don't really know if she tried to brake, or if she tried to steer around it. I don't know what was in the container, or if she died the moment she hit it, or if they took her to hospital and she died slowly.

I don't remember the funeral. Maybe I didn't go? Mostly I just remember things from here, from Lornea Island. I've figured out we moved here soon after it happened, but I don't know *why* Dad chose here. I don't think we'd been here before. We don't have relatives here. As far as I know we don't have relatives at all. I guess maybe Dad wanted to make a fresh start. Maybe he thought it was better if we lived in a place that doesn't have freeways? I don't know. Like I said, Dad doesn't talk about it, and I stopped asking him a long time ago.

We don't go back. To where we lived with Mom, I mean. Dad doesn't like to be reminded of anything from that time, and it's too far away anyway. So we don't go back, and we don't talk about it, and if I ever do ask, or if something comes up on TV that maybe reminds me of before, and what happened, Dad just tells me we've got to move on with our lives.

So now you know. And you can stop wondering.

18

"Hey, *Sammmmm*, how's it going, man?"

"Hey... buddy. How ya doing? You cool?"

We've just walked through the door of *The Green Room* surf shop, and that's the assistant and Dad talking and high-fiving the way surfers do. I don't say anything as I've gotten myself a little bit upset telling you about Mom. I'll be OK in a minute, though.

The assistant has got blond hair down to his shoulders, and he's wearing shorts even though it's cold. The yellow hairs on his legs are sticking up like fur. He's really excited to see Dad though. This often happens. It's because Dad's kind of a celebrity for the local surfers. Sometimes, there are surfing competitions, and when people persuade Dad to enter, he usually wins, especially when the waves get big. So they all like to hang out with him.

There's a strong smell of rubber in the store, from all the wetsuits, and there's a TV on the wall, playing a surf video. I don't get surf videos. They all show the exact same thing, just people riding waves over and over again. Actually, maybe that's why the assistant looks excited: he's just so bored from watching the video.

"Did you catch it this morning?" the assistant asks. "Pretty *awesome*, huh?"

"Yeah, it was OK. Until that wind came in anyway."

"Oh yeah. That was a bummer, man. So, you buying? Or just hanging?" He looks equally hopeful about either option.

"Actually..." Dad looks kind of awkward for a moment. He scratches at his ear. "Pete said he'd do me a deal... He let you know?"

"Yeah, sure. He said you might drop in."

"Cool. Well, actually, I'm looking for a board for my son here."

The assistant notices me for the first time. Or maybe he saw me when I came in but assumed I'd wandered in by accident. I look a bit out of place in surf shops.

"Yeah... Cool." I can feel the assistant's eyes on me, and there's a flicker of recognition between us.

"Hey, dude," he says to me, the first words he's *ever* said to me. "I never knew you were *Sam Wheatley's* kid." He tilts his head to one side, like he can't quite get past this. I don't say anything.

"So, you gonna be a local legend like your old man, huh?" I can hear the forced enthusiasm in his voice, and still I say nothing.

"You gonna win the Island Championship when you're older? Maybe even go on tour, yeah?"

A couple of times, after there's been a big surfing competition, I've overheard people say that Dad could have done the surfing tour. If he hadn't had to look after a kid, that is.

"No," I say finally, just to shut him up. I look at Dad. He's the one who brought me in here.

"Yeah, we're looking for a board, aren't we, Billy? Say hi to... um." It's suddenly clear Dad doesn't know the assistant's name. The guy jumps in quickly to put this right, like he's more embarrassed about it than Dad is.

"It's Shane. You remember, right? Shane," the assistant says.

"Yeah, yeah, sorry buddy." Dad hits the side of his head, like it just slipped his mind. "Yeah, say hi to Shane, Billy."

"Hi Shane" I say, raising a hand to wave. Then Shane launches into his sales pitch. Although he's looking at me, it's Dad he's trying to impress.

"So, you're after a new board? Well, you've come to the right place. We got these new Micro Machine boards for grommets. You thinking thruster? Quad fin set up - "

Fortunately, Dad interrupts him.

"Billy's not... He's not quite at that level yet," Dad says. "We're looking at something more at the beginner end of things. But nice, though. Something decent." Dad looks at me and smiles.

Just then though Big Pete himself comes in. He sees Dad and they start talking about the waves this morning, so for a few minutes, Shane and me are just standing there, until Pete suggests that Shane should show me the boards.

"Yeah, sure. Cool." Shane nods enthusiastically. "Billy, you wanna come with me and look at what we've got?"

I don't have much choice, so I follow him into the board room where the walls are lined with racks, each housing a surfboard resting on its tail. He goes to one wall and starts pulling boards out, looking at them. I don't know what he's looking at; they all look pretty much the same. I can hear Dad still chatting with Big Pete next door.

"So, what's the story with you then, Billy? How come you're only learning now, I mean?" Shane asks me. "I mean, it's cool and all. No big deal, I'm just wondering, with your old man being... You know."

I shrug and don't answer. I'm certainly not going to tell someone like Shane about my thing about going in the water. It's not because I'm embarrassed about it; it's not a big deal. It's just that Shane's an idiot. I'll tell *you* if you like.

The thing is, I'm just a bit scared of the sea, that's all. I know it's kind of odd for someone who lives on an island and all that. Especially someone who lives in a house overlooking the beach and who's going to be a marine biologist when they're older. But then, this kind of thing isn't that uncommon. Did you know, for example, that Neil Armstrong was afraid of heights? So are most airline pilots.

It's not that I'm scared of the water exactly, anyway. It's just I don't like going out of my depth. Or any deeper than my waist, really. Everything else is fine. I don't mind the rockpools. And I can swim OK if I need to. Dad saw to that. He made me go to swimming lessons for years. I'm OK in a pool, where there's lifeguards, and I don't actually go out of my depth. It's just the open sea I don't like. There's something about how big it is, and how deep it is, and the currents that can pull you out. It gives me the shudders. I just don't like it.

I feel my heart rate going up now, thinking about it. And I start to feel hot too. The room and all these surfboards begin to wobble in my vision. I can see Shane's face, too. Suddenly, he's looking really worried about something. He's not exactly spinning around, not yet anyway, but I can feel it going that way. White dots of bright light appear in front of my eyes, and I can hear my breathing sounds funny: it's gone fast and heavy. Suddenly, I feel a hand on my shoulder.

"Hey, Billy, you OK? Seen anything you like?" My dad's back. His voice sounds distant, though. I hear him talking to Shane. "Bill's a little nervous about the water. It's not a big deal. He can swim just fine, and we're gonna work up to it real slow. Aren't we, Billy?" He's crouching down beside me now. Then he slaps me on the back. "We're going to figure it out. Catch you some waves."

Slowly, my vision returns to normal, and my breathing slows. Dad's hand is still on my shoulder, and he's gripping me tight. Holding me up, pushing me on.

"How about that one?" Dad says, pointing to one of the boards. Shane pulls it out for us to inspect. It's blue, and it's got three dolphins painted on the top. When I was younger, I had a thing for dolphins. I wonder if he remembers.

"Yeah, that looks cool," he says. "What you reckon, Billy?"

One hour later, I'm all set with my new surfboard and wetsuit. We're driving back home, and Dad's telling me over and over how nice the rails are and how great the graphics look. I'm wondering how the hell I'm going to get out of actually using this stuff.

Oh. And I think dolphins are one of the most overrated animals in the sea. Just so you know.

19

It's late on Friday evening now. I've been at school all week. I was hoping I'd get the chance to go back to Mr. Foster's to pick up the memory card from the camera, but what with school and the evenings getting darker, I didn't manage it. And the weather's been bad too; it's hardly stopped raining all week. And now the weather's gone really crazy. I've got a weather station on the roof of the house. It tells me the average wind speed and the maximum gust. Tonight, it's averaging forty-four knots, and the biggest gust was fifty-five knots. That's an actual storm, as classified by the Beaufort Scale.

Storms are pretty scary up here on the cliff, but they're exciting too. With the big gusts, the whole house shakes, and the wind howls like we're surrounded by wolves. Sometimes, I like to go outside and lean into the wind, not too close to the cliff edge, though. The clouds scud through the sky like they're on fast-forward; and even at night the sea is more white than black.

The wind is supposed to peak about now, and then drop off quickly. I hope so, because I won't get any sleep until it does. Not with the wolves howling like that. And I need to sleep because Dad will definitely be up early tomorrow for the surfing. And that means I can get to Mr. Foster's house at last. There'll be a full week of recordings to pick up. Maybe Dad will even surf all day. Then I'll be able to go through the recordings tomorrow afternoon and pick out the best parts to give to the police. Then they can arrest Mr. Foster, rescue Olivia, and everything can go back to normal.

I'M SORT OF WONDERING, too, whether I should become a detective *and* a marine biologist when I'm older. I think I'd like to, but I don't know if you're allowed to do two jobs. I don't know anyone who does. Except Emily obviously. She's a waitress and a scientist, although what she does in the café isn't a real job for someone as clever as her. And thinking about it, I'd rather be a marine biologist than a police officer. Most of the time, the police just sit in their cars, eating donuts.

I'm tired now. I didn't have a very easy time of it in school this week. If I'm honest, I'm a little bit worried, too, because this is the first weekend since Dad bought me the surfboard. At some point, I'm going to have to explain to him that I'm not going to use it. I shudder a little at the thought of that. And under the sound of the wolves, I can hear the roar of the ocean, like it's trying to remind me all the time. Then my window rattles like someone's trying to break in. I know there isn't, really; it's just the storm. I check the reading from my weather station. That last gust was fifty-eight knots. I won't sleep until this storm dies down.

20

The storm blew itself out about three, but Dad's up at first light. The wind has gone, but the swell is *huge*. Obviously, I'm not going anywhere near it, but even so, the bay looks kind of awe-inspiring from up here on the cliffs. Out to sea, the swells are like great folds stretching right across the whole seven miles of the bay. Closer to the beach, where the waves break, they're forming into enormous round caverns that rear up and hang in the air for longer than looks possible. And then when they finally do crash down, each one does so with a bellowing *crack* that makes the windows rattle. Then, in the aftermath, all this crazy white water tumbles in toward the beach like a tsunami. Even the beach looks wild. It's covered in long streaks of foam, wobbling like jelly.

You'd think only mad people would want to go in the water today, but you should see Dad. He's singing to himself, and his eyes are open wide. I guess he looks like a mad person, come to think of it. But he loves days like this. Days like this are his thing.

It's colder after the storm. I'm shivering in my sweater, and I put my shoes and socks on before I come downstairs. But Dad's there just in bare feet and his jeans.

"Hey, buddy! You seen the swell?" He's eating a big bowl of muesli as I come into the kitchen. I glance nervously at the corner of the room, where my new surfboard has been leaning up against the wall since we got back from The Green Room. Dad follows my eyes.

"Whoa there. Sorry, big guy. I know I promised to take you out this weekend, but I don't think it's a day for you. It's kinda big out there today."

There's a *crack* from the bay below us as another wave explodes down. Both our gazes go to the window, which shakes in its frame. Beyond it, we can actually see the lines of waves; they're breaking that far out. Dad whistles.

"Maybe in a few years, huh? We'll get you out there on a big 'un. I tell you there's no feeling like it. Not even..." He doesn't finish the sentence but shovels the last few spoonfuls into his mouth.

"We might be able to do tomorrow. Later on?" He says when he's finished chewing. "This swell's not forecast to stick around too long. Maybe we'll get you in the water tomorrow huh?"

I don't say anything to this. There isn't much point because Dad isn't really listening to me. It's like he's not even here in the kitchen with me. He's only thinking about one thing.

"Anyway, we better get going. Get down there before the wind kicks in. You ready?"

I haven't had breakfast, but I nod anyway. If I hold him up, he'll only get frustrated.

I have time to grab my backpack and a chunk of bread before I hear the engine on the truck. Then I go outside. There's no question where we're going. No one could paddle out through the giant waves pummeling Silverlea, not even Dad. But at Littlelea, the rivermouth shapes the waves better, and the cliff gives some protection, so they're smaller - it's just where people go when the waves get big like this. So I chuck my bike in because I know I'm going to have to get along the beach to get to Mr. Foster's house and retrieve my memory card.

I CLIMB in the back of the truck, and take a bite of bread. I go to sit back against the cab, like I normally do, but my bike's in the way. Instead, I have to squeeze in down one side. And Dad's board bag is kind of pushing against me, so I shove it out of the way to get more room. And that's when I see something.

I don't know what it is at first, but it's flashing in the light, almost like a tiny mirror. It's something small, whatever it is, caught between the side of the truck and the floor. I try to get closer to get a good look at it, but at that moment, the truck bounces over a pothole, and I bang my head against the side of the truck. Dad's driving too fast. I rub my head and blink. I almost give up on the thing, but then it flashes at me again. Something shining and sparkling in the light.

I try again, more carefully this time. It's probably just a nail or a screw - there's always stuff like that from Dad's work - but then, it looks a little too shiny for that. I try to get my fingers in there, but they're too fat to get down the gap. I can't even touch it, let alone pull it out to examine it. But now I'm a little closer, I realize why it looks familiar. Why it looks so out of place. It's a girl's hairclip. The part flashing in the light is the diamond on one end.

Obviously, we don't have many hairclips in the house, between Dad and me. But the girls at school wear them, so I know what they are. And I know they don't have real diamonds in them too. That's not why this one interests me. It's not that I think I've found some treasure. I look around for something like a piece of wire or a stick to fish it out, but I can't see anything. By then though, we're already pulling into the parking lot at Littlelea. There's already four or five other cars there, all surfer friends of Dad. They all come out on days like this, although a lot of them stay on the beach watching when it's really big.

We skid to a halt on the loose gravel, and Dad's door is open before the engine has even died away.

"Hiya, boys," he shouts to the group, who are all watching the waves roll in. It's big enough that you don't even need to climb the dunes to see it today.

"Day of the year, huh? Day of the year!" Dad gives a kind of whoop and turns to me. "Jump out, Billy, I gotta grab the board."

So I don't get a chance to prize out the hairclip, if that's actually what it is. I'm a little bit frustrated by this, but not for very long. I've got important things to do today. I've got to get my memory card from the camera outside Mr. Foster's house and get my evidence. So I put the clip out of my mind and get my bike ready. I hang around for a little while, until Dad's suited up. It just seems polite since they're all so excited. Then I begin pushing my bike through the dunes.

21

The beach is quite busy. People come down to watch when the sea is rough like this. The tide's almost up, too, so everyone is pushed up together near the dunes.

I like storms. You always get strange things washed up when the waves get big. All the flotsam that's floating around in the ocean gets pushed in. And the jetsam too. (The difference is that one is accidentally put in the ocean, and the other is dumped from ships. I don't know why they need separate words for that.) One time after a storm, the beach was covered in dozens of plastic butter-containers, and the butter was OK to eat too. I collected tons of it, and we ate it for weeks. They must have come off a container ship. That's flotsam, I guess, although it makes more sense to just call it butter. Or plastic. Another time, I found an old fishing buoy that was covered in these really strange creatures. I'd never seen anything like them before: they looked like snakes. Or maybe aliens. Or alien snakes. They were stuck onto the buoy, but their heads were writhing around, like they were trying to get back into the water. I looked them up; they're called goose barnacles. Over in Europe they eat them as a delicacy and they're really expensive. I always look out for them now, not to eat, they look disgusting. But so I can sell them. But I've not seen anymore.

All I find today are a couple of coconuts, which I don't bother to collect because I've got lots of those already. Oh, and a big dead crab, which reminds me of my hermit crab study. It'll be good to clear up this Olivia business and get back to work.

So when I get to Silverlea, I hurry up a little and cycle through the town until I get to Mr. Foster's house. I can still hear the sea booming, even from up there, but other than that, it's eerily quiet, and it occurs to me that actually lots of Mr. Foster's neighbors' houses are just empty. In fact, when I look, all of the neighbors' houses look exactly the same as when I was here last week: the drapes drawn in exactly the same way, the driveways still empty. It gives me a chill to think of that.

Mr. Foster's van *is* in the driveway, though. I was hoping it wouldn't be, because it would be easier to switch over the memory cards that way. But no one said being an investigator would be easy. I lock my bike up like before and watch the house for a long time from behind the tree. The drapes are open, but this time, the lights are off, and I don't see any movement inside. Eventually, I go for it, running over to the front of the boat again, where I'm a little bit protected from view if anyone in the house does look out, and I sneak back inside the cover and inside the boat. Straight away, I see my camera setup is still there, and I crawl forward to where it's clamped on.

I wave my hand in front to see if I can hear the little noise it makes when it switches on, but there's nothing. The battery's dead. I'm not unhappy about this. The battery life depends on how much recording it's done. If there's nothing to record, it will last almost two weeks. It hasn't managed a week this time. That means it's done a lot of recording.

I unclip the camera, slide out the old battery and card and replace them with fresh ones, then refit the camera. The house is still dark. Perhaps Mr. Foster isn't there after all? Maybe he's gone for a walk. I hang around for a little while, but nothing happens, and what I really want to do is download my videos. So after a while, I roll back out the boat and sneak away.

22

I cycle all the way back through Silverlea and along the beach to Littlelea. The tide's fully high now, which means there's no hard patch of sand to ride along. I'm worn out when I get back to the truck.

"Yo, Billy. We've been waitin' on you," Dad says when I get there. He's in a good mood, sitting in the passenger seat of Pete's truck, which is the same as Dad's, but it's got adverts for *The Green Room* all down the side.

"Tide's got too high. We're gonna grab some breakfast, then head out again when it's lower," Dad says. Or he says something like that. The important thing is the word 'breakfast'.

I put my bike back in Dad's truck, and we drive all the way back to Silverlea again, the place I've just exhausted myself cycling back from. Honestly, sometimes, I can't wait until I'm an adult and can decide things for myself. I'd rather go home to download my card, but it wouldn't do any good to argue.

The Sunrise Café isn't busy, so we all sit together near the window. Dad and his friends are all going on and on about the 'drops' they took and how clean the wave faces were and how hard they had to paddle, and obviously, I'm not listening because I never listen to that kind of talk. I'm wondering if I can get away with opening up my computer here and looking through the footage from outside Mr. Foster's, and deciding I probably can't. Then, all of a sudden, I realize they've stopped talking about surfing, and now they're talking about Olivia Curran. But before I understand exactly what they're saying, Emily comes over to take our order.

"Hi, guys," she says, giving me a wink. Then she looks surprised. "Why the long faces? I thought you'd all be loving these waves?"

"Yeah, we are," Big Pete says. "But Karl here was just saying how it'll probably be a day like this that finally washes that girl's body in." Karl works for the Coast Guard, here on the island. But I don't know him very well because he's a bit strange.

"They're gonna step up the search for the body. Next week," Pete goes on, but then he stops. There's a moment of silence as everyone thinks about this, then Pete waves his hands like he's dismissing the subject.

"Hey. Forget I mentioned it. It's too nice a day. Say you got pancakes this morning Honey?"

Emily's smiles at him, like she's happy to move on.

"Sure do." She writes all the orders down on a notepad and walks back to the kitchen. I'm pretty sure she knows that all of Dad's friends are watching her walk away because she walks a bit funny. When she's out of earshot Karl opens his mouth again.

"Is she still seeing that lifeguard?"

"Think so," Pete replies, still watching her. "Why? You fancy your chances do you?" And he laughs. I kind of snigger a bit too because Emily would never date someone like Karl.

"Not me. I heard she's high maintenance," Karl says. Like I said, Karl is a bit strange.

* * *

A HALF HOUR LATER, and only a few moments after I finish eating my sausage sandwich, Dad pats me on the shoulder.

"Right, Billy boy," he says. It's the first thing he's said in a while and his voice sounds tense now, like his earlier good mood has completely gone. "We gotta get going. I gotta go to work."

"I thought you were going surfing again?" I say. I thought we'd be going back to Littlelea, and I would be able to walk up the cliff to the house to download the card.

"Don't have time. I gotta paint the chalets up at the hotel." I start to interrupt him to tell him he said he was going surfing again, but he talks right over me with what sounds like false cheeriness: "And *you* gotta help this time."

Big Pete gives him a look like he's surprised too. But he doesn't say anything. I think fast. I've got to download that card as soon as I can, but you've got to be careful arguing with Dad. Especially in public.

"Is it alright if I do my homework instead? I've got a ton of math to do."

"Do it tonight," Dad says.

"I was gonna do geography tonight."

Dad doesn't say anything at this, but looks at his friends and sighs. Most of them are married and sometimes he complains that they don't know what it's like having his responsibilities.

"*Shit.* Whatever, Billy. Whatever you want." He shakes his head like I'm being unreasonable; then he lays down a couple of notes on the table.

"Pete, give this to Emily when she comes out, will you?" Then he gets up and we leave, Dad and me, even though the rest of them are soon heading right back to the beach.

WE RIDE TOGETHER UP to the hotel. On the way, Dad starts asking me about what I'm actually doing in math, like he's sorry about getting mad but doesn't want to say so. But I tell him it's algebra, and then he doesn't know what to say because he doesn't know anything about algebra. Dad didn't even finish high school. It's probably not his fault, but that's why he's just a handyman. It's not really the point though, I don't actually have any math homework anyway.

WE ARRIVE at the hotel and park right in front of the chalets. There's two rows with five in each. He's still in his mood when he goes into one of the chalets with his paintbrushes and stuff. I go into another and set myself up at the little table.

I plug the card into the computer and set it to download the video. The window pops up: it tells me there's five hours of footage in 118 separate clips. That sounds like a lot, but actually it's less than normal. When you set up the camera traps, a lot of the time, they start recording just because the wind moves some leaves. It's a pain to watch it all. You can view it on double fast-forward speed to make it easier, but – actually - I've got a whole lot of footage I've never even watched yet.

I start watching them now, one after the other, thinking maybe I'll grab a Mountain Dew from the fridge. I noticed there's a packet of cookies on the shelf too. It's one of the perks of having access to apartments all over town. I can almost always get cookies wherever I am. But I don't get my soda. Because then I see a clip that makes me forget all about it. The cookies too.

23

I was right about most of the clips not being much use. There was a weed growing up the back of the boat - I told you it was overgrown there - and the top of it must have been moving in the wind. That did two things. First, it kept setting the camera off, so a lot of the clips only show this stupid plant waving its leaves around in front of the screen, and nothing else happening. But worse than that, there were times when the whole plant got stuck right in front of the camera, so you can't see the house at all, just a close-up of out-of-focus green.

For a little while, I worry that all the later clips are going to be just green, but then the plant moves again. I guess the wind direction changed.

The first clip where anything actually happened was this: Mr. Foster opens the front door, then shuts and locks it behind him, and limps to his van. Then you see the front of the van back slowly out of the picture. Thirty seconds later, the recording stops, which means nothing else happened. I save this clip to my investigation folder, although I don't know the significance of it yet. Then there's quite a bit more green where the plant gets in the way, and by the time the camera is working again, the van is back, and the lights are on in the house. The camera only seems to have picked up any movement from inside the house when Mr. Foster comes really close to the windows. There's a couple of other clips where you can just make out someone's moving inside the house, but I don't bother saving them because I get impatient and scan another clip a little later on. And that's the one that almost makes me stop breathing.

It was filmed at four thirty-seven on Sunday afternoon, still the same day I set up the camera. On the screen it's just getting dark. The lights are on in the house, both the kitchen and the living room, so you can see inside really clearly. The thing that sets the camera off is the drapes are moving in the living room window. Someone's shutting them. But it's not Mr. Foster. It's a girl.

It's only a short clip. For most of it, you can't see her face clearly, but you can see she's a teenager, and she's got long blond hair. Then, just before she closes the drapes completely, she pauses and looks straight out of the window. And in that moment, you can see exactly who it is.

I'VE FOUND HER. I've really found her.

24

———

"I disagree, sir. I don't think she drowned."

Detective Jessica West, a mainlander, was only in the meeting as a courtesy, she wasn't supposed to say anything, much less interrupt her commanding officer as he summarized the progress made in the month since Olivia Curran had gone missing. Lieutenant Langley kept talking, assuming she'd realize this and shut up. But Chief Collins held up a hand to stop him, turned to her.

"Why not?" he asked.

Now the small room went quiet and all eyes turned to her.

As far as most of the island officers felt, West shouldn't have even been there at all. The Lornea Island Police Department was small, but it was capable, and they understood better than most the nature of crime on the island. But when this case had come along the Chief had been quick to send out a plea for spare resources from neighboring forces. It turned out to be a good call. With almost the entire town of Silverlea present when the girl went missing it had been a stretch to take statements and organize the search, even with outside help. But that's why the Chief was the Chief, he tended to call the big decisions right.

"I JUST DON'T SEE why she would suddenly decide to go swimming." West began, wishing she had something stronger to say. "Without saying anything to anyone."

Langley looked as though he might just continue with his summary. He shook his head.

"Thank you for your input Detective, it's noted." He looked through his notes until he found something. Then he began reading again.

"We've had nine accidental drownings on the island in the last five years. Nearly half of those were folk who took a swim at night. In one case without telling anyone where they were going." He turned to West, as if hoping to pacify her. "People underestimate the currents. They get drunk. They think the ocean looks beautiful. They don't know how dangerous it can be."

"And in those other cases, how often did the body not get washed up?" This was Detective Rogers. He too was a mainlander, brought in to help the case, and he'd been assigned to work with West. But since he was an experienced detective, it had been easier for him to fit in. And perhaps because he was a man. Langley hesitated in answering him.

"Usually they're in the water about a week. Obviously in this case it's been longer. But that's not unheard of. The whole east coast of the island is a nightmare of cliffs and sea-caves. It could be anywhere along there." He turned to the chief now. "That's where we need to focus, keeping the search going. Not on some fantasy investigation."

THE CHIEF SAT behind his desk, his chin resting on one hand, listening. He drummed the fingers of his other hand a few times and observed his officers.

"OK. Tell me again about Joseph Curran. You're happy there's nothing there?"

"No previous convictions, not even a speeding ticket. We've spoken to his friends and colleagues. Nothing unusual about his relationship with his daughter. Just your typical family guy." Langley shook his head. "We've turned him inside out, the mother too. There's nothing there. If the Curran's did it they're goddamn criminal geniuses, without a motive."

The Chief nodded. "The boyfriend?"

"Luke Grimwald. They'd been seeing each other for a few months.

Friends said it wasn't anything serious. He was on the mainland. No way he could have gotten here."

"What about the brother? Have you looked into him?"

"William Curran? He's only fourteen sir."

"It happens."

Langley hesitated a beat. "The Currans left the party to take him back to their rental apartment. She was seen multiple times after they left. The mother reported she checked in on him before she went to bed."

"OK," the chief seemed satisfied with that. "And there's no one else here on the island she knew?"

"No."

"And there's nothing else you're following up right now? Nothing come up?"

"No."

The chief mused over this for a moment.

"All of which leaves two possibilities. Either something happened to her - she was taken by someone with no connection to her, who no-one saw even though the whole town was there. Or for some reason she went into the water." He drummed his fingers again.

"She went into the water," Lieutenant Langley said. "This is Lornea Island. We don't get people *taken* here."

THERE WAS a short silence in the room. West was the one to break it.

"What about her clothes? Where are they if she went swimming?"

Langley turned to face her. "It was a low tide. She would have left them near to where she went in. It's too far to walk from the top of the beach. So when she didn't come out, the tide washed them away too."

"And they disappeared just like the body?"

"Either that or she didn't even bother taking them off in the first place."

"There's nothing to suggest she was suicidal."

Langley shrugged. "It's the sort of thing parents hide."

Detective West and Langley glared at each other.

"But why didn't she *tell anyone* she was going swimming?" West said again.

"You've got to understand the nature of the island, detective." Langley was beginning to sound frustrated. "This isn't the mainland. We're not chasing serial killers here, no matter how much fun that might sound to you."

West opened her mouth to reply, but Detective Rogers shot her a warning glance. She closed her mouth again.

"I think that's enough Lieutenant, Detective." The chief interrupted them all. "We're going round in circles now,". There was silence for a few moments, apart from the rasp as the chief stroked the ends of his mustache.

"As you all know. The reason for this meeting is to make a decision whether to continue working this case at the current level of resources, or whether to scale it back to something a little more sustainable. Obviously in an ideal world we'd investigate every crime, and potential crime, to its natural conclusion. But I'll let you all know when we're operating in an ideal world." The joke did little to lighten the mood. The chief didn't seem to notice.

"The Currans have sought - and received - a lot of media interest in this case. I responded by focusing the entire investigative capacity onto the case. And bringing in outside help," he nodded to Rogers and West. "It's frustrating when that level of effort doesn't pay dividends." The chief drummed his fingers on the desk again. "However, this is the bottom line. Without anything concrete to go on I've no choice but to scale things back to a more sustainable level. I'm also inclined to agree with Lieutenant Langley that the most likely scenario is the girl went into the water and didn't come out." He stopped and turned to West.

"Notwithstanding your concerns Detective."

Langley was nodding his head.

"It's therefore a decision that makes itself." The chief turned to the two mainland detectives. I'll be certain to highlight to both of your commanding officers that you've been a big help over here." But I'll also be informing them that I'll be releasing you at the end of the week. I want to thank you both for volunteering to come over and help. I know everyone here shares the sentiment." He stopped and straightened the papers on his desk. The meeting was over.

25

Detective West and Detective Rogers sat at the near-empty bar as the late-evening news came on. The TV was a small, flat-screen model that looked too cheap among the mirrors, gleaming glasses and dark woods of the Silverlea Lodge Hotel bar. Neither West nor Rogers had been in the mood to talk anyway, so they both turned to listen. The volume was low, but the place was so quiet, they had no problem hearing.

The presenter had that overly made-up look you only really get on local TV news. She sat on a lime-green sofa beside a pile of newspapers. She held one up to the camera.

"A development came today in the case of missing teenager Olivia Curran." The presenter had the characteristic accent of Lornea Island locals: the thickening of the vowels that West still wasn't used to.

"It seems the girl's parents have taken out full-page adverts in major newspapers across the whole country. They're appealing to the public for any information about what might have happened to their daughter. Jim, what more can you tell us about that?" She turned, and the image cut to a man standing by a newspaper stall on a city street.

"That's right, Jenny," he said, pressing one hand to his ear and ignoring the irritated looks of pedestrians passing behind him who had to step off the sidewalk to get past. "This case is already one of the higher-profile investigations that Lornea Island has ever seen, and with full-page adverts in most of the major national newspapers, that looks set to continue. As you know, there have been *no* arrests so far, and police still don't seem to know what happened to Olivia, or even if she's still alive."

The man stood there, listening while the first presenter asked another question.

"Tell me, we've heard previously from the Lornea Island Police Department's Chief Collins that the police are scaling back the investigation, as no leads have come up. Is this in some way pushback from the parents on that issue?"

"Well, Jenny. Olivia's parents have not explicitly said that. Their only comment was they simply want to do everything they possibly can to find their daughter. But the timing of these adverts does seem a remarkable coincidence."

The report cut back to the studio and its lime-green sofa. The female presenter turned to face the camera. "And of course, if you have *any* information regarding Olivia Curran and what might have happened to her, you can reach the Lornea Island Police Department at the number below." She smiled sadly at the camera for a few seconds. Then her face brightened as she began a new story about a girl's football team.

West turned away. She'd seen the ad that morning. Everyone in the department had. It was simple enough, showing a large photograph of Olivia Curran's face and the words:

Have you seen Olivia?

Then there was a brief summary of what happened the night she went missing, and a number to call.

"You know, it's clever what they're doing," said Rogers. He was in his forties, a big man, but from what she'd seen working with him, straightforward. One of the good guys. "I don't know how much ads like that cost, but the fact that they've spent it makes it *news*. Gets it on TV. That'll spread it far and wide. You watch if it doesn't."

West thought for a moment.

"Well, they do run a PR company," she replied eventually. "What do you expect?"

Rogers seemed not to hear her.

"Even little things, like just using her first name in the ad. You notice that? You ever notice how the most famous people just go by one name? Elvis? Cher. I dunno... OJ. They're trying to do the same for the Curran girl." He shook his head. "They're not giving up. They're damn persistent."

"Persistent?" West said. "They've lost their daughter. They're desperate, and everyone knows we've gotten nowhere. Wouldn't you do everything you could to keep the investigation going?"

"We haven't gotten nowhere. We've followed up all the leads, and they go nowhere. Which points to the likelihood that she almost certainly went swimming and drowned. At some point, you've got to give up."

"Except that there's no evidence she went swimming. No clothes on the beach, no telling anyone what she was doing, and of course, no body."

Rogers looked at her. West went on.

"I'm only saying it to you since no one else will listen to me."

"You have to work the odds. The odds here - she probably went swimming."

West didn't answer but pressed her lips together.

"I told you, when we first got here. The secret to being a detective is solve the ones you can solve, and let the rest go. It's tough, but there it is." Rogers took a swig of his beer and turned back to the TV.

West kept watching him, feeling conflicted. She liked Rogers. She'd liked him from the moment they'd arrived together, on the same ferry, and been made temporary partners in the Curran case. It wasn't that everyone else here had treated her badly. On the contrary, even though she was young. Even though they all knew she had only just qualified as a detective, they'd still sent her out speaking to witnesses, taking statements. But as the leads dried up she had found herself assigned more and more to the monotonous tasks that no one else wanted to do. Her and Rogers too. The two mainlanders.

SHE SIPPED HER WINE.

"It could all be a bluff," she said, with little conviction in her voice. "Go all out in public about how desperately you miss your daughter, and that way no one'll ever believe you're the one who took her."

Rogers shook his head. "It's not him."

"What about the statistics? Four out of five cases where children are abducted, the Dad did it."

"Still leaves one out of five where he didn't. And she probably wasn't even abducted."

West laughed suddenly. Rogers looked at her surprised, then finished the remainder of his beer. Then he set the glass back on the bar top.

"You want another one?"

She hesitated - she was on her third glass of the night, and she rarely drank more than one.

"Come on, it's our last goddamn night on Lornea Island. And we've earned it."

"Have we? I don't think we have much to celebrate."

"Don't talk like that, Detective. First thing you've gotta learn in this job, you're never gonna win 'em all. You don't remember that, you're gonna go crazy."

West smiled. In the month she'd worked with Rogers there must have been at least ten "first things" she had to learn. Not that she minded. He had over ten years' experience of major investigations, while this was her first real case.

"Go on then. One more," she said, sliding her empty glass toward him.

ROGERS RAISED A HAND, the bartender came over. He was in his twenties, dressed in a crisp white shirt, and more used to serving tourists than the two detectives who had been staying in the hotel for the last month. It had been the bartender's hope to get the detectives to talk about the case since they'd arrived, but they'd barely made it into the bar, until this evening. Tonight, he knew, was his last chance.

"Same again, Detective Rogers?"

"Sure."

The bartender unstopped the bottle he'd opened for West earlier in the evening and emptied it into her glass, the golden liquid swirling round. When it didn't quite reach the full measure, he pulled the cork from a second bottle and topped it off comfortably over the measure line. Then, as he stood pouring Rogers' beer, he asked as casually as he could,

"So, I hear you guys are on the boat tomorrow?"

West waited for Rogers to tell him they couldn't talk about the case, but he didn't say that.

"That's right."

"What's that all about, then?" The bartender went on.

Rogers shrugged. "Like the TV said. You can't throw unlimited resources at one case. No matter how influential her parents are, or what stunts they pull."

The bartender used a flat wooden stick to wipe the creamy foam so that it sat flat and level on the top of the beer.

"So that's it? You guys are just giving up?"

"No one's giving up. There's still detectives on the case. Just not us."

The bartender set the beer down carefully in front of Rogers, then frowned. "I still don't get it," he said.

A look of irritation appeared on Rogers' face, and West smiled to herself; she felt she'd gotten to know that look over the last few weeks.

"Get what?"

"The whole thing. How come you guys are here... How come you're going even though the case isn't solved..."

Rogers sighed. "Look. It's like this. Lornea Island is a small place, right? So when a big, difficult case like this comes along, the police department has to ask for help from neighboring forces. That's where we came in." He pointed at himself and West. "We came over to help out at the start of the investigation. But crime doesn't stop elsewhere. We've done what we can, now we gotta go back. It's that simple."

The barman's head tilted to one side as he considered this.

"So you guys are like the special agents, the supercops?" he said. West looked at him more closely than she had before. She noticed a tattoo partially hidden under the sleeve of his shirt. She guessed the guy read a lot of comic books.

"I wouldn't say supercops exactly," Rogers was saying. "But yeah, it's something like that."

"Actually, we're more like the lowest of the low," West said abruptly. "We're the detectives our own departments could spare." She smiled at the bartender, aware that Rogers was screwing up his face, scowling at this description.

"It's more about who's available. You need guys who can up-sticks in a moment's notice. They can't be in the middle of a case. They gotta have an understanding family," he coughed. "Or not mind leaving their family for a while." The bartender began nodding.

"I get it. So now you gotta go back? Solve some more crimes?"

"That's right." Rogers looked happy for a moment.

"Before you know what happened to Olivia Curran?"

Both detectives went quiet.

"Yeah," Rogers said eventually.

WEST PULLED her glass toward her and sat stroking the stem. The bartender retired to the other end of the bar and resumed his slow washing of glasses.

"I know you're right, but it still doesn't feel great to have failed at my first real case," West said. "Leaving when we don't know what happened to her."

Rogers shrugged. "That's the job, Detective. You work a case. Maybe you crack it, maybe you don't."

"So it doesn't bother you, even a little?" she asked.

"Nope. And it shouldn't bother you, either."

"I know." West looked into her glass; the hotel bar was reflected on the surface of the wine. "It does, though. I guess I'd just like to know what happened to her."

Rogers watched her for a moment, then laughed. "Well, I guess you will now. The amount of media coverage her parents just bought, this case is gonna be in the papers if she does ever turn up."

She looked up at him, surprised at the sound. He had a nice laugh.

"Anyway. We're supposed to be talking about something else," Rogers said, forcing a more upbeat note to his voice. "Aren't you looking forward to getting back to the mainland? To *civilization*?"

Jessica West thought about what she was returning to the next day. An image formed in her mind, her one-bedroom apartment, in a cheap part of town, the lease signed in a hurry after it all went wrong with Matthew. Work was better though, she supposed. After five years in the

Hartford Police Department she'd been successful in her Detective Exams at her first try. The city was a curious mix, the home of many major insurance firms but fast-climbing the poverty rankings. Domestic abuse cases were common. So were random shootings. Was that really more civilized than here, where outside, she could smell wild heather and hear nothing but the sound of the ocean?

"I NEVER CLEANED OUT MY FRIDGE," she said thoughtfully. "Before I came here, I mean. I'm dreading what civilizations I'll find in there."

Rogers made a face. Then, watching her closely he went on.

"What about your boyfriend?" He looked away, as if he wasn't that interested. "What did you say his name was? Matthew? Doesn't he look after things like that?"

West had noticed him using the same voice when he'd be taking statements, when he'd thought the witness might be about to say something interesting. She bit her lip for a moment, then decided to come clean.

"He's not really a *boyfriend* as such. Not anymore." She watched him as she spoke, knowing it was the wine making her open up, but not minding so much. Rogers frowned again, his big, bearlike face revealing the effort of trying to fit what she was saying now, with how she'd described it when he first asked about her circumstances.

"We split up a while back. When I came here, I made out we were still together. I just thought it was simpler that way. I didn't want any complications. You know?" She looked at him, searching his face to see if he got it.

There had seemed good reason for the lie. Even back in Hartford, male officers outnumbered women by four to one, but the Lornea Island Police Department was fifteen years behind. It consisted entirely of male officers, most of whom had done little to hide the fact they were checking her out when she turned up. It was a small department, too, the kind of place where everyone knew each other's business, or expected to.

"I get it," said Rogers, nodding but still frowning because he didn't really understand. He waited a beat, then went on. "So what happened? With this Matthew, I mean?"

Normally, West would have steered the conversation onto other matters, but this was her last night on the island. It was almost certainly the last time she'd ever see Detective Rogers. And, she guessed, she was ready to talk.

"I had quite a different kind of life, before I joined the force. He's kind of a hangover from that. We tried to make it work but..." She stopped, changing her mind about getting into this. "We grew apart. Actually, it's one of the reasons I volunteered to come over for the case. He was having a hard time accepting it was over."

"What kind of a hard time? He get violent?" Rogers narrowed his eyes.

She smiled, but shook her head. "No, nothing like that. It's just my life changed a lot when I signed up. It was tough for him."

Rogers grunted but seemed to accept the explanation. He didn't ask what it was she had done before signing up. West guessed it didn't much matter. Once a police officer, always a police officer.

"How about you?" West asked, "Why'd you volunteer to come here. To be a *supercop*?"

Rogers glanced up at the word, then smiled.

"I used to come here as a kid." Rogers looked around. "We even stayed right here in Silverlea." He shrugged. "I guess that got my interest. Plus my ex-wife has recently decided to do everything she can to make my life a misery."

"I'm sorry."

"Don't be. But don't end up like me. I'm a walking stereotype. My ex-wife won't talk to me, and I see my kid maybe once a month." He grinned at her, and she found herself considering the man sitting opposite her again. He wasn't bad-looking; she'd thought that the moment she was assigned to work with him. Blond hair, receding a little. Maybe twenty pounds overweight, but he carried it well. Looking at him, she was once again reminded of a bear. A friendly bear with huge hands.

A silence stretched out between them, but a comfortable silence. They watched each other. The mention of Rogers' wife had triggered something in West's mind. She hadn't considered him as anything other than partner and colleague until that moment. Now another aspect of him came into focus. As a man. An apparently available man.

SHE TURNED AWAY. What the hell was she thinking? Throughout her short career as a police officer, and her even shorter career as a detective, she'd been warned by senior female colleagues not to get involved with anyone she worked with. The office gossips would ensure she'd never live it down. To date she had followed that advice. But she'd been with Matthew then. And there was an easy way to dismiss the warning voices. Come tomorrow she would never see Detective Rogers again. She would never see the guys at the Lornea Island Police Station. Tomorrow morning, she would pack up her gear and drive to the port. She would climb on the ferry and return to her old life, never to come back to Lornea Island. And the way she was feeling about that, a little human company might be welcome.

SHE SIGHED. She looked across at him wondering if he was thinking anything remotely the same as her. She finished her drink.

"Fancy a nightcap?" She asked.

26

It took a while for West to recognize the dryness of her throat and the bitter taste in her mouth, but then it had been a while since she'd drunk that much. And even then, she couldn't figure out why her hotel room seemed different. It looked more or less the same, but somehow reversed, like it had been turned into a mirror image of itself in the night. Then she remembered. It wasn't *her* hotel room at all. It was the one across the hall from where she had been staying the last month. She looked across the other side of her bed and sighed.

"Oh Shit," she said, but quietly enough that she didn't wake him up.

She covered her face with her hands as last night began to come back to her. He'd agreed to her suggestion for another drink. That turned into another, and they'd ended up taking the bottle of Jack Daniels from the bar. She dimly remembered sitting on the bed, staring at Rogers suitcases, packed and ready to go. What happened after that, she didn't want to think about. She glanced over at the bottle now, nearly empty.

It doesn't matter, she told herself. *I'll never see him again. I'll never see any of them again.*

She sat up in bed and looked across into the mirror. She took in her tired-looking face, the crumpled clothes surrounding the bed.

A swim, she thought to herself. *I need to go for a swim.*

TEN MINUTES LATER, and still driven on by the alcohol in her bloodstream, she was striding down the beach. The October air raised goosebumps on the bare skin of her arms and legs and the sun, still low, stayed hidden behind a thick blanket of clouds. For a mile to the north, and five miles to the south, she couldn't see another figure on the sand. She breathed in the freshness, questioned her sanity, and listened to the low roar of the waves.

The hotel had a heated indoor pool she could have used. But it was tiny, barely long enough to fit in five strokes before she had to turn around. And they kept it too hot, unlike the pools she was used to. No - if West needed to make peace with Lornea Island, with her failure on her first major case, and with whatever mess she'd gotten herself into last night - the ocean was what she needed.

She reached the lower part of the beach, where the wet sand was washed by the long surges of water, the final gasps of waves that had broken much farther out. She set down her towel where she thought the water wouldn't reach, and hoped the tide was going out. She took two deep breaths, then strode forward, still clumsy from the drink. Moments later, she was in the water, the coldness splashing up against her body. It made her gasp, but she forced herself to carry on. To focus only on keeping her legs moving.

When the water reached her stomach, she leaned forward and dived under. The cold knocked the breath from her body, and she came up at once. But after a few panted breaths she tried again. This time when she dived she forced herself to glide for several long seconds. She kept her eyes open, watching the green-yellow sand slide past underneath. Then she angled her body up and rose through the shades of green to the surface, where she fell automatically into a smooth, powerful stroke.

Under the water, her arms swung beneath her, pulling forward with an easy rhythm. Her breathing became light, just a subtle roll of her neck, alternating from one side to the other. Her movements were smooth, all trace of clumsiness gone. As if she belonged in the water.

She swam straight out to sea, powering through the small breaking waves as they rolled toward her. West swam until her body no longer felt the cold of the water. Then she stopped. Treading water, she looked back at the hotel. Already, last night felt washed away.

Then she widened her gaze. From out here, the beach was breathtaking. A vast sweep of sand, the little encampment of Silverlea midway along, the low cliffs of Northend feeling closer than they must actually be. She hadn't had the time to do the tourist thing of searching for silver, of course. Well, maybe she'd have to come back one day. She turned to the other end of the beach; the higher, more severe cliffs of Littlelea were half-lost in the mist.

She'd stood on those cliffs just a few days after she'd arrived. She visited a boy and his father who had been at the party. She'd taken their statements. A strange boy, what was his name? Billy. *Billy Wheatley.*

SHE GRIMACED AT THE THOUGHT, and began swimming again, this time along the beach. But as her head fell to the side she noticed a figure walking down the beach to where she had left her towel and clothes. The figure waved a hand. She stopped, brought back into the moment. On a whim she took a full breath of air and let herself sink down, feet first, into the water. Once her head was covered, she exhaled and looked up, watching the bubbles disappear above her to the surface, watching her hair swirl, until the water turned too dark to see. She felt a moment's fear, that her feet would never touch the bottom and she was letting herself sink forever, but then she felt sand under her feet. She bent her knees until her arms touched, too, in the darkness now, and she grabbed two handfuls of sand. For a second, she stayed there. Her eyes were open, but they saw nothing. She wondered what creatures might be observing her from the shadows. She wondered if Olivia Curran's dead eyes were somewhere staring back at her.

When she surfaced she swam fast back to the beach, enjoying the feeling when the swells picked her up and accelerated her towards the shore. When she felt the bottom she walked out. The cold made her skin feel like it was glowing.

"Thanks," she said, taking the towel that Rogers held out to her. She bent forward, rubbing the water from her hair.

"You swim pretty good, Detective West." Rogers took care to avert his eyes from the thin fabric of her swimsuit as she wrapped herself in the towel.

"I grew up swimming," she said.

"I grew up swimming too. I can't swim like that." He pulled his eyes back to her face and smiled at her.

"No, I mean I really grew up swimming. Since I was five years old, my dad decided I was going to be a swimmer. We went every morning before school. Then since I was seven, every day after school too."

"No shit? You were serious about it?"

"Dad was. He had this dream I'd win him an Olympic medal."

He watched her for a beat, to see if she was serious.

"So did you?"

West's childhood flashed before her eyes. The early years, when it was just Dad shouting at her from the poolside, stopwatch in hand. Driving to competitions in Dad's Volvo that smelt of chlorine from her constantly wet hair and towels. Then, later on, when it wasn't just her but Sarah too, and it wasn't just Dad but a team of coaches and nutritionists and physiotherapists. It might have ended with Olympic success - although she knew Sarah always had the greater chance. But it wasn't how it ended. It was too much to explain to Rogers. And did she even want to?

"No." She said, looking away.

"Why not? What happened?"

Without thinking West rolled her shoulders around, feeling for the burn she still remembered from after a race.

"I wasn't good enough." She turned away, not wanting him to see her face.

Rogers sounded dismissive. "Well you look pretty good to me. I had no idea I was working with an athlete."

West had heard the same sentiment before. It always annoyed her.

"I never achieved anything when I was a kid. Too busy getting drunk and chasing girls." Rogers went on, flashing her a grin.

"Can we not talk about it please?" West replied.

There was a silence, just the burr of the wind rolling down the sand.

THEY WALKED in silence for a while but West felt frustrated. Thinking about her past highlighted the sense of failing, again. By leaving Lornea Island and the case unsolved she was failing again. Just like she'd failed her Dad. Just like she'd failed Sarah. There had been nothing she could do that time, but now she was *supposed* to help. She was a police detective. She was supposed to put things right this time. Yet a girl was still missing. Another family left in limbo, not knowing whether their daughter was alive or dead. It didn't feel good.

WITH A JOLT she realized Rogers was speaking again.

"Anyway, I'm guessing you didn't check your cellphone this morning? Given how it's on the floor of my hotel room."

West brought her mind back to the present.

"No. Why?"

"The chief wants to see us."

She stopped.

"Why?"

"I don't know."

"How do you mean?"

"He didn't say. Just that he wanted us to come in."

"When?"

Rogers checked his watch. "He said to be there at nine. That's in about ten minutes. That's why I came down to the beach to get you. You think I just fancied a stroll?"

"He didn't say anything about why?"

"No. Just that it was urgent. Maybe he wants to say goodbye and thank us for all our hard work."

"Didn't he do that yesterday?"

"Maybe he wants to do it again?"

West didn't reply. But her mind latched on to the meeting. It offered a chink of hope.

27

It took just ten minutes for West to shower and get dressed. They drove the twenty minutes to the police station together. A few of the uniforms were sitting around, on a break. One of them, a guy named Deaton, gave Rogers a friendly shove as he passed.

"You just can't keep away from the place, can you?"

Rogers grinned back, but shrugged when Deaton asked what they were doing. West said nothing, and no one spoke to her, but Lieutenant Langley did glance up at her as she passed. He nodded in greeting.

"DETECTIVE ROGERS, DETECTIVE WEST..." The chief said from the window. He waved at two chairs in front of his desk and poured them coffees from the perculator he kept for his own use. They sat. West looked around his office, she hadn't expected to see it again.

He kept the small room neat. There was a well-stocked bookshelf, and the books looked used. Perhaps that was how he intended on spending the last few years before retirement? On his desk there was a newspaper.

"So, I understand you're both booked on the midday ferry?" Chief Collins said, taking his own seat and smiling at them.

"I'm sure you're both anxious to get back to family and friends." He raised his eyebrows. West felt Rogers glancing across at her. She nodded noncommittally.

"But I'm sure you'll also be aware of yesterday's little development." His eyes shifted to the newspaper, which lay open on the Currans' advert. His face remained neutral. He took a sip of coffee.

"I spoke with Joseph Curran by telephone yesterday afternoon," the chief went on. "He informed me he intends to purchase another round of adverts next week, then another *every week* until his daughter is found, or he runs out of money. Whichever comes sooner." He stopped, and sent the detectives a wan smile.

"As you know, the Currans have rather a lot of money." He gave a small laugh this time. Then he made a steeple with his hands as if praying.

"As of eight o'clock this morning, when I got in, we've logged twenty-seven calls. Tip-offs, from people who think they've seen her, across the whole country." The chief watched the two detectives as he said this.

"Anything relevant, sir?" Rogers asked, his voice gruff and low against the Chief's clipped, precise tones.

"Nothing obviously so, no. Langley and Strickland are looking into them as we speak. And if Langley's right - and the girl went into the water - there won't be anything relevant. Just a lot of work, following up dead end leads. But if Langley's wrong..." The chief's eyebrows flicked up on his face. "Well, there's just a chance something might come out of it. Which brings me to why I've asked you back here." His fingers started drumming on the desk.

"I'll get right to the point. I spoke to both of your commanding officers last night. I've explained how our circumstances have changed, and how we could benefit from your assisting us here a little longer. Ultimately, they're both willing to release you - if you're willing to stay on, that is."

West realized she'd been holding her breath. She took a gulp of air.

"You're not scaling back the investigation after all?" she said.

"Officially, no. Unofficially, yes. Clearly, I cannot continue to dedicate my entire criminal investigation division to a single case. There may not be much happening on Lornea Island, but we do still have other crimes to investigate." He smiled.

"Lieutenant Langley will remain in nominal charge of the investigation, as before, but if you agree, you two will become the main active investigative unit. The search of the Silverlea sea cliffs will also continue with the help of the Coast Guard."

"So we'd be digging into the leads the Currans' adverts generate?" Rogers said.

The chief took another sip of his coffee.

"That's about it. I'd suggest you also go back over the case. Review everything. It's possible something was missed."

"But unlikely?" Rogers questioned. The chief didn't answer him.

"We wouldn't be able to keep you in the hotel any more, but there's a number of apartments in Silverlea that become empty this time of year. You'll have a bit more space." He smiled again. "You'll still be neighbors."

"How long are we talking here?" Rogers asked.

Chief Collins shrugged. "Assuming we don't find anything and the Currans don't decide they're wasting their money, I'd look to review the situation after three months. Every case has limits. Even when the victim's parents run a successful PR agency."

There was a silence.

"I know you weren't expecting such a long stay on the island. And you're probably itching to get back to friends and family."

Two images flashed through West's mind. Her apartment back in Hartford, and an image of Matthew. They were gone almost as soon as they appeared. She felt the weight of disappointment lifting. This was a second chance. An opportunity to not fail. Then another thought occurred to her. Another image formed, this time it was Rogers' hairy back, turned away from her in the thick white sheets of the hotel bed. Was that going to be a problem?

SHE WONDERED if Rogers would stay. He'd been clear he thought the case was hopeless. If he left as planned that would be simpler, she reasoned. No worries about their night together becoming common knowledge.

But Rogers' voice interrupted her thoughts.

"I could stay here a little more sir. I don't have too much to get back to right now."

"Good man. Good man. Detective West?" The chief's attention swung over to her.

She tried to think fast. The idea of everyone in the department knowing she'd slept with Rogers didn't bear thinking about. But then she blinked it away. Who the hell really cared? There was never any doubt how she would reply.

"Me too, sir. I'd like to stay as long as it takes."

She glanced at Rogers, and their eyes met for a moment before both looked away.

28

My heart is beating like a drum as I sit and stare at the image on the laptop. I've got the image paused on the screen so she's frozen there, staring out at me. The girl the whole of America is looking for. Olivia Curran.

I've found her. I've caught her on my wildlife cam. I actually pinch myself because it doesn't feel real. I pinch both arms until they hurt, but afterward, she's still there, frozen on my laptop screen, looking out the window, right at the camera. But then questions begin to bubble up in my mind. She looks so normal. Why isn't she locked up in the cellar?

I check the date of the recording. Six days ago. I nudge the video a few frames forward. It's not *that* clear, actually. The windows are dirty, and because the lights are on in the house, she's backlit, so her face is in shadow when she looks out. And these few frames forward, her expression has changed.

I zoom right in to try and figure out if she looks scared or not. It's hard to tell, but she's definitely not smiling.

WHAT DOES IT MEAN? If she's in the living room, maybe that means she's just escaped from the cellar, or wherever he's keeping her? But if you'd just escaped from a murderer, you wouldn't go and close the drapes, would you? Why doesn't she run away? Why doesn't she make a run to the front door and escape?

Then something else occurs to me. Something obvious that you've probably already worked out, but it makes me feel really happy. *Olivia Curran is alive.* Even though the TV news people always talk like she might be alive somewhere, it's been obvious for months that no one really believed that. Even the parents, when they stare right at the cameras and pretend to speak directly to Olivia, saying how much they love her and how they just want her to come home, you can tell they don't believe it. You can tell from how much they're crying that really, they think she's already dead.

But she's not dead. She's alive, and I'm the one who found her!

I re-run the video a few more times, trying to take it all in. Maybe the police will want me to help on other cases? Will I be able to fit it in with my schoolwork? Will I be famous? Like that French boy, Tintin? I used to like reading those stories when I was little. Only he's not real, of course. Not like I am.

Then suddenly, I notice something in the video. Mr. Foster's van is in the driveway. I can't see him, but this means he must be in the house too. That brings me back down to earth. Wondering again what she's doing there? It sends a little shiver down my back too.

My next thought is I have to tell the police right away. But there aren't many other clips left, so I decide I'll just quickly look those over before I do anything else. And I'm glad I do, because the very next clip changes everything. And not in a good way.

CLIP NUMBER 00753 starts with the front door opening. That must be the movement that triggers the camera because the recording starts with it half-open already. But immediately, you can see something strange is happening. The inside of the house is glowing red, like the inside of a volcano, and all around it, it's black. It takes me a moment to realize what's going on, but then I get it. It's a *nighttime* clip. The camera is recording in infrared. The red glow coming from the house is just because the air in there is warmer than the outside. Then a monster with bright-white face and hands appears, limping into the shot. But it isn't really a monster. It's Mr. Foster, with his features all distorted by the heat signature. He comes out and props the door open with something that looks black against the red background; I guess it's a rock from the path. Then he goes out of shot, to the van. I guess he opens the back doors of the van because I see a little bit of red come into the corner of the frame, which is probably from the interior light, which gives off some heat. Then Mr. Foster comes back to the house, pauses on the doorstep, and has a long look around. Then he disappears inside, and then - and this is where it gets really interesting - he reappears. But this time, he's carrying something.

Actually, that's not the right word. He's *dragging* something. Something big, like a slightly bent trunk of a tree. It's hard to figure out what it is, since the colors are so strange, but I've seen quite a few infrared videos since getting that camera so I work it out. It's a carpet. A badly rolled-up carpet. It's bigger than he is, and Mr. Foster is holding onto one end and struggling to get it out of the front door. Then he drags it right past the camera, and it slowly disappears out of the left side of the shot. A moment later, the van door shuts again.

I can't see what's inside the carpet, but from the lumpy way it's rolled up, there's definitely something in there.

The clip ends with Mr. Foster going back and closing the front door, then getting into the van and driving off. Then there's thirty seconds of nothing while the camera runs in case there's anything else to catch.

I'm stunned. I watch the clip three times, and on the third time, I start taking screengrabs when there's a particularly clear shot of him with the carpet. It's obvious there's a body in there. It *has* to be her. It *has* to be Olivia. Sometime between 16:37 on Sunday afternoon and this clip from 02:12 on Monday morning, he must have killed her. All my excitement from before just evaporates. It's replaced by a kind of unreal horror.

And then a horrible thought hits me. If I wasn't a kid, if I'd done a real stakeout in a car, with coffee and donuts, then I could have rescued her. I would have seen her at the window. I would have called the police then. But it didn't happen like that. I used my camera instead, and now she's dead. I had a chance to save her, and I failed.

It's my fault she's dead.

I can't describe how it makes me feel. I've never felt it before. Crushed, I guess. Hollow. And horrified. But also panicky. My next thought is that I *have* to hide the evidence. Before anyone finds out that I could have known and blames me for it. My hand hovers over the *delete* key.

NO! Think Billy. Think.

I'm too late to save Olivia Curran, but Mr. Foster has a *history* of this. He's done it before, so he'll do it again. Unless someone stops him.

I REALIZE my mouth is dry so I go and get that soda. I eat the cookies too. I try to pull myself together. I've got to be professional. It's just like doing science. In science, you have to collect and present all the information you get so another scientist can see what you've done and come to the same conclusions. It must be the same with criminal investigations. I need to send the police all the information so they come to the same conclusion, and arrest Mr. Foster. I just won't tell them who I am. That way, they can't blame me. I mean, it's not as if I actually killed her; I did my best. I'm only a kid, and at least I *found* her. That's more than the police did.

And once I've made the decision, it's easier. My breathing slows down, and my fingers start working again. I open the Word document and start writing up my notes. I label all the important video clips and embed the screen grabs alongside the correct file names. I make a time-line of when each event happened, and figure out what time Mr. Foster must have killed her. Then I remember I haven't finished watching all the clips yet, so finally, I go back to viewing the last few, and sure enough, there's Mr. Foster returning to his house the next day. I note the time: 05:55. But I'm so engrossed in my work that I don't notice the door to the chalet opening behind me.

"Billy, can you..." a voice begins. Then, *"What's that? What the hell are you doing?"*

Dad's voice swings from calm to mad in the space of two sentences.

29

I've got the video player screen open in a corner and I'm pretty quick to minimize that, but all it does it give more space to the investigation file in Word open underneath. I fumble with the keypad, trying to close that. It's open long enough, I reckon, for Dad to read the title:

INVESTIGATION INTO THE OLIVIA CURRAN ~~MYSTERY~~/MURDER

"What the *hell* is that, Billy? You said you had math homework. You got out of helping because you had math. Did you lie to me?"

It's really hard to snap back into Dad's world after what I've been doing, and I can't understand why he's so *angry*. I could tell him that I finished, but then he'll be annoyed that I didn't come and help him. Anyway, I don't think of it in time.

"*Investigation into the Olivia Curran Mystery*? That's not math. What the *hell* are you doing?"

"It's nothing," I say, and I close the laptop screen. I feel my face flush hot. "It's just a project I have to do. For... for PD."

I don't know why I tell him that; it's just the first thing that comes into my head. It's not a good excuse, but I'm pretty sure it's better than telling him what I've really been doing. I can't imagine how mad he'd get if he knew she was dead and I could have saved her.

"PD? That Personal Development bullshit? You're studying that girl for *Personal Development*? That's sick." It turns out it was actually a good excuse because Dad always gets angry when he hears about PD. I think it's because they didn't have it when he was at school, so he can't figure out what it's for.

"Jesus. That's... That's not right."

Dad seems thrown off balance by this, so I keep going.

"Yeah, it's about keeping safe, you know, from pedos and stuff."

"Pedos?"

"Pedophiles. They're people who like to - "

"I know what a goddamn pedophile is, Billy." Dad cuts me off.

"I'm just not sure the school should be giving you projects on them." He stops for a moment, looking at the closed computer. Then he looks right back at me.

"You're not lying to me, are you, Billy?"

I hesitate for just a second. Maybe I should just tell him. After all, what I'm doing here is unquestionably adult stuff. Surely I can tell Dad? But I feel another flush of guilt that I was too late to save Olivia, and I push away any thought of telling him. I'm going to tell the police; then they can deal with it. Dad never needs to know. No one ever needs to know that I could have saved her. I shake my head.

"No."

For a little while, the only noise is the sound of Dad breathing, irregularly because he's still angry. I think I'm out of the woods, but he doesn't let up.

"Then let me see. Let me see what you were working on. Open it up. Right now."

He's called my bluff. I can't let him see the detail – it's all about Mr. Foster and how he killed her. And it's too late to be honest now. Not now I just lied to Dad. I can't let him see my computer, but he leans over me and lifts up the laptop lid. The screen comes to life.

Welcome Back user: Billy Wheatley

Enter Password:

"What's your password Billy? Put it in. Let me see what you're doing."

I hesitate. There's something about the way Dad's standing over me that's just plain scary.

"Put the goddamn password in, Billy. Put it in NOW."

His voice is so loud it makes my fingers jump onto the keyboard, but I stop myself just before they press out the word that's throbbing in my head. All my passwords are variations on one two-word root, with different endings and numbers to make them more secure. But Dad doesn't know the root. I start to type.

Incorrect Password

"Um," I say. And I try again. Typing the same word in a second time. The computer makes the same dud sound, and I'm still locked out.

"What the hell are you doing, Billy?"

"I can't get into it. I changed the password the other night, and I forgot what it is."

"Bullshit..." Dad slams the little table with his hand, and the empty soda can falls off and onto the floor. I freeze, not knowing what to do. Then Dad's anger turns to frustration. He can't figure out what to tell me to do.

"I've got it written down at home," I say. "I can open it again there. It's just I keep changing my password for security, and I forgot." I pretend to try again, still typing in the wrong word because, obviously, I haven't really forgotten my password. I'd never do that.

"Billy, are you lying to me? Are you really studying what happened to that girl for PD?"

There's not much else I can do but nod.

"I swear, Dad." He makes a big sighing noise.

"That's just... This whole damn town's gone crazy over that girl." He scratches his head, and I notice he's gotten white paint on his hands. Some of it rubs off on his hair. "The whole damn country. She just went swimming. She drowned. That's it. I don't know why people can't just *fucking* drop it."

"Do you want me to help you with the painting?" I say a few moments later. Clearly, I can't go back to working on the computer now, and if I help out, he's more likely to forget about asking to see my PD homework when we get back. Dad sighs again.

"Yeah, why not? I'm in chalet six. You can do some sanding."

30

I t's late now, and Dad's asleep. He didn't even remember about checking on my homework when we got home. I did a lot of sanding for him, and that made him forget, and my arms ache. I still had to run upstairs when we got home and quickly make some pretend homework I could show him in case he did remember. Just a summary of how the police have got nowhere. I copied and pasted it from Wikipedia mostly. But then, when I went downstairs, Dad was on the sofa with the TV on, one beer open, and another lined up on the arm of the chair, so I didn't even bother telling him about it. Instead, I went back upstairs and got on with what I really had to do this evening: organizing my information to give it to the police.

I KNOW where to send it. There's been these adverts in the papers for weeks, asking for information about her, and there's a phone number and an email address. It says you're allowed to be anonymous, but if you send a normal email, you're not really anonymous, are you? They could just reply and ask who you are, or at least see your email address. But I know a way around that. You can get email addresses that can't be tracked, and then you can send the actual email through lots of different countries like Russia and Australia and funny countries like Bolivia and

Poland too. I don't know exactly how to do it yet, but I've read about it, and I understand the basics.

This is what I write to the police:

URGENT

To the attention of Chief Larry Collins.

I am emailing to tell you Olivia Curran is dead. She was being held prisoner at 16 Speyside Drive by Mr. Foster, who is well-known around town as a pedophile. Most of the time, she was locked up in the cellar, but unfortunately, last Sunday she escaped, so he killed her. Here is a picture of her closing the drapes before he killed her.

Here is another picture of him hiding her body in some carpet and taking it out of his house in the middle of the night. It's not very clear because it is taken with the infrared mode of a Denver WCT-3004 Wildlife Camera (not the new version, unfortunately, which has the higher resolution).

I have also seen that Mr. Foster has a pink girl's backpack in his house, which probably belongs to Olivia. I'm sorry I don't have a photograph of this because I forgot to take one. But I expect you'll find it in the house when you raid it.

I do think you should arrest Mr. Foster immediately so he doesn't kill any other girls.

Signed

HK

I THINK ABOUT SIGNING IT "ANONYMOUS," but it's a hard word to spell so instead I put those initials that I just typed randomly (think!), and then I attach the two screen grabs and package up the email to send. After a little reading, I download a remailer program from the Internet. Then I set up a VPN (that's a virtual private network, in case you don't know) and install a new browser that doesn't track IP addresses. Finally, I use something called Guerrilla Mail to create a temporary email address, which I use to set up a *permanent* Gmail account in a false name (Harry King, so if they ever do track it, it'll match my initials). I didn't need to do that last step; I could have just sent my message with the Guerrilla account, but I didn't like the logo for the account much. It was a man with a bandana and a rifle. You'd have thought they'd just use a monkey.

It was a lot of work. It's now almost midnight, and I've finally hit "send" on my message. The police will get it in the morning. Well, they'll get it now; even though the message goes all the way around the world, it only takes a few seconds longer than a normal email, but I don't think there's anyone there at this time of night. What I'm trying to say is that tomorrow, the police will do a raid on Mr. Foster's house and arrest him.

It's a shame I was too late to rescue Olivia, but at least he'll go to prison, and then the town can get back to normal. The beach too. I've been worried about the Coast Guard search teams tramping all over my hermit crab study. I'd like to get back to doing that too. I like being an investigator, but I think I prefer being a marine biologist.

I get undressed and put my pajamas on. I can hear Dad snoring while I brush my teeth. When I get into bed, I find my mind is still buzzing, and I can't get to sleep. For some reason, I start thinking about my password again. I decide I'm going to tell you what it is. Not so that you can break into my files, of course, and not the *whole* password. I won't tell you the end part where I have some funny characters, but then, that part isn't very interesting anyway. I'll just tell you the first bit, because I feel like we're getting to know each other by now. And I don't really have anyone else to talk to. But you have to *promise* that you won't tell anyone.

You promise, right?

The first part of my password is: **BabyEva**

31

I check the local TV news as soon as I get up, but I'm not really expecting anything yet. Probably, the police are still eating their breakfast. They won't have even read my email yet. It's hard, but I try to forget about it.

Dad goes surfing again, from Silverlea, and with the tide being low, I decide I can get into the caves and do a hermit crab count. I make sure I've got all my gear and run up the beach to Northend as soon as we arrive. I feel I've neglected my study a bit. I hope Dr. Ribald doesn't mind. I guess she'd understand if she knew.

It's a beautiful day, the first good weather we've had in a long time. The sun feels warm on my back, almost like summer, and I run along that hard part of the sand you get just before the water, and sometimes, I have to make sudden detours up the beach when big surges of waves rush up the beach. It's fun, and by the time I get to Northend, I've stopped wondering if the police have raided Mr. Foster's house yet.

Then I take my shoes and socks off, put them on my usual rock, and roll up my jeans carefully. Part of me doesn't want to go in the caves, where it's cold and dark. It's too nice a day out here. But I do it anyway. I step into the cold, clear water of the rockpools by the entrance. They sparkle in the sunlight, and I see a shimmer of silver where a shoal of tiny fish darts away from my foot. I almost decide to stop and try to catch them. It reminds me of being a kid, searching for nuggets of silver. But I'm not a kid anymore. I've got work to do.

I step carefully through the seaweed until I get to the cliff face, where a small black opening marks the entrance to the caves. The water's pretty deep in the entrance, and you have to duck down, so it's kind of intimidating, but I've done it so many times now I don't even hesitate. I duck down under the rocky ledge, move forward with my back bent, and stand up inside the cave. In front of me, it's pitch-black at first. You'd think no light could ever reach in here, but the truth is a little bit of sunlight does get in through the cave entrance. Gradually, my eyes adjust until I can make out the interior shape of the cave. It's almost circular, this first chamber, with smooth bumps on the walls and ceiling, like the rock has been growing in here. Size-wise, it's about half a tennis court, but that's only the first chamber. It goes back further than that, but the rockpools don't, so there's no need for me to go that far.

I switch on my ultraviolet flashlight and start to shine it around at the water I'm standing in. Like usual, I'm a little worried that it's not working because it doesn't send out a beam of light like a normal flashlight. It's only when you catch something that glows in ultraviolet that you know it's actually on.

I focus my eyes on the bottom of the pools as usual, but all I can see at first are my feet glowing blue when the flashlight shines on them. And then I see some anemones. They look purple with the light, but they glow much darker, so they take a while to spot. I keep sweeping the flashlight from side to side, trying to catch the brighter yellows, reds, and greens of the crabs.

I search for a long time, until my feet feel cold and shriveled from the water, but there's nothing. For a while, I think I'm not going to find *any* of my crabs. That would be a disaster. But then I shine the light under a ledge of rock, far back into the cave, and a strange blue light shines back from under the dark water. It's pretty deep, and I have to put my whole arm in the water, so my sleeve gets wet, but I pick up the crab and pull it out to inspect it. It looks like just a shell; the little pincers and legs have retracted almost completely inside. I don't need to read the small number 13 painted on the back of the shell to recognize it as one of my favorites. For some reason, I called this one Gary.

I record Gary's position on a notepad hanging from around my neck.

Then I put him back where he was and continue my search, eventually finding two other crabs, one is number 27 and the other doesn't have a number because I haven't managed to paint them all on yet. Then I run out of time. It means a lot of crabs have gone missing. I stay a little longer to try and find them, but for some reason today, I don't much like being inside the caves. A long time before I really need to, I find myself ducking back out of the cave and back to the sunlight.

I sit down on the rock where I leave my shoes. My feet feel the warmth of the sun, and I decide to knot my shoes together and hang them around my neck. Then I just sit there for a while, thinking about things. Three crabs from the two hundred I originally painted isn't very many, and I wonder what might have gone wrong. The first time I tried to do this experiment in the rockpools at Littlelea, I had the same problem of losing all the crabs. I thought I'd solved it with my ultraviolet light idea, but now I'm not so sure. I ponder if it's a useful scientific result to say that hermit crabs actually move around a lot more than people think. I consider emailing Dr. Ribald and asking her, but she still hasn't answered my last email, and I was hoping to send her some actual results before bothering her again.

So I'm a little glum as I set off back down the beach to meet Dad. But with the sun still out, I go back to my game of getting as close to the surge of the water as I can without letting it catch me. Then, halfway back, I change the game and jump in the puddles of water left on the beach, which have now been warmed up by the sun. It's like jumping into little sandy baths. And slowly, my mood improves. The problem with my study, I decide, is that I haven't been able to give it the attention it deserves. It's pretty hard, doing a scientific study *and* going to school. And when you add on catching a killer on top of that, it's not surprising that things aren't going that well.

But now, I can get back to things. The police will definitely have caught Mr. Foster by now. And thinking about that, I remember that I have to recover my camera from Mr. Foster's boat. I'm excited about that because it will have captured the whole police raid. I think about whether I could put it on YouTube. If I used a false name.

But when we get home (it's Sunday, and Dad isn't working for once) and I check the local news, there's nothing about a raid. In fact, there's nothing at all about the Olivia Curran case. I look on my computer in my bedroom and search all the sites I can think of, but still, I can't find anything. I think about it for a while and decide that maybe the information is going up the chain of command. That's what happens to important information. And maybe specialist officers are coming from the mainland. Maybe the FBI. The ferry gets in at two on Sundays, so maybe they'll catch him after that?

32

It's Wednesday evening now. Four days since I sent my evidence to the police. Four days and *still* they haven't done anything. What worries me is that Mr. Foster could easily murder again.

If you looked at me and Dad right now, you'd think we were just sitting together watching TV, but actually, a new idea is forming in my mind. The program we're watching is one of those late night shows where grown-ups talk about news and politics. Normally, I'd be upstairs on the Internet, but I'm disappointed after not finding anything about the raid on Mr. Foster. Tonight, I wanted to see if there might be an update about it on the show. There isn't. But it gives me an idea all the same.

They're not talking about anything interesting. It's about a hospital where people keep dying, more than usual I mean. But what's interesting is *how* they came to be talking about it. Apparently, there was someone who worked in the hospital, called a "whistle-blower." This person spent a long time trying to tell everyone about the bad doctors, but no one listened. So eventually, they went and told the newspapers about it. Then the newspapers printed a story, and *then* the bad doctors got found out. That's how they came to be talking about it on this program too. And that gives me an idea. It's just the same as with me. If the police aren't going to arrest Mr. Foster on their own, I can force them to by being a whistle-blower. I can send the information to the *Island Times*. They'll make a story from it, and then the police will *have* to do something.

At first, I don't really think about it seriously. I just like the idea of it. I like the idea of doing something. But the more I think, the more convinced I become that it's the right thing to do. Look at it this way:

If I *don't* tell the *Island Times*, and the police *don't* do anything, then Mr. Foster could easily decide to kill another girl. He might be planning it right now. I did the wrong thing before, and Olivia Curran ended up dead. If I do the right thing now, I could save another girl's life.

There's also the question of timing. The *Island Times* comes out once a week, on Fridays, so I don't have much time to sit around thinking about it. If I don't send the photographs now, tonight, I'll miss this week's paper. That would give Mr. Foster a whole week to kill another girl.

The more I think about it, the more certain I become. I *have* to be a whistle-blower, *and I have to do it right now*, before I even go to bed. That way, the journalists will get it tomorrow morning, and they'll have all day tomorrow to put it in Friday's paper. Then the police will have to go and arrest Mr. Foster.

Upstairs, I open up my laptop and get to work. I couldn't figure out from the program whether it was illegal to be a whistle-blower or not, but I decide to use my new Harry King Gmail account again to stay anonymous. Then I decide it might be safer to set up another one, so it's different than the police one. By the time I've gotten all that set up, and routed the email through fifteen different countries, it's really late, so I don't have that long to write the actual email. But I know what I need to send them: the same photographs that I sent the police. Olivia Curran's face at the window, and then the picture of her dead body being dragged out of Mr. Foster's house, with his face looking all burning white like he's some kind of monster.

Just before I send it, I have a moment's worry that this isn't the right thing to do. What if I get into trouble? But I make myself stop thinking like that. Being a whistle-blower is scary; that's what the TV program said. But if I don't do it, someone else could die.

My finger hovers over the button. One click, and my message will fly twice around the world, then land in the inbox of the *Island Times*. I can't take it back. I screw up my eyes and press my finger down onto the keyboard. When I open my eyes again the email is gone.

33

West woke to the sound of rain battering the windows of the cramped, damp apartment which had become home. She was alone, the duvet on her double bed supplemented by two blankets. As long as she slept in pajamas, she was warm enough, just. She got up, pulled back the flimsy drapes above her bed, and looked out at the low, leaden sky. Fat raindrops ran down the glass, smearing the backs of the houses that blocked her view of the ocean.

She stumbled to the shower cubicle, where her elbows knocked the sides and threatened to break the thin plastic walls. She opened the tap, and a thin trickle of water leaked out. She let it fall on her hand until it got as hot as it was going to. With a grimace, she stepped inside.

As quickly as she could, she began washing her hair. Working the shampoo in, she heard the sound of the shower next door. Then next door's cubicle door shutting, the sound of water hitting a plastic tray identical to the one she stood in. Then, irritatingly clear, the sound of cheery whistling.

It was new, this morning optimism coming from next door. She put her head to one side and considered for a moment what it might mean. She'd only been inside Rogers' apartment a few times, but that was enough to know it was as unsuited to the onset of winter as hers was. And they had made almost no progress with the case. The Currans had made good on their promise, publishing their seventh round of adverts only two days previously, but all it produced was noise, nothing of value. That didn't explain Rogers' exuberance. She went back to squeezing the shampoo out of her hair.

He was alright Rogers. He'd not so much mentioned the night they spent together, not to her, or more importantly, to anyone else. And they'd slipped easily back to the working relationship they'd had before. Most of the time, when she looked at him, she was able to forget they'd spent a drunken night together. And when she didn't forget she felt a kind of warmth about it. It was something in the past, but she didn't exactly regret it. That didn't mean his good mood didn't irritate her though.

Once she'd dressed and gathered her things, she found Detective Rogers relaxing in the plastic sun lounger on her little porch, watching the rain drip down from the roof overhead, smoking his first cigarette of the day. He greeted her with a quick flick of the eyebrows, then stubbed his cigarette out.

"Morning," he said. "You ready to seize the day?" There was a breeziness to his voice that West studied, trying to see what was different about her partner. He climbed to his feet. The keys were on the table beside him.

"You wanna drive this morning?" he asked, noticing her looking. Rogers never asked if she wanted to drive.

West's first job of the morning was to pick up the mail bag from Sergeant Wiggins. He was a cheery soul who had taken to counting the letters for her each morning. Mondays were the worst, since she and Rogers didn't work weekends. Today was a Monday.

"Just twelve today. It's definitely drying up," Wiggins said. And it was true. Even with Joseph and Susan Curran's latest round of newspaper ads, and an appearance on a popular talk show, the public interest in their daughter's case was fading away. West thanked the Sergeant and carried the bag to her desk, clearing away two empty coffee cups before sitting down. Rogers was already sitting down opposite her, frowning at the screen of his terminal.

West pulled open the Velcro closure on the mail bag and pulled the letters out.

"How many you got?" Rogers asked.

"Twelve. You?"

He ran a finger down his screen, counting in his head.

"Twenty-seven," he said, when he'd finished. He didn't take his eyes off the screen, and she didn't expect him to say anything more, but his good mood that morning seemed to make him more sociable. He went on, leaning back in his chair.

"It's incredible, isn't it? Even now, two months after she disappeared, we've got twenty-seven crazy people emailing to say they've seen Olivia Curran. I mean, clearly, they haven't. They've just seen a teenage girl who looks a little like her." He glanced at her pile of letters, then looked at her. "You still think it was worth staying?"

She bit her lip before answering.

"There's still a chance."

THEY'D DEVELOPED a basic screening system. Green meant the tip-off was of the lowest possible credibility. They would do just enough work to confirm its status as junk, then it would be filed and forgotten. Nearly all the leads that came in were green leads.

Occasionally, a lead was flagged as orange. Orange meant there was some limited reason to think the information *could* be credible. Orange leads got scheduled for further investigation, although they would join a queue and wait their turn. An orange lead might require a phone call or a number of calls to be validated, or more likely invalidated. If they were particularly lucky, an orange lead might necessitate a trip out of the office. Real detective work, as Rogers put it. More often than not, though, the orange leads could quickly be downgraded to green.

Then there were red leads. Or rather, there remained the hypothetical possibility that red leads existed. A red lead – if it ever came in – would be one that contained information that was obviously credible or immediately relevant to the investigation. But in nearly a month of searching, there'd been no red leads. No one in the station really believed that one would turn up now. Too much time had passed. Except

West. Even after all this time she still felt some belief, when she opened a letter or email, or listened to a phone message, that it might lead them somewhere. Rogers had taken to mocking her about it, although he did so with a grudging respect for her dedication.

THE FIRST ENVELOPE West opened that morning contained nothing but a handwritten note on a sheet of stationary that had a watermark from *City Garden Grand Hotel*. It was hard to read the spidery black ink, but after a moment, West deciphered the words. An anonymous sender claimed to have seen Olivia Curran in an open-air swimming pool in Manila in the Philippines. There were no details, not even the date the sighting was supposed to have taken place. Her gut feeling was this information was worthless, but she turned to her PC and typed "Manila" into the search bar of the investigation database. Nothing came back. She tried "Philippines", then "City Garden Grand Hotel" with similar results. She tried different spellings, in various ways that people might have gotten wrong. Nothing. There had been no previous sightings of Olivia Curran anywhere in the Philippines.

On a whim, she typed "swimming pool," and five listings came back. Five other people believed they had seen the missing girl in swimming pools. Three in the United States, one in Argentina, and one in France. Satisfied, she clicked the button to create a new listing. She scanned the letter and attached the digital version to the entry, then filed the original copy in the day's file - should it ever need to be reviewed, it could be found linked via the date. She typed the details of the "sighting", added the keywords "Manila", "Philippines", and "swimming pool", then coded the entry as green. Then she reached over and picked up the next envelope.

Three hours passed.

"HOW YOU GETTING ON? I'm getting hungry here." Rogers' voice interrupted her work.

She flicked through the remaining envelopes. "I got three to go. I want to get them done before lunch," she said, expecting him to let her get back to it. But he didn't.

"I got another two sightings in Paris."

"Paris?" she said. She searched her mind. Paris had come up before, was it...something?

"Yeah, but don't get excited. They're worthless. They both took photos. Wrong age, wrong height. One of them was fat. How's she going to get fat in two months? They reckon she's been hiding out eating donuts on top of the Eiffel Tower?"

"France, though," West said, remembering. "I had some sightings in France the other day." She looked thoughtful.

"And you're still wondering if it can really be a coincidence? Well, it's not. I'll tell you what it is." Rogers leaned forward.

"What you've got is three hundred twenty million Americans who know this girl's missing and think that's tragic because she's *pretty*. Then, when these people go on vacation, which sometimes they do, they stop staring at the floor and look around them for a change. And when they do that, suddenly, they start noticing people. Including teenage girls who are pretty and look a little like Olivia Curran. Believe me. That's why France keeps coming up. A lot of Americans go on vacation to Europe at this time of year."

West had heard this theory from Rogers before, but he was refining it as time went on. She had to admit it seemed to match the evidence they were building up.

"I thought you were supposed to go to Paris in the springtime?" she asked, but he ignored her. Her concentration broken, she asked another question.

"Anyway. How come you were whistling in the shower this morning. Isn't yours cold?"

He looked up, pretending to be surprised, but unable to restrain a grin.

"Cold?"

"Yeah."

"No."

"What do you mean '*no*'?"

"I mean it's not cold. Well, not anymore it isn't. I got Tommy's brother to take a look at it. He's a plumber. If anything, it's a little hot now." He mimed shrinking back from hot water.

"Tommy? Who's Tommy?"

"Tommy! You know, the skinny guy from Patrol. We were in the bar the other night, and I was moaning about the shower. He said his brother could take a look for me."

West thought for a moment, feeling a little snubbed that no one had invited her. But then she'd not made much of an effort with the guys.

"You didn't get him to look at mine as well?"

"I didn't know yours was cold." Rogers made a face like this was obvious. "Was I really whistling?"

She ignored that.

"Did you get the guy's number?"

"No." Rogers shrugged. "You *heard* me? You were listening to me in the shower?"

"No. I wasn't listening. I was in the shower at the same time, and I heard you in there, whistling."

"Did you have the toothbrush glass up against the wall to hear better?"

"Don't be an idiot."

Rogers just grinned at her.

West shook her head and looked away.

"Come on." Rogers said.

"Come on where?"

"It's lunch time. My stomach's rumbling."

34

Rogers drove this time, even though the diner was only a few minutes' walk. They sat in their regular booth and Rogers chewed slowly through his usual turkey sandwich. West watched him, not feeling hungry enough for her order of chicken soup.

"Can I ask you a question?" West said after a while.

"I dunno. Can you?" Rogers replied, not looking up. West was used to the sarcasm and barely heard it.

"If you're so sure we're wasting our time here, why did you stay? "

Rogers didn't answer at first. He picked up a paper napkin and wiped the grease from his mouth, then he folded it and placed under the edge of his plate. He looked at her.

"Who says we're wasting our time?"

"You do. All the time. You complain about how all the leads are junk."

"They are junk."

"So why are you here?"

Rogers shrugged.

"I told you."

"When?" West frowned.

"That night," he glanced at her for a moment then looked away. He went on quickly.

"I told you, I'm in no hurry to get back home and face my ex-wife." He looked thoughtful for a moment. "And maybe you've taught me something."

"What?"

"I dunno. Don't give up? There's always a chance? You seem to believe it anyway."

A frown appeared on West's face and Rogers laughed.

"Are you finally realizing that detective work isn't very glamorous? Not like they show in the movies. Feeding a database and hoping to come across the needle in a haystack. That *is* the job. And it's the same job here or back in New York. At least here I can take refreshing walks on the beach." He smiled. They both knew he'd yet to take a walk on the beach.

"Seriously. I'm not a complicated guy. I like it here. I like the people. It makes a nice change from the city. And it's a long way away from my ex-wife."

"So you don't think there's any chance of solving the case?"

He plucked a toothpick and scraped at a gap in his teeth. "It depends if there's a case to solve." West looked away.

"How 'bout you? You ever going to tell me why you stayed?"

The question surprised her.

"What do you mean?"

"Back on the beach that day, you started telling me something, then you clammed right up."

She felt her face redden slightly.

"No I didn't."

"Yes you did. You were saying how you were all set to be a swimmer. But then you stopped and joined the police. That's not exactly a natural jump. And you're just about the most determined person I ever came across. So there's gotta be something behind it."

West was about to tell him he was wrong. But then she'd started with the heart to heart. It seemed only fair to give her side.

"Go on," Rogers said, still picking at his teeth.

"OK," West said slowly. "If you really want to know. It happened when I was nineteen. I'd done quite well. I was swimming in the Nationals. They were being held in Florida that year. We were swimming there..."

West paused and looked down at the table for a moment. Rogers narrowed his eyes but let her take her time.

"I was there with my best friend, Sarah. We grew up together. Like, we were never apart. Never. We went to the same school. We both swam. We pushed each other on. We were... Close. Very close."

Rogers waited.

"Sarah Donaldson. Do you know the name?"

"Should I?"

"Maybe. Maybe you would've. She would have medaled in Beijing, no doubt." West stopped talking suddenly. There was no reason to tell the story she had begun. It only caused her pain.

"Would have? What happened?" Rogers prompted..

FOR A LONG MOMENT West said nothing. She considered brushing him off again. But she knew that now she'd begun he wouldn't let it go.

"We were sharing a room together. Sarah and I always shared. The night before the competition, she was restless, full of energy. She was always like that before she raced. Usually she'd use the gym or something, to bring her down a bit. But the hotel didn't have a gym. So she decided to run a few K's. She asked me to go with her, but I preferred to rest before races." West looked up at the ceiling of the diner, as if the story still hurt. Then she looked back at Rogers and continued talking.

"IT WASN'T late or anything. The hotel was in a good part of town. There was no reason to worry about it, no reason to think twice. But when she wasn't back an hour later, I started to get worried. I told my coach. We waited for her together. And when she wasn't back by midnight, we called the cops.

"I'LL NEVER FORGET that night. No one could sleep. We were just waiting. Just praying that she would walk back in the door. And everything would go back to normal." West paused for a long time. Rogers gave her time.

"But it didn't. They found her body the next morning. Dumped behind some bushes in a park. The guy - *the monster* - raped her and then strangled her." West's voice cracked a little over the final words.

"He get caught?" Rogers asked after a pause.

West nodded. "Not at the time. A few years later he did. A traffic cop caught him in the act. He did it four more times in the meantime."

"Jesus."

"IT WASN'T JUST THAT." West said, a moment later. "I'm not drawing a direct link between Sarah's murder and me joining the force. That would be... An oversimplification. But at the same time... You could say I never really had the same focus after that. I never lived up to my potential." She shrugged. "Not that that matters."

This time Rogers looked confused.

"Swimming. I didn't qualify. My times went way down. Eventually I got dropped from the team. It never seemed important after that."

"Shit." Rogers said.

"How 'bout you?" West said, trying to force her voice to sound brighter. "Why did you join up?"

"Dad was a cop. Granddad too. I never had much imagination as a kid."

"Good reason. Better than mine," West said.

"Jesus Jessica, I'm sorry. I shouldn't have teased. About you being determined. You've got good reason."

She flashed him a smile, breathing a little deeply.

"You wanna get back to it. You wanna keep searching for that needle?" Rogers asked, and West nodded.

Neither of them knew it yet, but the needle they had been hunting for so long was sitting waiting for them at their desks.

35

They found it right after lunch. West finished up her remaining leads and looked up, intending to offer Rogers help with his. She had to wait though, since he'd gone to get more coffee. There was a vending machine in the corridor with which he had developed a love-hate relationship. He walked back. Placed a cardboard cup in front of West.

"How many damn shirts am I gonna wreck before figuring that machine out?"

West smiled her sympathy and took her drink. "I'm all done here," she said. "You want some help with yours?"

"Sure."

She pulled her chair around the pair of desks so she could see his screen. He was still fussing over his shirt so she clicked open the next email and began to read it out loud to him.

"OK. Here we go. Urgent, written in capital letters. *To the attention of Chief Larry Collins*. Yeah, right. Like he's going to read this personally. *I am emailing to tell you that Olivia Curran is dead. She was being held prisoner at 16 Speyside...*" Suddenly, her hands stopped, and she read on in silence. She felt him stiffen beside her.

"Shit. Ollie, what's this?"

The email filled the top half of the screen; an image took up most of the bottom. It was too dark to make out what it showed at first, but it looked creepy. They both looked closer. It showed a man dragging a carpet from a bungalow in what must be the middle of the night, the image captured by infrared camera.

"The hell is that?" Rogers said, leaning in close. They both read the rest of the email.

URGENT

To the attention of Chief Larry Collins.

I am emailing to tell you Olivia Curran is dead. She was being held prisoner at 16 Speyside Drive by Mr. Foster, who is well-known around town as a pedophile. Most of the time, she was locked up in the cellar, but unfortunately, last Sunday she escaped, so he killed her. Here is a picture of her closing the drapes before he killed her.

Here is another picture of him hiding her body in some carpet and taking it out of his house in the middle of the night. It's not very clear because it is taken with the infrared mode of a Denver WCT-3004 Wildlife Camera (not the new version, unfortunately, which has the higher resolution).

I have also seen that Mr. Foster has a pink girl's backpack in his house, which probably belongs to Olivia. I'm sorry I don't have a photograph of this because I forgot to take one. But I expect you'll find it in the house when you raid it.

I do think you should arrest Mr. Foster immediately so he doesn't kill any other girls.

Signed

HK

"SCROLL DOWN," West said, and when Rogers did so, a second image came up. A girl's face at a window, this time taken in the daytime, but the same bungalow.

"Jesus!" Rogers spilled more of his coffee. "Is that her? Is that Olivia Curran?"

36

"We should do this more often," the woman said, resting her head on the man's shoulder. She was late thirties, him early forties. Her hair showed gray at the roots; he was no longer lean and fit like when they met, but growing a gut. Their girls, now four and six, ran onto the beach, oblivious to the cold weather.

"It's good to get away," he said, letting her head stay there for a while. "We all need to reset every now and then."

THE GIRLS HAD DONE their best on the journey, but three hours in the car and then two more on the ferry were plenty. Now they were like wild animals released from months of captivity. Running this way, then that, bending down to inspect pebbles and dig holes in the sand with their hands.

"So WHAT DO you want to do?" the woman asked. The man watched his children for a while before answering. "I think we should just tire them out and make sure they get an early night," he said at last, and she lifted her head to look him in the face.

"Oh yes?" She cocked an eye curiously. "And why would that be?"

"Don't you get all coy on me. I'm talking about a quiet meal in the hotel restaurant with a good bottle of wine. I'm not proposing anything after that."

She smiled. After a moment, she spoke again.

"When did we last have a meal out together?"

"Oh, a decade ago. Maybe more. Come on." He got up and strode down the sand to join his daughters. "Let's do a competition. Who can find me three types of shells? The winner gets a piece of chocolate cake."

In less than ten seconds, the older girl had presented her father with three types of shells, two white and one blue, and the younger girl was almost in tears at the thought of missing out. But he diffused the situation by resetting the challenge.

"OK, now you have to tell me what *types* of shells they are."

"What types of shells?" the girls asked, confused.

"Yeah, I'll help you with the first." He picked the blue shell from the girl's hand and held it up so they could both see. "This is a mussel shell. When they're alive, there are two of them, like this." He found a second blue shell on the beach and held them together.

"The little animal would live in here, and when it gets hungry, it opens up like this and lets the seawater flow in, and it filters out little bits of food."

"Daddy?"

"Yes, Chloe?"

"What's this shell here?"

She held up a second shell. He peered at it, confused. Then he pulled an iPhone from his pocket and began tapping on the screen.

"I'll have a look. You find some more shells," he said while he worked, and the girls went away, used to such interruptions.

His wife watched him from where she sat, on a patch of pebbles so her trousers wouldn't get sandy. She was a little disappointed that he was on his phone so soon, but it was probably a work email. Best to answer it so he could focus more completely on the family. She enjoyed watching him with the girls, when he did find the time.

"Chloe?" he said.

"Yes?"

"It's a slipper limpet," He showed her the screen on his iPhone. "Do you see? Apparently, they live in big clumps like this. The bottom one is always the female - that's the girl - and the little ones on top are the boys. When she dies," he stopped, corrected himself, "or just goes away for some reason, then one of the boys becomes the new girl. What about that? Can you imagine? So all the girl slipper limpets started off as boys."

As weird as this fact was, Chloe was used to the world not making sense, and simply held her head to one side for a moment to consider it, and then moved on.

"Where do they live?"

The man consulted his phone again, but it didn't immediately help, so he guessed. "In the rockpools, I guess. Tell you what. We'll have a real competition. We'll take our shoes off, and whoever can find the most interesting thing in the rockpools, they'll win the piece of chocolate cake."

Excited screaming greeted this suggestion, and the girls pulled off their shoes and socks and picked their way carefully through the pebbles to where the bigger rocks began. Only the woman stayed where she was, stretching out her legs and letting the low November sun warm her face.

IT WAS HER IDEA, the mini break to Lornea Island. She'd come a couple of times as a child, and she liked the thought of taking her children, too, but it had never happened. Then a pretty hotel with an indoor pool popped up on her Facebook feed. It looked lovely, and when she clicked the ad, she saw it was on Lornea Island. It's funny how coincidences work, she'd been thinking, what with Lornea being in the news so much these days. So she booked it. Her only caveat was she didn't want to go to Silverlea - the town where that poor girl actually went missing. Instead, they were on the other side of the island, facing the mainland, the sea here calm and unthreatening. Not many people came to Lornea in the off-season, meaning the hotel was cheap. The family room was actually two rooms, one with bunk beds for the kids, and a door dividing them and the main room. She and Peter would be able to dine in the hotel restaurant while the girls slept. A rare chance for an evening together. What happened after that was on her mind just as much as it was apparently on his.

She watched the three of them now, picking their way across the rocks, stopping by the many pools and bending down to investigate. Her husband had his trousers rolled up to just below the knee; their younger daughter, Sarah, had taken her leggings off completely. She shook her head in exasperation, the girl would get cold, but her excited whoops filtered back up the beach to the woman, and she let it slide for now. She breathed in the smells of the beach. The salt and the muddy odor of the seaweed.

Suddenly, a scream broke the quiet calm. And when the noise should have stopped if, say, one of the girls had seen a large crab, or splashed herself, it carried on, getting louder and more piercing. More desperate.

The woman was on her feet and moving without knowing how. She ran down the sand, ready to throw herself upon whatever danger her daughters faced but not yet understanding what it was. Her attention focused on Chloe, standing in the middle of a deep pool of water, her hands on her face, shaking in terror. The man was running toward her, too, as well as he could over the uneven surface.

"What is it?" the woman called out, but no one answered. The only noise was the screaming. She got to the rocks and didn't pause to remove her shoes, but carried on, crashing right through the first pool. She looked up to see her husband sweep Chloe off her feet and carry her to a large flat rock, away from where she'd been standing. Moments later, the woman was there as well, terrified at the look on the faces of her family. Her husband was still holding Chloe, and she lifted Sarah too, asking over and over as she did so,

"What is it? What happened?"

His face was white with shock. He looked at the children for a moment before answering, as if he didn't want them to know. But they were the ones who'd found it.

"It looks like a hand. A human hand. Chloe found a hand in the rock-pool over there."

37

I t's Friday now, and there's still nothing in the *Island Times*.
        I checked online this morning. Nothing. Then, just after registration, I sneaked up to the library before class. I had to ask the lady if today's paper had come in yet, and she looked at me really funny because she was actually reading it, at her desk. I told her I needed it for a school project, and she sighed but let me look. I skimmed through the whole paper really quickly, and there wasn't anything about Olivia Curran. I don't understand it.

I'm sitting in math now, trying to make sense of it. There's two possible explanations. The first is I didn't send the email correctly. I realized I can check that tonight. It's a bit complicated though, not just a case of looking in the "sent" folder of my secret Gmail account. It has more to do with tracking to see that the email didn't get bounced from any of the foreign servers I routed it through. It's hard to explain, but trust me. The second possibility is that I sent the email fine but just too late for the *Island Times* to include in this week's paper. You'd think they would be able to manage it, but one thing I've noticed about adults is they always take *forever* to do anything. Even important things.

It's like with math. I like math, but the stuff we do at school is so basic. Today, we're doing fractions. I could do fractions when I was six. We're only halfway through the class, and I've finished both worksheets already. I'm about to put up my hand and ask for some more work when the door of the classroom opens.

I glance up automatically, not really to see who it is; it's just that the noise gets my attention. It's probably one of the boys, coming back from the restroom. They all pretend they need to go all the time; I think it's a kind of joke. But that's not what it is. It's the principal, Mr. Simms. And I can see him looking right at me.

He mouths something to my teacher. I think he says: "A quick word." Then the teacher, Mrs. Walker, goes over to the door, where they whisper to each other. Then she looks over at *me*; I'm sure of it this time. Then I see there's more people behind them. A man and a woman. I don't know who they are.

"Billy," Mrs. Walker says then. Her voice sounds funny. "Could you come out here for a minute?"

I feel a pang of alarm. A few of the kids in class are looking at me now, wondering what I've done. But there's nothing I can do. I push my chair back, and it squeaks on the floor, drawing even more attention. I feel the eyes of the whole class on my back as I walk over to the door.

When I get there, Mr. Simms puts his hands on my shoulders and guides me out into the corridor. Then he closes the class door so it's just me and him and the two strangers in the corridor. Mr. Simms nods to them.

"Billy Wheatley?" one of them says, the man. He's really big, with blond hair on the backs of his hands. "My name is Detective Oliver Rogers, and this is my colleague, Detective Jessica West. I believe you two already met?" There's a hardness in his voice, like he's being sarcastic.

I fight to hold back the panic. Detectives? The police? My mind is buzzing, trying to figure out what's going on. Then the man's words register, and I look at the woman. I don't recognize her. I don't know what's going on.

"HELLO, Billy. I took your statement when Olivia Curran first went missing. Do you remember?"

I stare at her face. Dimly, I think I might recognize her. She was the one who didn't think my evidence was significant. The not-very-good one. Is that what this is about? They've finally realized the mistake they made?

I nod, then look down at the floor, waiting to see what happens next.

"Billy," the man says. The man detective; I've already forgotten what his name is. "We'd like to ask you some questions about an email you sent to the Lornea Island Police Department and later to the newspaper, the *Island Times*. We'd like to ask those questions at the police station. Your principal has agreed to accompany you there until we can track down your father, and then he can sit in with you. Are you OK with that?"

There's this heavy silence in the corridor. I don't know what horrifies me most: the thought of going to the police station, or going with Mr. Simms. I've never even spoken to him before.

"Do I have to?" I ask, my voice coming out in a squeak. The two detectives look at each other.

"Come on Billy. We just need a little chat," the woman says. She puts her arm out, like she's inviting me to go with her, and reluctantly I start walking.

38

I t's not a real police car, just a red Ford, but they put me in just like they do in the movies, pushing my head down so I don't hit it on the roof, even though I've gotten in lots of cars before without any problems. Then the woman detective gets in beside me. Mr. Simms goes in the passenger seat. He doesn't say anything. He just pretends to be interested in the view.

We drive to the Newlea police station. It's on the main road, and I've driven past the front with Dad lots of times, but we've never gone into it before. We drive through these big black gates, and I'm a little surprised to see there's just a small parking lot inside; I don't know why, but I was expecting something more. There are lots of real police cars here, though, with the black-and-white markings of the Lornea Island Police Department. The man drives to the end, but there's no spaces, so the woman detective says she'll take us in, and he goes off to park somewhere else. I never knew the police had to do that; I always just assumed they would be able to park anywhere they liked.

The woman detective leads us inside into a kind of front desk area, where a policeman in uniform is sitting behind a big desk. The woman stands next to me while he asks my name and address, and writes it down. Then he asks Mr. Simms' name and address. Mr. Simms isn't allowed to call himself Mr. Simms, and I find out his first name is Paul.

The policeman writes all this down in a book, an actual book, not a computer. Then the woman detective starts talking to Mr. Simms.

"We're going to take some fingerprints from Billy now. They'll help us eliminate him in the event that he's contaminated any crime scenes."

Mr. Simms nods like he thinks this is a good idea, and we all go into another room. My brain is working really fast, but I don't understand. Why do they want my fingerprints? Do they think I might have been involved? Do they think I might be Mr. Foster's accomplice? I try to think of what I might have touched. There was the boat, of course, and the windows - when I checked to see if the windows were locked. Why didn't I wear gloves? I've got lots of pairs of gloves.

"Billy, could you follow me, please." The woman detective's voice cuts through the chaos in my head.

There's no computer in the fingerprint room either. The woman detective tells me to roll up my sleeves, and then she presses each finger into an ink pad, and then on a piece of paper with a little square box for each finger. We do both hands, and after that, she takes palm prints too.

"OK, Billy, you can wash your hands now." She points to a sink on the opposite wall, and I wash them really well. I don't like the feel of the ink on my hands. It makes me feel guilty of something.

Then the man detective comes back. He sticks his head in around the door, so I guess he managed to find a space for the car.

"The dad's on his way. We're gonna take him straight in."

I get led to a room with the words "Interview Room 4" stenciled on the door, with a lightbulb inside a little grille just above the entrance. It's switched off at the moment. There's not much inside, just a table and chairs, an old-fashioned tape recorder on the table. There aren't any windows.

Before we've even sat down the man detective starts talking to Mr. Simms.

"Thank you for coming sir, but Billy's father has now just arrived, so we won't be needing you after all. I'll arrange for you to get a ride back to the school."

Mr. Simms nods at this. I glance over at him and think he looks disappointed all of a sudden. But then another policeman leads Dad into the room, and I can't really pay any attention to Mr. Simms anymore, because Dad's in a crazy mood. I mean, I know this isn't a normal situation, but Dad's real mad.

"What the hell's all this about?" he says at once. He seems to take in the detective who's still standing by the door.

"You. What's this about? Why has my son been dragged to the police station?"

"He hasn't been dragged here sir. He's agreed voluntarily to answer some questions."

"He's not under arrest? Then you can't hold him, he's just a kid anyway. Whatever he did. Come on Billy. We're getting out of here *right now*." Dad walks right around the table to where I'm sitting and goes to take my hand, but the man detective manages to get in between us.

"We'd prefer you do this voluntarily," the woman says. "But if you refuse, we can arrest Billy for attempting to pervert the course of justice and obstructing a police investigation."

No one says anything for a few beats.

Then the man detective speaks.

"Sir, I'm going to need you to calm down and take a seat."

For a moment I think Dad's still going to push past him. I'm holding my breath.

"*Right now sir.*"

I've never seen Dad look like this before. His eyes flick around the room like he's trying to figure out if he can escape through a window or something, and then he just stares at me, shaking his head. Slowly Dad takes a seat.

The detectives sit back down again too. Across the other side of the table from us. They're both still breathing hard though. Then the man detective presses some buttons on the tape recorder.

"For the tape," he says. "The Officers present are Detective Oliver Rogers and Detective Jessica West." I make a point of remembering this time. When he's finished giving our names too, he slides a piece of paper across the desk to me.

"Billy. This email was sent to Chief Larry Collins of the Lornea Island Police Department on Sunday, November nineteenth. Do you recognize it?"

I look down at the paper. It's a printout of my email. Underneath are the two photographs I sent. All signed by HK. I try to think really fast, to work out why they think I sent it. Whether there's any way they can trace it back to me? I'm pretty sure I routed the email the right way. I glance up at Detective Rogers' face. He looks angry still. The woman looks a little bit friendlier. I do remember her better now. She gives me a little smile, just for a second, like she's encouraging me. But I shake my head.

"No? You don't recognize it? You sure about that?" While Detective Rogers talks he reaches for a clear plastic bag from the floor. I hadn't seen it there until now. But as he fiddles with the ziplock I get a dread feeling in my stomach.

"You did a good job with the email Billy, I'll give you that. We tracked it through..." He glances at his papers. "Here we go. Azerbaijan, Russia, Bulgaria... Then we lost it in Colombia. So instead, we visited Philip Foster to see if he'd noticed anyone unusual watching the house." He fiddles with the bag a bit more.

"And this is what we found." He pulls my camera out of the bag and turns it over and over in his hands. Eventually he stops playing with it, and when he does he's got the label at the top. He holds it up and shows it to Dad. I put it on for when I was recording animals. In case someone found the camera and thought it was lost. It says:

Property of Billy Wheatley
Clifftop Cottage, Littlelea
IMPORTANT SCIENTIFIC WORK
DO NOT TOUCH!!!

"Bit of a schoolboy mistake wouldn't you say?" He smiles at me, but I just look down at the table.

"And then there was the second email. You didn't do such a good job with that one, the *Island Times* was able to trace it all the way to Venezuela before they lost it. Fortunately, the editor has a good relationship with the chief here and passed it over at that point. If they'd printed this," he shook his head and glances at Dad. "If they'd printed this, we'd all be having a very different conversation here today." He pauses.

"Billy... Look at me." Reluctantly I pull my head up, and eventually I nod.

"Billy this is a very serious situation. We could be looking at juvenile court, Youth detention facilities. But this gets a whole lot easier if you cooperate. Now did you send this email?"

This time I nod.

"For the benefit of the tape, Billy Wheatley is nodding his head."

"AND THIS SECOND EMAIL," Detective Rogers holds up another sheet of paper. "To the editor of the *Island Times*. Did you send this one as well?" Rogers slides it towards me so I can see better but I don't need to. I nod right away this time, and I'm surprised when a tear plops down onto the table in front of me.

"I was only trying to help," I say. "I wanted to find Olivia Curran because no one else could find her. Only when I did, it was too late, but that wasn't my fault. I didn't do it, I didn't help him kill her. You believe me, don't you?"

"Again, for the benefit of the tape, Billy Wheatley is nodding."

"I only sent that one because you weren't doing anything. I know she was already dead by then, but he could still be out catching another girl. Have you arrested him yet? He could be killing someone right now - "

"Is that the missing girl?" Dad asks suddenly. He's looking down at the email in amazement. "What the hell is going on here Billy?"

THE TWO DETECTIVES look at each other. Detective Rogers is the one who breaks the silence.

"If you'll let me sir I'll explain. Your son here has formed the opinion that Philip Foster is connected with the disappearance of Olivia Curran. With these emails, he's wasted a large amount of police time. Had the *Island Times* printed those photographs, he could have caused irreparable damage to any trail resulting from this investigation. That's why he's here today."

"But that's her isn't it? That's Olivia Curran?" Dad interrupts him. "If he's found her, what does it matter how he did it?"

There's another silence and I take the opportunity to fill it.

"She was in his house. I saw her at the window. That's why I sent the emails. I push the emails back across the table to the detectives, so the picture of Olivia is right in front of him.

Detective Rogers doesn't even look at it. "Billy. Philip Foster has a sixteen-year-old daughter who comes to visit him on weekends. We've confirmed that your photograph of the girl in the window is of Mr.

Foster's daughter. You also mentioned a pink bag you saw. That also belongs to Mr. Foster's daughter."

I stare at Detective Rogers. I can feel my mouth hanging open. Out of the corner of my eye, I see Dad rubbing his face.

"What about the cellar? Didn't you find anything in the cellar?"

"There's no cellar in that house, Billy."

"Well..." I screw up my face in confusion. "The carpet, then. What was he doing taking a carpet out in the middle of the night if he wasn't disposing of a body?"

Detective Rogers gives a really big sigh and pours himself a glass of water.

"The mystery carpet." He shakes his head. "Would you like a drink, Billy? Mr. Wheatley?" He looks at Dad, who nods; then he pours us each a glass. When he speaks again, it's more Dad he's speaking to.

"Philip Foster is in the process of renovating his Silverlea property as a vacation let. It seems he wanted to avoid paying any charges to dispose of the carpet at the dump site." He pauses for a sip of water.

"Mr. Foster took the carpet to the dump in the middle of the night and left it in front of the gate. We've confirmed with the site that a carpet was found there in the morning after your son took this photograph. It was carried inside by the site staff when they arrived at work. They're sure it didn't contain a body. Furthermore, we've had a team of officers searching through the garbage to find that carpet." He pauses. "A lot of garbage. We finally located it yesterday. There are no traces of blood, or anything suspicious." Rogers turns to Dad again. "It seems Mr. Foster used it to wrap up some damp plasterboard. That's why it looks heavy in the image your son sent."

"So in a way, Billy, you have drawn our attention to a crime. But it's a crime of illegal waste dumping. Not murder. Meanwhile, the investigation has had to divert resources from legitimate lines of inquiry, to this wild-goose chase."

There's a long pause while they all seem to take this in. Then Detective Rogers turns back to me.

"You've caused a lot of people a lot of hassle. And you've accused an innocent man." Detective Rogers sits back and makes a steeple with his fingers. Then he looks annoyed when Detective West asks me a question.

"What was it that made you think he was involved, Billy? Philip Foster, I mean?"

It's the first question I've actually been asked to answer, and it takes me by surprise. There's so many reasons, I don't have them ordered in my mind.

"At school," I say before I've really thought about it. "At school, they call him a pedophile. And I saw him at the beach that night. He was fishing. And he walks with a limp. It's weird." I didn't mean to say the last part. I look down at the table.

West sighs. She glances across at Rogers, who shakes his head.

"Look, Billy," she says. "We understand you've tried to help. You've gone about it precisely the wrong way, but we understand your intentions were good."

She glances at Detective Rogers, and he nods at her before she goes on.

"Philip Foster used to be a schoolteacher. On the mainland, and in a pretty tough school by all accounts. There was a child - a fourteen-year-old girl – who made an accusation against him." She pauses to take a breath.

"We've checked it out. There was nothing in it. No evidence, no witnesses, no history, nothing. And the girl involved had a reputation for inventing stuff." She looks up at Dad. "Maybe the girl just took against him for some reason? We don't know. But there was no action taken against him. The complaint wasn't upheld."

She takes another breath, like the next bit is difficult.

"But it seems the girl's father wasn't satisfied. He followed Philip Foster home from school one day with a baseball bat. He managed to break his leg pretty bad before someone pulled him off. Mr. Foster and his wife came to the island to try to start afresh."

Then Detective Rogers butts in. "Until you came along Billy."

He gives me a hard look. He's about to say something else when I think of something.

"But I *saw* him," I hear myself interrupt. "Even if he didn't do the thing on the mainland, I *saw* Mr. Foster's van the night Olivia went missing. And his fishing light on the beach. He was on his own, at the beach where she went missing. In the dark. So how you can you be sure he didn't do this?"

Detective Rogers stares at me for a long time. Then he shuffles around in the pile of papers in front of him until he finds the one he wants.

"Philip Foster *was* on Silverlea beach that night. He was fishing until 22:30, at which time he gave up, having caught nothing. Between 22:30 and 23:15, he was drinking with several people at the beach party, including one Brian Richards." Rogers looks up at Dad. "He's a neighbor of yours, I believe, Mr. Wheatley?" Dad says nothing.

"Mr. Foster's daughter was also at the party, and they left together, at about 23:15, driving directly to Newlea and arriving at his home just before midnight. His wife confirmed that he stayed there the rest of the night.

"Philip Foster is not involved in the disappearance of Olivia Curran."

AT THAT MOMENT there's a knock on the door. I barely register it, but Detective West gets up . Detective Rogers' eyes stay fixed on me.

We sit there in silence for what feels like forever. And then, just when Detective Rogers opens his mouth to speak again, Detective West calls out to him from the door.

"Rogers. You better come out here. There's been a development."

39

Detectives West and Rogers barely had time to grab more coffee before they joined what looked like the entire Lornea Island Police Department in the small briefing room. At one end a pull-down screen had been deployed, and projected onto it was the faded image of a hand, roughly cut off halfway down the forearm. Even though it was packed full, the room was quiet. Lieutenant Langley and Chief Collins stood at the front, waiting for everyone to file in.

"Can we get those blinds down, please," Langley ordered, while the chief watched the room. "And hurry up."

The room darkened. The image on the screen changed from a half shadow to a clear, full-color image, the skin's yellows, purples, and greens deepening. The colors were all wrong. The image sickening.

"Well, I guess I have everyone's attention," Langley said. He didn't wait for anyone to reply.

"As some of you know, the hand and partial forearm from a young white female was recovered from the rocks to the west side of Goldhaven beach earlier this morning. We won't have the full pathology report for some time, but from a birthmark on the wrist here," he tapped the screen, causing it to wobble and the image to distort, "there's little doubt it belongs to Olivia Curran.

"Moreover, we don't need to wait for pathology to tell us the hand was cut off deliberately. Which means this inquiry will now become a murder investigation."

A few hushed murmurs started up, but Langley talked over them.

"It's also clear from the advanced state of decomposition that Olivia died at or about the time she went missing, on August twenty-eighth this year. But the arm was removed later, probably within the last week. We'll get more precise timelines as they come in."

Langley paused and looked around the room. "I want to be clear. This is not in any way connected to the information received by Detective Rogers and Detective West relating to the Silverlea resident Philip Foster. I know a lot of you have worked hard on that, but we need to move on from there." He gave Rogers a sympathetic look, which seemed to have hardened by the time it moved across to where West was standing.

"So. Any thoughts on what we have?"

There was a momentary pause. Then they all came at once.

"How was the arm removed?" One of the other detectives asked.

Langley turned to him. "We'll have a better idea later for sure, but I'd say a saw or some kind of serrated knife."

"It couldn't be an animal? Bitten off by a shark?"

"No."

"A boat or something? It get chewed off by the prop?"

"No. You can see the marks from here." Langley pointed at the screen, and it *was* obvious. "Whoever did it wasn't an expert either. Unless they were working blindfolded."

"Where exactly was it found?" This was one of the patrolmen.

"It was partially buried in the rockpools. Some kids found it. They were pretty freaked out."

"Where was it exactly?" West interrupted.

"Goldhaven beach." Langley replied.

"That's the ferry port right?" Rogers asked.

"Yeah." Langley sounded impatient. Like everyone there should know this.

Then the patrolman came back. "The coastline up past Goldhaven is full of ravines and crags. It's a great place to hide a body."

"And a hell of a place to search for one," another said.

"It's going to be even worse if we're looking for lots of different body parts." Langley said.

The patrolmen looked at each other. They knew they'd be the ones doing the searching.

"What are the currents like around there?" The first asked. "I mean, could it have washed up there from this side of the island?"

The other patrolman answered by shaking his head. He was one of the oldest on the squad and an avid fisherman. He knew the currents. "I wouldn't say so. Anything that goes in the water here is either going to go north or south, not around the back of the island."

"I want that checked out. Get onto the Coast Guard about that," Chief Collins interrupted, directing his order to Lieutenant Langley, who nodded.

"I don't want any other civilians coming across body parts." Collins said, and there was another pause. Longer this time.

"What if it's *just* an arm?" West said into the silence. "What if there's no other parts to find."

Langley looked at her.

"What?"

"I mean, why would someone just cut an arm off? And the arm with the birthmark too?" West asked. She was aware that all the heads were turned to look at her.

"What are you saying?" Rogers cut in. "I don't get it."

"I don't know. But why cut off an arm weeks after you've killed someone?" West said. "What would be the point?"

"The killer went back to try and tidy up?" Rogers replied, but he didn't sound convinced.

There was another pause. This time, Langley interrupted it.

"Clearly, we need more information. The chief and I have discussed our next move. One," he jutted a finger in the air. "Let's get her found, either the rest of her body, or any other parts that may be washing around. Speak to the Coast Guard. Speak to local fishermen, oceanologists at the university if you need to. Draw me up a plausible area where that arm could have come from, and then a plan to search it. I want her found before anyone else does.

"Two. Goldhaven is now an area of interest. We've had no reason to focus our attention there until now. Well that changes. Let's go door-to-door. Let's find out if anyone saw anything suspicious. Either in the last two weeks when we think the arm was removed, or back when she first went missing. Rogers. West. I want you on that.

"Three. This case is now this department's number one priority. Everything else is on hold. Everything. We already have the attention of the entire nation on us, thanks to Mr. and Mrs. Curran. We can expect that attention to explode when this news gets out. Well I want the next headlines to be about how we've captured her killer. Is that clear?"

No one moved when he finished speaking, but he let the silence draw out for a few seconds.

"Well, go on, then. We're not going to catch anyone sitting here. Get organized and get going." He snapped off the power to the projector, and the image faded to white.

40

Rogers drove them both to Goldhaven, they sat in near silence, lost in their thoughts. They arrived to find the beach closed, with patrolmen from the mainland stationed every fifty yards along the short promenade. They were turning away the few tourists who still remained.

THE TIDE HAD COME in by now. The rockpools where the arm was found were hidden underwater. Still, a police team worked in a rough line, performing a fingertip search of the high tide line where dried curls of seaweed lay mixed with sticks and random pieces of plastic. It wasn't a pretty beach: a few patches of sand, then rocks that extended to the heavy stone wall, forming the entrance to the harbor. It was the first time West had been back to Goldhaven since arriving on the island. It made her realize how beautiful Silverlea was, with its white sands stretching unbroken for miles in either direction.

"Come on. We better get on with it," Rogers said.

THEY SEPARATED, each with a list of streets to work, and West began the task of knocking on doors. About half of the houses were empty. Where people were home they knew nothing. Then one woman invited her in. She told West in a low whisper how she'd noticed a green van parked in front of her house for about a week, around the time Olivia went missing.

"Why did you think this was strange? West asked.

"Because I hadn't seen it there before," the woman whispered back.

"Do you know who it belonged to?"

"No."

"Is there any other reason why you think it might be relevant?"

The woman screwed up her face in thought for a long moment. "No," she said.

"Okay... I don't suppose you got the license plate?" West asked.

The woman shook her head sadly as if this failure could cost the police dearly.

It was probably nothing, it was *clearly* nothing, but it all had to be noted down, along with everything else. Vehicle make, color. It would all have to go in a new database, similar to the one West and Rogers had worked on so diligently for the previous three months, and which was now worthless.

And so it went on. Door after door, resident after resident. Hour after hour.

"Anything?" Rogers asked when they met up again, once it was too late now to knock on any more doors.

"Uh huh." West said.

"You alright?" Rogers asked.

"Sure." West said.

Neither of them spoke much on the drive back to Silverlea. After a while Rogers switched the radio on. A voice was explaining with a note of excitement how he was standing on Lornea Island, where the police were now focusing on the port town of Goldhaven.

"Earlier today, we saw Chief of Police Larry Collins confirming the dramatic news that Olivia Curran, the missing teenager, is now known to have died at or around the time she disappeared - the worst possible news for her

parents. And it was on this very beach where the grisly discovery of Olivia's hand was found sometime yesterday.

"Chief Collins wasn't able to say whether this discovery means the police are any closer to solving the mystery that has gripped the island for the last few months. But there's no question that this find will only increase pressure on a police department already heavily criticized for having made little or no progress in this case."

Rogers switched the radio off and sighed.

"I need a beer. You wanna stop off for one?"

West rolled her neck around as far as the car's headrest would allow.

"You go. Drop me off at the station if you like."

"Come on. Come for a beer."

West didn't answer.

"You sure you're alright? You seem kinda quiet. I thought you'd be happy. We got a lead. This is a real case at last."

"Happy?" West replied sharply. "The girl's dead. We're too late."

Rogers drummed his fingers on the steering wheel.

"Come on Jess. We knew that three months ago. But there's a real case to investigate now. And a real lead. There's a chance of catching this guy."

"Is there? Maybe that's the problem," West said, suddenly much more vocal. "What are we doing here going door-to-door? And why isn't Langley doing it? We're the ones who've worked this case. And he just steps back in and takes over..." She stopped.

"Langley was always in charge of the case. What'd you expect? This thing explodes into the highest profile case the island's ever seen and he's just gonna hand it over to a couple of mainlanders? Come on. Come for a beer. You look like you need it."

West didn't answer.

"Look I'm not saying I disagree with you. But at least things are moving. Come on. Come for a beer and we'll be grumpy together."

"I can't." West replied. "I need to get to the station to finish up on the paperwork from that kid."

Rogers frowned at this. "What you gotta do?"

"Type up a report," West sighed. "And get the kid's fingerprints in the system. I don't suppose it matters now, but the chief asked me to put them in there, in case the kid's been sticking his nose into a crime scene."

"Christ, Jess, you don't need to do that. First thing you learn in this job: when the shit hits the fan, you *delegate*. Stick a note to Diane. Get her to do it. Come on. One beer." He sensed he was winning and gave her a weary smile.

"One measly beer."

"Oh what the hell," West said. "One beer."

Rogers laughed.

"What?" West asked.

"Nothing. I was just thinking: we sure scared the crap out of that poor kid."

41

When they come back into the room, Detective Rogers doesn't even sit down before he starts talking again.

"Billy. Let me be crystal clear with you. I do not want to see you again. I do not want to hear from you again. You don't go *anywhere near* Philip Foster, or anywhere near this investigation. At all. Ever. Do you understand me?"

I don't say anything. They don't tell us what they were talking about outside the room, but suddenly they seem in a hurry.

"And you, Mr. Wheatley. You better keep your kid on a much tighter rein from now on, or you're gonna lose him. Do we understand each other?" I look at Dad and after a while he nods.

"Good. Detective West will sign you out." He leaves the room. The next thing, the other Detective is leading Dad and me out of the station. Dad has to sign some papers and then we walk outside. Suddenly it's just Dad and me. I can't believe how quick that just happened.

I FEEL A BIT BETTER OUTSIDE, but also I feel scared because Dad's obviously still mad, and there's no one around now to calm him down. Dad doesn't have his truck, the police brought him in without it, so we have to get a cab. Dad asks the driver how much it'll be, and the man says thirty dollars. I can see this makes Dad madder than ever, and he doesn't talk to me the whole way home. So I just sit there, looking at my feet all the way and trying not to snuffle. When we get home, I try to walk upstairs, but Dad doesn't let me.

"Sit the *fuck down*, boy. Now it's my turn to set you straight on a few things."

I do what he says, taking the furthest seat I can at the kitchen table. Dad doesn't sit, though. He paces up and down. He's shaking. I've never seen him like this.

"Do you know what you did today? You almost fucked us. That's what."

He sits down, but it's like he can't contain himself if he's still. He gets up and starts pacing again. Now he's slapping the wall when he gets to each end.

"The police. The *goddamned* police. I don't know why the hell they let us go like that. I thought we were fucked. Jesus fucking Christ. I thought they were gonna..." He stops, he comes really close to me.

"You *cannot* go around drawing attention to us like that, Billy. You just fucking can't. Not with..." Suddenly, he turns and slams his fist into the wall cabinet where we keep the mugs. It jumps so it's not level any more on the wall, and there's a huge crashing sound inside. It stops his rage for a moment, though. He stands there staring at it, then looks at his fist. There's blood on his knuckles. Then there's more smashing as the more glasses make their way to the bottom of the cabinet. Neither of us says anything about it.

"You just can't do it, Billy. You just can't draw attention to us like that. Haven't I taught you that? Haven't I told you hundreds of times how we need to keep our heads down? You *don't know* who might be looking for us."

I don't know what he means by that. I don't feel like saying anything, but I don't like the silence either.

"Who's looking for us?"

Dad doesn't answer me at first. Instead, he sits down again and puts his head in his hands so I can't see his face. He's still doing that when he does speak.

"No one. No one's looking for you, Billy. No one's looking for us."

I don't understand what's going on, so I don't say anything. Then, after what seems like forever, Dad takes his hands away and looks at me again.

"How come I didn't know what you were up to? Haven't I been looking after you right?"

I don't know if Dad wants me to answer this, so I don't know what to say. It doesn't really make sense. Dad doesn't look after me; I look after myself. I screw up my face in confusion.

"I'VE TRIED to do right by you, Billy. It's just you're... You're not like how I expected you would be. You know? If you knew how much I gave up for you" Dad shakes his head, he gives a little laugh. There's a little smear of blood on the tabletop from his knuckles.

"We're going to do better. You and me. We're going to do so much better. We're going to *do* stuff together. Like we used to. You remember how we used to search for silver up at Northend? We'll do stuff like that." His eyes travel to the surfboard he bought me, still propped in the corner of the room, unused, and I sort of hoped, forgotten. "We'll go surfing. That's what we'll do. I'm gonna teach you to surf. I'm not good at much in this world, boy, but surfing's one thing I can do." And with that, Dad starts to cry. Big, fat tears appear in his eyes and roll down his cheeks. He doesn't seem to care at first; then he wipes them away and sniffs loudly.

"Come on, fuck off upstairs, kid. I got to clear up this fucking mess." He walks over to the cupboard and opens it. A shower of broken pieces rains out onto the countertop and the floor. He swears again, then laughs.

"We'll talk again later, huh?"

Thoroughly bewildered, I go upstairs before he changes his mind.

42

I 've just seen the news. I might have been wrong about Mr. Foster, but I was right about Olivia Curran being dead. They've just found part of her body in Goldhaven. It must be why the police stopped interviewing me so suddenly. They must have just found out.

I CRY for most of the night. I just can't stop myself. I think about all that happened in the police station and all that Dad said, and although I don't understand why I'm crying, the tears still come. I don't sleep at all.

I don't even go downstairs the next morning. I'm missing school, but to my surprise, Dad doesn't even come up to tell me to get dressed. When I do finally go down to the kitchen, Dad's already gone out. He's tried to tidy up. The cabinet has been taken off the wall and placed on the floor; I guess he'll fix it later. The bin is full of pieces of broken mugs, and there's an opened can of soup on the countertop, with a note from Dad propped up behind it. I sit back down at the table and read it.

Hey Billy,

Sorry I lost my temper yesterday. It was just the shock, that's all. I gotta go out today, but we'll spend time together, just you and me. We'll get your new board wet, OK?

Love,

Dad

I eat the soup, tears still flowing from my eyes every now and then. I try to think. I try to make sense of everything that's happened.

I think first of all about Olivia Curran. She *is* dead, but not like how I thought it happened. Mr. Foster didn't do it. I got that all wrong. And just thinking about it now makes my face burn red. How much I messed that up. But then it wasn't my fault, there was so much evidence. And if Mr. Foster didn't do it, then who did.

Then my thoughts turn to Dad. Why was he so angry? I mean, I understand why he'd be a little mad, but I've never seen him like that before. He hardly ever swears in front of me and he's *never* used the F-word like that, so many times. And that thing with the cupboard. It was like he wanted to hit *me*. *Why?* I don't understand. And where's he gone now?

I DON'T LEAVE the house the whole day. I just sit and think. And after a while I don't feel comfortable downstairs so I go back to my room. I don't have a lock, but I shift my desk so it blocks the door. I just think the whole day. I sit and think. And some things start to come clearer in my mind.

43

Dad made me go to school again today. It was OK, though. No one knows about what happened at the police station, and to be honest, no one there really cares about Olivia Curran. It's harder at home. Dad keeps trying to talk to me; like he's pretending that suddenly he's really interested in everything I'm doing. It's weird. It's kinda creepy.

It's Saturday morning now. Or at least it will be when I get up. Dad will want to go surfing, but I'm not going with him. I'm going to sneak out before he gets up. I'm just going to try and stay out of his way until I can work out what's going on. I just think it's the best thing to do. So I get up an hour early and as quietly as I can I go downstairs. I can't stay the whole day without food though, so I pour some cereal into a bowl, and I've just added the milk when I realize he's there in the doorway, watching me.

"Hey, Billy," Dad says. "You're up early."

His voice sounds wrong. Like he's suspicious of me. I freeze with my spoon in the air, milk and Cheerios dripping back into the bowl.

"I was trying to tell you yesterday," he goes on. "We're gonna get you in the water today. Try out your new board." His tone changes. There's a false cheeriness now, like he's pretending that everything's OK, when really, the last few days have been horrible.

"We won't get too many days this late in the year when it's OK for you. So we're going to do it. OK? You and me."

I regret having my breakfast now, just the sight of it makes me feel sick. I slowly put the spoon back down.

"I was going to check up on my hermit crab project," I manage to say. My voice sounds croaky. But Dad ignores me.

His voice stays calm but I can hear he's mad underneath it. Like he's planned out exactly what he's going to say if I try to object. "Listen, Billy. What you did the other day, with the police, that's serious. OK? It means things are going to change around here. No more running around on your own. No more crazy *projects*. You're going to come out with me today, and you're going to come surfing. And you know what? You're gonna enjoy it. You and me. Together. OK?"

I don't know what to say back to him. There's a hardness to his voice that I don't recognize. For some reason it worries me. It scares me. Normally if he said this I'd try telling him how I've got schoolwork that has to be done, or that Dr. Ribald really needs my results this afternoon... Or something. But today, I don't say anything. Maybe I'm just worn down by all that's happened.

"I understand about your thing with water. Believe me, I do. But you'll be fine. I'm gonna take care of it. I'm gonna take care of everything." Dad's still talking. I don't even hear the rest of what he says, until he finishes with:

"So no arguing, eh? No feeling 'sick'. No urgent schoolwork. We're going surfing this morning. That's all there is to it."

I DON'T EAT any more. Instead I wait in the yard while he gets the gear ready and loads it in the truck. I look out over the bay and it occurs to me that I might not find a way out of this. It's not a big day for waves, not a huge day at least, and it's milder than it's been for a while. But the thought of having to go out there into the water makes my stomach feel like someone's kicked it. I hear the snap and rumble as the waves break and roll in towards the sand. I begin to imagine myself walking out there, the water creeping higher and higher up my body until I can't even touch the sand any more with my toes. I feel that dizziness around the edge of my vision. I hear that buzzing.

"Get in the truck Billy," Dad says.

44

Something makes me rebel just a little bit and I climb into the back, along with the surfboards. I guess I just don't want to travel in the front with him while he's in this mood.

He's already got the passenger door open for me, and he kind of sighs when I ignore it, but he doesn't say anything. He just shoves the door shut, a bit too hard, and gets in on his side.

I feel the truck vibrate as the engine starts and we roll out the drive and down the bumpy lane to the main road, taking the turn-off to Little-lea. I'm relieved by this, at least. The waves will be smaller there. Before I know it, we're pulling into the parking lot. We're here so early there's no one else around. Dad's door jerks open and he jumps out.

"Get your suit on, Billy." He snaps the words at me.

"Aren't we going to have a look at it first? To see if it's OK" I ask, because sometimes, Dad does this and decides the waves aren't good enough to go in.

"No need. It's perfect for you."

I don't move.

"Jesus Billy, you're almost twelve years old. Now get your goddamn suit on."

I try to think of anything I can say or do to get out of this, but I can't.

So slowly I start picking at my shoelaces. Dad keeps talking. I don't really listen though.

"You know Donny? His kid's only eight, maybe nine years old, and he's *ripping*. Absolutely ripping." Dad pulls my board out from the back of the truck and puts it down on the grass, talking all the time. And that's when I see it again. That thing I saw before, stuck down in the gap between the side of the truck and the flatbed. I thought it was a hairclip before. Maybe the bumps we've driven over have jiggled it a little looser, because it's easier to see this time, and it *is* a hair clip; I can see that easily now.

"Billy. *Get your suit on!*" Dad says again. He throws the suit at me and then he goes to his seat to put his on. I do what he says, but as I pull the rubber suit over my legs, what I'm actually doing is scanning the floor around me for a piece of wire, or a nail, or anything I can use to dig that hairclip out. I don't even know why I suddenly think it's so important. Actually, that's not true. I've got a horrible feeling I do know.

These last few days, when I've been thinking about things, I spent a lot of time online, reading all the news about the Olivia Curran case. It's everywhere again, now they've found a bit of her body. In one story I saw a photograph of her, taken on the day she went missing. It was taken by one of the friends she made that week. It shows Olivia standing with another girl, their arms around each other's shoulders. I didn't know why but something made me study that photograph. Something made me look at her hair. It was pinned up. It was pinned up by a hairclip with a flower decoration with little diamonds in it. And I remember it from when I gave her the hotdog roll that night. And it looks exactly like the one lodged in the back of Dad's truck.

"Right, Billy," Dad interrupts me. "Listen up,' cause this is important. We're going to walk out until you're about waist deep, and then we're both going to paddle right out the back. We'll use the rip from the river to get us out beyond where the waves are breaking. OK? You might have to duck under a couple of waves, but not many. OK?" He stares at me now, and his voice changes, goes quieter.

"Jesus, Billy, don't play the sick card on me now. I don't know what you're doing to look so white, but just pull yourself together. Huh?" Then he sits down next to where I'm pulling my boots on. He tries another approach.

"Listen, buddy, I know you get a little worried about the water. But it's OK. It really is. I'm gonna be with you the whole time. And as long as you listen to me and keep out of the breaking waves, you'll be absolutely fine. You'll love it."

I don't say anything. My brain's making connections faster than it ever has before. I'm still thinking about that hairclip. What it means, stuck there. I get this strange sense that I'm about to understand the whole thing. That it's all just about to fall into place. It's like suddenly, the world around me has become transparent, coherent, understandable. But then Dad's voice changes back to the harsh tone it's had all morning.

"Billy. You've caused a *shitload* of trouble recently, and I'm trying really hard with you. Really, I am. Now, you're going to get in the water today, and you're going to give it a good shot. You understand? No fu - "

He stops, mid swear word, as another car drives into the parking lot. It stops a few yards away and a man gets out and whistles to a dog. It's not anyone we know, but he gives a friendly wave as he shuts the car door. Then Dad leans in close to me, and his voice is a low growl.

"Christ. Just don't fucking embarrass me. OK, Billy?"

I feel like I'm going to cry again. I can feel my bottom lip trembling, and that whole sense of understanding disappears in a puff. I tell myself I'm not going to cry. I sniff a little, but then I nod my head. Dad puts his hand on my head and ruffles my hair.

"Good boy. It's gonna be fun. I promise you. Good-sized, clean waves. No crowds to worry about. That's the beauty of getting here early. There's hardly anyone else around. Not like later on. Come on. I'll wax your board for you."

Dad jumps back down and crouches next to my board. His board is already waxed and ready to go, the truck keys hidden behind the wheel. While his back's turned, I take my chance. On the ground near the back of the truck is a small piece of wire, and I jump down and grab it, then climb back into the truck, and on my hands and knees I try to wiggle it into the gap behind where the hairclip is. It's not quite long enough, and all I can do at first is move it. I pull my wire out and try to straighten it to make it a tiny bit longer. It almost works. Twice I snag the clip and think it's going to come loose, but something is holding it in place. I try again, my hands beginning to shake with nerves because I know Dad will be finished any second. And then I get it: my wire catches firmly on the decorative flower with the diamonds in it.

"*Billy*! What the hell are you doing now? Get out of there!" Dad's voice sounds loud. He's right behind me. I don't have time to look at the hair-clip, but I press it into my palm and turn around so he can't see what I've got, or what I've been doing. He's right there, his face near to anger.

"Billy. Come on. Get down. We're going *right now*."

I climb off the truck again, the hairclip pressed into my palm. Dad thrusts my board at me, and I have no choice but to take it, and try to tuck it under my arm. He picks up his too, and leads me away from the truck.

At first, Dad's behind me, and I don't dare open my hand to look at what I've got. I can hear Dad's breaths right behind me, and then his board bangs into mine.

"Fucking hell," Dad curses, stopping at once. "Jesus, will you not stop right in front of me?" He overtakes me, inspecting his board where they bumped, but there's no damage; it was just a knock.

"Come on, speed up."

With Dad in front of me, I finally have a chance to look at the hair-clip. I unpeel my fingers and look at it. It's just a silver girl's hairclip, a flower pattern on the top with diamonds arranged where the petals would be. I think back again to the photograph I saw the other day. It's the same design; I'm sure of it. The same clip Olivia Curran was wearing. But what's worse, now that I've gotten it loose, I can see what was keeping it stuck in place in the truck. On the other end of the clip is a small but recognizable clump of hair and skin, colored black with dried blood.

45

The Records Division of Lornea Island Police Department employed two people: Sharon Davenport, a young technician in her thirties, and her boss, Diane Pittman, an older woman who had worked there for longer than anyone could remember, and who had a reputation for ruthless efficiency. Had the task of processing the paperwork generated by Billy Wheatley's activities fallen to Mrs. Pittman, she would almost certainly have acted upon it more quickly. And that might have made all the difference.

Unfortunately, Diane Pittman didn't work Saturdays. So it was Sharon Davenport who found the paper card imprinted with Billy Wheatley's fingerprints in her in-box, with Detective West's handwritten instructions to enter them into the national fingerprint database. The detective hadn't stated that this was urgent, so Sharon delayed acting upon it until she had written a long email to her sister, answering a series of questions about the plans for her upcoming wedding.

With that done, Sharon turned to the fingerprint card. Sharon had grasped most of what went on with Billy Wheatley, and she didn't fully approve. In her view, he seemed a nice kid who had simply tried to help. To be rewarded by being marched around the station and given a talking-to by those detectives from the mainland was a bit much. The boy had been close to tears, and that father looked mad enough to near kill him. And now he would have his fingerprints locked away in the database until he was sixteen.

But she did understand *why* they had to be entered - there was a possibility his prints might have contaminated a crime scene, especially now the poor girl had turned out to be dead after all. So there was no question of Sharon not fulfilling her duty. And so, at about half past nine, she picked up Billy's fingerprint card and walked over to the terminal with the scanner.

The computer used to input fingerprints in the Lornea Island police station sat at the back of the technicians' office. It wasn't the most up-to-date piece of equipment. It looked like a standard scanner and computer, in fact it was – the only difference was the software loaded onto it. The scanner converted the inked prints into digital files, and the computer could then upload them to the central database. They would be indexed and filed, and then could be searched for by any authorized internet-connected computer. Should a fingerprint containing the same pattern of loops and swirls be found linked to any crime or investigation anywhere in the United States, and in a great number of other countries, too, it would come up in a matter of minutes. All Sharon had to do was create a new entry, with Billy Wheatley's details as written on the card. But when she tried to do so, an error message came up that Sharon hadn't seen before. Eventually, she reached for a telephone.

"Langley. What is it?"

"Oh, I'm sorry, Lieutenant Langley. It's Sharon here from the tech office. I've had something strange come up on the Billy Wheatley file."

"Wheatley? Who the hell is that?"

"Billy Wheatley. He's the boy that Detective West and Detective Rogers brought in the other day."

"Then you need to talk to Detective West or Detective Rogers." Langley was putting the phone back down when Sharon spoke again.

"I think it might be important."

There was a sigh. "As important as looking for whoever cut Olivia Curran's arm off? Because that's what you're interrupting here."

Sharon paused, not sure how to continue, but she realized that the lieutenant was still on the line.

"It's just, I was adding his fingerprints to the system. But something strange happened."

There was another sigh, then: "What?"

"Well, it's strange, really. He's already in there, but under a different name, and the entry under it doesn't make any sense."

"Like I said, I'm kinda busy here. Are you planning on getting to the point?"

"Well, it's just... It says he's listed as a missing person. And he's at risk because his father has tried to kill him on at least one previous occasion."

46

It feels like the world should freeze, but it doesn't. My legs are still working; I'm still following Dad down to the water. Now we're at the bottom of the dunes stepping onto the hard, wet sand of the beach. Ahead of us, the ocean stretches out, a set of waves now coming in and breaking with the steady roar, like airplanes taking off from a distant airport.

I can hear my breathing, fast and panicky. The hairclip is burning in my hands. Part of me wants to drop it, to recoil in horror from the blood and just *get it out of my hands*. But I can't. If I do that, Dad will see it, and he'll *know*. He'll know I know.

But what do I know. Thoughts begin to flash through my brain like flickers of lightning. Too fast to properly understand them. What does this mean?

Dad killed Olivia Curran?

No. No. That's just crazy.

My legs work automatically. Following him down the beach toward the water. The open sea that I hate so much. That so terrifies me.

Dad killed Olivia Curran?

It kind of explains things. The moods. Why he got so angry in the police station.

No.

I shake my head and the thought is gone. I almost laugh. It's so crazy. But there's water pressing behind my eyes.

"So I'm gonna stick real close to you, OK?" Dad turns to me and waits a moment so we're walking in step. He suddenly looks different. So big and strong, so in his element, readying to enter the water. This is his world. He must see how my face looks, but if he does notice, he deliberately ignores it.

"You just paddle hard at first. We've gotta punch out through these little waves."

We reach the end of the beach. Dad places his board on the sand to fix his leash. I can't do the same, because I still have the hairclip in my hands. I look around, desperate for somewhere I can put it. Not to throw it away now, and not just because he'll see, but because I know how important it is now. But there's nowhere. It's mid tide at the moment, and all the beach around me will soon be covered by water. If I leave it anywhere here, I'll never find it again, and I can't think of any excuse to return up the beach to someplace where I could hide the clip. Wait, there's one thing.

"Dad. I need the bathroom," I say.

"Just go in your suit," he replies.

"Not that type," I say, almost openly crying now.

This stops him for a breath or two, but not long.

"No way. No way, Billy. You're getting in there right now. No excuses. We're gonna bust this stupid phobia of yours right now. You hold it in, or you take a shit in your suit. I don't much care which right now. Now put your leash on."

Dad stands there watching me, and I've got no choice. I bend down and put the board on the sand, and then try to wrap the Velcro around my ankle, but I can't with the hairclip in my hand. I do the only thing I can do. I reach up to where the suit is tight against my neck, pull it out as if I'm adjusting it because it's uncomfortable, and I drop the hairclip down inside my suit. As I do so I catch a glimpse of the end, the sliver of hair, skin and blood. I feel it lodged there, trapped between my chest and the suit.

"Let's go. Let's get some waves." Dad tries a final attempt at making this sound like something fun, and we push forward into the water.

I've got boots on but even so the water flows in and runs up my leg. I register it's cold, but distantly, like it's not affecting me. Like I'm watching someone else wading out. Then the first wave hits me. This close in, it's only a line of frothy white water, but it still goes right up over my thighs. It feels like it's reaching up to grab me and pull me deeper. My breaths come fast. Suddenly the cold hits me. It's icy. I feel the panic rising.

THINK. I've got to think. What does it mean, the hairclip? The question is hammering in my brain. Does it mean Dad is involved? Does it mean Dad killed her? *Dad killed Olivia Curran?*

I know it makes sense. He was there on the night she went missing, he parked his truck out of sight on the beach. He said it was so he wouldn't get a ticket, but what if there was another reason?

And then, when I wanted to go home, he wouldn't take me. He said he wanted to stay. I went home with Jody's mom. But he made me tell the police we came home together. Dad made me lie to them.

The thoughts come rushing at me so fast I can't even think them all. I'm being crazy. Dad told me he got back a half hour after I did, about eleven. Olivia Curran was seen lots of times after that. So it couldn't have been Dad. Unless he was lying. I was asleep. I don't know when he got back.

My hand goes to my chest. I feel the outline of the hairclip with my fingers. Olivia Curran's hairclip. That was stuck in the back of his truck, glued there with dried blood. I feel like I'm going to be sick.

DAD KILLED OLIVIA CURRAN.

ANOTHER WAVE HITS ME. It's deeper now, and it almost washes me off my feet, but I feel his hand in the small of my back, keeping me upright and pushing me forward. I try to recoil but I can't. Dad's behind me, pushing me out towards the waves. Horrible, freezing waves pulling at me and trying to hold me underwater.

A THIRD WAVE HITS, and it rips the board from my fingers. I feel Dad's hand move quickly to my head as my feet slip from the sand. Dad pushes me down under the water, and suddenly, vision turns to green and bubbles as my face goes under. I pull in a breath of salty water. I kick out, panicking wildly. My foot connects with the seabed, and I push off. My head is above the water again, and I see Dad right there, close to me. I suddenly understand. Suddenly, the full horror of it hits me. Of course Dad killed Olivia Curran. That's obvious. And he knows I know it. That's why we're here. Here too early in the morning for anyone else to see us. Here in his world. He's going to drown me. He's going to kill me so I don't tell anyone.

HE SAYS SOMETHING, I don't hear what. My brain is racing all of a sudden, thoughts zapping around my head like the finale of a fireworks display. Maybe it's my life flashing before my eyes before I die. I suddenly see Mom's face. Clear as if she were really here. I see her eyes, cold and empty. I can't help myself. I scream. My mouth floods with salty water.

I cough and splutter, and I try to fight through the water to get away from him, but I'm too deep now: the river rip is pulling us out to sea fast. And now another wave is coming. Some of Dad's words break through into my brain.

"Duck under. It's easier if you duck under the wave." But I don't. I try to stand and jump at the approaching wall of water. This time, it totally knocks me off my feet, and I'm pushed backward and underwater. I feel my bottom hit the sand this time before the wave's energy passes and I fight my way to the surface. Only to see Dad striding purposefully through the water - barely waist deep for him - toward me. He takes my arm and leads me forward.

"There's a rip here. Get on your board and paddle."

I hesitate. I wonder if I could run to shore, escape him. But what then? And in my hesitation, my body responds to his command almost on its own. Maybe the result of my whole life with Dad. Listening to him, doing what he tells me.

My dad is taking me out to sea to drown me. And I'm doing exactly as he says.

47

I lie on my board and start to paddle. I almost slip off, but the wax grips my chest. I register the hairclip pressing against me, but my attention shifts to the arrival of the next wave. Lying down on my board, it suddenly looks much bigger. A wall of white water that towers above me.

"Dive. Duck now," Dad shouts, and my arms try to do what he says, to copy the way I've seen him and a thousand other surfers duck underneath the waves as they paddle out. I press down on the board's nose, but it hardly responds at all, and when the wave hits, it smashes into the gap between the board and where I'm performing an awkward press-up above it. It sweeps me off at once, and I get a second mouthful of water, and suddenly, I'm rolling around. I don't know which way is up. My head grazes the sand, and I can feel my board pulling against my leg. I surface again, and I hear my own voice crying out. But Dad's there again. I feel his strength shoving me back on top of my board. His voice telling me we're going to do this. He's not going to let me fail.

"Paddle. Come on, Billy. Just move your arms."

Gasping for breath, I do what he says, straight toward another wave. But this time, when it almost hits, I feel Dad giving me a mighty shove on the back, and the energy he gives me pushes me into and then through the wall of water. I'm not paddling or ducking this time. I'm gripping the sides of the board for all I'm worth.

"Now. Paddle again, Go left a little. That's where the rip is."

My fear of Dad is outdone by the terror of this moving, roaring water, so I do what he tells me. And it's slightly easier now. Around me, the water is bubbling and fizzing in a way I've never seen before, and the next wave hasn't broken yet: it's coming toward me like a low hill. Although I stiffen and ready myself for another tumble when it reaches me, this time it just lifts me up, and then I slide down the back as it rolls underneath. Dad's still beside me and a little bit behind. I feel my speed through the water surge every now and then as he gives a shove from behind. Two more unbroken waves come toward us and pass underneath. I can feel the power of the rip now, pulling us out, as if on a conveyor belt.

Dad's alongside me now, encouraging me to keep going. My throat is hurting from where I've swallowed the water. My arms hurt from the paddling; it's the rip pulling me out, not my paddling. But even so, I can see we're making progress.

Dad's pulled ahead, and he stops for a moment, sitting up on his board to look around.

"Come on, Billy, a little more. We're almost out." My pathetic strokes pull me closer to him, each one an effort now. I'm out of breath and stop when I draw level. I look at his face, and part of me wants to feel reassured I'm here with him, but part of me is terrified. Is he going to push me under again? What does it feel like to drown?

"Don't stop. Keep going in case another set comes in." He gives me another shove, further out into the ocean, further away from the safety of the beach. This time, I just put my head down and try and do what he says. I try to ignore the way my arms burn. I kick my legs like they taught me in the swimming pool, even though I can feel they're out of the water and doing nothing. Slowly, painfully, we creep further out to sea.

Finally, Dad stops us.

"That'll do. Take a rest."

I stop paddling but stay lying down on my board, my breath coming hard from the effort and the panic.

"Sit up, try to breathe slower."

I ignore him. If anything my breathing speeds up.

"Sit up, Billy. Like this. Sit on your board."

His voice brings me back, and I try to do what he says, sitting with my legs dangling down into the water. It's hard. After a few lurches to either side, I fall off, and my head goes under again. To right myself, I put my legs down, expecting to feel the sand underneath, but this time, it's not there. I sink right under and still don't feel it, and then, panicking again, I try to reach the surface, coming up spluttering and crying.

"That's it. Try again. You'll get it," I hear Dad say.

I grip my board like I'm some drowning sailor whose ship has sunk. Then, when my breath returns, I clamber back on, and try again to sit like Dad. This time, I manage it, although I don't feel secure, like I could fall off again at any moment. But I look around. I try to get my bearings.

We're about four hundred yards from the rocks, and maybe the same distance away from the beach – it looks miles away though. There's no other surfers out here with us. No one on the beach would even see me - I've tried to watch Dad from the beach a thousand times. With the waves, you can't see anything. Dad could push me under right now. No one would see. No one could stop him.

The only thing in my favor is the ocean has gone flat. It's off-set. While we were paddling out, it was like the waves would never stop coming, but now it's like a flat, calm day.

Dad's just sitting. Looking out to sea. He seems to be ignoring me. Maybe I could paddle away from him? But I know all the strength in my arms is gone.

Instead I just sit there, wondering. Why did he kill Olivia Curran? What does he get out of it? Maybe he's just one of those people who like it. Maybe he kills people all the time. Maybe our yard is full of dead people that he's buried there.

Maybe he killed Mom.

THAT THOUGHT hits me like electricity. A while back I tried to find out more about Mom online. He wouldn't tell me anything, so I went through all the newspaper archives. I thought of all the keywords that would have been used when the accident got reported. *Nurse, freeway, jackknifed truck, accident, killed, Laura Wheatley.* All I really wanted was to see what she looked like. Dad doesn't keep any photos of her, and I just wanted to see her face.

But I didn't find anything. Well, that's not quite true. I found plenty of nurses who had crashed on the freeways, over the years. But never one named Laura Wheatley. I couldn't figure it out at the time. But now I know. Mom didn't die on the freeway. Dad killed her. Now he wants to kill me.

I look at him now. He's still watching the horizon, and now lumps are beginning to define themselves - a new set coming in. And this time, my arms move without my thinking at all. Dad's distracted, and this is my only chance to escape him. I start to paddle as fast as I can. I don't even think which way. I'm not sure I think at all. I just paddle away from the man who wants me dead. But I haven't gone ten strokes before he sees.

"Hey. What you doing? Billy!" he shouts after me. Then I can sense him moving back into the paddling position on his board. Almost instantly, he halves the gap I've built up, just from a few strokes.

"Billy. Where are you going? There's a set coming. Stay with me."

But I don't. If anything, I paddle harder, and my panic must be flooding my body with adrenaline because now it doesn't hurt, and I feel my hands begin to grip the water better, begin to pull me forward better than before. I don't quite hear what Dad says next, only random words piercing my head.

"Wrong way... Get washed... Stop..."

I look up and see I'm heading in, towards the sand. Good enough. If I can make it to the beach, I can run to the rocks. I know the rocks. There are places I can hide, places where Dad might not be able to find me. It's my only chance.

For a strange half minute, it's just the two of us paddling, me a few yards in front. I can hear Dad behind me, his voice becoming angrier and angrier. If he catches me now, I know he'll do it now. He'll hold me under until I drown.

"Billy, there's a wave. Turn around."

But I don't turn around. It's a trap. And then I feel my legs rise up above my head. And then everything seems to happen in slow motion. The wave hits me from behind and from the side, and I get pulled up its face. But it's not a broken wall of white water or an unbroken glassy hill this time: it's actually breaking right here. It picks me up in an instant. It sucks me inside it, turns me upside down, and then it throws me forward and slams me down into the water. The violence of it is numbing. I didn't have any time to take a breath of air, and now it's too late. It's just a whirlwind of water and sound, and I'm tumbled this way and that way, and this time, I don't hit the bottom at all. I'm just stuck there underwater, rolling over and over, no breath in my lungs.

My eyes are open. I can see cascades of bubbles all around; I have no idea which way is up. I just keep spinning. Flailing around with the bubbles.

It goes on forever. It feels like it holds me for minutes, the water roaring around my head. And I can feel it happening. I can actually feel myself drowning. I realize I've got my eyes shut again, and I open them in a desperate attempt to see where the surface might be. But it's black this time, none of the green water I saw earlier. I suck in a half breath of water, desperate for anything, but my body stops me. I feel vomit flood into my mouth and throat. I'm running out of oxygen. I'm going to die. To drown. I can feel it. It's like I'm split: exactly half of me doesn't care, wants to suck in a lungful of ocean and let it happen, but the other half is still fighting, terrified of what comes next. Terrified of the darkness that I'm sinking toward.

And then something touches me. My board? Dad? I don't know. Whatever it is, I feel it push down on me, sending me deeper. But then it slips off, and I'm alone again. It's too late now. I open my mouth a little; it floods at once, and a reflex makes me close it again. And maybe I can start to feel the power of the cyclone of water reduce just a little, and around me I can see bubbles in the blackness. But instead of rising up around me, they're falling down. Down toward the bottom of the ocean.

I suddenly get it. *I'm upside down.* I'm upside down. I've been swimming toward the bottom to try and get to the surface. I fight to twist my body around in the water and change direction. It's my last fight. If this doesn't work, I know I'll give up. I'll give in to the screaming from my lungs, and I'll take a final breath of salty water, and then I'll die. I almost feel it already.

But I do fight, and I do feel it's easier, swimming upward, and the water isn't black anymore, it's green again, and that gives me a boost, and then it's almost white where it's just foam and bubbles, and suddenly my head breaks clear. I snatch a gasp of air before I sink under again, but it's enough to have me kicking my legs like crazy, and the next time my head bursts clear, it stays there, and I draw in a mix of water and air, coughing and sputtering. I stay like that for a minute, holding onto the side of my board, which is still there beside me, tied to my leg by the leash. Then I see Dad. The wave must have rolled me quite a long way in toward the beach because he's thirty yards away now, further out to sea, and another wave is about to hit him. I watch as he turns to meet it and ducks neatly under. Then he's lost from sight behind the rolling wall of water.

I know I have to take the opportunity. I climb on the board and start to paddle again, this time heading directly toward the beach. If I can get ashore, I can get to the rocks. I know places I can hide there. I don't know what I'll do after that, but I'm not thinking about that now. I just don't want to drown.

I feel the wave pick me up from behind, like before, but it's less violent this time. For a half second, I'm riding the foam, but then it tumbles me off again. The panic returns, but I keep my mouth shut this time, and the wave returns me straight to the surface. My board is right there again, waiting for me on the end of its leash, and I can climb on again, and I keep going to the beach. I hear Dad calling out to me, but a long way away. I can make it. I know I can. Then another wave hits. This time I'm ready for it. I grip the front of the board and I hold on. The wave catches the surfboard and picks it up, sending me sliding along in front of it, and suddenly, I'm racing toward the beach, covering the distance fast. I've seen how surfers do this when they want to come ashore. They just lie there, waiting, while the wave carries them in. I do it now, and I hold on for maybe twenty seconds before I'm pitched sideways and off again into the water. But this time, I immediately hit the bottom. I've ridden the final wave back to the shallows. I don't dare turn around to see where Dad is. Instead I struggle to my feet and try to run, but the water is like treacle, and it's flowing back out to sea, so I move like in slow motion. Then I hear Dad again, shouting. He must have ridden a wave in too. I glance behind. He's thirty yards away from me. I have to run. I have to reach the rocks. I have to get there before Dad catches me.

At last I'm free of the water, on the sand. I make a final effort. I drop my head and try to sprint. But I only get a few steps before something grabs at my leg and I fly forwards. My arms flail through the air, and I fall heavily, gritty sand grates against my face and goes in my mouth. What tripped me? Did he throw something? I try to move, but already I can hear Dad's footsteps closing in on me. I hurt all over. I try to crawl but something tugs at my leg again. I look down and follow the black line of the leash to where it anchors me to the surfboard. That's what tripped me up. I think to unstrap it, but there's no time. Dad's running towards me now. I crawl anyway, towards the rocks, dragging the board along behind me but he closes the distance in seconds. He steps on the leash and grabs my leg, pulling me back towards him. I scream. There's no one to hear me but I do it anyway.

I'm not going to go quietly.

48

" C an you say that again please?" Lieutenant Langley said.

"It says he's listed as a missing person. And he's at risk because his father has tried to kill him on at least one..." Sharon Davenport began.

"Where are you?"

"I'm in the records office."

"Wait there. I'm coming down now."

TWO MINUTES later Langley was leaning over the younger woman as she sat in front of her terminal. Langley peered at the screen.

"Do you see here, where I tried to create a new file for William Wheatley, yet his prints are already in the system? They're under the name of Benjamin Austin..." Davenport began again. She rotated her chair to give the lieutenant a better view.

"Yeah. Uh-huh. Who's the father? I don't see that."

Sharon Davenport typed quickly into the search box. An hourglass icon appeared, rotated, and a few moments later the screen refreshed.

"Jamie Stone," Sharon Davenport read. "Wanted by Oregon State police for murder, attempted murder, perverting the course of justice and - oh my - child abduction." She turned now and looked at the lieutenant.

"Print that off. Right now." Langley said, as he picked up the phone on the woman's desk.

* * *

THE FIRST TWO police cars arrived at the clifftop cottage just after eleven, ninety minutes after Lieutenant Langley finished his call. West was in the second car, her weekend canceled at short notice, not that she'd had any plans. It had picked her up from Silverlea and then driven, sirens-on, until they reached the bridge that led to the spread-out settlement of Littlelea. There they'd switched the noise off so as not to alert the residents of the clifftop cottage of what was about to happen.

THE PATROLMAN at the wheel swung into the long driveway too fast, scraping the side of the patrol car down an embankment lined with blackberry bushes, but no one inside the vehicle mentioned it or even seemed to notice. They already had their pulse rates maxed out. You could taste the thumping adrenaline in the air.

The first police car drove right up to the house, the driver of West's car stopped a little way down the drive, blocking it off as a potential exit in case Stone tried to escape. West pushed open the door and continued on foot, her firearm heavy in her hand. She reached the little front yard of the cottage just as the occupants of the first car were banging on the door. She scanned the scene, her heart pumping so hard the noise of it was a distraction. She waited, breathing hard, readying herself to give covering fire as she'd been trained to.

There was no response to Langley's shouts. He thumped on the wooden door one more time. Then, with a signal to an uniformed officer next to him, he retreated out of the way. The uniformed officer was standing ready with a heavy steel battering-ram, painted bright red. She remembered it from training, they called it the BFK, or Big Fucking Key. The door resisted the first blow, but on the second, there was a splintering of wood, and it swung inward. Langley entered first, his gun held in front of him. West's training came back to her again, entering half-finished properties where plywood villains and schoolchildren would swing out mechanically for her to either blast or ignore. Her mind raced. Would the boy be here? A flesh-and-blood version of the simulations.

She nodded to Rogers, who was standing beside her by then. Then she went through the door.

It led straight into the kitchen, smaller than she remembered. A few cups and bowls were left on the countertop. There was a faint smell of coffee. One of the wall cabinets was resting on the floor, a faded patch above it showing clearly where it had hung until recently. There were stairs leading directly from the kitchen, and from there, she heard the shouts of "clear" as the men before her searched the rest of the cottage. Now the stairs creaked as Langley came back down, his shoes thumping on the bare wood.

"Not here." He shook his head. Then he turned to the patrolman. "Get on the radio and report it." Langley went outside.

"Well, where the hell is he, then?" Rogers said to no one in particular. "*Shit.*"

THEY CHECKED AROUND THE HOUSE, then Langley made them wait outside while he organized the scene. They stood by the low wall, looking out over the beach. There were dots in the water, swimmers perhaps, surfers more likely.

"What a fucking disaster," Rogers said, kicking at the wall. "I can't believe we had the son-of-a-bitch. Right there in front of us."

West frowned. "You reckon it's him? You reckon Stone is responsible for Curran too?"

"You reckon he isn't? You saw him. He was..." Rogers screwed up his hand, searching for the right word. "He was *tight* when we talked to him. Like he was holding something in. Didn't you see it?"

West didn't reply.

"I reckon he was just waiting for us to spring something on him. I bet he couldn't believe his fucking luck when we let him go."

West thought back to the interview with Sam and Billy Wheatley - as they'd known them at the time.

"He did seem kinda nervous," she said.

"He'll be halfway to fucking Mexico by now," Rogers replied, not really listening to her. He puffed out his cheeks, fat like a hamster.

"Maybe," West replied.

"Not maybe. For sure. Wouldn't you be?"

"I'm just saying I don't know." She looked around. "This doesn't look like a place where everyone's left for good."

"What does the place need to look like, then? You hoping for a goodbye note?" Rogers turned away and stared out into the void that dropped away in front of the cliff. A silence hung in the cold air.

"No," West said eventually. "I'm just trying to get my head around this. This guy kills Olivia Curran, and his son comes up with some elaborate, crazy tip off about someone else killing her. Does that make any sense?"

Rogers was spared from answering because Lieutenant Langley came up to them.

"Stone works for the guy who owns the big hotel in town. James Matthews. He may even be working today. I'm gonna tear this place apart. You get over there. See what you can find out."

They turned to go, but Langley had one more thing to say.

"Oh. And if you find the fucker. Try not to let him go this time, will you?"

49

They took the squad car and drove down the hill toward Silverlea. Coming up to the bridge, they had to slow down. Ahead, another squad car was parked side-on, blocking the road. Two uniformed officers were standing in the road, stopping all cars and checking the occupants. Rogers flicked on the siren for a couple of seconds until the civilian cars in front cleared the way.

"Anything?" he asked, slowing beside the officer, who shook his head.

"No sign of either of them, sir," he replied.

"Well, keep looking." Rogers bit his lip and drove on.

THEY DROVE in silence down the pretty lane that led to the Silverlea Lodge Hotel.

"You reckon they'll remember us?" Rogers asked as they came to a stop outside. West didn't answer. Instead she pushed open the door and jogged up the steps.

The receptionist looked up from her desk, and her face broke into a smile.

"Good morning, Detective Rogers, how nice..." she began brightly, but Rogers cut her off.

"Hi, Wendy. Afraid this isn't a social call. We need to speak to the boss. You know where he is?"

"Mr. Matthews?" She looked flustered for a second but gathered herself.

"Well normally he'd be playing golf on a Saturday, but I did see him pop in earlier. Would you like me to check if he's still in his office?"

"Yeah. Do that." Rogers said, and waited right in front of her as she picked up the phone.

"Small place," Rogers said to West.

"What?"

"Small place. Lornea Island. Everything's connected to everything else."

Before West could reply, Wendy spoke again.

"You're in luck, Detective Rogers. Mr. Matthews is still in his office." She paused, covering the receiver with her hand. "Would you like to see him now?"

"Yeah, we would. It's this way, right?" Rogers didn't wait for her to reply, instead walking behind the desk and into the corridor behind it. West followed him, the flustered Wendy a few steps behind. A few yards away, they came to a door labeled 'Manager'. Rogers knocked three times and was about to knock again when a voice from inside said to enter. They did so without hesitation.

"James Matthews?" Rogers asked of the man seated behind the desk. Matthews was dressed in golf clothes and he still had the phone in his hand. He returned it to the receiver, a look of confusion on his face.

"DETECTIVE ROGERS and - "

"Detective West, sir," West said. She pulled out her badge and flashed it. Rogers did the same. "Is there a problem?"

"You might say that," Rogers said. "Can you confirm that a Sam Wheatley works here at the hotel? He gave your name as his employer."

"*Sam*? What's this about?"

"If you could just answer the question," Rogers said.

"Well, I could, but I'll need you to tell me why first."

"We're investigating the murder of Olivia Curran. Could you tell me if Sam Wheatley works for you?"

Matthews looked like he was beginning to anger. "Look, Detective Rogers, I think I should advise you I'm a very close friend of your boss, *chief* Larry Collins."

"And I advise you I'm losing patience fast. Does Sam Wheatley work here at the hotel or not?"

James Matthews stared at Rogers, growing red in the face. West interrupted the two men.

"Mr. Matthews. It is urgent. And important."

For a long moment, Matthews continued to stare at Detective Rogers, but then he looked across at West and gave a tiny shake of his head.

"Of course, have a seat."

There was only one chair in front of the desk. Rogers grunted at it, and West sat down. Matthews took a deep breath, then exhaled slowly.

"Detective West." Matthews held up a finger as if he'd just placed her. "You're the two officers who stayed here at the beginning of the Curran inquiry." He tilted his head to one side.

"That's right."

"Well, I trust you had a comfortable stay? I made the rooms available to the police department. I wanted to do my part."

"We appreciate it, sir. Now, about Sam Wheatley. Can you confirm that he works for you, and do you know his present whereabouts?"

Matthews raised both hands as if in defeat.

"He does work for me, but not here. He looks after the maintenance of my vacation cottages. But I'm sure he's not involved in any way."

"And is he working today?"

"Look, I've spoken with Larry; I know all about the poor girl's hand being found in Goldhaven. And I'm sure Sam Wheatley has nothing whatsoever to do with that."

"If you could stick to just answering the questions," Rogers said, now pacing up and down at the back of the office. There was another chair here, and Rogers pulled it forward to the desk and sat down.

Matthews frowned again. He turned back to Detective West.

"I'm afraid I don't know. He does work a lot of weekends, but he essentially arranges his own schedule. I could call him if you'd like?"

"What number do you have for him?" Rogers cut in. There was a pause.

"I'll check," said Matthews. Another pause while he searched on his computer and then his cellphone. He found a number and showed it to Rogers, who wrote it down in a notebook he produced from his pocket. Rogers nodded at the phone.

"Try it."

Matthews dialed the number. The others waited while Matthews listened in silence for a few moments. Then he hung up.

"No signal."

"OK," West said a few moments later. "We're going to need a list of all the places he could be working. The cottages you mentioned. Can you get that for us right away? We can have those checked out."

Matthews sighed lightly, but he picked up the phone again, dialing a single digit on the phone's keypad, and gave clipped, clear instructions to whomever was on the other end.

"It'll be here in a few minutes." He smiled thinly at the two detectives.

"Thank you, sir."

Rogers dug his cellphone from his pocket and checked for messages. There were none, and he shook his head at West.

"What can you tell us about Sam Wheatley? How long have you known him? How did you come to employ him?" West asked.

The manager stayed silent for a while before he answered.

"I wouldn't say I do know him *well*. I think I met him... seven, eight years ago. Maybe more. As I remember, he came to the hotel, asking for work. Our old maintenance man was retiring at the time. I said I'd give him a chance."

"And did you perform any background checks? Check his references?"

Matthews paused. "It's a long time ago, but for a position like that, I wouldn't normally dig too deeply. May I inquire why you're asking?"

Both detectives ignored the question.

"And do you know him socially?" West asked. "Could you give us the names of any family here on the island? Or close friends?"

Matthews shook his head. "We've never really socialized." He thought for a moment. "I believe he's a surfer. You could try asking around that crowd."

West glanced at her partner.

"Does the name Jamie Stone mean anything to you?"

"No. Should it?"

Again, the detectives ignored the question.

"Is there anything else you can tell us about Sam Wheatley? Anything that might tell us where he is?"

Matthews shook his head again. "I only know he's extremely reliable, and he's never been any trouble. To be honest, I know his son a little better, he's something of a computer whiz kid. He fixes the Internet connections in many of our cottages."

West glanced across at Rogers, who had looked up from his phone at this.

"Billy Wheatley?"

"That's right."

There was a knock at the door, and it opened a crack. A girl hovered outside, holding up a sheet of paper. Matthews waved her in, and she approached the desk, glancing at the two detectives but not making eye contact.

"Thank you, Cheryl," Matthews said, then waited until she had left the room. He studied it for a while, then picked up a pen and began to scribble on it. When he'd finished, he held it out to Detective Rogers.

"This is a list of our properties. I've circled the ones that Sam's working on at the moment."

Rogers took it from him and glanced at it. Then he dialed a number on his cellphone and began issuing instructions for patrolmen to visit the properties Matthews had indicated. When he'd finished, his cellphone beeped loudly.

"Thank you, Mr. Matthews. You've been most helpful," West said, rising from her chair.

"Well, I hope so. I hope you're able to find him. Although I say again, I don't believe for a moment Sam Wheatley has anything to do with whoever killed poor Olivia."

"Well. Thank you anyway." She rose to leave, but Rogers stayed in the chair beside her. He was staring at the screen of his cellphone.

"We got it," Rogers said to her.

She didn't reply, but his eyes flicked to her face, and he spoke again.

"Langley's got his truck. Abandoned by the river."

50

It was late on Sunday evening when Chief Collins called the meeting. He had one of the patrolman fetch take out, and the four of them - Langley, Rogers, West and the chief - sat in his small, neat office, eating pizza in silence. It had been a long day with no opportunity to eat. When they'd finished the chief kicked things off, summarizing what they knew so far about Jamie Stone.

"I spoke today on the phone with one Randy Springer. He's chief of police out in Crab Creek, where this all happened. He was pissed about me calling on a Sunday, but he remembers Stone well enough."

"Springer is certain Stone is our man. He says he knew he'd resurface sooner or later. Stone's the type that's always gonna offend again." The chief paused and appeared to think for a moment.

"He says Stone is violent and extremely dangerous. He'll be armed, and if he's cornered he won't hesitate to shoot his way out." Collins paused again for a beat or two.

"Springer made a big point of that. He said to shoot first and ask questions later." The chief looked around at his team. "So I don't want anyone taking unnecessary risks. Especially with the boy involved. Assuming the boy is still alive."

There was quiet in the room as all the detectives considered this. Even though she hadn't eaten all day West hadn't touched the pizza. She'd listened to what Stone had done with a growing sense of horror. She thought of how it must have been for the boy to live with him. But more than that, she thought about how she had missed two opportunities to rescue him. It twisted her stomach. The chief went on.

"OK, let's get to some details. Langley. The pickup truck. What do we know so far about that?"

Langley pushed himself off the wall where he'd been leaning and read from his notebook. "It's a red Ford, '97 plates. Discovered unlocked in a rural parking lot down by the river. Fresh mud down the side like he'd been off-roading this morning. River water in the footwells."

"Anything in it? Any sign of the kid?"

"Surfboards and wetsuits in the back. They looked like they'd been used this morning too. Other than that, not much. We saw footprints, though, a large male boot and a kid's sneaker. Leading straight to the highway. I'm thinking they went surfing this morning, came back to the house and saw we were there, then fled through the backroads. Abandoned the pickup when they realized we had roadblocks set up."

"OK." Collins thought for a moment. "No cameras out that way, I suppose?"

Langley shook his head.

"Forensics?"

"There's no lab on the island big enough to take it, so it's being wrapped to go on the ferry tonight. We should have something by tomorrow afternoon."

"OK. Keep on that. I want to know the minute there's anything back. How about the vacation places he looks after? Anything there? Rogers?"

"He's not hiding out in them. We're keeping an eye."

"Keep on that too. It's cold out there tonight. If they're on the run they're going to need somewhere to hide out. Empty properties are going to be mighty tempting." Collins said. "Escape routes off the island?"

Langley took this point up. "We're watching the port and going through the CCTV. No one matching their description got on the boat today. Course, he could have a private boat we don't know about, but there's no sign of one. And nothing's reported stolen. We're working on the assumption he's still on the island somewhere"

"How about the house? Anything?"

Langley shook his head. "Nothing. We'll keep looking, though. We'll tear it apart."

"Alright. There'll be time for that."

Collins stayed quiet for a moment, not looking at any of them. He stroked his mustache.

"OK. Let's think back to his alibi. West, you took his statement didn't you. What did he say?"

Detective West had printed out copies; she handed them around now. She cleared her throat.

"He claims he didn't meet the Currans when they began their vacation. They picked up the key to the cottage from a strongbox. He claimed he didn't even know who the daughter was, not until it made the news. He *was* at the party though." She hesitated.

"He told us he left around eleven p.m. To take his son home. Olivia was seen after that time, so it wasn't followed up."

"The son confirm they left together?"

"At the time he did," West said. "But then I found this. Take a look." She handed out a second statement.

"This is from Linda Richards. She's lives nearby to the Wheatleys. She says she was taking her daughter home from the party and offered to take Billy Wheatley back at the same time. Stone was talking with friends and wanted to stay longer. So the boy did come home when he said he did. But Stone didn't."

Langley leaned forward, skimming the document for himself. "How did this get missed?"

No one answered him.

"Who took Linda Richard's statement?" the chief asked.

"Strickland, sir." West replied.

The chief stroked his mustache and blew out his cheeks. There was a silence in the room.

"You didn't pick up anything weird about Stone? When you took his statement?" Langley asked.

"Like what?" West asked.

"Like it was *bullshit*." There was anger in Langley's voice.

"No. Not at the time." West replied. "There was no reason to."

"And how about when you had him sat in front of you. Here at the station? You didn't sense anything then?"

"We were focused on the boy. There was no reason to consider his father a suspect at that time."

"Jesus, what a fucking mess." Langley said.

West opened her mouth to say something but the chief stopped her.

"That's enough. We need to look into this. If Stone didn't leave at eleven, when did he leave? Who saw him after that? We gotta build a case against this guy as well as catch him."

WEST LISTENED as the chief gave his orders, but she wasn't fully focused. She couldn't get Langley's anger out of her mind. Was it her fault they'd let Stone slip through the net? Should she have realized there was something not right about Billy and his father?

"OK, let's wrap up for now," the chief said, interrupting her thoughts. "Langley, Rogers, go home, get some rest. I want the search back on as soon as it gets light. West, you wait here for a moment. I'd like a word."

THE OTHER OFFICERS gathered their things and filed past her. Langley gave her a stare as he walked past. Rogers raised his eyebrows. When they'd gone, Collins quietly shut the door. Then he went back to his desk.

"Sir?" West asked a few moments later, concern written on her face.

The chief didn't answer at first. Finally, he looked up.

"Detective West. You need to know something. In addition to speaking with Chief Springer this afternoon, I've also been called by two journalists. It's only a matter of time before they discover we took a statement from Jamie Stone two months ago and did nothing, and then had him in the station this week. And let him go." He glanced up at West. His face was grim.

"Sir..."

"When that happens," Collins talked over her. "We're going to take a hammering. If they get your name – and I may not be able to prevent that - it's possible *you're* going to take a hammering." His eyes rested on West. She couldn't read his thoughts.

"If it does indeed turn out that you interviewed a killer on two occasions, there are going to be people, inside and outside the department, who hold that against you."

West felt her face flushing hot. There was nothing she could do to prevent it. She opened her mouth to speak again but he held up a hand.

"DON'T MISUNDERSTAND ME, Detective West. I'm well aware that killers can make very good liars. I'm also aware that this department is under extreme pressure." He paused. Then swung on his chair, and looked out of the window.

"You know, I came here thinking I'd see out my years away from the limelight," he said; his voice suddenly a lot lighter. "I'd had enough of psychopathic child killers and the media circus they exploit. You realize, after a while, however many you catch, there'll always be more. It's a sickness within our society." He turned back to her.

"This is a small department, Detective. On a small and isolated island. The people here have conservative views. A woman detective. A black chief of police. These are difficult concepts for some people here. We both need to be aware of that."

West didn't answer. She didn't grasp what the chief was telling her, and he didn't give her the time to process it.

"Detective. I believe it would be advantageous if you were out of the way for a little while, just until we catch Stone. Should it take longer than I hope, there's a danger of attitudes toward you hardening."

West still didn't understand.

"Out of the way? What do you mean?"

The chief stroked his mustache again. "I've made some arrangements. I want you to look into Stone's background. Speak to the boy's mother, the rest of the family. Reassure them we're doing everything we can to find him. Last thing we need is them throwing their weight around. And they knew Stone. Maybe someone there will know something to help us find where he's hiding."

West frowned. It seemed like a longshot.

"But sir I want to find him. I want to be here."

Collins spoke sharply. "No. Langley has that covered. He'll search the whole damn island. If Stone is still here, Langley will find him. In the meantime I want someone on the mainland. I want to hear firsthand what this guy did."

"But..." West opened her mouth to voice another objection, but Collins stopped her.

"No buts Detective. I've told Chief Springer to expect you tomorrow lunchtime. You should speak to him first. He sounds like the kind of man who would demand that."

"*Tomorrow lunchtime*? How can I even do that?"

As if on cue there was a knock at the door. At Chief Collins' command it opened, and Diane Pittman put her head in around the door. She glanced at West to check who she was before speaking.

"The helicopter is on its way, sir. They say half an hour. They're asking where to head for?"

Collins' eyes flicked to West.

"You're still staying in Silverlea, aren't you?"

"Yes, sir."

"Can you be packed and ready to go in half an hour?"

She blinked at him twice before replying. "Yes sir," she said.

"Good." He turned to the older woman, still standing holding the door half-open. "They can land on the beach." The chief looked back at West. "They'll pick you up there."

For a moment, she didn't understand that he was dismissing her. Then she got it, and stood up slowly, her mind whirling. But he called her back.

"Oh, and Detective?"

"Yes?"

"If anything doesn't smell right over there, you let me know, won't you?"

51

Outside the chief's office, the building was quiet, but not the normal Sunday evening quiet. Tonight, the place had the feel of being deserted, the entire department having been involved in the day's search. Coffee cups stood full and cold on desks. Computers, left on, looped *Lornea Island Police Department* screensavers.

Detective West entered the office in a state of shock. She almost didn't see Rogers waiting for her. Lounging in a chair that wasn't his own, and twirling a pencil around his fingers.

"What was that all about? He's not pissed we didn't see through Stone when we interviewed the boy?"

"No."

"It's not what Langley said is it? 'Cause the guy can be an asshole. And it wasn't just you. If there's an issue there, it's on both of us, and I don't mind telling him that." Rogers was getting up a head of steam. West interrupted him.

"He wants me to go out to Crab Creek - where Stone first killed. He wants me to look into all that. In case there's something there that could help."

Rogers frowned.

"How's that going to help? He's *here*. We need to catch him here."

West didn't answer.

"Well. When?"

"Now. Literally now. Tonight. The chopper's picking me up in a half hour."

Rogers screwed up his face in confusion.

"I guess you need a lift then."

THEY DROVE TOGETHER to the apartments. West packed quickly, throwing two changes of clothes into an overnight bag. As she zipped it up her cellphone beeped as Pittman send through messages about her flight details. Then Rogers drove her down to the Surf Lifesaving Club and right onto the beach. West waited in the front seat, her bag at her feet. They barely spoke.

Moments later, a bright light appeared in the sky, coming over the headland from the north. Only as it came close was it possible to make out the rotor blades and the shape of the helicopter. And then, when almost overhead, it slowed and descended, with a flood of noise and raising tiny tornadoes of seawater from the beach. It looked clumsy from inside the car, a little bit unreal. The left sled touched the sand first.

"Well, I'll keep you informed," Rogers said when it had settled. The rotors continued to thrash around and he had to raise his voice against the noise. Inside the chopper the pilot gestured at them.

She nodded, then glanced over at him. He had a distant look in his eyes, like he was itching to get back to the search for Stone.

"Yeah, me too," she replied at last. She put her hand out to open the door.

"We'll catch him for you," Rogers said hurriedly. "We'll nail the bastard."

West hesitated for a moment, remaining silent, then pushed open the door.

OUTSIDE, the noise was deafening. A wash of hot, exhaust-laden air was billowing toward her, heavy with sand that stung her face. West stooped down and covered her head to protect it from the blast. Around her feet, small puddles of seawater shivered like they were alive. She ran toward the helicopter, reached its glossy painted side, and slid the rear door back. She climbed in and hauled the door closed, having to use both arms to get it to move. When it thumped into place the noise was cut by half. It was warm inside too. The pilot turned to look at her and said something she didn't hear. Then he pointed to the earphones resting on the hook above her seat. She reached up to retrieve them.

"Welcome aboard, Detective," a voice said into her ears. "Could you strap yourself in, please? We'll take off right away." His mainland accent surprised her. She'd become accustomed to the islanders' way of speaking by now.

"Boston Logan, right?" the pilot said, and this time, she nodded at him.

"What time's your flight?"

"Ten forty-five."

"Gonna be tight, but we'll do our best. First time in a chopper?" he added, and she nodded.

"How do you know?"

"You can always tell by the look of terror." In the dim lighting of the aircraft's cabin, she thought she saw him smile, but then he turned back to his controls. She had barely finished fitting her belt before the engine note rose. Slowly at first, but gaining in speed, the helicopter lifted off. The ground, the beach, the sea, all dropped away below them. It felt like being drunk in an elevator. Then they spun around so the view from West's window changed. The town slid away. Instead, she could see the darkness of the dunes and then the ocean. She found herself gripping the armrest, then forced her hand to relax. They gathered speed, flying out over the water to skirt around the cliffs. It didn't feel like it, but by now they were moving fast, because they were already at Littlelea. She tried to see the boy's house, on the clifftop, but couldn't find it. Then she realized she was looking in the wrong place. It was disorienting.

Then she saw it. Billy Wheatley's clifftop cottage, the home he had shared for so long with a murderer, a child killer. From up there, it looked even more precariously perched, right on the edge of the cliff. It was fitting somehow. The boy had lived such a precarious life. Was that life over already?

NOW LEVEL WITH THE COTTAGE, she could see the lights of the search team, still working, two – no – three squad cars in the narrow driveway. Then the pilot banked hard around to the right and out to sea, so that the black rocks of the cliffs were flashing past their left hand side. West flinched and pulled herself back from the window, as if that might help should the pilot lose his grip of the aircraft's controls and send them smashing into the dark rock face.

Then the cliff disappeared behind them, and they roared past the smooth tower of the lighthouse that squatted on the rocks. And then there was just water below them. A dark sea, flecked with flashes of white where the chopper's lights reflected off the waves. West turned to look behind. She could see the island, the lights of the towns, shrinking away. The pilot made another course adjustment and increased the power. The engine note changed. There was a whine of hydraulics. A clunk. The pilot's voice came through the earphones again, clear and familiar, without its island drawl, yet somehow missing something as well.

"I'm gonna explain your situation to Boston Flight Control. They should give us a good route in but I'm not promising." He adjusted one of the controls above his head. "Whoever booked your flight must really want you to get to wherever it is you're going," he went on. "Or maybe just get you away from here."

It was just a light hearted comment but West didn't feel like replying, and it was dark enough in the cabin that she got away with silence. Outside, the darkness blinked to the navigation lights and she watched the patterns in the rolling waves below. She wondered whether there was any real reason for taking this trip. Or if she had just been sidelined.

52

After the isolation of three months on Lornea Island, the mainland felt enormous. The two runways of Boston's airport reached out on giant arms into a harbor filled with ships, their superstructures lit up to make them look like a watery extension to the skyscrapers of downtown. The city itself stretched out behind the airport, yellow ribbons of freeways snaking around it. A billion tiny points of light, each one of them representing a human life, just like her's with its unique path around the spinning planet. She was back in civilization, and she didn't know if she wanted that.

THE SECTION of the airport reserved for helicopters was to the north, nearly a mile from the passenger terminal, but West found an airport security car was waiting for her. It raced across the tarmac, orange light flashing, dwarfed by the jet liners trundling into position to disgorge their passengers into the terminal or launch them shooting into the sky. The car dropped her off at a side door, the driver getting out to unlock it for her. When he closed it behind her she found herself in the main passenger check-in area, so bright it hurt her eyes. She shouldered her bag and ran for the desk.

HER SENSE of dislocation continued when she got there. In her line a family argued over the weight of their suitcases. Everywhere was a mass of people. People all living their own lives. People too busy to care about the strange, quiet Lornea Island that lay out in the Atlantic darkness. Out of sight just over the horizon.

SHE KNEW she should interrupt the family, explain to the check-in clerk how she was about to miss her flight, but she held back. The sudden vastness of the airport intimidated her. To her relief a second desk opened up, and the clerk called her forward.

WEST FELT a little better when she boarded her flight. Maybe it had something to do with getting out of the airport, where so many people milled around. Maybe it was just relief for catching the plane. Whatever, they took off, and she found herself straining to see Lornea Island through the small window. She thought she'd caught a glimpse of it before they bumped their way through the cloudbase up into the night above.

IT WAS a short flight to Washington Dulles and there was drizzle when she was back on the ground. West had to wait an hour in the concrete and marble for her connecting flight. The only reminder of where she had been now were the newspapers, a few of which carried small articles reporting the developments in the Olivia Curran case. When she took off again she tried to sleep but the cramped seat wouldn't let her body relax. So instead, she read the file, cover to cover. Then she flicked through the in-flight magazine, before finally feeling her eyes heavy enough to let her sleep. She rested her head against the window and outside the massive engines powered her across the mighty American continent.

HER JET LANDED at two thirty in the morning, Pacific Time. But that was five thirty in Lornea Island, off the East Coast, so it left West fresh enough to rent a car right away and begin the four-hour drive south to

Crab Creek. She got there at seven and checked into a motel. By then, she didn't much care that the room smelled damp. She set her alarm for nine, then lay down on the lumpy mattress and went straight to sleep. Her breathing, still gunked up from the aircraft's stale air, was the only sound to accompany the low buzz of the refrigerator.

53

"I don't know what you expect to achieve by coming here, Detective. Like I told your boss, it's all there in the file."

Crab Creek's Chief of Police Randy Springer had rolls of fat barely held in check by his uniform shirt. His forehead glistened with beads of sweat. He shook his head now, or tried to; the thickness of his neck limited its available movement.

"Chief Collins wanted me to come and speak to you personally. It's such a high-profile case."

"Yeah. I know all about that," Springer said, looking annoyed. "I just reckon you'd be better off over there catching the bastard rather than sitting here." He fixed her with a stare but then didn't seem willing to hold her eye. He snorted, like something from his throat had gotten stuck in his mouth.

"Well, I'll tell you what I told your boss. Jamie Stone is a sick son-of-a-bitch. One of the worst I ever came across. A lot of folks around here will be happy if you shoot him dead the moment you lay eyes on him." He sniffed this time and looked around. West wondered if he was going to spit out whatever had entered his mouth.

"Could you tell me about it?" she heard herself asking.

"I told you. It's in the file. You *have* read it?"

"Yes. I read it on the flight, but it would still help to hear it from you. You actually worked the case, right?"

"If you've read the file, why are you asking me that? We do have crime to solve here, you know."

West waited, unsure of what to say next. She wondered if he was actually going to refuse to tell her.

"OK." He appeared to give up. "Where you want me to start?"

She thought fast. The file had been poorly written; it assumed the reader had background and sometimes inside knowledge.

"Maybe start with the family. They're well-known around here. Is that right?"

Chief Springer took a deep breath, but then, before he replied to her, he picked up a telephone on his desk.

"Laura, bring me some coffee, will you? I'm going to be here awhile." He made it sound like that wasn't his choice, and he didn't ask West if she wanted any. He put the phone down and looked at her.

Suddenly, he smiled. West didn't smile back.

"Yeah. You could say the family are known." He spoke as if only a fool wouldn't be aware of that. "The Austins own a lot of real estate around here. Hotels, couple of shopping malls. Then Bill Austin served as mayor. Stepped down last year. He'd be the boy's grandfather."

"So an influential family, then?"

"A reputable family. A good family. Tell me again why is this important to you?"

"I'm just... building a picture."

He sighed. "Building a picture," he repeated to himself, then blew out his cheeks.

"What about the mother?" West asked. "What do you know of her?"

"Christine?" He raised a pair of pink, oily hands in a shrug. "She was a good girl. Never in any trouble."

"Did you know her? Before it happened?"

"Knew of her. Least a little bit. Most folks did. Pretty girl like that... Hard to miss." Chief Springer's eyes strayed to West's face, and she felt him examining her with a casual gaze. He didn't seem to like what he saw.

"The file says she was committed to a psychiatric hospital after it happened. Is she still there, or has she been released now?"

"Why do you wanna know that?"

"Excuse me?"

"Why is that relevant?"

West frowned, "I'd like to speak to her. I'm trying to establish her whereabouts. The file doesn't actually give the name of the hospital..." She began paging through the file to show him, but he just shrugged. West stopped looking.

"So is she still there?"

"I wouldn't know."

"Well what's the name?"

He shrugged again. "Have to ask the family, I guess."

There was a pause. West took a deep breath, telling herself not to get frustrated.

"She was young, wasn't she? When it happened? Twenty-one, twenty-two, something like that?"

"If that's what the file says..."

"And he was too?"

In response, the chief pointed to the folder she was holding.

West looked down at her lap and smoothed the fabric of her skirt down her knees.

"Perhaps you could just tell me what happened? In your own words?"

"I could, Detective West. And I will, just as soon as I get my coffee." He smirked at her.

A FEW PAINFUL MOMENTS LATER, there was a knock on the door. The girl West had seen sitting outside the office walked in, carrying a cardboard holder with two take-away cups planted in it. Someone had written the word 'Chief' on one of the cups. Chief Springer pulled it out of the tray and flipped the lid off, while Laura handed West the other cup, smiling conspiratorially at her as she did so. Once she'd gone, the chief made a thing about pulling open his desk drawer and adding sweetener to his coffee. Only then, did the chief start speaking again.

"OK. Here we go. Yeah, he was young. And he wasn't exactly the kind of guy anyone would want coming home with their daughter. Least of all a society guy like Bill Austin. He was a nobody, a high-school dropout. Beach bum, you know? No job, imagined he was going to make a living for himself from surfing. But that was just fantasy. He was going nowhere, fast. And then he lucked out by getting Christine Austin pregnant, and then he even managed to screw that up."

He paused for a moment and sipped his coffee. West just waited for him to continue.

"No way she wanted his kid but she left it too long to do anything about it. And then when it came out there were two of them. Twins. Non-identical. Obviously, *he* couldn't provide for them - no job, no family money to fall back on. So it all turned sour. Christine and the kids moved back to the parents' house. A big old place out of town. Nice place. That's where the lake is. Where he did it. He was still living... I forget, somewhere in town." He waved his hands like this wasn't an important detail.

"He'd visit them, but it was always difficult, you know? Stone didn't get on with the family. You can't blame them. Guy like that ruining their daughter's life and still hanging around. Like a bad smell." The chief stopped again, as if he was thinking about this.

"I notice in the file," West said to prompt him, "there's nothing on what his motive might have been."

He scowled at her.

"Motive, opportunity? That's what you look for when you don't have solid witnesses who can tell you who did it."

"Yes..." she replied slowly. "But we're wondering if it might help us understand more about what happened in the Curran case."

The effort of speaking seemed to have left the chief out of breath. He was almost panting now, his forehead shiny with sweat.

"What about you let me finish up, now as you got me started?"

West was surprised at the unmasked distaste in his voice, but she nodded quickly.

"So like I was saying. It went on like this for a while, him hassling the family, her trying to move on. But it wasn't sustainable - you know what I mean?"

West nodded again.

"Christine has a brother. Smart guy. Paul Austin. Works for a law firm up in the city." Chief Springer sipped his coffee again. Then he sighed.

"And he came down to visit one weekend, and when he gets there, the front door is unlocked. He can't understand. It's never like this. He goes inside. He searches the house, but there's no one there. *That's strange*, he thinks. And then he hears screaming coming from the grounds. He runs out there, and that's when he sees it. He sees this guy who's been hassling his sister. This *Jamie Stone*. He's standing in the lake. He's holding Christine Austin down under the water, trying to drown her. One of the twins is on the bank, strapped into a stroller - that's Ben. His sister, Eva, she's floating face down in the lake. *Stone's already drowned her.*"

It was nothing that West hadn't read already, but hearing the words spoken gave them a power she'd not felt before. It was warm in the room, but she felt cold. Her brain furnished her with the file image of the dead baby photographed on the banks of the lake, the skin yellowed except where the purple bruises shone out. The girl hadn't gone without a struggle. West said nothing and waited.

"Paul runs straight into the lake. He tries to get Stone off his sister. But Stone sees him coming. He times a punch and lands Paul on the head with it. They fight, but Paul comes out on top. He drags Christine to the shore. She's conscious but in no state to do anything. Stone's picking himself up by now, but Paul can see the other kid, Eva, floating out into the lake. He knows Stone could get away, but what choice does he have? He goes for the baby, but once he gets there, he finds it's too late for her. And by the time he gets back to the shore, Stone's disappeared. And he's taken the other kid with him. Ben's gone.

"We searched the whole state for them. Looked everywhere he might have dumped a body, but we didn't find anything. He got away." Chief Springer looked away for a moment, a wistful look on his face.

"I was the first on the scene."

West said nothing. The chief looked back at her. "So like I said. There's a lot of folks around here who'll be very happy if you find Jamie Stone and put a bullet through his evil skull."

54

For a few moments the only sound is our breathing, both of us out of breath. Slowly I open my eyes to look at Dad. His face is fixed in a crazed smile. Then he laughs, throwing his head back to the sky.

"That was one hell of a wipeout buddy! I thought you weren't gonna come back for a while out there!"

He laughs again. The noise of it fits the empty beach, just the two of us here, slick in our wetsuits.

"C'mere, kid. Come here." He grabs me now, he pulls me close to him, so that we're stuck together like two seals.

"Hey stop it. C'mon. Stop crying," he pulls back and looks at me, still holding onto my shoulders.

"I guess it was a little bigger out there than I thought." He laughs again, then slaps me around the shoulder. "But you did well. You went out there. You caught a wave. Shame you tried to run up the beach afterwards. But it's progress."

SLOWLY I LIFT MY HEAD. I look at my Dad. I don't really know what's going on. One minute he was trying to kill me. The anger written on his face. Now he's acting like nothing happened, nothing like that anyway.

I'm limp like a doll as he squeezes me again.

"But I get it. I get it now. I really do. You don't like the water. Some people don't. If that's you, that's you." He laughs again. "The way you panicked out there... I've never seen anyone react like that. You looked like I wanted to kill you." He laughs and squeezes me harder.

Dad kneels down beside me and undoes the leash that's still wrapped around my ankle. Then he picks up my board and his, and tucks them both under one arm, and wraps the other arm around my shoulder.

"Let's get you changed; then we'll get some breakfast. Not the cafe. We'll go someplace different. Someplace nice."

I walk with him, not sure what to think. It feels like suddenly my old dad is back. The dad I remember from when I was little. The dad who used to take me rockpooling, who had time for me. The dad who would sit in my room because I was scared the monsters under my bed would eat me while I slept. Then, with a sudden empty feeling in my stomach, I remember. I put my hand to my chest, feeling for the hairclip. The clip with the bloodied hair that I pulled from the back of his truck. The proof that tells me that version of Dad really has gone forever. I feel myself shrinking away from his grip again, and he looks at me, worried. He smiles, as if that's going to reassure me. I keep my hand on my chest, trying to feel for the bump under my suit that tells me the clip is still there, but all I feel is my chest rise and fall, in time with my too-fast breathing.

WE GET BACK to the truck, and Dad turns the radio on. It's playing Jay-Z and he turns it up louder. Dad still likes the kind of music that's meant to be for younger people. He throws me a towel, and then pulls open his door to get changed.

I pat my chest again, feeling for the bump of where the clip is. I can't feel it. So I reach behind my back to pull the zipper down on my suit. Carefully, I pull the rubber off my shoulders and then look down at the space where my chest has been. There's no hairclip. I study my chest. I look pale and skinny, even more so than normal, like the seawater has shriveled me up. There's a faint indentation that I think shows where the clip was, but the actual hairclip isn't there. Hurriedly, I pull the rest of my suit off, wrapping a towel around my waist even though there's no one else in the parking lot. Still no clip. I turn my suit inside out and inspect it, then look on the ground around me. But I know it's not there. It must have gotten flushed out of the suit when I was being rolled around underwater. It's out there somewhere, sunk to the bottom of the ocean, where it'll never be found again.

Suddenly, I feel pressure on my nose, and just in time, I lean my head forward. A run of water comes flowing out of my nose, not just a few drops, but enough to fill a cup. Dad sees and laughs.

"That's a good one, Billy. You've swallowed half the sea out there, buddy."

I don't answer. I look at my chest again, but now, where I thought I saw the indentation from the hairclip, there's nothing, except a faint reddish patch on the skin. It could be nothing, could just be where the wetsuit rubbed against my skin. As I get dressed, I look again in the truck, to see if there's anything more where I found it. The little gap where it was stuck is still there, and when I close my eyes I can see how the clip looked, when it was lodged in there. But when I open them again, it's gone. Gone forever.

"Tell you what, Billy. I've got to head into Newlea later anyway, so how about we grab an early lunch there? We'll drop the boards off at home, then go get some burgers. How's that sound?" Dad asks, and I nod slowly. I don't know what to think anymore. So once we're changed, Dad loads the boards up and flings the suits in the back in a big wet heap. Then we get in and drive back up the hill to drop the boards off. And that's when everything goes really crazy.

55

Dad's whistling as he drives. I don't understand why his mood has changed. From trying to kill me, to wanting to buy me lunch. And I'm just sitting here next to him, not saying a word. It's like I'm floating or in a dream or something. I'm sitting next to Dad, but at the same time, I'm sitting next to a murderer. Part of me wants to push the door open and escape; the other part wants to tell him everything and let him hug me and tell me it's crazy. In the end I do nothing. I just wrap my hands around myself against the cold. I can feel my body shaking.

We turn off the road and into our little driveway. The only place it goes is our house, but there's a bend halfway along which hides the house from the main road. We go around the bend now, and Dad's whistling stops. He hits the brakes.

Up ahead, there's two cars, both painted black and white, with the blue police lights on the roof going slowly around, even though there's no one inside.

"The fuck...?" Dad says, and we just sit there for a moment. There's a gap in the hedge a little bit further on, and you can just see the house through it. Dad quietly rolls the truck on so we're level with it, and we both look through. There's more cars, some marked, some not, and there are people going in and out of the house.

"Shit," Dad says, and he puts the truck into reverse.

I'M THINKING NOW, not fast enough, but I'm thinking. The police are here. This is real. It must be. And I have to act. The police are here. *They can save me.*

I look down at the door handle, and I wonder what would happen if I open it. Would I have time to run to the police? Or would Dad catch me before I could get there?

But I'm already too late. We're already moving backward.

"Fuck it," Dad says. He's instantly angry again. "The fucking cops." He spins around in his seat so he can see behind better and speeds up. I'm worried we're going to veer off into the hedgerow.

He doesn't slow down where the lane meets the road. It's an awkward turn, even when you're going forward. But he goes for it anyway, backing out onto the road and spinning the truck around. We're lucky, though, it's clear. Then he rams the truck into first and accelerates so hard I get pushed back in my seat. He's checking in his rearview mirror all the time, and I turn around, too, expecting to see the flashing blue lights chasing us, but there's nothing there. The road is empty. He doesn't say anything. He doesn't say where we're going, or why. He doesn't say why there are police at the house. And I don't ask. Neither of us needs to say anything. The silence says it all.

When we get to the woods, he pulls off the road into the area where there's picnic tables and you can park to go for a walk. He drives behind some trees and stops. But he leaves the engine running. I look over at him and wonder what he's thinking. I realize he's checking the road again. We can't see it clearly because the branches of the trees are in the way, but we could see if any cars go past. Finally, I say something, mostly because it'll seem weird if I don't.

"Why are there police at our house, Dad?"

He looks at me suddenly, like he'd almost forgotten I was there. He's about to answer, but then we hear a siren. We both sit there for a moment, trying to hear where it's coming from, and then Dad pulls the truck forward so we're deeper behind the bushes. Then he kills the engine. I can see the flashing light now, bright though the gloom of the forest. The car flashes past, not coming from our house, driving toward it.

"What's going on, Dad?" I ask.

He stares at me again, like he can't believe I'm here. I guess he thought I'd be dead by now and he wouldn't have to worry about me.

"Billy... This is going to sound weird, but we've gotta go somewhere for a while."

"Why?" I say.

"We've got to get off the island."

"Why?" I say again. Even though I know the answer, I can feel the panic rising in me. I can hear it in my voice.

"I don't have time to explain now. Just trust me." Dad starts the engine again. "We're gonna go get the ferry."

We spin around again, and this time, Dad looks both ways before rejoining the main road. He keeps the speed down, and he checks in the mirrors almost as much as he looks out of the front.

"We'll get to Goldhaven, we should make the midday boat. That gets in by four. We can find a motel somewhere, figure out what to do," Dad seems to be talking to himself, but then suddenly he stops. We're out of the woods now; it's open land around us, and up ahead, the bridge over the river. And there, blocking the road in both directions, are two more police cars.

"Motherfuckers," Dad says. He slows to a halt and then puts the truck into reverse again, and backs up the main road into the woods. Then he stops again and just sits there with the engine running, thinking.

"Do you think they're looking for...?" I don't know how to finish my question. *You? Us?*

Dad doesn't answer anyway. Then, suddenly, he beats the steering wheel with his fists and swears again. Then he smiles at me, a manic smile.

"Want to do a little off-roading, Billy?" he says.

He doesn't wait for an answer. He spins the truck around so we're facing back into the woods, and we drive on for a half mile, until we come to a track on the left. It's not a real road; you're not supposed to drive on it, but it's wide enough for the truck. We bump our way down it, and eventually break free of the trees. It's kind of marshy land here; no one comes here much, except maybe some bird-watchers.

Eventually, we come out by the river, about a mile upstream from the bridge where the police are waiting. It's not a big river. In the summer, it sometimes dries up, but this time of year, when it's been raining a lot, it's pretty full.

"What are you going to do?" I ask.

"I told you. We're gonna get the ferry."

"Won't they be waiting there too?" I ask, and Dad just looks at me. We drive along the riverbank for a while and then we come to a section where the banks are low. In the summer, you can easily get across here. I'm not sure about now. Dad edges the truck forward, down toward the water. He doesn't hesitate. He just drives right in.

The truck lurches from side-to-side as the wheels find hollows hidden under the water. I grip the door, worried we're going to roll at one point. The water's right up to the grille on the front of the truck, and out on my side, I can see water, almost up to the window. Dad's revving the engine hard, and we're pushing through the water, a big wave rolling out in front of us.

"C'mon, c'mon," Dad's muttering as we go through the water. I see water coming in through where his door shuts, but he ignores it. Then I feel the same is happening on my side. We hit something, and the truck stops dead, rocking back and forth. Dad swears again, then turns the wheel full lock, and somehow we edge past the obstruction. We're more than halfway across the water now, and heading back uphill, almost on the other bank. Dad's still muttering. Willing the engine to keep going. I can see we're going to make it now. We hit the bank, and the big truck struggles to grip, but with the engine roaring, we climb out of the water and over the neat grass where people come for picnics in the summer. There's another little parking lot here, and a track that leads back to the main road, past where the police are waiting.

There's woods this side of the river, too, although they're not as thick, but they protect us from the police on the bridge. We're going to make it. But suddenly, there's a roar above us and the sound of rotor blades hammers through the air. The helicopter seems to appear from nowhere. I guess it must have taken off from the beach, and now it's flying upriver, straight toward us. Dad guns the engine until we're in the trees again, and then he slows to a stop and stares up through the wind-shield, trying to spot it. We both see it together, coming overhead and banking into a turn. We don't see it clearly, just glimpses through the branches, but it looks like it must have spotted us, but then instead of staying overhead, it keeps on going, and we see it following the road out of town, the road we need to take across the island toward Goldhaven. There's no need for me to ask if Dad thinks the helicopter is there to catch us.

He doesn't move for a long moment. The chopper is hovering stationary now, not too far away. It seems to be keeping an eye on traffic on the main road. I guess they know what vehicle Dad's got, and they're looking out for it.

"Come on," Dad says suddenly. He pushes the door open and steps out. I don't move, so he says it again.

"Come on, Billy. We're gonna walk from here."

"To Goldhaven?" I ask, but he shakes his head. "No. They'll be watching the port anyway. We'll take the back way into town. I know somewhere we can hole up. Until I find a way out of this."

I still don't move, but he's already at my side of the truck. He pulls open the door.

"C'mon, kid. Let's get going." I unbuckle my seatbelt and step out of the truck. Then he leans in after me and opens the glovebox. Inside, there's his wallet and phone, and tucked under the folder where he keeps the car's documents, I catch a flash of black metal. My mouth falls open. It's a gun. I've never seen Dad with a gun before. He hates them. For a moment he tries to hide it, but then he sees there's no point. He kind of shrugs like what did I expect, then he tucks it into the waistband of his jeans.

It's cold, but Dad makes us walk fast, under the cover of the woods, and we get to the main road in no time. I've driven along this road lots of times in Dad's truck, but I've never been here on foot. I'm surprised how fast the cars are going as they zoom past. It's not busy, but there's always a car or two in sight. The helicopter is still visible, too, but it's a mile or two away. Dad takes my hand, like I'm still a kid, and he pulls me across the road.

"Where are we going?" I ask, stumbling behind him as we push through the undergrowth into the cover of the woods the other side.

But he doesn't answer.

56

Detective West drove back up the ocean highway she'd driven down only hours before. This time, in the day light, it was beautiful; the sunshine bounced and glittered on the waters of the Pacific. The climate was drier here than Lornea Island, the ocean seemed fresher, the air cleaner.

After an hour, the road snaked inland, cutting through huge fields. She was flanked on her journey by towering power lines that guided her toward the edges of the city. She had the road to herself at first, but as she neared Portland the traffic increased, and soon she had to concentrate, hands gripping the rental car's plastic steering wheel. She followed the GPS to the city center, where the traffic thinned a little, till it was mostly just cabs. Towering above her, tall buildings of glass and steel spoke of money and power. She pulled into a parking garage, left the car and continued on foot.

The offices of Austin, Laird & James occupied two floors high up in a smoked-glass tower. The atrium was so big there were full-size trees inside, presumably to make the experience of passing through metal detectors under the watchful eyes of security guards feel a little more natural. If so it didn't work. For West, as she rode the elevator up to the law offices, it felt like an environment designed to protect the wealthy and the powerful, and to send a message to everyone else. Don't challenge us. You don't belong here.

THE RECEPTIONIST WAS VERY PRETTY and looked very bored. She was filing her nails as West flicked open her badge and ID. Judging from how she kept on filing, nothing about West impressed her.

"I'm here to see Mr. Paul Austin," she said, trying to smile confidently. "I telephoned earlier."

The girl raised one finely-plucked eyebrow and took West's ID. She examined it carefully, then did something on her computer. There was sound of a printer and a she pulled out a visitor's card with West's details on it. The receptionist slipped the card into a plastic wallet and asked West to clip it to her lapel.

"Mr. Austin's in a meeting at the moment. I'm afraid I'm not able to disturb him." She smiled like this rather pleased her.

West checked her watch.

"We arranged to meet at three. He said he could fit me in."

There was an unmistakable challenge in the girl's answer.

"But you only made the appointment this morning. Normally, it wouldn't be possible to see Mr. Austin at all on such short notice." She smiled again. "If you'd like to wait, I can have some coffee brought over." West looked around, wondering who would do it if the receptionist wasn't going to move herself. She declined the offer anyway, and went to wait where she was told, on a suite of black leather sofas and smoked-glass coffee tables that matched the windows. There was nothing to read there except the company brochures, which explained the firm's specializations. Or rather didn't explain it, since West wasn't able to get past the language of *derivatives manipulation, disintermediation, discretionary trust protection* and *estate efficiency frontiers*. West flicked through the glossy document, then tossed it back down on the table and watched the receptionist, who moved onto her other hand. After twenty minutes, West returned to the front desk, only for the girl to repeat that Mr. Austin would see her as soon as he was able, but that she couldn't say when that might be. West refused another coffee.

Back on the sofa, her cell chirped, and she dug it out of her bag, happy for the diversion. It was a text from Rogers:

Call me if you get a minute.

SINCE SHE APPARENTLY HAD PLENTY OF minutes, she hit the button to call him. He answered at once, his gruff voice taking her straight back to Lornea Island.

"I thought you'd want to know," he sounded tired. "It's Stone's pickup. The lab found traces of blood and hair in the back."

"Olivia Curran's?"

"Right blood type. And the hair's the right color. We should have the results of DNA tests in a couple days. But it looks like it. And that will positively link Stone to our case. If there was any doubt." There was a pause on the line. "Are you getting anything useful out there? Where are you now?"

West lowered her voice. "I'm just about to meet with a Paul Austin. He's the brother of Billy's mom, Christine. He's the one who disturbed Stone drowning the family in the lake. Or at least, I think I'm meeting with him. He's an hour late already."

"They not treating you right out there?"

"The chief out here thinks I'm wasting everyone's time. We should be putting everything into catching Stone."

"Well, if he'd caught him, Stone wouldn't have been able to murder Curran in the first place. You remind him of that if he gives you shit," Rogers said.

They were quiet for a second or two. West noticed the receptionist was on the phone; she hadn't heard it ring.

"Anyway, I'll keep you informed. I just thought you should know." Rogers sounded like he was preparing to hang up.

"I am confused about one thing, though," West spoke quickly, not wanting to end the call yet.

"Go on," Rogers said after a beat or two.

"I still don't get why Stone would drown one of his children, and then disappear with the other, and apparently try and bring him up as normal. Does that make sense to you?"

There was another pause while Rogers thought this over. At the same time, the receptionist put her phone down and stood up to walk across to where West was sitting.

Rogers sighed. "Some sort of psychopathic guilt? You're over-thinking this, Detective. If he's the kind of guy who can drown a baby, and murder a schoolgirl then go back and cut off her arm, we don't need to wonder too much about his motivations. The guy's a sick fuck. That's it."

The receptionist stopped just short of where West was sitting and waited. She was close enough to overhear her and West felt a buzz of irritation.

"I gotta go. Text me when you hear about the blood," West said, loud enough for the girl to hear. She killed the call and looked up with a smile.

The receptionist smiled back, but it was less self-satisfied than before. West felt a small victory that the 'blood' might have just unsettled her.

"Mr. Austin will see you now."

"Why thank you," West said.

PAUL AUSTIN'S office was at least four times the size of Chief Springer's, but the view was a hundred times better. Floor-to-ceiling walls of glass revealed half the city and the river that wound its way through. Low hills dusted in mist graced the horizon. It was distractingly beautiful. Then she saw Paul Austin, and she was distracted further. He wasn't just handsome, but ridiculously so. Like a model from a Christmas perfume ad.

"I'm sorry to keep you waiting, Detective West." His voice purred, soft and sensual. "My two o'clock meeting ran over." He shrugged with a knowing look. As he did so his features softened slightly giving him an edge of vulnerability. West had to fight not to stare at him. He was her age, tall and tanned. His white teeth were perfect, set within unusually red lips. His eyes were so bright and so blue they almost looked fake, like a movie star touched up for a poster. He wore a dark blue suit that complimented his eyes, and underneath, a thick, cream cotton shirt, with slim silver cufflinks peeking from the sleeves.

"I'm afraid I'm normally booked up for weeks in advance," he explained. "But this is important so I've canceled my three thirty. I hope that's OK? Do have a seat, please." He held out a hand to an informal area of his office where more sofas were arranged. West felt herself sinking down, and any irritation she'd had in the waiting area slipped away. Paul Austin picked up a phone and ordered coffee in a quiet voice. Then he sat opposite and leaned in toward her.

"So. I understand Jamie Stone has resurfaced at last?" He was close enough that West couldn't help but catch the fragrance of his aftershave. Fresh and musky. She had to resist breathing it in.

"WE BELIEVE SO," she said.

"And he's now implicated in the Olivia Curran homicide case?"

West fought to maintain her sense of sharpness. "That information hasn't been released yet. May I ask how you became aware of it?"

"Chief Springer. He telephoned me this morning. He thought I might not be able to clear space in my schedule unless I was told the importance of the meeting." There was a slight roll to his eyes, as if to acknowledge the police chief's deficiencies. "The family has maintained a very good relationship with the police." His blue eyes watched her face.

"I see."

"We've never stopped searching for Stone. To get justice for Christine. It's just terrible we weren't able to locate him before he could strike again. I understand he was hiding as a janitor?"

She answered before she realized he'd flipped things so that he was asking the questions.

"He was working for a hotel in the resort town of Silverlea, on Lornea Island. Do you know it?"

"I'm afraid not," Austin shook his head. He continued with his line of questions.

"And I understand you interviewed an eleven-year-old boy you believe to be Benjamin Austin? Christine's son?"

His voice was so soft she couldn't tell if his use of the word 'you' implied the Lornea Island Police Department, or her personally. "That's correct," she said carefully.

He didn't say anything. Instead, he brought his hand to his mouth and pressed his knuckles into his lips. Then he looked away. West thought she'd seen a tear appear in the corner of his eye, but when he looked back, it was gone.

"I'm sorry, Detective. I was only informed this morning. It's a lot to take in. Could you tell me what he was like? Did he appear abused? Was he healthy?"

"Physically, he seemed normal. Healthy. He... You may know, he contacted the police anonymously with information regarding the Curran murder. It turned out to be false, but given the subsequent development of his father now being implicated..." She stopped.

"I'm not an expert, but I would assume that hints at some... psychological issues."

"Of course," Paul Austin said. Then he continued in an even voice that West was unable to read.

"And you don't know where either of them are right now?"

She tried to answer in a positive way.

"We're looking everywhere we can. The search underway is the biggest in the history of the island's police department. We've brought in dozens of officers from the mainland," West said, uncomfortably aware of how inadequate that might sound in such opulent surroundings.

He nodded. "We'd like to do everything we can to help. I'll say that right away. If Ben can be brought back to us, that will be something positive to come out of a horrible situation. That's the priority for the family." Austin stopped. There was an undercurrent to his words that suggested that if Ben couldn't be brought back, he wasn't ruling out further action. Or perhaps West simply imagined it, intimidated by the display of wealth. Then Austin smiled. "Baby Ben," he said. Suddenly, he looked lost in thought.

"That's what we used to call him. And his sister. Baby Ben and Baby -" He stopped and screwed up his eyes, only to be interrupted by a knock on the door. The receptionist came in, carrying a silver tray loaded with coffee.

"Thank you, Janine," he said to the girl, his voice a little husky with emotion. West caught the way she looked at him, an expression that revealed such glances were why she turned up for work each morning. And probably why she spent so much time on her face. When she'd poured the coffee, her body seemed to pull itself into him as if attracted by a magnet. If he noticed he hid it well.

"Thank you Janine," he said, then waited till she left the room. "Anyway. How exactly can I be of help to you, Detective?"

It was a question West didn't welcome, given she didn't really know herself.

"I'm here to speak to everyone involved in the original case. To see if there's anything that might help us locate him now."

"Such as?"

She hesitated. What clues could possibly exist from a ten-year-old open and shut case?

"It's more about getting a better understanding of the crimes he's accused of here."

"*Accused of*? That's an interesting choice of words, Detective."

West hesitated. "I only say that because he hasn't been convicted of anything. Just a point of process."

"I witnessed him trying to murder my sister. There's no doubt as to what he is. He's a cold-blooded killer." West felt the blue eyes fixed on her, and she had to look down to avoid their stare. She pulled out a notebook and pen. It was more a prop than anything she needed, but it helped her change the direction of the interview.

"Did you know Jamie Stone well?" she asked. "Before he disappeared?" She clicked the pen so it was ready to write.

"No."

"But he dated your sister? They had the twins together?"

"Clearly."

"Well. You must have met him? Spoken to him, many times, I'd have thought?"

For a second or two, West thought he wasn't going to answer.

"Yes." He said at last. He seemed suddenly tense, then he made himself relax. He smiled at her.

"He came to the house once or twice when I was there. At garden parties and so on. We were very different."

"How so?"

"He was... rough. He wasn't the kind of man any of us expected Christine to become involved with. He was... more like a guy you'd meet in a sports bar. The type that would get into fights."

"He was violent?"

"Evidently so. Murderously violent."

"But you saw him being violent?"

"I saw him drowning my sister."

West glanced up from the notebook.

"I'm sorry."

Paul Austin was holding his head up high. She looked down again.

"Mr. Austin, where is your sister now?" She looked down at her notes. "I understand she's in a private institution, but I don't have the name?"

"Why would you need to know that?"

The sharpness of the reply surprised her. "As I said, I'm just trying to talk to everyone who knew Stone before he disappeared. He doesn't have any family so she knew him better than anyone else. I'd like to ask her if there's anything she might remember that might help us."

"I'm afraid that won't be possible."

West didn't respond at first, and when she did, she chose her words carefully.

"Mr. Austin, I'm investigating the murder of a teenage girl. It's possible your sister could assist in that - "

Austin cut her off.

"It's not possible."

"Excuse me?" West felt her voice rise in indignation. She told herself to cool it.

"It's not possible that she could help. She doesn't know anything about where Stone went after he disappeared. Believe me, I've asked her many times."

"Nonetheless, I'd like to ask her myself." West met his eyes once again. She felt she had to fight to maintain her focus against their piercing intensity.

Paul Austin was the one who looked away first.

"Detective," he began, then paused to allow himself a small sigh.

"I doubt anyone can truly understand the experience my sister went through. Stone *drowned* her daughter, in front of her eyes. He was in the process of drowning her, too, when I happened upon the scene. Christine was moments away from death. Perhaps some people might have come back from that, but not Christine. I'm afraid my sister hasn't yet recovered. She is not able to answer questions. It's unlikely she ever will be."

There was the buzzing sound of a cellphone, and West looked expectantly at the lawyer. But he raised his eyebrows.

"Yours, I believe," he said.

She realized he was right and scrambled for it, further flustered to see it was only a text and she needn't have rushed. She was slipping the phone back when the contents of the message flashed up on the screen.

Positive ID on the blood in Stone's truck. It's Curran.

SHE HESITATED FOR A MOMENT. Her mind absorbing the words. Then she pushed the phone back down into her bag. She noticed Austin watching her, as carefully as ever. She found her mind had gone blank, and it was Austin who spoke next.

"Detective, I appreciate this is going to be difficult to handle, but I have spoken to my father already this morning. He's agreed that for the sake of Christine, and for my mother's sake, too, we would like to remain as far away from this case as possible. Whatever this Stone creature has done this time has, mercifully, nothing to do with our family. Therefore, I'll be putting a team together to ensure that the Austin family is kept at arm's length from any trial and from media attention. I trust you'll understand why we feel like this." Paul Austin leaned forward and clasped his hands together. West breathed in another breath of his scented air.

"What about the boy? Billy - Ben?"

The lawyer didn't miss a beat. "Our thinking is further predicated upon the boy's case. He'll be returned here to the family. That's exactly why we insist our family is kept out of this as much as possible. It's vital that he is protected from any untoward media interest." Austin paused.

"That's assuming you're able to recover him before Stone goes on another killing spree, of course."

Paul Austin checked his watch. It was a slim, gold-bracketed model. West was reminded of the in-flight magazine she'd fallen asleep to the night before. It was full of ads for expensive brands, models pretending to be people just like Paul Austin. She realized how tired she was.

"I appreciate your coming to see me in person, Detective West. And I will further appreciate your keeping me personally informed, but alas, I do now have another meeting."

Before she could stop herself, West found she was getting to her feet. At least she stopped herself from walking to the door.

"Mr. Austin, if I could just get the name of the hospital where your sister is staying?"

"As I say, she's in no condition to answer questions on this matter."

Austin continued ushering her out, but something made West stop. She felt like, despite her best efforts, the entire meeting had been undertaken on his terms. She shook her head and refused to move.

"Sir, if and when Stone is captured alive, your sister will be a key witness in any trial that takes place. I *need* to see her."

The lawyer answered quickly, for the first time not picking his words as carefully.

"Detective, we both know you have no jurisdiction in this state and are in no position to insist upon anything."

They stared at each other, both breathing hard.

"The state police have agreed to cooperate fully. It feels to me like you're not," West heard herself say.

Austin looked away. He sighed again.

"Detective. You're trying to do your job. I'm trying to protect my sister." He looked down at the floor, as if considering what to say next. He seemed to come to a decision.

"I apologize. As I say, this has been an extremely challenging morning. My sister is staying at the Paterson Medical Facility. It's a private hospital. I can arrange for you to visit if you would like?"

"Thank you, sir." West felt flustered, unsettled. "I *am* just doing my job." She said. She didn't understand what had triggered the sudden change in his approach. She felt like she didn't understand much of the exchange that had just taken place. But Austin nodded as if the matter had been settled entirely amicably.

"I will telephone her doctor to arrange the visit. Janine will give you the directions."

"Thank you, sir."

West was about to leave when another question occurred to her, just one of the many she'd meant to ask.

"Does she know? Does your sister know about Billy, I mean? That he's still alive?"

A strange thing happened with Paul Austin's deep, blue, powerful eyes. They filled with water. He blinked and looked away. When he looked back, the eyes were back to normal, and she wasn't sure if she'd seen them wet at all.

"Detective West, if you're able to answer that question for us, my family will be most grateful."

57

Dad keeps us walking at a fast pace, so we don't talk much, and we stick to the woods. The noise of the helicopter fades away, leaving just the sounds of leaves and sticks cracking underfoot. We don't see anyone the whole way, even though it takes nearly two hours to get into Silverlea by the back way.

Dad looks more nervous when we get into the streets, there are a few people around but they don't pay us any attention, and we don't see any police. Even so I wonder about shouting to them, screaming for help, but I don't trust my voice, and I know Dad's still got the gun. It's tucked into his waistband, hidden by the hem of his jacket.

At one point, I see Mrs. Roberts, from the store. She's in her car. Dad sees her, too, and he turns me sharply so we're looking into the window of real-estate agents. I watch the car go past in the reflection, and only when it's out of sight does Dad get me moving again. Then we turn off the main street, and we're in the quieter residential area again.

"Where are we going?" I ask. I'm getting tired, my face feels tight from where I was crying earlier, and I feel like I'm about to start again any minute.

"We're almost there" is all Dad says.

And then, a couple of houses further on, Dad swings open a little gate, and we walk up a path to the front door of a little bungalow. I don't understand, though. I know who lives here.

"Why are we here?" I ask, but Dad just rings the bell; then he raps on the door with his fist, real urgently.

I hear a voice inside telling Dad to calm down, that she's coming.

58

"Sam? What the hell are you doing..." Emily starts asking when she answers the door. Then she notices me. *"Billy?"*

"Are you alone?" Dad asks, and she doesn't answer, just screws up her face in confusion, still holding the edge of the front door.

"Are you here alone?" Dad asks again, and this time, Emily nods.

Dad doesn't say anything. Instead, he grabs my hand again and pulls me inside, pushing past Emily, who gets pushed backward out of the way.

"Shut the door," he says.

"What the hell? What the hell is going on, Sam?" Emily asks.

Dad doesn't answer. He lets go of my hand and paces up and down in the hallway. Then he disappears into the other rooms, and I hear him closing all the drapes. I just stay with Emily, waiting for whatever is going to happen next.

"Hi, Emily," I say.

She's breathing really hard, and she stares at me for a minute.

"Hi, Billy. Do you know what's going on here?"

I shrug. "Dad killed Olivia Curran, and now he's trying to escape from the police. He tried to kill me too."

She stares at me like I've gone completely crazy. She opens her mouth to say something back, but doesn't get the chance because Dad comes back into the hallway.

"Em, I need your help. I wouldn't ask if I wasn't desperate, but there's police all over our house, a roadblock on the bridge. There's a helicopter looking for me. You've gotta help us get out of here. We've got to get off the island. Can you drive us to Goldhaven? Right now?"

Emily is breathing really hard, and she pulls her eyes off me like it's a struggle and focuses on Dad.

"*Goldhaven*? Why?"

"I'll explain on the way. There's no time now."

She opens her mouth again a couple of times and then closes it again. Finally, she manages to get a sentence out.

"I can't. I'm meeting Dan," she says and looks at her watch. "In about half an hour. It's my day off."

"Fuck Dan," Dad says in a low voice, like he hopes I don't hear. "This is important. This is serious."

They stare at each other.

"But won't they be watching the ferry port, if they've got all that looking for you?" Emily asks in the end.

That's what I said, I feel like saying, but I don't say it.

Dad doesn't speak either. He just looks around, like he suddenly feels trapped by the walls around him.

"What's going on?" Emily asks. "Billy said - "

"I'll tell you later. I'll explain everything. Just not right now." Dad's eyes flick across to me as he says this, and I know he means he won't say it in front of me. He doesn't want to admit he tried to kill me.

"You've got to help us, Em. There's no one else I can turn to."

We all stand there for a moment. Still in the hallway.

"I'll call Dan, say I'm not feeling well. You can stay here and work something out. No one's going to look for you here," Emily says. Her voice still sounds incredulous, like she can't believe we've just walked in.

Dad's suddenly nodding. "OK. And let us borrow the car. We'll leave it for you at Goldhaven. You can pick it up later - "

"*Sam!*" Emily almost shouts this, and Dad shuts up.

"*They'll be waiting for you at the port. You can't just run like this. You've got to think, Sam. You gotta be smart.*"

I've never heard Emily talk like this before. She sounds scary, and it stops Dad dead.

"Sit down. I'll make coffee. I'll call Dan, tell him I've got a headache."

We all go into the kitchen, and Dad and me sit, watching Emily as she goes around putting the coffee together. About halfway through, she looks up at me and smiles.

"How about you, Billy? Do you want your usual? I think I've got some chocolate here somewhere."

I nod and smile back at her. She says it like we're in the café and everything's normal. She says it to make me feel safe. But my smile doesn't last long. I've got so many questions, and although I'm scared to ask most of them, the confusion is even worse.

"Dad," I start, cautiously. "Why are we here with Emily?"

Dad looks away from the wall where he's been staring, lost in his own world. He looks up at me and half laughs. Then he shakes his head. He says to Emily,

"Christ, I've got half the island's police force chasing me, and he wants to know that. Do you want to tell him, or should I?"

"I think you'd better."

I look at them both, mystified. "Tell me what?" I say.

A few moments later, Emily puts a mug of hot chocolate in front of me and a coffee in front of Dad. She sits down, takes a sip of her coffee and holds the mug in front of her, blowing the steam away. She doesn't say anything, but she looks at Dad.

"OK. Billy," Dad begins. But then he stops and looks down at the table. "I don't know how much they've taught you about this at school. I guess it's that Personal Development class, isn't it?" He rolls his eyes. I just wait.

"The thing is, Emily and me, we've been... kind of..." He scratches his head. "We've been kind of seeing each other. For a little while now." He glances at me to see how this is going.

"In the café?" I ask.

"No. Well obviously, yes... Look, I'm not talking about in the café. I mean, it's been here mostly, at Emily's house, when Dan's not around." He stops and looks at me.

"You know what I mean by *seeing* each other?"

I know what "seeing" means, but it doesn't make sense.

"Like Emily's your girlfriend?" I say, although that doesn't sound possible.

Dad sounds relieved. "Yeah. That's it. Sort of. You're OK with that, aren't you?"

"But Emily is *Dan's* girlfriend," I say.

Dad looks at Emily. She looks away.

"Yeah. That's right. But sometimes, people don't really want to be with the person they're with, and they see other people too. Just to see if that works better," he says. Then he sounds a little more certain.

"That's why I haven't been able to tell you. I didn't want to hide it from you, I swear to you, Billy."

"I'm sorry, too, Billy," Emily says.

I look over and see her blue eyes watching me, her mug half-hiding the rest of her face. I think of everything we've shared. All the times we've discussed my projects, and her research. She puts the mug down. She looks so pretty. I can't help but think of my daydreams. I've never told her. I've never told anyone, but sometimes, I can spend hours imagining what it would be like if I were a bit older, how Emily and I would go off around the world, doing science. How maybe we'd even get married. I feel my face going red. I feel - I don't know - angry? Angry and awkward and kind of embarrassed. But also just confused.

"You're Dad's *girlfriend*?"

She smiles at me now, then nods her head. "Not exactly, but I guess that's a way of looking at it." She smiles at me again, her eyes all big. "Oh, Billy, I'm sorry I couldn't tell you. Adults are such funny creatures." She reaches her hand across the table and takes mine. Her hand feels soft; she's got pretty, slim fingers. I let her squeeze my hand for a while.

"What about Dan?" I ask, a moment later. Emily gives my hand a final squeeze and pulls her's back.

"Dan doesn't know," she says. "No one knows. Apart from you, now, obviously. We had to keep it a secret at first to see if it was going to work." She looks at Dad now. "If it does, then maybe we'll tell people. You and... and Dan too."

Dad glances at her, looking troubled still. But mostly, he's watching me. I feel like I'm about to start crying, so I look down at my hot chocolate. I try to pick it up, but my hand shakes, and some goes on the table.

"Sorry," I mumble, and Emily makes a big thing of cleaning it up with a cloth. Then they're both sitting down and looking at me. I try again to drink the chocolate, but it's not good; it tastes old. I look at the carton, and I can see it's the old branding. They changed it years ago; it's got new colors now and everything. Actually, now I notice, the whole kitchen is really old-fashioned. I saw it in the hallway too. It looks like an old lady should live here, not Emily.

"Why is your kitchen so old?" I ask suddenly.

Emily looks confused for a moment, then laughs. It's amazing how much it lightens the heaviness of the atmosphere, that laugh. Her face is so pretty when she smiles.

"This is my grandmother's cottage, Billy. Or at least it was. She passed away earlier in the year. I haven't gotten around to sorting it out yet."

There's a silence, and the magic of her smile fades throughout the room. Then Dad takes over.

"Look, Billy. Em and I need a little space for a while. How about you go and find the science channel or something. Leave us to have a talk?"

Part of me wants to say no. Wants to ask what's going on, why we're here. Why he's suddenly pretending to be nice to me. But I can't quite get over what Emily just said to me. Normally, I'd be able to talk to her; I can tell her anything, or I could. Now, I'm confused. I need some time to think about everything. And I haven't forgotten the gun in Dad's jeans.

I look at Emily, hoping she might help, but she's nodding along with Dad. So I just do what he says. I pick up my drink with two hands and get up from the table.

"Good boy," Dad says, and he shuts the door behind me.

59

I go into the living room like Dad says. I kind of hoped I would be able to hear what they're talking about, but they're talking quietly. The living room is decorated like the rest of the house. The walls have flowers on them, but they're stained yellow. The floor is brown carpet. There's a window, but when I go to look, it's locked, and I can't find the key anywhere. I guess Emily's grandma was one of those old people who worried all the time about burglars. A lot of old people are like that.

I wonder if I should try to escape anyway. I could just open the front door and run away. Maybe I could go to a neighbor and ask them to call the police. For a long time, I think about it. But it's scary. Maybe Dad would come after me. Maybe he'd shoot me this time. And now that we're with Emily, maybe I'm safe again. Maybe he's decided not to kill me after all. I don't know; it's all too much to think about. So I stop thinking. I sit down on the couch and wait for whatever is going to happen next.

I don't drink my hot chocolate, though. There's definitely something wrong with it, probably because it's so old. It's probably something her grandma had in the cupboard for years. I feel a bit sick about drinking it, but I don't want to offend Emily so I pour it away into a plant pot in the corner of the room. I mash the dirt around so you can't see where I did it, then wipe my hands on the carpet. It's brown anyway.

I think I'd better do what Dad says, so I look for the TV remote, but instead of finding it, I see Emily's laptop on the sofa, half-hidden under a cushion. I stare for a moment at its bright blue lid. Normally, I wouldn't think of looking at it, but I wonder if I could get online. Maybe I could find out what's happening. Glancing at the door to make sure Emily hasn't come in, I quickly open it up. Emily's icon is a starfish. I stare at that for a moment before I notice the cursor blinking, asking for the password. I have no idea what her password is, so I shut the laptop, feeling guilty for even trying. I slip it back under the cushion and sit back on the couch. I get the sudden feeling of everything hitting me at once.

Dad and Emily are like *boyfriend and girlfriend*. I remember things that have happened. Things that seemed a little strange at the time. Like when I wanted her to come and see the whale with me, and she said she had to work. Emily doesn't work Saturday afternoons. She never has. Did she say no to looking at the whale because she was with Dad? I think how often Dad's come home late from work recently. Crazy late, really. I feel my face going red as I think about it. He was with her. And the part that really gets me is I was at home, daydreaming about her and me going off together on a research trip or something. My face gets hotter still.

I tell myself to stop. I hardly ever had that daydream, really. And I never meant it. I see the remote at last and turn on the TV. I start to flick through the channels like Dad said, to find something with science in it, but instead, I find a cartoon. It's been years since I watched any kids' TV, but I find I can't make my finger press the button to move on. The sound is down low, but it's just a bunch of cartoon animals anyway, a dog and a rabbit running around. I put the remote down and leave it on. I'm surprised to suddenly feel my cheeks are wet. I grab the cushion and wipe my face. Then I pull the cushion close and wrap my arms around it. I let the tears flow.

IT FEELS like hours later when Emily comes in. I'm curled up on the couch, still watching cartoons. I've been flicking between Cartoon Network and Disney Junior, and I've almost forgotten where I am and why I'm there. Emily's got her hair tied up behind her head, and she's gotten changed. She's wearing a baggy sweater and leggings. She still looks nice.

"Hey, Billy, how you doing?" her voice is soft.

She reaches out and puts a hand on my head, ruffling up my hair.

"This is all a bit much, isn't it? How are you feeling?"

Because I don't know what to say, I don't say anything, and she goes on talking.

"What you said earlier. About your dad... about Sam somehow being involved in that girl's death. That's not right. That's not what this is about."

I look at the cartoons for a moment before suddenly answering. I don't feel ready to talk about it.

"How do you know?" I say, because I can't exactly ignore her completely.

"Sam's told me everything. It's not about Olivia Curran. And I promise you it's not about you, Billy. He didn't try to kill you, Billy. That's just crazy. He would never do anything to hurt you."

I hear her words, but against the pull of the TV they sound weak. The cartoon world seems so much easier to face. The truth is I'm exhausted by it all. I want to turn away from Emily and pretend this isn't happening. But what happened this morning flashes through my head. I can't pretend.

"I've got evidence."

She does this funny thing where she tries to give me a comforting smile but also frowns a little.

"What evidence, Billy?"

My nose starts running, so I sniff. "I found Olivia's hair clip in the back of Dad's truck. It had blood on and everything."

Emily touches the hair on the back of her head. It's not like Olivia's. Emily's got brown hair. She touches her fingers on her own hair clip.

"Billy, you couldn't have." Her voice is reasonable and calm.

I shrug. "I did."

She smiles at me, but it looks fragile.

"Billy, sometimes, people imagine things that aren't really there, or make mistakes, think something is important when really, it isn't. When we're under a lot of pressure, I mean."

"I didn't imagine it." Suddenly, my voice sounds angry. It surprises me. "It was the clip she was wearing that night. It had blood on it."

Emily stays quiet for a moment.

"Can you show me, Billy? I'm sure there's an explanation. If you can show me, I can help explain."

I shake my head and look away. "I put in inside my wetsuit. It got washed away when Dad took me in the water."

"So it's gone?" she says slowly. Then she's quiet again for a moment, thinking. I think I know what she's going to say next, that this probably means I imagined it, but she doesn't say that.

"Did you look on the beach for it?"

I'm surprised by that.

"I didn't get the chance," I say. "But I lost it out in the water. No one will ever find it now."

She nods. Her eyes go big, and then she smiles. She slips down and sits next to me on the couch, putting her arm around me and pulling me close. She's never done this before, and I'm a bit uncomfortable because my face is close to her boobs. I feel like it's wrong but I try to remember how they feel. Soft and warm. I can smell her perfume really strong now. Flowers.

"Look, Billy." She squeezes me harder so my whole face is pressed against her side "You remember how things went with Mr. Foster? You were so certain he was responsible in some way. And then... Well then he wasn't. Well, this hairclip - if that's what it actually was - it's probably the same. I don't know what, exactly, but you must have the wrong idea."

I want to believe her. I want to believe I've got this all wrong some-how. To just press my face against her and make this alright, but that won't work. I'm here. In this strange room. Everything's changed. Different now. I push myself away from her.

"But I saw it, Emily. I *saw it*." For some reason, I'm pleading with her now. "I held it in my hand." I snatch up my sweater and show her my chest, where the imprint has now long since faded away. "I put it right here. It had blood on it, and *hair*, like a little tuft of blond hair. It was the same clip that Olivia Curran had. And then, right after that, Dad tried to drown me. He pushed me underwater. Just as a wave was coming. He chased me." The tears are flowing now, and I don't care. I don't even wipe them away.

"*Billy, no.* Stop it. Your dad wouldn't do that. He didn't do that."

"I saw it, Emily. I saw the proof."

"Then where is it now?" Her voice is sharper now. "Did anyone else see it? Did you take a photograph?"

I don't say anything to this. Just shake my head.

She bites her lip.

"Look. Your dad's explained a lot of things to me that do make sense. He's very nervous about telling you. God knows I can understand why. He's cooking some food. He's going to tell you everything once we've eaten, and then - "

"There's something else that will prove it," I interrupt her. "Tell me your password, and I can prove it."

"What?" Emily looks startled. I pull her laptop out from under the cushion.

"Tell me your password," I say, opening the lid.

She looks uncertainly at her computer. Then, without saying anything, she leans over and quickly types a word. I try to see what it is, but I'm too slow. The computer boots up; the desktop photo is an underwater shot of a coral reef that she took herself. She emailed the same photo to me from her last trip on the *Marianne Dupont*. She looks at me.

"Open the Internet," I say.

She does so, and we wait together.

"Now what?"

"Give it here."

I pull the laptop onto my knees and type in the address for my weather station, then I log in to the admin account. It's not just an online thing; it's something I've actually got fitted to the roof of the cottage. There's an anemometer which measures the wind direction and strength, a thermometer, and best of all, there's a webcam. I was the first person to set up a webcam on Silverlea beach. At the start, I would get tons of hits from people wanting to have a look at the surfing conditions, or just look at the beach, before they came here. But then the Surf Life-saving Club copied my idea and put up their own weather station. And because they had a better camera, and you could see the waves better from where they are, they get all the hits now. But I still kept mine going because you can use the data for research.

The webcam takes a photograph every fifteen minutes. Every photograph gets uploaded to a database that you can access online. So you can go back and see exactly what the beach looked like at any time you want, for the last three years.

Unfortunately, though, when I bought it, I couldn't afford a very good webcam. Mine is just a static image with a wide-angle lens. That means you don't only get to see the ocean. You can also see the edge of the cottage roof on one side of the frame, and down to the yard on the other.

The back end of the site loads up. I click into the search box and set it to load the images from August 29, earlier this year.

"This is the view from our house on the night Olivia Curran went missing," I tell Emily. "You remember we were all at the Surf Lifesaving Club Disco?"

Emily nods, watching what I'm doing.

"About ten thirty, I got tired, and I asked Dad to take me home. But he wanted to stay and drink more beer. So Jody's mom said she'd take me home. Then later, when the police asked me about it, Dad made me lie. He said he'd get into trouble if they found out I was home alone."

"GO ON, BILLY," Emily says. I select the right time. The cam's view looks normal again, dark and empty.

"That's eleven o'clock. Just before Jody drops me off." I click forward. In the next image, there's a pool of light on the yard.

"Eleven fifteen. The light is from the kitchen window. I left it on for Dad because he said he wouldn't be long."

I flick through the next image, and the next, and the next.

"One a.m.," I say. "He's still not back. He told me he got back at about eleven thirty." I show her the next eight images. Finally, I get to the 5:00 a.m. image. This time, the pool of light has gone, but there's another difference. Even in the darkness, it's possible to see that Dad's truck has appeared in the driveway.

"Dad told me he got back at eleven thirty that night. I remember really well because that's the time he made me say to the policewoman. But *he* lied to me. He actually got back at five a.m. Because he was out there doing whatever he did to Olivia Curran. Then hiding her body."

There's this really long silence. Emily is staring at the laptop. When she finally says something, her voice is really quiet and soft.

"Oh, Billy," she says. "Oh, my poor boy." She takes the laptop, and it looks like she's going to shut the lid, but in the end, she just puts it back down on the coffee table and puts her hand on my hair again.

"Oh, Billy," she says again. "The reason your dad didn't come home until five that morning. He was with me. That was the night we got together."

60

The receptionist gave West the address for the Paterson Medical Facility and told her an appointment had been made for that afternoon. West made her way back to the rental car and drove for three hours. At first, she passed several small towns, but for the last hour, she seemed to be driving through entirely empty country. And then, when she arrived at what her GPS said was the right location, West found nothing but an empty stretch of single-lane road, fields on either side, with only a few stands of trees to break the monotony of the horizon.

She stopped, not bothering to pull off the road, since she hadn't seen another car in a half-hour. She left the engine running. She must have overshot by a few hundred yards since the GPS told her over and over to turn around where possible. So she switched it off. She held onto the steering wheel for a moment, thinking, but then she realized how tired she was, and how it was affecting her thinking. She killed the engine and got out of the car.

She felt a little better right away in the fresh air, but looking up and down the road, she still saw nothing that looked like a hospital. She pulled out her cell, hoping to google the place, maybe find a number to call, but she had no Internet connection. There was reception for a call, though, so she dialed Rogers. Maybe he could locate the place and tell her where it was. He could update her on the search for Stone at the same time.

The phone rang, and she held it to her ear, waiting to speak. But on the sixth ring, it clicked over to voice mail. Annoyed, she shut the call off. She leaned on the hood, wondering what to do next.

Then she noticed a small tarmac road that led off the main highway. It looked far too small to be of consequence, but just before it, there was a sign; whatever it said was obscured by a tree. For want of anything better to do, she walked back down the road toward it, then squinted up when she reached the front of the sign. In small letters, it spelled out the words:

Paterson Medical Facility

Private Road

Still a little confused, West walked back to her rental car and backed up. She used her turn signal out of habit and drove into the lane.

It took her through a stack of trees, and beyond these it dropped down into a hollow. At the bottom, she saw the facility: a plain, characterless building. As she pulled up, a man in a white doctor's coat walked out and stood waiting for her.

SHE PUSHED OPEN the car door and he stepped forward and stretched out his arm. "Welcome. I'm Dr. Richards. We've been expecting you." The jacket was open and underneath it West saw an expensive blue shirt. He wore metal-framed glasses with thin lenses. He smiled.

"I'm Detective Jessica - " West held out her badge, but the doctor waved it away.

"Detective West. Yes, I know. Paul's explained everything. Please come inside."

They climbed the steps and walked inside. The room was smaller than West had anticipated, and a man sat watching a bank of security screens. He didn't move as the doctor pulled a form from a plastic tray and began to fill it out with the date and time of her arrival.

"What exactly is this place?"

"The Paterson is a private residential medical facility. We offer a safe and secure environment for clients with very specific needs."

"You're pretty hard to find."

He slid the form across the desk for her to sign.

"Yes. Our profile is deliberately low key," the doctor said. "It helps our residents."

West hesitated, then signed the form and passed it back.

"I'm sorry, how do you mean?"

The doctor scooped up the form, then slid it into a plastic holder and held it out to her again.

"Our location here is part of our appeal. We cater to residents who are unable to cope in an uncontrolled environment. They benefit from not coming across too many people they're not familiar with."

"Like a secure hospital?"

"No, quite the opposite. We're out here so that our clients are free to roam almost wherever they like without running into danger. You can walk ten miles in any direction without coming across a house or a farm." He smiled.

"Please, can I get you a coffee, or perhaps something to eat?"

"I picked something up on the way." The refusal was automatic, and West wasn't sure why she said it.

"*Really*? I don't know where." Dr. Richards looked perplexed for a moment. "Like I say, there's not a lot around here." He smiled again and shook his head, as if this wasn't relevant to anything.

"Anyway, perhaps we could have a quick chat inside my office before we go to see Christine. I understand Paul already told you this may be a wasted trip?" He opened another door and led her into a spacious office, with a large antique wood desk. She took a seat and waited.

The doctor offered her coffee again before settling his side of the desk. "I understand you want to ask Christine a number of questions about what happened to her, and the man who attacked her. Is that right?" The doctor raised an eyebrow.

"I'm hoping she might have some information that will help us locate him."

"I think that's unlikely."

"Why?"

"Christine doesn't like to speak about what happened..." Dr. Richards paused. "I don't know how much Paul explained to you, but Christine is suffering from post-traumatic stress disorder." He waited until she shook her head to show he hadn't said.

"Many people misunderstand the disorder; they believe it's a temporary reaction or that it can be cured. Both assumptions, unfortunately, are false. In Christine's case, her reaction was very strong: it resulted in a permanent change in her brain. The best we can do for her is manage it with medication, and shield her from triggers by avoiding unsolicited social encounters.

"Are you saying I can't see her?" West asked.

"Not necessarily. But I am saying you're unlikely to gain anything useful from doing so. And that your questions will upset her."

West thought for a moment.

"I'd still like to see her. To ask if she's able to help."

The doctor nodded.

"I can't prevent you. I'll need to stay with you while you speak to her."

"OK," she said, then paused. "Can I ask you something before we meet her?"

"Of course."

"Has anyone told her whether her son is still alive?"

"Yes," the doctor said. "Yes, we've tried to speak with her about that."

"And what did she say?"

The doctor sighed. "She said very little. Perhaps if the boy could be brought back, they could be reintroduced to one another over a period of time. But I understand he's now missing again. Is that correct?"

West hesitated, then nodded.

"Well, perhaps we should get on, and then you can get back to trying to locate him. Shall we?"

Dr. Richards rose and showed her out of the office. They went down a long corridor lined with black-and-white photographs of fields and farmland. Eventually, they came to a door. It had a small window with wired glass.

"Are you ready, Detective?"

61

"Billy, Billy?"

I look up. I don't know how much time has passed. It might be five minutes; it might be an hour.

"Did you hear? Your dad just said dinner's ready."

I don't move. I'm not hungry anyway.

"Come on, Billy, you've got to eat. And your dad wants to say something to you."

I want to stay where I am, but I find myself following her back to the kitchen, like a lost puppy. Dad's wearing an apron with an image of a kangaroo on it, with a little joey poking out of the pocket. He gives it a little shake and looks at me like I should be laughing. I just stare at him.

"I made spaghetti," Dad says. "Come on, you'll feel better once you've eaten." He opens a drawer and rummages around for a spoon. The food smells nice. I can see the waistband of Dad's jeans. I wonder where he's put the gun.

We all sit down, like we're all part of a happy family. Dad spoons the spaghetti onto the plates like this is how we always eat. He's got a beer open, and I notice Emily is drinking wine. There's a glass of water in front of my place.

"Cheers," Dad says, lifting up his can. "This was a little unexpected, but let's say thanks to Emily for helping us out." She picks up her glass and tings it against the can. I don't move. They exchange a funny look.

I poke around at my food, because that's better than looking at Dad. I still don't understand. I'm trying to make sense of all this. If he didn't kill Olivia Curran, then why are all the police after him? What's all this about?

"So Emily told me," Dad starts talking. He sounds all casual, like I'd just mentioned to her how I'd bought a new motion camera, instead of thinking he was a murderer. "About what you think this is all about."

He gives a little kind of half laugh, but then his voice gets more earnest.

"Billy, I understand how confusing all this must be. What happened today with the police." He stops. He hasn't even picked up his knife and fork yet.

"But I promise you, it's not what you think it is. It's got nothing at all to do with that." He shuts up and watches me for a moment.

"I don't know *anything about* Olivia Curran. I swear to you. I never even laid eyes on the girl. Never met her, never spoke to her. I've got nothing to do with it."

His voice sounds like honey, thick and smooth. I want to believe him. But I know what I know, so while he's speaking, I do my best to think about the hair clip. I try to remember exactly what it looked like. But it's hard. I can sort of see it, but it's not clear anymore. A fleeting thought occurs to me: Maybe Emily's right. Maybe I did imagine it all, or just made a mistake...

"And this thing about trying to push you underwater..." Dad's still talking. He's smiling at me, in a way he hasn't smiled for a long time.

"That was me being... just being an *idiot*, Billy." I see his eyes flick to Emily, then back to me.

"It's just that there was this big wave coming. That's how you get through the waves; you duck under. You know that, right? 'Course you do. You gotta hold your breath, and then you pop right out the other side." Dad starts tapping the table.

"But you panicked. That got you caught in the impact zone, so every other wave caught you too."

"But you were right. It was way too big a day to try and get you out there. I was just... I was frustrated. I feel like we should be doing more together. Father and son." He stops and shakes his head.

"Billy, you've got to believe me. I would *never* hurt you. You're the most important thing in my life. Bar nothing." He sighs. "Look at me, Billy. I'll never hurt you. You gotta believe me on that."

I want to believe him. He's Dad. I want to believe every word he says. But I'm not sure. I look down at my pasta; the cheese is melting over the top. I haven't eaten for hours. I don't feel hungry but my stomach is growling now I've seen the food. I nod, mostly just so he'll let me be.

"I'm gonna eat my dinner now," I say. He smiles.

WE DON'T TALK about any of it after that. Instead, Emily starts talking about her next trip on the *Marianne Dupont*. That's the name of the research ship she goes on; I told you about it. But with everything that's been happening I kind of forgot - she's going again later this week, back down to the Caribbean, to do more research into her jellyfish. If things were normal I'd be jealous. But now I just don't know.

AFTER WE'VE EATEN, I help Emily clean up the kitchen, and Dad sits, drinking more beers. By that time it's late, so Emily shows me a room where I can go to sleep. It's old and musty, and it smells of old ladies, but I don't really care. I don't have a toothbrush, so I have to use my finger, and then obviously, I don't have any pajamas, so Emily lets me use one of her T-shirts, and that smells a lot better than the bed. I can smell her flowery perfume on it, and I use that as a kind of defense against the old-lady smell from the bed linens and the pillow. I'm so tired I'm asleep in seconds.

62

Christine Austin was sitting in a wingback armchair with a blanket over her knees. She was nodding her head to the TV show in front of her, which was on mute. A line of drool was hanging from her lips. The doctor noticed and wiped it smartly away. West was shocked by the age of the woman. She would be in her mid-thirties, but she looked much older. Her jowls hung from her face, and her skin was pallid and sickly. Her eyes were unfocused. She didn't appear to notice them come in, didn't react when the doctor used a paper tissue to wipe her mouth. He glanced at West, as if to say: *Don't say we didn't warn you.*

"CHRISTINE? Chrissy? There's someone to see you. Do you feel like talking today?" Dr. Richards spoke loudly but kindly. To West's surprise, the woman turned her head and looked in her direction.

"Chrissy, this is Detective West. She's from the police. Do you mind if we sit with you for a while?" Without waiting for a reply, the doctor sat down on a sofa next to Christine and indicated to West to do the same.

"Chrissy, Detective West is the policewoman who found Ben. The one I told you about. She'd like to ask you some questions." The woman's eyes moved across to West, but they were heavy and dulled.

The doctor stopped speaking and smiled at West as if encouraging her to go ahead. West opened her mouth to speak.

"Christine..." It felt strange, speaking with the doctor watching her. Almost like she was being judged. West pressed on anyway. "I'm part of a team investigating the murder of a teenage girl in Lornea Island. We believe your former partner, Jamie Stone, may be involved in some way. Can I ask if he ever mentioned Lornea Island to you? Did he have friends there, or relatives? Anywhere he might be able to go and hide out?"

It was impossible to say whether Christine heard what she was saying or not. She watched West speak, but gave no reply.

"We're searching for him now. And for your son... Ben. If there's anything you know about Stone it might help us find him..."

Still Christine said nothing. West glanced across at the doctor, who smiled sadly at her. She felt frustrated. This was clearly a waste of everyone's time. Just like Paul Austin had said. And the doctor. Just like she knew herself.

"Anything at all might be useful. Did he ever talk about going anywhere special? Did he own any property anywhere that he might go to?"

Still Christine said nothing, and then she turned back to the television. The doctor began shaking his head. He opened his mouth to speak, and West sensed he was going to tell her it was useless. Even though she knew he was right, it still irritated her.

"CHRISTINE, I saw your son, Ben. I saw him last week. I spoke to him. He's eleven years old." She reached out and took Christine's hand. "I just wanted you to know, we're going to do everything we can to find him. To bring him back for you." West squeezed the hand gently, and saw the woman turn back toward her. Deep within, behind the swirl of clouds in her eyes, she thought she saw a spark.

"Ben?" Christine said. When she spoke, her voice was weak. West nodded and held her breath. "That's why I'm asking for your help. We believe he's still with Stone."

The woman seemed to consider this. She moved her head in a slow nod, then it seemed like she forgot why she had started nodding but kept on doing it anyway, nodding over and over. Then she turned away from West so that she was watching television again.

"We're trying to find Ben," West continued, trying to regain her attention. "Is there anything you can tell us to help find Ben?" But this time, Christine appeared to ignore her. There was a pause. Then Dr. Richards interrupted quietly.

"I think we should probably leave it there." He didn't wait for an answer before going on.

"We'll leave you to enjoy your afternoon, Christine. The detective is going now." West felt her irritation harden, but she didn't argue. Instead, she pulled out her card, meaning to give it to Christine. But she hesitated, passing it from hand to hand.

"Dr. Richards, is she able to use the telephone?"

He saw the card and guessed what she had in mind. "It's better if I take it. If she talks to any of the staff, they'll come to me, and I can call you." He smiled.

West nodded, then turned back to Christine.

"Is that OK? If you think of anything that might help, you can talk to Dr. Richards, and he'll call me. We'll do everything we can to find your son. I promise." She reached down to touch Christine's hand again, but she seemed to be gone, sucked back into the silent world of her TV show. West was about to pull her hand away, but then something happened. With a speed that seemed impossible given the woman's condition, she suddenly twisted violently in her chair. She grabbed West by the arm, nearly pulling her off the chair she was sitting on, and before Dr. Richards could react, she thrust her mouth up against West's ear.

"Tell him I'm sorry," she said, in a low, rasping voice. "Tell him for me. Tell him I'm sorry."

West was startled. She had one knee on the floor where Christine had pulled her down. She saw Dr. Richards was moving toward them, clear alarm on his face.

There was just time for Christine to spit a few more words into West's ear before Dr. Richards reached her shoulder and pulled her sharply away.

"Chrissy," he hissed. Then when he'd separated the two women, and Christine had gone back into her passive state, he apologized to West.

"I'm so sorry, Detective. She doesn't normally do that. Are you OK?"

West was still kneeling on the floor. She looked at Christine, now back to watching the TV, nodding slightly to the tune in her head as if nothing had happened.

"I'm fine. It's fine," she said, getting to her feet. She stared at Chrissy, wanting to ask her what she had just whispered into her ear. But something stopped her. The doctor's presence stopped her.

"I do think we should leave Christine now. She's clearly tired," Dr. Richards said, and this time West didn't argue. The doctor lead them away. He continued to talk all the way back down the corridor, and it was only when she'd left the hospital that West realized she hadn't given her card to the doctor. When Christine had lunged at her, it must have fallen onto the floor.

63

There was no helicopter flight back to Lornea Island for Detective West. Instead, she caught the ferry for the final leg of her journey. She texted Rogers from the boat, and he was there to pick her up.

He talked the whole way back to the police station, explaining the detailed searches of the empty self-catering apartments that Stone might have access to, the discovery of the boy's treehouse, in the woods set back from the Littlelea beach parking lot, with its camouflaged sides and its basic camping equipment. But ultimately, the failure to locate Stone.

"There's something we're missing," he said when he was finished. "Some connection we're not seeing yet. But we'll get him. We'll get the bastard."

West listened to him in silence, and now sat staring blankly out of the windshield.

"You OK?" Rogers asked.

She shook her head as if he'd woken her from a trance.

"Yeah. Yeah, I am. Just tired."

"Long flight, huh?"

"Long everything."

"So how about you? You find out anything useful out there? Anything that might help us find him?"

She answered slowly.

"I'm not sure. At first, I thought maybe the chief only sent me out there because he wanted me out of the way for a while."

"And? What do you think now?"

"I still think that. But one strange thing happened."

"What's that?" Rogers asked, as he swung the car into the police station's parking lot. He took the corner too fast and had to brake sharply to avoid a patrolman who was walking to a car. The patrolman was near retirement, a man in his sixties. He walked around to the open driver's window and called in with mock seriousness.

"Don't think I can't book you for dangerous driving just because of your shiny detective badge." He laughed at his own joke.

"I'm just testing your reflexes Bill. Get you ready for your next medical," Rogers shot back.

The patrolman noticed West and nodded at her stiffly. He backed away and Rogers edged the car forward into a space.

Rogers forgot to ask West what she found strange. She didn't bring it up again.

WEST REACHED the end of the office where her desk stood. She looked out of the window, at the familiar view of the parking lot and the back of the stores opposite. It was all as it had been before. Not surprising given that she'd only been gone a couple days. But it felt wrong somehow, as if the distance she'd traveled ought to be marked in some way.

ON HER DESK WAS A NOTE, telling her to report to Chief Collins when she got in. She found him talking with Lieutenant Langley, who stayed while she talked through who she had seen, but their focus was clearly on the local search for Stone. When she was done, Langley told her to help Rogers, who was checking through the boy's laptop computer. He did little to conceal his opinion that this was unlikely to produce anything of value, and went back to talking with the Chief. She left the office and found Rogers slouched back in his chair, his big hand toying with the mouse.

"What have we got, then?" she asked.

"Pull up a chair, Detective," Rogers said, sitting up straighter. "Pull up a chair."

SHE SAT NEXT TO HIM, opened a fresh page in her notebook, and clicked her pen so it was ready to use. He raised his eyebrows at this.

"It's possible you're being a touch optimistic," he said. "It's a hell of a mess in here."

"How do you mean?"

"I mean, welcome to the inside of Billy Wheatley's head. Take a look around."

West leaned in toward the laptop screen; it was filled with folders. She took the mouse from Rogers and clicked a couple at random. They opened into new folders, each just as packed and chaotic as the last.

"Wow. He's got a lot of stuff in here," she said.

"Yeah. So here's the story. The kid's laptop was found in his bedroom. At first, no one could get into it because it's got a password set up. So we give it to the IT boys. No problem, they go in via a different route, or whatever they do, disable the password - I dunno. But what they can't do is restore any order. It's just a mess of files, random names, pretty random content too. Check this out." He clicked back a few times and opened a file named "Weather Sensor." A screen of thumbnail images popped up.

"What are they?" West squinted at the screen.

"They..." Rogers smiled and opened one. "Are hermit crabs painted with fluorescent paint." He watched her face, then laughed as she turned to him, her face screwed up in confusion.

"It's some experiment he was doing. Don't ask me. There's tons of this kind of stuff, though. He's like some schizophrenic version of Charles fucking Darwin."

"Is any of it relevant?"

"That's what I'm trying to figure out. I don't think so is as far as I've got. I did find this, though." This time, Rogers pointed to a printout on the desk. It was headed:

INVESTIGATION INTO THE OLIVIA CURRAN
~~MYSTERY~~/MURDER

BELOW THESE WORDS was a summary of what happened to Olivia. Mostly, it looked lifted from the internet.

"What's this?"

"He was running an investigation, or trying to. He had this in a folder about limpets."

West looked at him questioningly.

"They're little triangle things that cling to rocks."

"I know what a limpet is. I just don't see the connection."

"Neither do I. The boy's nuts; I told you. And I'm not finished yet. Then there's these." He turned back to the laptop and clicked open a new folder.

"I think you'll enjoy this, Detective," he said.

The new folder opened to show six more folders, and when Rogers opened the first of those, it showed a long list of video clips. Rogers clicked one at random, a file called 00013_07_07_16 12:34. The little laptop ground its gears for a while. Then a video player box appeared.

"Here we go," Rogers said.

The image was of a small clearing in a wood. The horizon was unsteady, and there were drops of water on the lens, which made it confusing to see what was going on at first. But then a small red fox wandered into the frame, and sat on the ground in front of the camera. It began to scratch itself with its hind leg. When it was finished, it looked around casually, and eventually, it got up and walked on, this time out of the other side of the screen. The image didn't change at all for thirty seconds. Then the clip ended.

"What the hell?" West asked.

"Hey, that's a cool one," Rogers said. "I like that." He clicked another one. It opened to show the exact same forest clearing, but this time, a black rook was hopping through the frame.

"It's his wildlife camera files," Rogers said. "I kind of wondered after we'd interviewed him why he had that camera-trap thing. Well, this is why. This is what he did with them when he wasn't spying on people. He spies on animals."

"Have you watched them all?"

"Christ, no. There's far too many. Thousands. Tens of thousands, maybe. He's pretty into it."

He quickly clicked back through to the desktop. "I found the files from where he was spying on Philip Foster in a different folder. I guess he watched all of those. Fucking loony."

Rogers clicked away and opened another folder. He scrolled right down to the bottom and opened the last file. It showed the front of Philip Foster's house, with a patrolman in the foreground. He appeared to notice the camera and then leaned in close until his face filled the screen. Rogers laughed. "The moment we found the camera." He closed the file so there was just the folder visible. "Say, what were you saying outside? Something strange happened..?"

West found herself distracted and didn't answer. Something about the files had occurred to her, but she couldn't tell what.

"So what was it? The strange thing?" Rogers prompted.

She shook her head to clear the half-thought. She tried to focus properly.

"It's something the kid's mom said."

"The mom? You said she was a wacko too. PTSD? Never recovered from the attack?"

"I didn't say she was a wacko."

Rogers lifted his hands from the desk in mock apology. He waited for her to go on, but West didn't say anything.

"Well, what'd she say?"

West made a face.

"I'm not sure. It was a strange thing. She seemed to want to say it without her doctor hearing. She kind of whispered it, right in my ear."

"Whispered what?"

"I'm not sure; I didn't hear it clearly. But it might have been: *don't trust them.*"

"Don't trust them?"

"Yeah."

"Don't trust who?"

"I don't know." West shrugged. "I've been wondering that all the way back. But then I'm not even sure that I heard right. It could have been something else." West let her eyes rest on the screen. There was something about that folder that bothered her. Something she still couldn't place.

"You said she was in a state, drugged up and whatever. It's probably nothing."

"I know."

"I mean, you're not seriously questioning the case out there, are you? We've all read it; it's watertight. Two eyewitnesses who knew him. Stone fleeing like he did. And now what he's done here too..."

West didn't answer.

"Come on Jess, don't find problems where they don't exist. That's the first rule of detective work."

"No, I'm not doubting it," West's voice was tight and she heard herself sounding uptight. She softened it before she went on. "It just affected me, I think. To see how much damage you can do to someone with a single crazy act. She's my age, Christine Austin. But she looks twice that. And they say she'll never recover. It just makes it seem more real, actually seeing her like that." West paused and looked at Rogers, as if searching for something in his face, a sign that he understood. But he looked away.

"Yeah, well. It makes it all the more important that we catch the son-of-a-bitch."

West was silent.

"Jess? You hearing me?"

"Shit. Ollie, give me the mouse," West said.

"What? What is it?"

"Just give it to me."

64

———

Silently, Rogers did what West asked. She leaned in closer to the little screen, clicking as she went.

"There."

"What?"

"Look at that column there." Her finger pointed at the two files they'd just played.

"What?"

"It gives the date it was last accessed. Today."

"So?"

"Well, look at all the others."

Rogers looked. After a while, he turned back to her.

"I don't get it."

"They're all the same. All the same dates. Same times too."

"OK. I can see that, but so what?"

"Well, either he looked at each and every one of these files on the exact same time and day he downloaded them off the camera - which is impossible - or more likely, just like you, Billy hasn't watched these files."

Rogers sat back in his chair and tapped his fingers on the edge of the desk, his eyes narrowed in thought.

"OK. But so what?"

West hesitated now.

"I'm just wondering if he had any of these camera traps set up on the night Olivia Curran went missing."

Rogers turned to look at her, then burst out laughing.

"Jesus, Jess, I've heard of long shots, but that's ridiculous."

"Why? These are *hidden* camera traps, set up around the town. Why wouldn't he catch something?"

"Because... Well, I don't know. But how do we check anyway?"

"Well, that's easy enough. They've all got the date and time on them."

IT ENDED up being harder than West said. It took them two hours to understand that Billy had four cameras, two which worked in daytime only, and two which also recorded in infrared. Between them, he'd collected and saved tens of thousands of video clips. The vast majority were apparently unwatched. They also ascertained that two of his cameras were deployed and recording on the night the teenager went missing. They created a new folder and copied all the clips from that night. Then they arranged them in chronological order starting with those captured around the last time Olivia was seen alive.

"So. Detective," Rogers said when they were finally finished. "Are you ready for this?" He rubbed his hands together.

"Shut up Ollie," West replied. "We've been looking for a needle in a haystack for the last three months. We've got to find it sooner or later."

He raised his eyebrows and grinned at her.

"Just play the damn files."

The first dozen clips showed nothing of interest at all, perhaps the wind had moved vegetation to trigger the camera. The thirteenth clip showed a small mouse-like creature. Rogers spent some time debating whether it was a mouse or a vole. West ignored him. Then the next clip began.

The view the camera had recorded showed a scrubby open-heathland setting; the camera appeared to be fixed by a vague pathway - the sort of track made and used by animals as much as humans. West suddenly realized she could place it.

"This is somewhere around the Silverlea Lodge Hotel, isn't it?" she said. "I recognize the landscape." But Rogers didn't answer, because at that moment, a figure entered the frame.

It was a male, young - late teens or early twenties - and he was stumbling along the path. Then he stopped, put his hands to his mouth, shouted something, looked around for a moment, and then carried on. He looked drunk. The time of the clip was 12:47a.m.

The two detectives watched until the clip stopped. When it had finished Rogers immediately clicked to play it again.

"What's he saying?" West asked.

Since the only sound up to then had been wind noise, they'd had the sound turned down low. Rogers found the laptop's volume control and increased it. Then he replayed the clip for a third time. Again, the figure stumbled into frame, looked around, and put his hands to his mouth. This time, they heard what he said, a loud call:

"Where are you?"

"I know who that is," Rogers said.

West looked at him in surprise. "Who?"

"It's Daniel Hodges. He works at the Surf Lifesaving Club in Silverlea. Some people thought he'd shown an interest in Curran before she went missing."

"What's he doing?"

"I'd say he's looking for someone."

"Who?" West asked the question automatically, but she wasn't surprised that Rogers didn't answer. He turned to his own computer and typed the man's name in the investigation database. Quickly, he pulled up the statement that had been taken from Hodges in the days after Curran went missing. They read it together quickly on screen.

"He says he was at the disco all night, then went to the party on Princes Street."

"No mention of going wandering around the heath, looking for someone?"

"No."

"Then what's he hiding?" West asked. "We gotta go see him. Find out who he's looking for."

"We'd better get Langley first," Rogers said.

West made a face. "Really?"

Rogers shrugged. "It's his investigation."

* * *

SOON, there were four detectives crowding around Billy's laptop, viewing the clip over and over again.

"How about the other clips?" Langley asked after a while. "There anything else to see?"

"No. Just this one. You make anything of it?"

Langley thought for a long moment, then shook his head.

"I don't see that it changes anything. We've got Stone, a fugitive with at least one previous murder on his record, plus he's got Curran's blood in the back of his truck. So what if this guy was running around drunk?" He shook his head. "I don't think it's anything." He stood up from where he'd been leaning in to see the screen.

WEST FELT A BURST OF IRRITATION. She opened her mouth to argue, but then stopped herself.

"You mind if we go check it out anyway?" she asked, keeping her voice calm. "At least find out who he was looking for? It might tie in somehow."

Langley looked at her for a moment like he suspected some sort of trick. He shrugged.

"Be my guest."

West glanced at Rogers and grabbed her coat.

65

They found him in the first place they looked, the Silverlea Surf Lifesaving Club. He was dressed in a one-piece blue overall, pulled down to his waist to reveal a sleeveless white vest and the arms of someone who worked out. It was cold inside, with the door open and a cold breeze blowing off the sea. He stood at a workbench, attaching a buoy to a shiny new shackle that was wedged in a vice.

"Daniel Hodges?" Rogers said.

He looked up, his brows knitted together. "Yeah?"

"I'm Detective Oliver Rogers, and this is Detective Jessica West. We're investigating the murder of Olivia Curran." They both flipped open their badges. Hodges didn't move, but his eyes widened.

"I already spoke to the police. When she went missing."

They both ignored him, but Rogers went on.

"The door was open; I hope you don't mind us just walking in?" From his voice it was clear he didn't care whether Hodges minded or not. West watched the young man's face carefully as her partner spoke. She noticed a look sweep over his features. It could have just been irritation at Rogers' manner, the normal reaction anyone would have to the words 'detective' and 'murder'. But it looked like something more.

Hodges shrugged unconvincingly. "Whatever. What do you want?"

"I wonder if we might ask you some questions."

Hodges put down the large wrench he was holding and wiped his hands on a rag.

"What about?"

"What are you doing?" Rogers asked suddenly, pointing at the buoy.

Dan Hodges looked at him warily, as if he couldn't understand why the police would want to know this.

"They mark the bathing zones. We take them in for the winter. I'm servicing them." He pointed over at the wall, where a row of similar buoys lay with their chains laid out.

Rogers stepped forward as if this was something of interest to him. West hung back, still watching Hodges' face.

"So what's this about?" Hodges asked again. "I gave a statement when that girl went missing. I said I didn't know anything about it. Anyway, I thought you'd found the guy you wanted? Sam Wheatley? It's all over the news."

"You're a friend of Sam Wheatley, aren't you? You wouldn't know where he was, by any chance?"

"No." Hodges seemed to recoil at the thought of this. "And we're not friends. I just see him around. I never liked the guy."

"Oh, really?" Rogers said quickly. "Why's that?"

Hodges seemed to sense he'd made some kind of mistake. He hesitated but then fudged an answer.

"I dunno. He's just... He's kinda weird. Too quiet. Like he's always judging you but never coming out and saying it."

The two detectives exchanged glances. For West it confirmed her partner was getting the same bad feeling she'd had since she walked in here. It seemed to rattle Hodges more. Rodgers didn't back off.

"What do you mean exactly?"

Hodges looked more uncomfortable. "He's kind of full of himself. Thinks he's God's gift just because he wins a few surf competitions."

"You ever fought with him?"

"*Fought?* No."

"You ever argued?"

"No..."

"Why not. Are you scared of him?" Rogers leaned in close to Hodges.

"No, I'm not scared of him... I just, I mean we just kinda keep away from each other."

"You sure about that? I mean you're clearly in good shape." Roger's nodded at Hodges' bare arms, "but then Wheatley looks like he can take care of himself too."

"No, look you've got the wrong idea. I hardly know the guy. It's just from what I've seen, he looks the type that's capable of doing something like this."

THERE WAS NEAR SILENCE, just the sound of Hodges breathing too fast, and the whistle from the wind outside. Rogers - who was nearest the workbench - reached out and ran his finger down the upper surface of the buoy, where it was faded by the sunlight. Then he continued past the clearly defined waterline to where it was coated with a film of dark green seaweed. He pulled his hand back and inspected the surface of his finger, turned slightly green from the algae. Hodges watched him in silence.

"You can't always tell from how people look on the surface, what's hidden underneath." Rogers said, apparently suddenly fascinated with the algae. Then he looked at West, and held up his finger to show her too. She took it as her cue and stepped forward.

EVEN THOUGH, she felt nervous as she pulled a notebook from her jacket pocket. She sensed the importance of this moment. She flicked her note-book open to gain a few seconds thinking time. She riffled through a few pages.

"Mr. Hodges," she began, her voice neutral but feeling the tension underneath. "In your statement, you said you spent the night of August twenty-ninth here, at the club disco, and then went on to Princes Street for the after-party. Is that right?"

He nodded.

"You made no mention of going anywhere else."

"No."

"But you did go somewhere else, didn't you?"

She looked up at him, as if she were simply checking a fact they were all aware of. Hodges' face was white. She didn't give him any time to reply, but carried straight on.

"Daniel, when you gave this statement, we were dealing with a missing person inquiry. It's now a murder investigation. You're aware of that, aren't you? You understand how much more serious that makes it if you lie to the police?"

"I didn't lie. I didn't go anywhere else. I don't know what you're talking about," Hodges said, his voice thick and deliberate. He had his feet planted squarely apart, and for some reason, he picked up the wrench he'd been using again. It was a heavy, oversized tool, painted red and well-worn. He seemed to realize at once how this must look, and he quickly set it back down again. But if he hoped West hadn't noticed, he was wrong. She hadn't planned to do what she did next, but something about his eyes, so clearly full of panic, made her take a risk.

"Mr. Hodges, you also stated you didn't know who Olivia Curran was. That you had never spoken to her. That wasn't true either, was it?"

Hodges' answer to this was hard to hear, a sort of grunted denial. West ignored it.

"You see, the problem is, Mr. Hodges, we have a videotape of you and Olivia Curran going off together, around midnight. Up toward Northend."

She sensed rather than saw Rogers swinging around to stare at her, but she didn't take her eyes off Hodges' face. She didn't know why the lie had come to her, but she knew right away it was right. His eyes widened, then flicked to the left, toward the door. For a crazy second she thought he was actually going to run for it. His mouth dropped open. He swallowed.

"How?" He said.

West fought hard to keep her face neutral. It felt like the floor was dropping out from underneath her. She heard her voice reply.

"A hidden, infrared wildlife-camera captured you both. It recorded the time and your exact coordinates. Very unlucky on your part." She offered him a sympathetic smile, more confident now with every passing moment.

"What happened, Dan? Did you have a fight? Did she do something to make you angry? Was it an accident?"

"No. *No.*" Hodges put his hands to his hair and let them fall slowly down his face, scraping on the stubble he wore on his chin. For a long moment, he just stared at West.

"You don't understand. It wasn't me. It wasn't. I didn't do anything to her. You gotta believe me." He looked around the room. Piled up against the far wall were stacks of blue plastic chairs.

"I need to sit down," Hodges said, and West nodded. Silently, Rogers stepped across and got them all chairs, placing them in the center of the room. He managed to catch West's attention as he did so, his eyes full of questions.

Hodges sat down and leaned forward, his hands on his knees, arm muscles bulging. Forehead creased in concern.

"You *were* with her? With Olivia. That night?" West asked.

Daniel Hodges swallowed again. He looked past the two detectives at the open door and the sea beyond it. He ran a hand through his hair again.

"Look, I couldn't say anything. My girlfriend would have found out. She gets crazy jealous, even when it's nothing. Something like this she'd probably kill me." He laughed a little, like this was an attempt to lighten the mood. But then he seemed to regret it. "That was stupid, I know. But at first, no one really believed anything serious had happened to Olivia. People thought she'd just run off. Like teenagers do sometimes. And once everyone knew it was serious, it was too late. If I'd have said something then people would have suspected me. And I didn't do anything. I swear to God. I didn't do a thing."

"What were you doing with Olivia Curran that night?"

Hodges sat there breathing hard for a long time. Eventually, he spoke.

"Look, she and her friends had spent the whole week sunbathing down by the lifeguard tower. And she'd been giving me the eye." He glanced across at Rogers. "You know what I mean?" Rogers just stared at him. Hodges looked away.

"Well, that night, she was doing it again. Looking across at me. It was obvious what she wanted."

"What did she want, Daniel?" West asked.

He looked at her, still breathing hard.

"She said she wanted some air. So I took her out on the beach."

"Did she resist?"

"*No.* No. It was *her* idea. Look, I swear to you, it wasn't like that." He shook his head, frustrated. "When she said *air,* she was... up for it. She had *condoms* and everything." He said the word quietly, then stopped and stared up at the ceiling.

"There were quite a few people hanging around outside that night, so I said we should go up the beach towards Northend. You can go in the dunes up there..." He stopped, suddenly aware of how this might sound.

"Not that, I don't... I don't do this all the time, just... Sometimes."

"Then what happened?"

Hodges was breathing so hard now it was as if he'd been running.

"We were making out on the beach; we were lying down on the sand. Then she said she needed to go do something. At the time, I thought she meant she needed the bathroom. So she went up into the dunes - and that's it. She disappeared. I figured she'd changed her mind. Went back to the party, I don't know. It said on the TV she had a boyfriend back home. I figured in the end, she must have felt guilty."

"So what did you do? When she didn't come back?" Rogers asked.

"I waited a while. Then I went looking for her. But when it was obvious she'd gone, I went back."

Rogers and West exchanged questioning glances. Rogers turned back to him.

"And you didn't think it was important to tell any of this to the police?" Rogers said. "Even after her *severed arm* was found?" He stared at Hodges. West could hear the anger in his voice.

Hodges turned to face Rogers. "I'm sorry, man. Like I said, I was scared. I was scared half to death. But I don't know anything. You gotta believe me."

There was a long pause during which no one spoke. Hodges broke it.

"So what happens now? You guys gonna have to arrest me or what?" He looked around, as if he was worried about who was going to close up the club. West was recording what he'd said in her notebook.

"You say you didn't come forward at first because you were worried about your girlfriend finding out?"

"Yeah."

"What's her name?"

Hodges didn't answer at first. He stared at West.

"Does she really have to know about this?"

"I'd say your girlfriend knowing about this is a very, very long way down your list of problems."

Hodges continued to stare for a moment, but then he looked away.

"Emily. Emily Franklin." He buried his head in his hands.

* * *

"YOU TOOK a hell of a risk there, Detective," Rogers said when Hodges was out of earshot. He'd asked to be allowed to get changed before they took him into the station. Rogers had checked the changing room carefully before agreeing, and now they stood outside - the only possible exit - waiting for him.

"I don't know," West said, her eyes still wide from the shock of what they'd heard. "You were pushing him pretty strong. His reaction just seemed wrong."

"Well, it worked," Rogers said. She didn't know if he meant his approach or hers.

"So you believe him?" she asked a moment later. She knew they didn't have long to talk together before he would be back, able to hear them again.

"I don't know. You?"

She shrugged. "The thing I don't get: If Hodges killed Curran, how does her blood and hair get in the back of Stone's pickup?"

Rogers frowned in thought, but shook his head.

"I don't know. There's something else that's strange too."

"What's that?"

"*Emily Franklin.* I recognized the name. The kid, Billy, there's a whole chain of emails between him and her on his computer. It's like they're friends."

"Why's that strange?"

"Apart from the age difference? Because she knew about his crazy-ass investigation into Philip Foster. He sent her updates. And she didn't exactly dissuade him from it either. I'd say she egged him on."

They both thought for a moment.

"You know what's gonna happen?" West said a few seconds later. She said it before she'd really thought about it.

"We're gonna take Hodges in, and Langley's gonna take over. He'll say thank you very much, take all the credit and we'll be back to tidying up the damn station." She could see in his eyes that he agreed with this, but he looked uncomfortable.

"So what're you saying?"

"Just that... that we've gotten this far. Let's dig a little bit more."

Rogers glanced at the changing room door. They could hear footsteps behind it; Hodges was changed and coming out.

"Franklin lives a street away from here. I looked her up earlier. You want me to wait here with Hodges while you go talk to her?" he said quickly. Then the door opened, and Hodges stepped out, this time dressed in jeans and a worn wool-sweater.

West thought for a moment. Then nodded. Rogers acknowledged her with a scowl.

"Right. Change of plan, Dan! You and I are going to wait here till a squad car picks us up." Rogers checked his notebook and found the address for Emily's house. He scribbled it on an empty page, then ripped it out and handed it to West.

"This is gonna piss Langley off," he said, raising his eyebrows.

66

When I wake the next day, I don't know where I am. I have this weird feeling that something's not right, and then I remember that everything's not right, and I wish I was still asleep.

THERE'S a knock on the door. Emily opens it and asks if she can come in. She's got a cup of hot chocolate in her hand. She smiles at me and asks how I am, then sets it down on the bedside table and sits on my bed. It's the same hot chocolate as the other night, so I can't drink it.

We have breakfast, sitting around the table in the kitchen again. But this time, we all sit in silence. Dad's in a really bad mood, and although I've still got lots of questions, I'm too scared to ask them. Then Dad tells me to go back to my room. He says I'm not allowed to go into the living room in case someone looks in from the street - he thinks it would look strange to leave the drapes closed. I think it's because he doesn't want me to watch TV, though. I saw him watching something on the news, but he turned it off when I came in. So I sit in my room. Only it's not my room, it's Emily's dead grandma's room. There's a stack of old *National Geographic* magazines in there, the ones with the yellow covers. They're really old; they go right back to 2005. Eventually, since there's nothing else I can do, I sit and read through them.

I make three piles of the magazines. The first is ones I haven't looked through; the second is ones I've skimmed through, and there's an interesting article I want to read. The third is ones where I've read all the interesting articles. There's a couple of good ones, something about lobsters and how they go to deeper water when a storm approaches. They line up in little columns, each one searching for the lobster in front of it with its feelers. I don't know how the one in front knows where to go.

Even so, it feels like the day really drags. A couple of times, I leave the room, but both times, Dad tells me to go back. He's really worried about anyone seeing me from the road. Him and Emily spend the whole day in the kitchen, talking, sometimes really loudly, but not clear enough for me to hear. We have takeout later on. I eat it in my room.

The next day is pretty much the same, apart from Dad going out. I don't know where he goes. He borrows a baseball cap and sunglasses from Emily, and he goes in her car. Emily tells him to be careful, and he just looks at her, but I can't tell how he looks because of the sunglasses. When he goes, he locks the door from the outside. I ask Emily if I can watch TV. She says no at first, but then she lets me. We watch it for a bit, until the news comes on. And Dad's the first story. There's a picture of our pick-up being loaded onto the ferry, on the back of a big, flat-bed truck. You can't see it properly because it's under a tarp, and the newsreader says it's going to a laboratory on the mainland because Olivia Curran's DNA was found in the back. I want to watch more but Emily turns it off. Then she comes to sit with me in my room and read *National Geographic.* I try to ask her what's going on, and where Dad's gone, but she won't tell me. Instead, she just says how when she was a girl, she used to come and visit her gran, and she would look forward to the latest issue of *National Geographic,* and how it got her interested in marine biology. Normally, I'd be interested in stuff like that, but I don't really care at the moment.

Dad comes back about four. He and Emily disappear into the kitchen to talk where I can't hear, and they stay like that until it gets dark. Then they come out, and Emily shuts the drapes in the living room. We eat dinner in front of the TV, but Dad won't let us watch the news. We watch sitcoms instead.

We're all sitting there, just the noise of canned laughter and the clattering of our forks against the plates, when Dad suddenly starts talking. It's been so long since anyone really spoke to me that I'm surprised.

"We can't stay here. You know that, don't you, Billy?"

I jerk my head up, then look back down at my dinner. I'm not ready to talk. I go on eating like I didn't hear.

"I said we can't stay here, Billy." He picks up the remote control and turns the volume right down. I look at him, and he just watches me carefully.

"At Emily's?" I say.

"Here. On Lornea Island. We can't stay. We've got to get away."

I wonder about asking why, but I don't really want to think about all that again. It doesn't feel nice to think about it. I nod instead.

"I know."

"Emily and I have come up with a plan. I need to tell you about it," Dad says.

I can feel my heart start beating real fast. I don't want to talk about it. I want to go to bed.

"It's going to be a big change for us. But we can make it work. It's a good plan."

I don't say anything to this. I want to look back at the TV, but I feel this might make him mad. Eventually, he continues.

"I'm sure you know that Emily is going off on this research ship this week. She's going down to the coast of Central America. Did you know that, Billy?"

"Yeah," I say. "She's looking at the venom in jellyfish there, and why some fish survive and some don't."

"Yeah, I guess so. Well, Billy, how'd you like to go with her?"

I don't know if it really does, but it feels like my mouth drops right open.

"What?" My mind races. Like, as a scientist? How would that be possible? What about the police? What about *Dad*?

"The ship docks here on the island Thursday night. Emily reckons it'll be easy enough to get aboard. Then she's got her own cabin, so we'll stay in there. We'll keep hidden. She'll make sure we get plenty of food and water. It'll be fun. Like going on a cruise." Dad smiles at the thought.

"THEN WHAT?"

Dad stops smiling. He takes a deep breath in, then holds it for a long time.

"Well, Emily thinks there are plenty of smaller places where it'll be easy to get off again, maybe in Mexico, maybe Venezuela. We'll sneak off the ship. Then we'll find somewhere nice where we can be safe. We'll start over."

I blink at him. "But what about school?"

He holds up a hand. "We'll find you another one. I'll get some work. We'll find a nice little place somewhere." He gives me another smile. "Billy, I had a little stash. Some cash, some other bits and pieces, hidden out in the woods. That's where I went today, to dig it up. My emergency stash. That'll see us through for a few months. Long enough to find somewhere nice. Somewhere we can start again."

"But they speak *Spanish* in Venezuela! I don't speak Spanish."

I look over at Emily. "Are you coming?" I ask. I feel a little angry. I get the sense this is her idea. She hesitates.

"The idea is that I come back and try to help from here. You and your dad will be somewhere safe, where the police can't bring him back easily. But I'll be working with lawyers and things, helping them to understand how they've made a terrible mistake."

"How long will that take? How long will we have to stay there?" I turn back to Dad.

Dad takes a very long time to answer this.

"Not forever, kid," he says finally.

67

I lie in bed thinking for a long time. I'm going to live in South America. That one fact just keeps pressing into my mind, crowding out everything else. I try to imagine what South America is actually like. Ironically, there were lots of articles in *National Geographic* from South America; it all looks like rain forest and people living in little huts. Little brown children in a classroom with an old-fashioned blackboard and no glass in the windows. Actually, that might have been Africa, but really, what's the difference?

I CLOSE my eyes and try to imagine what it might be like. Me and Dad living in a hut somewhere. Just outside the front door, we'd have the beach - fine, white sand - then a wide bay of turquoise water, so warm you can be in bare feet all year round, and protected by a coral reef offshore. I can almost see the hut: bamboo roof, a balcony with a hammock. Shaded by coconut palms that I climb every morning to get breakfast. There'll be a village nearby, but I won't go to school there. If Dad can get away with whatever he's done, there's no way he can make me go to school. Instead, I'll do my research. But this time, it'll be really important research. I'll do something on turtles. We'll be on the kind of beach where they bury their eggs. I'll tag them; maybe I'll paint their shells with the ultraviolet paint. I'll still have email and the Internet and everything. Maybe visiting scientists will come and stay with me. They'll sit on the balcony in the evenings and listen to how it all began with hermit crabs in the silver rockpools of Lornea Island.

But I can't hold the daydream in my mind. It's like a bike tire with a slow puncture. Reality keeps piercing it so it deflates, and I have to try and blow it up again. I can't make it stay feeling real. I try to build from what I know. Emily's research ship, the *Marianne Dupont*. I've seen tons of pictures aboard there. Both official ones from the websites and the ones Emily's taken on her trips. Whatever happens, I'm going to go on the *Marianne Dupont*. I know I'll have to stay in her room, and I won't be able to see all the science happening and everything, but that's something, isn't it? Through the whirlwind in my head, I'm able to make myself a little bit excited about that. I try to hold that in my mind as I fall asleep.

I GUESS I must doze off for a while because something wakes me up and brings me right back into the room. I don't know what the time is, but then there's a sharp click, and I see the door opening, light from the hallway leaking in. I see Dad peering in at me. Quickly, I pretend to be asleep. A moment later, he pulls the door softly closed again. But the latch doesn't work very well, and once he's gone, the door stays open.

The bungalow is all on one floor, so Emily's room is next door. And for a while, I lie there, listening to the soft sounds of them going to bed. My thoughts about South America are still fresh in my mind; it's nice to let the images play in my head. Just to lie there, not really thinking at all. Then the hallway light clicks off, and the bungalow goes dark. I turn over and try to go back to sleep. But now that I'm awake, I can't. The sound of Emily's grandmother's house is so different from our house. There's some light still, from streetlights outside, I guess. We don't have those. At home, if there's clouds and you can't see the stars or the moon, it's just pitch-black.

And I can hear murmured voices, too, coming from next door. Dad and Emily. I kind of expect them to go quiet in a minute, but they don't. I try to go to sleep anyway, but I've kind of got myself awake now. I wonder if going to get a glass of water might help. I do that sometimes at home.

I try to just forget about it, but once I've got the idea in my head, it becomes all I can think of. I'm not really thirsty, but on the other hand, I haven't really drunk much all day. I know I'll just sleep badly if I don't get up. For a long time, I try and resist it and go to sleep, but eventually, I give up. I push the covers off and pad to the door. I push it open and step out into the quiet of the hall.

Only it's not that quiet. For some reason, they've left the door open to Emily's room, pushed to, but not closed. And I can hear them still talking. There's still a glow of light coming from the door. I don't mean to listen. It's just I have to go past their door to get to the bathroom.

"You've gotta tell him sooner or later." It's Emily's voice, soft and concerned. "I don't understand why he isn't demanding to know more now. I guess he's just... overwhelmed by it all," she says. I freeze.

"He's scared, I guess." That's Dad's voice, lower, gruffer. "Scared of what he thinks he might find out."

"That's why you've got to tell him, Sam. He'll understand. That's why you've got to tell him the truth."

I can't hear Dad's reply, just the low murmur of his voice. Then Emily replying. I realize I've crept right up to their door now; I'm still out of sight behind it, just listening, struggling to hear what they're saying.

"Alright. Alright. He's your son. You know him best," Emily says. Then there are more noises, like the covers moving.

"God, you're tense." Emily gives a half laugh. "Come here."

I half-turn to go onto the bathroom, but I don't move away from the door. I realize I can see though the crack between the door and the frame. They've still got a light on, Dad's bedside light. I can see them both in bed. Dad's sitting up, staring at the ceiling. Emily's lying beside him, in a T-shirt like the one she lent me; she's rubbing his shoulders.

"Em, no. I don't think I can tonight," I hear Dad say, but she doesn't stop.

"Come on, Sam. When am I going to get another chance?"

Then, to my surprise, she stops what she's doing, reaches down, and pulls her T-shirt up and off over her head. For a stunning second or two, I can see *everything*. I have to slap my hand over my mouth to stop myself gasping out loud.

I'VE SEEN BOOBS BEFORE; on the beach in the summer, sometimes, girls take their bikini tops off when they're sunbathing in the dunes. But they're not supposed to do it, so they always go a long way away to do it. You're not supposed to look either, but sometimes, you can't really help it, can you? One time, I was birdwatching, and I had my binoculars, and this woman was sunbathing very close. I looked at her for a long time, but in the end, I felt dirty, so I stopped. And anyway, that woman was lying on her back, so it was kind of hard to make out where her boob started and the rest of her stopped.

EMILY'S BOOBS are really white, except for the middle bits that are pink and sticking out. They're swaying from side to side. I only see them for a few seconds then she leans in close to him, pushing herself against his back. She puts her arms around him, slides them down his belly.

"Em, not tonight, come on," Dad says.

I'M STILL SHOCKED. I've just seen Emily's boobs. I've heard Dad's surfer friends saying she's got nice boobs. Though they call them tits, but I don't like that word. I realize I'm holding my breath. I try to remember what they looked like. Like white wobbly coconuts. I force myself to breathe.

"Em, no. Come on," Dad says again, a bit more forcefully this time. I'm staring through the crack now, my face pressed up against the doorjamb. Emily rolls on top of him now. I can see her long hair falling over both their faces. Then, with one hand, she reaches behind her and pulls the covers looser.

"Come on, Sam." Her voice has changed now; it's gone deeper. Breathy. Then she lets out a big sigh.

"I've missed you, Sam Wheatley," she says. Then she reaches out again, and this time, she turns the light off, and everything goes black. I still don't move, and all I hear is the sound of them moving on the bed, the mattress creaking a little bit.

I'M NOT AN IDIOT. I know what's happening. I know what they're going to do. Everyone talks about it at school. We've even done lessons on it, although the teacher was so embarrassed he just handed out worksheets and pretended to mark homework while we filled them in. And obviously, animals do it all the time; otherwise, they wouldn't be there, would they? I know *what* they're doing, and I know I shouldn't watch. I should just get my drink and go back to bed. But now, my eyes are adjusting to the darkness. Emily's room looks out on the yard, so there's no streetlights, but the moon is really bright. As I watch, Emily rolls off Dad so she's lying on her back; then she arches herself up and pushes her underwear down and kicks them off her feet. Her limbs glow almost white in the gloom, but there's a darkness where they meet her stomach. There's hair. I catch my breath when I see it.

Then she does the same to Dad, laughing as his shorts get stuck. I have to look away when I see it. He's never tried to hide anything when he's getting changed, but it looks totally different now. Horrible. Huge. Then Emily does something disgusting: it looks like she's going to put it in her mouth. I can't look at that. I have to look away.

When I look back, he's lying on top of her, and I can hear him panting. Fast and short. I can see him going up and down; it almost looks funny. I can't see much of Emily, just her legs, stretched apart and wobbling in the darkness. I know I really can't watch any more now, but as I'm about to move away at last, Dad starts jerking like he's in pain. I see Emily's hands scratching at his back.

And then I see something I hadn't noticed before. There's a mirror next to the bed, and in the reflection, I can look around Dad and actually see Emily's face. And in the half-light, I get the scariest feeling she's looking in the mirror. Not at Dad, not at herself, but looking right at me. I feel her eyes locked on mine, and as I watch, the tip of her tongue comes out, and she runs it around her lips. I'm frozen to the spot. Then she closes her eyes and starts twisting and writhing, like a fish when you pull it out of the water. Suddenly, she screams so loud that Dad stops and tries to get her to be quiet. I use the moment to run away, back to my room and back into my bed. I lie there in silence, still thirsty and panting and shaking. All I can see are her eyes in the mirror, staring at me. That tongue running around her lips. And with every breath I take, I can taste the warm summer flowers of her perfume embedded in my T-shirt.

68

The next day is Wednesday. It turns out to be the longest day of my whole life. Everything changes on Wednesday.

It starts badly enough. I'm really embarrassed as we eat breakfast; I can't even look at Emily or Dad, so I just stay quiet. But Dad's not talking much either. Emily is trying to be sweet like normal, but I won't look at her. Then her cellphone goes off, and instead of answering it in the kitchen, she takes it into the other room. She's gone for a long time, and we can hear her voice rise more than once during the conversation. When she comes back, it's obvious there's something wrong. She looks at me, like she wants me to go away, and she says to Dad,

"Sam, we've got a problem."

"What?"

"That was Dan."

Dad sighs. He looks at me, too, but he doesn't get up from the table. Do you remember I told you once that people sort of forget I'm there? It's why I thought I'd be a good detective. Well, that's kind of what happens now. Or maybe because they've told me the plan now, they think it's OK that I hear. Anyway, they keep talking even though I'm right here, listening to it all.

"What does he want?"

"He's wondering what's going on. He wants to see me."

"Well, just say you don't want to see him."

"Sam, I can't do that. I'm going away for five weeks. We planned to spend some time together before I go. I can't have a headache forever."

Dad looks annoyed.

"Well, go see him, then."

Emily shakes her head. "He wants to come here, Sam. You know what his place is like..." She says the next bit more quietly, "there's no *privacy* there."

Dad gets up now. He paces up and down the kitchen.

"Well, he can't come here, can he?" he says in the end. Emily just looks frustrated. She made coffee before I got up this morning. She sees Dad's cup is empty and fills it up again.

"Sam..." She stops. She looks sad. "Sam, I really want to help you, but I didn't ask you here. I'm risking everything to help you out. I'm risking going to prison. All because I believe you didn't do what they're saying you did. But you've got to help *me*. He's already suspicious." She stops suddenly and covers her face with her hands. I wonder if she's crying. She sits down at the table. I wonder if Dad is going to hug her or something, but instead he just stares out of the kitchen window.

"I'm sorry," he says. "Look. When can we get on the ship?"

Emily sniffs a little, but when she takes her hands away, there's no tears I can see.

"Tomorrow. They're getting into Goldhaven tomorrow lunchtime; then we sail Friday at nine a.m. We can drive to the port and sneak you on tomorrow night. There's no security, just a key to get into my cabin. And I can pick that up before."

Dad nods. "OK. So what about Dan?"

"He wants to come around today. I think he wants to spend the night."

There's a silence after she says this. I think about what I saw last night. I can't help but imagine Dan in place of Dad.

"OK," Dad says. "OK. Well, maybe we could go to one of the cottages. They're mostly empty this time of year."

"Yeah," Emily says, but her brow is furrowed as she says it. "Only..."

"Only what?"

"Well, it's just - well, you've seen the news. Don't you think they'll be keeping an eye on them? They know you keep keys to them." Emily's eyes are round like stones. She bites her lower lip, and Dad stares at her. Then he rubs his head, like he's got the beginnings of a headache.

"So you don't think that's a good idea?" he says, and holds up his hands. "So tell me what *is* a good idea, will you? Just tell me what you want us to do." It sounds like Dad is getting angry, but he seems angry with himself, like maybe because he's not thinking straight. Emily looks a bit shocked and shakes her head.

"We can't go home!" Dad rubs his head again, wincing. He does sometimes get headaches. He looks pretty ill. I wonder for a moment if sex does that to you?

Emily watches him for a while. Then it's like she remembers I'm there.

"Billy, you know the old mines up at Northend?"

I look up, surprised.

"Yeah?"

"Did you ever go right inside? Past where the tide gets to? You can get to the old bunk room. In the old days, it took a long time to get up and down the shafts, so they put living quarters down there. It's a little dark and dusty, but it's all still there. You could hide out there tonight and during the day tomorrow. Then, when it gets dark, we'll go to the ship."

Her words seem to hang in the room. It feels like my brain can't quite make the leap from the photographs of South America, and the *Marianne Dupont*, to how the old mines look, pitch-black and the floor covered with pools of water. I can see Dad's struggling with it too.

"The old mines?" I say. My voice sounds squeaky all of a sudden.

"Not where you've been doing your experiment, Billy. You keep going up the old shaft and you get to a room. It's dry. It's..." She stops.

"Look, Nan had a thing for candles." She gets up and opens the cupboard under the sink. She pulls out three packets of thick white candles, not the decorative kind. "Nan was always prepared for power outages. There's enough here to keep lights going for a few days. She's got battery lanterns too. And I've got sleeping bags. Camping gear."

Dad doesn't say anything. He looks like he's thinking. He takes another swig of his coffee, then looks at the cup, a puzzled expression on his face.

"Sam, you've been here for *three days*. You need to move. It's only a matter of time before the police show up. You need to get away. Think of Billy. What's going to happen to him?"

There's a long pause.

"What's going to happen to me?" I say.

Emily pushes her chair back so fast it makes a loud squeak on the floor. "Nothing, Billy. Nothing's going to happen to you. We're going to get you on that ship, and then your dad's gonna figure everything out. I promise you." She gives me a hug, and suddenly, I've got her hair in my face, sweet and soft. I can feel her heart beating against me.

When Dad speaks next, his speech sounds slurred. Like he's just tired out by everything that's happening.

"You know this place? You've been there?"

I can't understand him at first, so it's Emily who answers. "Yeah, I know it. I used to go when I was a kid. A few of us used to hang out there. But hardly anyone else knows about it."

Dad stares at her for long minutes. I can't tell what he's thinking, but it doesn't really look like he *is* thinking. I'm a little worried about him.

"It's the safest place for you." Emily's eyes flit down to Dad's coffee, which is empty again. She glances at the coffeepot on the side, but doesn't offer a refill.

"How do we get there?" Dad asks, and I know he's really considering it. I don't the thought of it. Emily lets go of me and steps away.

"We'll have to go this afternoon. The tide's low at four, and from the beach is the only way in. It'll be almost dark by then. We won't see anyone. Even if we do, they won't be able to see our faces."

Dad nods.

"OK," he says. "OK. I guess it's the only way." His voice still sounds odd and he presses his hand against his forehead. Like he's trying to squeeze a headache away.

I don't say anything. I'm wondering how Emily knows that low tide is at four o'clock, without needing to look it up.

69

E mily already has a big backpack filled with things she needs for her *Marianne Dupont* trip, but she empties it and puts all that in a holdall. Then we fill the backpack with supplies for our night in the caves: food, two sleeping bags - we're lucky that she has an old one and a new one at the house - extra blankets, lots of candles, and water. In a way, it's fun, but Dad's weird all day. He comes in and out like he wants to help, but then it's like his head hurts so much he can't do anything, and he goes and lies down instead. Emily gives him aspirin. She looks worried about him, but he tells her he'll be fine. He wants to rest now so he can stay up tonight and watch out for us.

The day goes by real quick. And at three, Emily makes a flask of hot coffee, and another one of hot chocolate. She gets me to pile all the gear in the hallway. She tells me how we've got to be gone by four to catch the tide.

THE LAST HOUR ticks by real fast, because I don't want it to. At 15:45, I check my watch and hope Emily doesn't notice the time. But she looks at her cellphone.

"Come on, Billy, help me get the car loaded," Emily says. She opens the front door. But it's cold outside and I shiver. Emily sees and shuts the door again. She goes to the hall closet.

"Here. I'll lend you a coat, Billy. You'll need it for the caves." Emily smiles at me and holds a jacket out. It's the one Dad lent her on the night of the disco.

"I borrowed it from your Dad. I wanted to wash it before I gave it back. Never got around to it," she says.

I just stand there, staring at the jacket.

"Come on, Billy, put this on. We gotta load the car up." She pushes Dad's coat into my hands. Her voice cuts into my mind. Then it keeps on cutting. Her voice is a razor blade slicing through skin. I feel myself free-falling. I don't answer her. I just blink.

"Billy?" she says. "Are you OK?" She opens her arms to give me another hug, and it's all I can do to not shrink away from her in terror, because something horrible happens. It's like her skin and flesh have vanished from her face, and all I can see is a skull, her eyes still there but red like a demon's.

"Billy?" her voice says, but it's not her voice. It's a demon's voice, deep and pure evil.

"Put the coat on, Billy. It's time to go."

I shake my head, and the apparition is gone. In front of me, it's just Emily again, holding out Dad's summer coat.

WE GO out to Emily's car. It's the first time in three days I've been outside, and the air tastes fresh and cool. It's like when you've been thirsty all night, and you wake up and have a drink of water. It clears my head. I stand there for a minute in the driveway, just looking around.

"Come on, Billy, get in," Emily says, holding the back door open. I know I'm supposed to lie down there so no one can see me. She's going to cover me in a blanket.

"Hang on," I say. I run back inside. Into my room. I look around wildly, but there's no paper. Nothing. But the window's fogged. It's the best I can do.

"Billy!" Emily's at the bedroom door before I realize it. "We've got to go."

"Where's Dad?" I ask.

"He's already in the trunk. Come on. I don't want to leave him in there too long."

I go out to the car and climb in the backseat. Emily arranges the blanket over me. Even so, it's cold. I feel the car sink as Emily gets in the driver's side, then the chassis shuddering as she turns the key.

70

Emily Franklin lived nearby and West drove slowly down her street, squinting in the rapidly approaching night to see the house numbers. It was a quiet road. No traffic at this time of day, this late in the season.

Forty-nine.

Franklin's address was further up and West accelerated. A car came toward her, its headlights on. West tried to get a look at the driver, but she couldn't see until the car drew level. A woman, youngish. No one else in the car. West hoped it wasn't Franklin. She followed the numbers down until she found Franklin's bungalow and pulled up just short. The lights were off, there was no car in the drive. West thought again of the woman she'd seen driving away.

SHE GOT out and walked up the short pathway to the front door. She knocked. When no one answered, she knocked again, louder this time.

"Damn," she said out loud. She looked around, hopeful that maybe a neighbor would be available to tell her where Emily might be, or when she might return. But the street was empty, the night drawing in. The windows in the neighboring buildings were blank, either dark or with the drapes drawn.

She walked to the bungalow's front windows and tried to peer in. The drapes were drawn here, too, but there was a space at the side where they didn't quite close properly. It was dark inside, but she could make out a couch and a gas fireplace. It looked like the kind of place you'd expect a grandmother to live in, West thought, not a twenty-two-year-old.

She carried on. There was a passageway that led around the back of the house. The gate was shut but not locked; even if it had been, the fence was low enough to jump over. She pushed it open and carried on, into the bungalow's backyard. She came to a door and tried the handle, but that was locked. There was another window, though, and she peered in. A double bed, slightly more modern furniture here, a dresser with various bottles and products on it. She squinted and saw a few she recognized. They shared the same brand of shampoo.

THERE WAS ONE MORE WINDOW, on the other side of the back door. She almost didn't bother with it, since the drapes were closed here as well, but when she did, the frown on her face deepened. She dug in her purse for a flashlight but couldn't find one; then she realized she could use the light on her cellphone. She spent a moment remembering how to turn it on; then she shined it at the window with the closed drapes. And what she saw made her pulse jump forty beats a minute. For a long moment she stood there, rooted to the spot, the adrenalin beating through her body.

71

I'm lying on the floor in the back of the car, breathing through a blanket that smells of mold and cats, and for some reason, I'm thinking about what happened in Mr. Foster's boat. That all seems like such a long time ago now. It all seemed fun then.

I can feel - I don't know how, maybe from how the car's tires are still running smooth - that Emily is still driving through the town. I think of the stores and houses we must be passing. I don't know why I have to lie down here; there won't be anyone around now anyway. It's almost dark, and Silverlea will be empty. Then the car accelerates, and I know we're on the road out to the hotel. Soon, we'll slow down and turn onto the track out to the heath. You're not supposed to drive down it, but us locals do sometimes. There's a little part at the end where you can leave a car and hike the last mile out to Northend.

Northend. The caves. Just thinking about them now gives my heart a jolt. I don't want to go into the caves. I don't really know why; I mean, maybe it's obvious, they're dark, and wet, and kind of claustrophobic. But what I mean is, I don't want to go into the caves with *Emily*.

KERRUMP.

THE FLOOR DROPS away beneath me, then comes back hard, knocking the breath out of me. That's the drop-off from the tarmac onto the forest road; Emily's taken it too fast. I think of Dad in the trunk; is he going to be ok? What about the exhaust fumes? He already looks ill.

EMILY SLOWS A LITTLE, and the car rolls around as the wheels find the potholes. It's a long road. I walk it sometimes when I'm going to check my projects. I mean, I *walked* it sometimes. I guess that's all finished now.

I feel the car shudder and roll around as we go down the lane. It makes me feel sick. Suddenly, I think I'm going to be sick, and I don't care anymore what Emily says. I push the blanket up off my head and climb back up to the seat. I'm panting hard, and I roll the window down to get some air. Emily turns to look at me.

"You should stay hidden, Billy," she says. Outside the window is just heathland now. It's almost dark; the car's headlights pick up the potholes in front of us. I ignore Emily and put my face to the open window. The air streaming in feels cold, but it helps wash away my nausea.

"Well, I guess it doesn't matter here. There's no one around."

I sit back on the seat. We're near the end of the lane now. At the little area where you can park, and Emily slows, but she doesn't stop. Right at the end, the lane continues onto the beach, and that's where she goes. We slow for a minute, and the rear of the car slews around when we hit the sand, but she guns the engine, and moments later, we're on the hard sand below the high tide mark. You're not supposed to drive on the beach.

EMILY ACCELERATES HARD NOW, and we're flying along the sand. We're heading directly for the first headland at Northend. It's weird, being here in the dark, and driving here. She slows when we get to the rocks and she picks her way carefully. And then when we're round onto the hidden beach she accelerates hard and then slows. We fetch up next to the rock-face at the final headland. We're there. Right by the entrance to the cave. My cave.

EMILY'S DOOR OPENS, and I see her walking past the back window. She pops the trunk and helps Dad out. He looks drunk.

"Come on, Billy. Get out, grab your bag," Emily says. I do what she says, getting out of the shelter of the car and stepping onto the wet sand. It's cold outside. I push my arms into the straps of the backpack. Emily swings my door shut, then locks the car with the key remote.

She switches on a flashlight. It's still not really dark enough, but it's comforting anyway, to see a little pool of light. I look at the cave entrance. It's dark in there, I know. It's just one night, I tell myself. It'll be alright. Then we'll be on the *Marianne Dupont*. We'll sail down all the way to South America. Where there are turtles. And I won't have to go to school. It'll be OK, I tell myself.

Emily was right about the tide. It's real low, at least twenty yards from the cave entrance. It's so low there's not much water in the rockpools at the entrance. We don't even need to take our shoes off. Emily digs out another flashlight and gives it to Dad. He tries to take it but drops it, and it clatters onto the rocks and goes out.

"Dad?" I say.

"It's alright, Billy. He's just tired. Once we're inside, he can lie down. He can rest. We all can. I'll stay a while before going back to see Dan." I ignore her. I don't want to hear it.

"Dad, *Dad*," I say to him. "I don't want to go in there."

I don't know if he hears me. He's fiddling with the flashlight, flicking the switch on and off, but there's no light coming out.

"Dad." I hear my own voice cutting through the gloom. The blackness of the cave entrance seems to be sucking me in. I know what it's like in there, but it's never felt this threatening before.

"Billy." Emily's voice is sharp, determined. "You've got to do this. You've got to help your dad. Sam, will you tell him?"

Dad's light suddenly flicks on, and he grunts in surprise, like he hasn't been following anything else. He points it around, at the cliff face, at the sand and rocks at our feet. He points it into the cave, but the light is swallowed up by the blackness. I can hear him panting.

"Em, I'm not sure," Dad says slowly, his speech slurring again. "I don't know what's wrong, but I don't feel too good. I'm not sure..." He stops, and there's a silence, apart from the wind blowing around the rocks.

"It's fine, Sam. You're fine," Emily says. She sounds frustrated. "We've just got to get you inside, get you laid down on a bunk. Come on. Sam, you go first, Billy in the middle. I'll go at the back. I'll show you where to go with the flashlight beam."

"Em, I'm not sure about this. Not sure at all." Dad doesn't move.

Then Emily snaps. She leans in close to Dad and starts talking to him hard and sharp. I don't catch all of what she says, but it's stuff about how we have to hide, and how there's nowhere else to go. How it's not too bad inside. That there's bunks to sleep on. When she stops, there's still enough light for me to see he's nodding. Then he turns to me and gives me a squeeze.

"OK. Come on, Billy. Let's get in there and get set up." He lets go, and he starts walking into the cave entrance.

"Be careful, it's low there," Emily says from behind me. I feel a light push in the small of my back, and she prompts me forward after Dad. I follow the yellow beam of his flashlight into the hole in the cliff face.

72

The message was written backward, stubbed into the condensation in the glass by a shaky finger. Childish letters. Even so, the first word was easy enough to understand:

HELP

Then the writer had obviously realized the need to conserve space. Next, it said:

Northend Caves
She wants to kill us

THERE WERE droplets of water beginning to run down from some of the letters, in some cases fresh enough that West guessed this couldn't have been written that long ago. An hour, maybe less? Maybe much less. She thought again of the car she had passed moments earlier. Then, with her phone in her hand anyway, she snapped photos of the message. As she did so the droplets continued. Her mind was racing.

Northend caves? She'd never heard of them, not specifically. She knew about the rockpools. You couldn't spend any time in Silverlea and not know about the famous rockpools, but she didn't know there were caves too. But it wasn't a big surprise; it was the right kind of coastline. She tried to think clearly. The rockpools were only exposed at low tide; you couldn't get to them otherwise. Presumably, that would be the same with caves? That was just a guess. But she did know it was low tide now. Very low, she'd noticed it when she was at the Surf Lifesaving Club, the surf had seemed further away than usual. It hadn't meant anything at the time, but now...

Now it would be coming in! How long would it take to get back to the station and organize a response? Too long, she knew at once. She had to move now. She ran back around the bungalow, dialing Rogers' number as she did so. When she got to her car, she looked around again at the street, wishing it weren't so quiet and empty.

Her cell connected. She held it up to her ear, willing it to give her Rogers' gruff voice. Instead there was just a busy signal.

"Shit," she swore. Then she tried to think. She got into the car and sat, scrolling through the contacts until she got to Langley's number. She dialed it and waited, wondering how she could explain everything to Langley so he'd actually act. When she got an identical busy signal, she slammed her fist down hard on the steering wheel.

"Fuck it." She killed the call again. She realized it would be each other they were speaking to, discussing what Dan Hodges had revealed. She could try someone else, but she didn't want to waste any more time. If Billy Wheatley was being taken into the caves at Northend, then every minute counted. She felt for her gun, holstered around her belly. Normally, she resented the hell out of wearing it there. But now she felt grateful for it. If Rogers was on the phone to Langley, they wouldn't be long. She texted Rogers to say where she was going. Then she started the car.

73

It's cold and black inside the caves. I can hear our feet scuffing on the rocks, and splashed though the rockpools. There's the occasional plop of water falling from the roof.

"Keep going back. It gets drier further in." Emily's voice comes from just behind me. My own path, deeper into the cave, is illuminated by her light. My giant shadow dances on the walls ahead, like an ogre luring us in.

"The cave gets tighter, and there are rocks to climb over. There's a way through," Emily says, and we push on. We go deeper inside than I've been before. She's right, though; the floor is mostly dry now, and the walls are bare. Dad stops. He shines his light around in front of him, but it's just solid rock. There's no way forward.

"Where now?" he asks, his voice still thick.

"Keep going," Emily replies.

"I can't. There's nowhere to go," Dad says.

She doesn't reply for a moment, but then her flashlight plays on the wall in front of us. The tunnel is blocked. We can't go any further. Emily fixes the light on Dad instead.

"Hey," he says, squinting into the light and putting his arm up.

She sounds different. "Then I guess we must be here."

Dad's voice sounds strained with the effort of talking.

"Em, what's going on. Where's the room?"

Emily ignores his question.

"You don't sound too good, Sam. How are you feeling?"

"I... I..." There's confusion in Dad's voice. "Em, what the hell are you doing? Where's the room you talked about? Get that goddamn flashlight out of my face."

"And how about you, Billy?" I still can't see her in the darkness. "How are *you* feeling? You seem to be coping a little better than Sam here. Aren't you feeling sleepy?"

I don't know what she's talking about. I'm not sleepy. I'm just cold and scared.

"Emily, where's the room? With the beds?" I say.

"Here." I feel Emily's hand touch me in the darkness. She pushes something toward me.

"Here. Light some of these. Let's all see what we're doing here, shall we?"

It's the candles. She's given me a bag of them; then a moment later, a lighter. Her flashlight shines at the plastic bag but then she brings it up to my face. It hurts. But I take a candle out and use the lighter to guide a flame onto the wick. I notice how my hands are shaking as I do it.

"Put that one on the floor somewhere and light a few more," Emily says. "You can melt the bases to make them stand up."

I do what she asks, and soon the cavern around us is illuminated with pockets of a wobbly yellow glow. The outlines of the walls and roof are visible around the candles; they look wet and lined with slime. I can't see anywhere where we can go deeper. I can't see any rooms. Then Emily flicks her light off, and slowly, the puddles of light seem to grow stronger as our eyes adjust. Now we're standing in a narrow cavern, blocked at the far end.

"Emily, where's the room?" I ask again. I can see her now, instead of just her flashlight, but she's still a vague shape in the gloom.

"Haven't you got it yet, Billy? I had an idea you'd worked it all out."

I don't answer. I've seen what she's holding, but Dad hasn't yet. "Em, what the hell's going on? We can't stay here. Where's this room you talked about?"

"Shut up Sam. Shut. The. *Fuck.* Up." Emily spits. Then Dad sees what

she's holding too. Emily has backed away a few feet. In her hand is Dad's gun, pointed at him.

"Em, what's...? What are you doing?" Dad says; it's a struggle for him to speak. "How'd you get that?"

"I said shut up, Sam. Take your pack off, sit down, and shut up."

"No. How'd you - "

"I said *shut up*." She lifts the gun out in front of her. "I want to do this in a way that doesn't cause you any pain, but it works just as well with the gun. So don't think I won't shoot you. *Sit down.*" She screams the last words, and Dad struggles to do what she says.

"You too, Billy. Take your pack off. Sit on it. Next to your dad." The floor is flat rock, slightly sloping toward the cave's entrance - a long way away in the darkness.

"It wasn't hard to get the gun, Sam. I pulled it from your waistband as you got into the car. You're so drugged up you didn't even notice."

"Drugged?"

"Don't tell me you're not feeling it?"

"What?" Dad's breath comes short and fast. "How?"

She laughs. "How? You've been in my house, expecting me to cook and feed you the last three days. I've been increasing your doses all the time."

"With what?" he asks after a while.

"Sleeping pills mostly. Poor old Gran left all sorts in the bathroom when she died. I mixed in some rat poison this morning. It works slowly, should be kicking in now."

Dad doesn't answer. Even in the gloom, I can see his face is astonished.

"Why?" he asks.

I can hear Emily's breath now. It sounds like she's hyperventilating. Or maybe it's me. I can't take my eyes off the muzzle of the gun. A black hole in the blackness. She doesn't answer Dad.

"Billy, there's two flasks in your bag. Get them out."

"Why, Emily?" Dad's voice rasps out beside me. Then he bursts out coughing; it echoes through the darkness around us.

"Get the flasks, Billy."

"*Why?*" Dad begins to struggle to his feet.

"Sit back down," Emily says at once, but Dad doesn't stop.

"*Sit back down,* or I'll shoot your stupid-fucking son through his stupid-fucking head."

Dad stops. I turn to look at him, and his mouth is open as he stares at Emily.

"Get the flasks, Billy. There's coffee and chocolate. They'll send you to sleep. It's a painless way out."

I still don't move. I can't process what she's saying. A painless way out of what?

"Billy, I'm giving you five seconds."

"One."

"Two."

"Three."

"*Four.* Last fucking chance, Billy. I don't want to do it this way."

"Do what she says, Billy. Just do it."

On hearing Dad's voice, I finally move. I almost can't open the backpack, my hands are shaking so hard, but I manage it. I slide out one of the flasks, the bigger one. I set it on the ground and dig around for the other. I'm not sure, but it feels like I might have wet myself. I'm glad it's dark so neither of them can see me. My hands close around the other flask. I pull it out and look at Dad.

"Now each of you are going to have a nice hot drink and then this'll be over."

"Emily," Dad starts; he sounds a little more with it, I hear this and feel a tiny burst of hope. "What is this? What are you doing?"

"What am I doing?" She sort of laughs "I'm trying to get my life back."

For a moment there's just the sound of her breathing hard.

"Drink up. Drink up and I'll tell you." She shines her flashlight at Dad's flask.

"Come on. Do it now."

Slowly, Dad opens the lid and pours enough to fill half the cup. Wisps of steam disappear into the cold cave air.

"More. Right to the top, please."

Dad adds a little more.

"Now drink."

Dad doesn't move. "What's in it, Emily?"

"Drink it now, or I shoot Billy. It's your choice, Sam." She aims the gun at my head. "Alright," he says. He raises the cup to his lips. He winces, and lowers it again.

"Drink it.

"It's too fucking hot."

Emily laughs again, manically. "Jesus does it matter?" I can hear her breathing again.

"OK. Well let it cool down. It won't take long." She stops.

"You want to know what this is about? You want to know? Get up Billy. Get up."

I hesitate, but then I hear my own voice ask:

"What?"

"Take your dad's light and go over to that wall." She shines her own light a little way from where we're sitting. "See that pile of rocks? Move them out the way. See what's underneath."

I don't move. I look at Dad, still holding his cup with one hand. For a moment, we just stare at each other. Then he hands me the flashlight and nods at me.

Unsteadily, I get to my feet, and I make my way to where Emily said. Where the cave's wall meets the floor is a pile of loose, flat rocks; not big rocks, the size of a head at most. They sit in a small pool of water; the cave floor is low here. There's a smell too, and I can hear something, a kind of dull scratching. I shine my light on it. The gray rocks have flecks of quartz that reflect the light.

"Pull the rocks off, Billy. Your investigation is about to be successful. You're going to solve the mystery of what happened to Olivia Curran."

Slowly, I put my fingers on the first rock. It's not really on the main pile, but I pull it back, and it clatters to the floor beside me. Underneath is just the rock floor, an inch of water, and when my flashlight sweeps over the area, I see color.

At first, I don't get it. There's something red, something else that's bright green. Whatever they are, they're *moving*. Then I see. They're *shells*. Cockleshells, snail shells. Hermit crabs. *My* crabs. I see a number, black paint on a circle of white. Number 13. Most ignore my light. A few scuttle away back to the darkness.

"Keep going." Emily's instruction comes from behind me. "Just a few more stones."

I lift another, and there's a new color, purple, some kind of cloth. The smell is horrible. And then I lift one more rock. Underneath, there's a human arm. The hand is missing, and the white bone is poking out of the end. But it's the rest of it that's truly horrible. The skin is moving so much it looks alive. Only it's not skin: it's a carpet of crabs, all kinds, some painted, most not, latched on and feasting away.

I drop the stone and stagger backward. Then I trip and fall to the floor. I feel a sharp pain in my back. My light goes off, and I panic. I scream into the gloom, and I crawl back to Dad as fast as I can. I grab him, knocking the cup from his hand.

"What is it, Billy? What's there?" Dad asks.

"What do you think it is, Sam? It's the stupid little bitch that caused all this."

"What? Who are you talking about?"

"You still don't get it, do you? Who has everyone been looking for around here? Who are the police accusing you of killing, Sam?"

"Olivia Curran?"

"The very same."

"I don't understand. *You* killed her?"

Emily doesn't respond for a moment. Then she uses her light to pick out Dad's cup.

"Don't think I didn't notice that Sam. Fill it again, and this time, you can drink it hot. Then we'll talk."

Dad does it as slow as he can, but all the while, she's got her flashlight trained on his hands. The gun, too. Dad hesitates before raising it to his lips, but Emily seems impatient to talk.

"She was flirting with Dan. The whole week. Silly little bitch. He thought I didn't notice. But I could see them from the café. Don't you think Dan would know that? If he wasn't thinking with his dick. And then the night of the disco. She was like a bitch on heat. They tried to slip out together; I knew they would. Dan's done it before. Well, this time, I followed him. I didn't plan to hurt the stupid girl. I just wanted to confront them. They walked a long way, though. North, toward the dunes. That's where Dan likes to take them. Silly little tourist girls. To fuck them. How's the temperature, Sam? Still too hot for you? Remember, that's the easy way out here."

Dad doesn't move, but she doesn't seem to care now.

"They were on the beach. I was in the dunes, watching. She said she needed to go pee. She came right toward me. I couldn't move without her seeing me. She was going to discover me there, watching them. It would have looked like I was in the wrong, and I couldn't have that. There was a stone at my feet. I picked it up. I didn't decide to do it - it just happened. I swung it at her head. I didn't even mean to do it hard, but it was heavy, my arm swung faster than I intended."

Emily laughs, her voice eerie and weird with the shadows and flickering lights of the candles. Me and Dad are silent. My whole body is shaking now.

"I was at a total loss for what to do for a minute. I thought about trying to stop the blood, but when I touched her head, I could feel the skull was broken. I could press bits of it right into the brain. I knew then I had to sort it. I thought about just leaving her there, but we were halfway up to the caves anyway. It was low tide. I figured if I could get her in here, no one would find her. People would think she went for a swim and drowned."

"How did you get her here?" Dad asks. Emily's beam of light is slipping down from Dad's cup. I see what he's doing, trying to distract her.

"I was wearing your jacket. Do you remember you lent it to me? Your keys were in the pocket. I'd already passed your truck on the beach, so I knew where it was. I ran back. I drove it with the lights off; I almost couldn't find her again - God, that was a moment. Then I did find her, and I managed to get her in the back. I drove to the cave entrance, and it was easier there because I could drag her through the water.

"Then I got back to the party. You asked me where I'd been. I don't know, I must have looked pretty wild - I *felt* wild. I *needed* something to take me down. I told you to come home with me. You barely stopped to worry about poor Billy at home on his own. Do you remember that night, Sam? Do you remember what we did? The way we fucked? Death and sex, who knew they were such a combination?" She laughs again.

"And once I've dealt with you two, you know what I'm going to do? I'm gonna go fuck my boyfriend's brains out. What do you think about that?"

"You're not going to drink that, are you? Well, time and tide wait for no man, Sam."

Three things happen all at once. There's a spurt of light from where her voice is coming from, I feel Dad's body jerk, and there's a huge bang that echoes back and forth. It's the gun. She's fired it. I can smell it at once. A smoky, oily smell. For a second, I wonder if I'm hit. If I'm dead already, or dying, but I know I'm not. But Dad's grip on me has changed. It's almost gone.

"Well, well. I wasn't sure your gun would actually work," Emily says. She shines her flashlight over Dad's body again. I can see his hands have gone to his stomach. Even with the light, I can't see much. It's too dark, but I can hear him gasping, fighting for breath.

"Turns out it does," Emily says. "Now, where was I?"

No one else says anything. It's just Emily. Only it's not her, it's a monster in her place.

"I had to come back. To cut the bitch's hand off. Do you remember?" Emily says, but somehow Dad interrupts her. His voice sounds terrible, but he's speaking. Interrupted by shallow breaths, but loud enough to hear.

"Emily, you don't have to do this. You blame it all on me. Everything. Take Billy and go to the cops. Tell them it was me. Don't hurt Billy - "

She listens for a moment but then cuts him off.

"I *said*, I had to come back and cut the bitch's hand off. The police were searching this side of the island, they'd have found the body. My first idea was to move the whole thing, but that proved impossible. So I sawed her arm off. I dumped it in Goldhaven. I knew that would change where they were searching. And it did. Everything would have been OK." She stops.

I turn away to look at Dad. His back's slumped against the cave wall, but he's leaning on me now more than anything. I can see there's a black stain spreading out from his belly, but he's still breathing. I can hear it. Then he coughs, and I feel a spray of something wet on my face.

"Dad, are you OK?" I say. He doesn't answer.

"And it would have stayed OK if you hadn't turned up at my door. What was I supposed to do? The whole island is searching for you, thinking you killed the Curran bitch and you come to hide with *me*? Can you imagine what that was like? Can you imagine what I was thinking? And then we saw the news, didn't we Billy? We saw how the police found her blood in the back of your truck. I couldn't let you go then. They'd have caught you – they were always going to catch you – and you'd have told them that I had the keys that night. They would have worked it all out. I couldn't let that happen Sam. So that's *why* we're here. It's your fault. It's all your fault."

She almost yells this last part, but then makes an effort to calm herself down.

"But now. *Now*, when they finally find Olivia Curran's body they're going to find two more bodies. One of them Sam Wheatley, *already* a killer. The other his son, his final victim. They'll think you killed the girl Sam, because no-one else knew where she was. Do you see? They'll think something drove you to return to the scene of your latest crime. Perhaps the guilt of it finally got to you? Perhaps you always planned it this way? I don't suppose they'll care too much. The little flask of hot chocolate laced with drugs will tell the story well enough. That bullet in your stomach isn't perfect, but they'll just assume Billy did it. Do you hear that Billy? They'll call you a hero. The tide will wash any other evidence away. There'll be no trace of me." I can see her face in the gloom. She's smiling. She's triumphant.

"And talking of the tide. We need to hurry up. I've got to get out before the tide gets too high. Which means Billy, it's your turn. How do you want to go, Billy? A nice cup of hot chocolate, or shall we get this over with? It's time to choose."

74

The sweep of the car headlights picked out the sign:

DANGER!
Do Not Pass This Point
On Rising Tide!

West barely noticed it; her eyes were fixed on the impression of tire marks in the wet sand. She'd picked them up as she drove along the beach, a diagonal track leading from the dunes down toward the headland at Northend. For some reason, they were easier to see from a distance: they stood out as something unnatural, not part of the regular patterns of the beach. Close up, they were harder to see. In places, they stopped completely, where the sand was covered with a shimmering layer of water in the dull moonlight. Only on the drier patches could she see them clearly, light impressions in the hard sand. But it was easy to see where they led, up to and around the headland at the north end of Silverlea's great sweep of beach.

She kept the gas pedal pressed to the floor until she reached the headland. Here there were barely twenty yards of beach left exposed at the foot of the cliff and the sand was pockmarked with rocks that stood in little pools of still water. The headlights picked them out and West steered between them, feeling the proximity of the ocean and the surf. She didn't know where she was going now, just that the tire marks led this way.

Around the headland, the beach widened into another beach. A kind of secret cove she hadn't known was here. It was too dark to see for sure, but it looked cut off on the land side by looming cliffs to her left. For a moment, she didn't know where to go - the tracks had vanished - but then her headlights picked out the shape of a car ahead of her, stopped by the cliff face at the far end of the cove.

It wasn't moving; its headlights were off. West switched hers off as well, plunging the beach around her into momentary darkness. Quickly, her eyes began to adjust to the moonlight. She saw the car was parked hard up against the cliff face. She couldn't see any people. No figures near the car or in it. But there were plenty of hiding places.

She drove on slowly, stopping twenty yards from the other car and feeling exposed and vulnerable. As she watched it, the final reach of a wave washed right up to its tires, then pulled back, like the ocean was reaching out to it, testing the strange object nearly in its grip. West guessed this meant the tide was coming in, probably it had got closer to the car since the driver left it there. But what the hell was a car doing parked here in the first place?

West swallowed, then pulled out her gun. She adjusted her grip around it; the weight giving her some comfort. On a whim she leaned across and searched inside the glove box. Among the papers, she found a flashlight. She pulled it out and mentally crossed her fingers that it had full batteries. She aimed the flashlight at the floor and clicked it on, relieved to see the car's foot-well flood with light. She clicked it off again. Then she took a deep breath and pushed the car door open. In a single movement, she stepped out and dropped down. She moved to the back of her car, using the body of the vehicle as protection in case of attack. But nothing moved. The only sound was the low roar from the ocean. West realized she'd been holding her breath and forced herself to exhale. Still from behind the car, she flicked the flashlight on. The beam shone powerful and yellow through the darkness. It picked out shadows in the cliff face; the other car's lights reflected back as if they'd been switched on.

Still nothing moved. There were no signs as to where the car's occupants had gone. Then she saw the entrance. In the cliff face beside the car, a black hole of a cave entrance, partially blocked by a low roof. *The Northend cave.* She hesitated for a moment. Then, with her gun supported over the flashlight, she closed the gap to the cliff face in a run.

She crept up to the side of the car, then shone her beam inside. It was empty. Casting the light around, she saw nothing of interest, just a blanket balled up on the back seat. She glanced up. In front of her, the cave entrance seemed to draw her in, a deeper shade of black even than the darkness of the cliff face. She approached and peered in, the flashlight sent a shaft of yellow inside. It picked out the wet rock wall in places, but in others only seemed to accentuate the darkness. She hesitated, unsure of what to do. Then there was a sound that made her jump.

AT FIRST, she didn't understand it. The noise seemed to 'pop' out of the cave entrance, followed by a lower sound. But then her brain placed it. It was a gunshot, muffled by the millions of tons of rock pressing down on the cave. She listened for more, her own weapon trembling slightly in her hand now. She considered for a moment, barely believing she could really be in this situation. A part of her mind was screaming at her not to go inside the cave. She felt the cold grip of fear. And yet... Another part of her felt something else. A rush of something – exhilaration? Duty? Somewhere inside the blackness of the cave something terrible was happening. And this time she wasn't a helpless teenager searching the midnight streets of Miami too late to help her best friend. She felt the fear, but she pressed it aside.

She turned around and swept the light across the beach one more time, hoping that maybe Rogers was on his way, or Langley and the guys. But there was no one. She was on her own. She took two deep breaths and stepped cautiously into the darkness.

SHE USED her hand to shield the beam from her flashlight, giving her just enough light to move carefully into the cave. The floor was made up of irregular rock, some parts filled with pools of seawater. The water was so clear and still, it was nearly impossible to see which were filled with water, and she stepped into one that soaked her shoes, the water was cold, but she kept going. The walls were wet too, her light picked out the colors of minerals dissolved in the rock. The ceiling was low and it dripped water onto her. She shivered. Then she stopped and listened. There was a sound up ahead, hard to make out yet as it was coming from much deeper inside. The only other sound was her breathing, it felt frighteningly loud. She pressed on, deeper into the cave.

WHEN SHE WAS MAYBE fifty yards into the cave, the sound became clearer: a woman's voice speaking, then laughing, then the voice again. West stopped again and listened.

"So how do you want to go, Billy? A nice cup of hot chocolate? Or shall we get this over with?"

West gently snapped off her light again. She tried to pick out which direction the words came from in the darkness. She'd seen how the cave seemed to narrow toward the back, and with her own light extinguished, she now saw the glow up ahead of her. The cave had narrowed into more of a tunnel, and she'd come to a bend. From beyond the bend, there seeped an eerie glow that changed in intensity, almost seemed to flicker. It was enough light that she could creep forward, one hand on the slimy wall to guide her passage. She could hear the voice more clearly now.

"Come on, Billy. Time's running out. I don't want to shoot you, not after all we've been through. But I will. Then I'll put the gun in your dad's hand, and that's how they'll find you. They'll think he shot you. I'll put your prints on it, too. They'll think you got a shot into him before he got you. You'll be a hero, Billy. Shall we do it that way? So you can be a hero?"

The cave was silent for a moment. There was no answer to the woman.

"Of course, you won't be Billy the hero, because you're not Billy. Do you even know that? Do you even know your real name? I can tell you if you like. We've got just enough time for that story. If you'd like, Billy?"

The woman paused again. Then there was the sound of her laughing. It echoed around the cave.

"It's Ben. Ben. Your dad ever tell you that? He ever call you that by mistake? In the early days maybe. I guess you'd be too young to remember." There was a pause.

"You don't even know why you're here, do you? You don't know what any of this is about. It's a shame. It's a shame that you need to die."

West crept forward, right up to the bend in the tunnel as the woman spoke, hoping all the while she wouldn't dislodge any stones to give her position away.

"Do you want to know? Before you go? I've got a few minutes Billy, but no more. I feel like you deserve to know. After all we've been through. When you were born, Billy. When you were Ben, you had a sister. A twin sister. Do you remember that? Do you remember her?" Another pause.

"No? Well your Daddy killed her. That's what this is all about. He went mad. He murdered your sister. He drowned her. And he was right in the act of drowning you, too, when he got caught. It's all over the news, if only he'd let you watch it. That's why you came here. To Lornea Island. Your dad was trying to escape justice."

West flattened herself against the rock wall. She held her breath and risked a glance around the rock. She caught sight of a bizarre scene. The end of the cave was illuminated by flickering candles, creating an eerie light. In the center, a woman stood with a gun, casting obscene shadows on the rock walls. She had the gun pointed at a shape on the floor. It took West a moment to see what this was, but then she picked out a pair of eyes. It was the boy, Billy Wheatley, and something else, an adult body, slumped against the wall.

"It wasn't Dad." The voice was so quiet West almost didn't hear it.

"What?" The woman replied.

"It wasn't Dad."

It seemed the woman didn't hear Billy because she went on.

"Your Dad's a killer, Billy, a killer no different to me..."

"It wasn't Dad that hurt Eva."

The woman stopped what she was saying.

"He tell you that did he? Because he gave me the same bullshit story. He said he was framed. That your mom did it. She had postpartum depression or some bullshit excuse. He tried to explain it all away. How your mom's family were embarrassed about it, wouldn't let her see any doctors..."

"I said Dad didn't do that. I remember. It was mom. I remember it all."

There was a silence in the cave, only broken by the dripping of water from the roof somewhere. West found she was holding her breath again.

"That's a lie." The woman's voice rang out, angry now. *"You were too*

young to remember. You're just saying that because that's what he told you to say...."

"It not a lie. He didn't kill anyone." The boy's voice was clearer too. Defiant. *"It was Mom. She was singing while she did it. She'd been singing the whole day. That nursery rhyme, Row Your Boat. Only she wasn't singing it right. She was singing it like this."* The boy's voice broke into verse.

> *Row, row, row your boat,*
> *gently down the stream,*
> *Drown your babies in the lake,*
> *life is just a dream.*

"We were having a picnic by the lake and Mom wouldn't stop singing, even though it was making Eva cry. And then she picked her up and walked into the water. Eva was screaming and struggling but Mom just kept singing and smiling. And then she was pushing Eva under the water. I was strapped into my chair. I couldn't move. And then Dad turned up, with Uncle Paul. They stopped her but it was too late for Eva."

There was a moment of silence.

"Dad's not a killer. He's a good person. You're a killer. You're evil."

"Shut up."

Another silence, before the woman went on.

"Well, well, well. Maybe poor old Sam was telling the truth after all. He said to me your mum's family knew their reputation would never survive what happened so they blamed it all on him. He said they had friends inside the police. They had contacts. Power. They all closed ranks against him. He didn't stand a chance.

"But it doesn't change anything Billy. You know that don't you? The whole country believes Sam is a violent killer. When they find him in here, with you dead and Olivia Curran rotting away in the corner there. There's only one conclusion they can draw. I'd like to tell you otherwise. I'd like to say I'll clear your dad's name for you, but I can't. It doesn't fit with the plan you see. The only plan, once stupid Sam came knocking on my door. I'm sorry Billy. It's nothing personal, but we have to get back to business now. The tide's coming in Billy. It's coming in fast. It's time."

West felt her pulse climbing fast. She took a breath.

"No? Nothing? Nothing more to say? After all we've been through. I'm a little disappointed. Well goodbye Billy. Maybe I'll see you in the next life."

The woman straightened her arm, aiming the gun. But West was already moving. Her gun came up, too, and with her other hand, she switched on the flashlight, sending the powerful beam toward the woman.

"Armed police! Drop your weapon!" She screamed the words out in a voice that sounded terrifying even to her. But there was so much adrenaline surging through her, she barely felt in control of her limbs. She dropped automatically into a lower firing position, but as she did so, her front foot slipped out from underneath her on the slime-covered rocks. For a split-second, she fought to keep her balance as her foot skidded away, but in a sickening moment she knew her weight had gone too far. Her foot flew out in front and she slammed down onto the hard rock, her back hitting first. Her flashlight beam drunkenly slewed up to the roof then went out. She lost sight of the woman.

THE NEXT THING West saw was red-orange light splashing from somewhere in front of her, then the cave exploded with deafening noise. West heard the whistle of bullets, and fragments of rock flew past her ear. Then something hit her shoulder. It didn't hurt at all but it felt substantial, spinning her around like an angry shove, and knocking her back to the ground. It knocked her gun from her grip, too, and sent her flashlight flying so that the head of the light hit her in the face. There were more shots. More noise. A scream.

WEST KNEW at once she was hurt, already the pain was coming in waves, each more extreme than the last. She was still on her back on the wet floor. Gasping for air, shock coming on, but knowing the next few seconds would be her last if she didn't do something. She couldn't believe the element of surprise had been taken away so cruelly. She ordered herself to ignore the pain, and began feeling around the rock floor, desperate to find her gun. She splashed through pools of water blind; her eyes were still replaying explosions of red and yellow light. But somehow her senses had registered the direction the weapon had gone, and with an audible gasp of relief, her fingers reached it. She pulled it toward her, holding it in two hands now, pointing it wildly into the darkness. She swung around, her eyes now beginning to readjust to the gloom of the candlelight. She saw where the boy had been. He was gone. The woman too.

AND THEN SHE saw something else. Or rather she sensed it. A shadow, a figure behind her in the darkness. She tried to turn. To get her gun up, but she knew she was moving too slow. There was a noise, weird at first, as the micro-seconds played out. West felt like she had time to wonder what the woman was swinging at her, a rock? Her own gun? And how would it feel when it connected with her head? But there was no time. No time to move, no time to get her own gun up, much less to fire it. And then West felt something connecting hard with the side of her head, snapping back her neck. For a blinding moment, she felt the shock of it smash into her brain, but then she felt her legs go underneath her, and there was nothing she could do to keep consciousness.

75

When she came to, West saw a single pool of light. It took her a moment to work out what it was, then her brain forced it to make sense: a candle illuminating a crevice in the rock face. Surrounded by darkness. The effort of it made her head throb, and when she tried to move, lightning flashes of pain exploded from her shoulder. She cried out into darkness, her own shouts bouncing back at her from the walls. She let her head fall back on the rock floor and lay there panting loudly. She knew where she was, but something about it felt different. She couldn't understand what.

THERE WAS A NOISE. Then a blinding light burned into her face, she cried out again and screwed her eyes shut. She pulled her good arm in front of her face. There was nothing she could do now, no way to escape. Her mind presented her with how she must look. Lying broken on the floor. The woman standing above her, holding the gun, above it the flashlight blinding her against the darkness. Her finger squeezing against the trigger, her eyes empty. West barely had time to gasp before the bullet hit her. She could almost feel it cutting through the flimsy, hopeless protection her hand would offer, before it ripped through into her face.

"Are you alright?" a quiet voice asked her. It sounded quite wrong. Devoid of threat. West managed to quell her panic.

"Who's that?" she panted, a few seconds later, trying to push the light away.

"It's Billy," the voice replied. "I thought you were dead."

West fought to make sense of the wild inputs of information into her brain. The training she'd done kicked in. She remembered specific phrases, drills meant to help her focus on what was important, to allow unnecessary details to pass for now.

"Billy, the light. Don't shine it in my eyes," she said, and when he lowered the beam, she went on. "The woman with the gun. Where is she?"

"Emily? She went."

"Went? Where? Where did she go?"

"I don't know. She just went."

"When? How long ago? How long have I been unconscious?"

"I don't know. Not long. Half an hour maybe? A bit more." The boy's voice was quiet, calm but mournfully sad.

"Are you hurt?" West asked, struggling to sit up a little. The pain in her shoulder kicked in again, but it was manageable this time. "Did she hurt you?"

"No. I hid. When all that shooting started, I hid behind a rock. Down there somewhere." The boy pointed the flashlight out into the gloom, but the beam stopped where the chamber curved around. "She looked for me. She was real mad looking for me. But she couldn't stay long, because of the tide."

West's professional senses were still flooding her with information. With options. The need to assess and stabilize the situation she found herself in.

"The man on the floor. Your dad? Where is he? Is he..." She found herself stopping. Not wanting to say the word 'dead'.

"He's over there. She shot him." The boy's voice sounded tiny inside the blackness of the cave. She remembered, the noise that drew her inside the cave. The gunshot. Christ, that felt like a lifetime ago.

West fought to focus. Jamie Stone was dead. Not a priority. So what was important now? The whereabouts of the woman. She presented the danger. She was armed. An active killer.

"Where did she go?" She asked. "Where did Emily go?"

"To the ship. She had to get out before the tide came in. If you don't get out in time, you get trapped. Like we are."

Finally West understood. "The tide?" She remembered how, outside the cave's entrance, the waves had already reached the car's, tires. "We need to move. We need to move now." She struggled further to pull herself up, wincing as her shoulder gave way underneath her.

"We're already cut off," the boy said, deadpan and with no urgency. "The sea's already coming in. I went to look."

THAT WAS IT. That was what felt different. The noise - of the waves crashing into the rocks outside the cave - it was different now, to how it had been. Louder, and there was the sound of water moving inside the cave. And now that she looked, the floor was wetter. Not just from the pools of standing water, but there was flowing water on the floor. West struggled to her knees, sending more pain shooting back from her shoulder. She gasped and made an ugly, wounded noise.

"Are you going to die too?" the boy said now, his voice pure misery this time. "Are you going to leave me alone?"

WEST MADE a huge effort and got to her feet. As she pushed herself up she saw stars from the intensity of the pain, but she clenched her teeth until she was upright and the pain receded.

"No. I'm not going to die, and neither are you. We're going to find another way out." West took a few steps further into the cave, seeing through the gloom by the single remaining candle. The boy followed.

"There isn't another way. That's why she took us here. She told us it was to hide until she could get us onto the ship, but that was a lie. I started thinking it might be yesterday, but I didn't really know. It was all really confusing. I didn't know what to do. Then when we got here she started telling us all about it. Like she was proud. And then she shot Dad because he wouldn't drink the poison. It was in the coffee flask. But I wouldn't drink it because I don't like coffee and the hot chocolate was old..."

West fought to cut through the boy's words to what was important now.

"Wait. Then, we'll wait here. We'll stay here until the tide goes back down." Even as she said those words, West wondered if she would be able to do that. Her shoulder felt cold and useless. She still didn't know if the wound was a gunshot or a ricochet. And now she was standing, her head throbbed where it had been struck. She didn't know if she was losing blood.

"We can't do that," Billy said. "The barnacles go right to the roof of the cave. Look."

West didn't answer. But her eyes followed the beam of Billy's flashlight as he shined it up at the ceiling. He was right. There were different levels marked out on the walls, different zones populated by different types of life, but a few shells clung on, even at the highest parts of the roof. As Billy swung his beam around, West saw her own flashlight, and she reached down to pick it up. With the two beams, the cave felt slightly less threatening, the darkness less dense. But what it illuminated was more threatening than anything. From behind them, the ocean roared as it flowed in and out of the cave's entrance. The floor ran with seawater. West turned away from it for a moment, as if not looking could make their situation different. She saw the crumpled figure of Sam Wheatley, lying on one of the few remaining dry patches. She moved closer.

"THAT'S DAD. SHE SHOT HIM." Billy said, keeping close to her. He seemed to take care not to let his light fall upon the figure lying on the floor, but West swung hers down. She barely recognized the man who she'd last seen in the interview room. She crouched down and put a trembling hand to his throat, feeling for a pulse. There was no sense of hope, just the demands of procedure. She closed her eyes to concentrate, expecting to feel nothing, just a cold, clammy softness. But she felt movement, the throb of life.

"He's alive, Billy. Your dad's alive," she said. Even in their situation, it felt a relief to say the words. She reached out and pulled the boy to her. He didn't resist and she felt his small, frail body shaking against her. Then she put her head down and tried to think. The desire to delay, to consider the options, to rest a little, was so strong. But she heard the sound of another set of waves pouring into the cave entrance.

"BILLY, how deep was the water in the entrance, when you looked?"

"I dunno. There's a rock that you have to duck under. It's already beyond that, so we can't get out."

West remembered it: the rock she'd struck her head on. "Then we've got to move *right now*. We'll have to duck under it and swim out. You can swim, can't you, Billy? I bet you're a great swimmer aren't you, living here on an island?"

He didn't answer at first. When he did, his voice sounded more uncertain, sadder than ever.

"I can't swim in the sea."

West heard the words with a sense of growing disbelief. That was the last thing she needed to hear. She thought fast. He wasn't a big kid; in open water, she'd be able to carry him easily enough. How hard could it be to pull him through the cave entrance?

"I'll take you. Just trust me."

"But what about Dad? Please don't leave him here." She realized he was sobbing now.

There was a booming sound. West guessed what it must be: waves crashing into the entrance of the cave. If the waves were still hitting the entrance, it couldn't be that deep yet.

"We'll find a way, but we've got to move *now*. Hold the light on your dad." West set her own flashlight down and pulled off her top. She fed it underneath Stone's back and tied it as hard as her shoulder would allow against his stomach. Then she put the flashlight between her teeth and she slipped her arm beneath the man's shoulder. She began to pull. She almost stopped at once, the pain in her own arm was so intense, but she choked it back and tried again, managing at least to adjust his position. To her surprise, he moaned. He was conscious.

"Billy. Help me," she said.

The fact that the floor was both slippery and already awash with seawater helped and hindered them. It made it possible to move the weight of Jamie Stone's body, but only with repeated falls. Ignoring the pain in her shoulder, West kept trying, the boy helped, too, and together they succeeded in dragging him out from the back of the cave and into a wider area that was now knee deep with water. Here, it was easier. Although they kept stumbling, the man's body was fully afloat here, and she could pull him much quicker away from the end of the cave.

IT WAS EASY NOW to pull Stone through the water. But more of a challenge to keep his head above the surface. The water was getting deeper. Already, it was up to her waist. She could see Billy ahead of her, struggling as the surges came up to his chest. But where to go next, she didn't know, and her flashlight beam was zigging crazily around the walls and the roof.

"Show me the way out Billy. Show me where to go," she panted. She could hear him breathing hard behind the light. She reached down and gripped his father's shoulder again, lifting his head out of the water. There was almost no pain in her arm this time.

A rush of water flowed in against them. He shone the beam ahead of him, showing the way, but their way ahead became blocked. There was nowhere else to go. The water ahead was too deep and roof too low. Billy stopped. He held the flashlight above his head and let the angle from its beam drop until it played upon the moving water.

"It's through there. The only way out is through there."

West focused on the black water surging and retreating. She was up to her chest now, the boy almost up to his neck. The powerful current ebbed and flowed as waves pushed in and pulled back out.

WEST THOUGHT BACK to when she'd walked into the cave, an hour or less before. The roof had been low in one part, she'd had to duck. This must be where they were. But it hadn't been low for long. If they could just get under the restriction they'd be outside. Safe. They just had to get past this restriction – under the water.

"Billy, we're going to have to swim. You're going to have to hold your breath."

The boy didn't move.

You'll be OK, Billy. You can do this."

"No, I can't."

"Come on, Billy. It looks worse than it is. You just need to swim a short way. Please, Billy." West heard the desperation in her voice. She wondered if it was possible to swim out with the man, then come back for the boy. Or maybe she should do it the other way around. Whichever way would leave one or the other alone. Would she ever find them again?

"Billy, you've got to do this." For some reason, her mind conjured up a memory from her childhood. A young version of herself exhausted in the shallow end of the pool, her father shouting at her from the side. Just another length. Do it. You've got to do it. It was such a vivid memory she could even remember the way the warm water from the pool's pump would flow out against her body. With a jolt, she came back to the present.

SHE REALIZED HE WAS NODDING. Then his voice rang out, louder and clearer than she'd heard it before.

"Dad didn't do it. He didn't do any of it."

West had almost forgotten what Jamie Stone was accused of. It seemed irrelevant to the circumstances that she'd found him in.

"I know," she said.

"Not just Olivia Curran. Everything else people are saying. I was there. No one knows I know, but I remember. I remember..."

"Billy, I know. *I know.* But tell me outside. We'll tell everyone when we get outside. But you've got to come *now.* You can do this. Just duck under the ledge. It's a short swim. I'll be right behind you."

He shook his head, the flashlight shaking as he did so.

"I can't do it," he said. His light slipped an inch under the water, the beam turned the water from black to a deep green. It almost looked beautiful.

"You've got to do it. Do it for your Dad," West said.

76

The boy swayed in the darkness, the surges of water reached his mouth, causing him to splutter. Then he shook his head.

"No. I can't do it."

West fought the desire to scream at him. Every moment they delayed, the water got deeper, the distance they had to swim underwater grew longer, and the currents against them grew stronger.

"I can help you. I can help you do it Billy. But I can't do it for you."

"No."

"Billy, you either go now and live, or you die in here."

West's light played on Billy's face. She saw it crumple in misery. But this time he nodded at her. As she watched he gulped at the air. Then he nodded. He breathed again, and then he dived under.

For a second, West was so surprised he went she wasn't prepared to follow him. She saw his light sliding under the water toward the rock face. She almost panicked when she saw it dimming as it moved away from her. Then she snapped into action. She clamped her hand over Stone's face and took a deep breath of her own. Then she dived forward, keeping her eyes wide-open to follow the light.

UNDERWATER, the noise was horrible, a constant roaring, and she could see almost nothing – just a gleam of Billy's flashlight ahead of her. She failed to sink deep enough, and she felt her back and her arm scraping up and across the roof. She felt the man's body catch on the roof too. But she kept going, fighting to make progress against the water that flowed against her. Then it went dark as another wave struck. She felt herself sticking as the power against her increased. She began to panic, not knowing which way to fight toward. But Billy's light was a constant, guiding her onwards. She strained toward it, feeling how the air in her lungs was running low. She tried to tell herself to stay calm. She could swim up and down an Olympic swimming pool underwater, Dad saw to that. But this was different, much harder than she'd imagined. She smacked her head against the side and nearly cried out, losing a gulp of air as she did so. And then suddenly Billy's light disappeared. The burning in her lungs was doubled by a panic she couldn't control, but then she felt the flow against her reduce. The power of the waves was weakening, Billy must have made it out, and she couldn't be far behind. She made a final, desperate effort and felt herself scrape forward once again, still dragging Stone behind her. And then she broke the surface. Just for a second. She gulped at the air before another wave plunged over her. But it was enough to give her another burst of life, and she swam now, more strongly. There was no cave roof above her now. She saw the moon, still low in the sky, oblivious to the drama it was illuminating.

"Billy," she called, swimming away from the cliff face and looking around. Her feet touched bottom, there was firm sand underneath her feet. She looked up at the black cliff face. After the darkness of the cave's interior, the night felt almost like daylight. Immediately, she could see lights, on the cliff top and out to sea. Boats, she realized. A thudding sound hammered overhead. A helicopter.

Most of the lights were on the tiny strip of beach that still remained, at the foot of the cliff. There were people there, visible from their flash-lights. As she swam towards it, Stone's body began to spasm. She knew she had to get him out of the water. She released her grip from his mouth and nose. She fought her way through the water, willing the searchers on the shore to spot her. She called out to them, but every time water filled her mouth. Her shoulder throbbed from keeping him afloat.

"THERE!"

A spotlight from the beach shone onto her. A figure waded out into the water. Moments later she felt Rogers arms around her. She leaned into him. Whatever it was he was saying, she was too tired to hear. Too far gone to focus.

"Jess, are you OK? - I need some help here!"

Somehow she nodded.

"Christ," Rogers said. He began pulling her towards the shore as others came to help.

"We've got her," Rogers said. "Emily Franklin. We saw a car tearing back up the beach. She opened fire when we tried to stop her. But we've got her."

She nodded again.

"Is he alive?" Rogers took over pulling Stone's body. They were nearly at the beach now.

"I think so," West said, then the scene on the beach became more clear. Men with flashlights, shocked faces. "Where's the boy? Where's Billy?" Rogers hesitated. He shook his head. "He's not with us."

West stopped. "What? Didn't he come out? He was ahead of me."

Rogers hesitated again and West made a noise like a wounded animal. She turned around, looking around desperately at the dark boiling ocean. She realized she was still holding Jamie Stone's body. She pushed it over to Rogers.

"Here. Take him, get him ashore. I'm going back for the boy."

"No. It's too late," Rogers began, but she didn't hear him.

She dove back into the black water, towards the cave entrance.

77

When West regained consciousness, she was in bed in a private hospital room, her shoulder heavily bandaged and arranged in a hoist suspended from the ceiling. An ECG machine on her bedside tracked her heart rate with a soft rhythmic beep. A TV on the wall in front of her played silently. Outside the window, she could glimpse a city, she didn't know which one. By the foot of her bed, Detective Rogers lay asleep in an armchair; he'd pulled up a small plastic chair to raise his legs, and he was covered by a light blue blanket.

"Hey," West said, but her voice was so weak he didn't wake up. For a moment, she considered trying to shout louder, but her throat hurt. And she realized she didn't know how long he'd stayed awake. She didn't know how long she'd been here. Nor how she came to be here. Let him sleep, she thought. In search of some answers she picked up the TV remote control, which was sitting on her bedside cabinet. She tried to raise the volume on the TV, but the batteries weren't good. So instead, she threw the control at Rogers. It hit him in the chest and then clattered onto the floor.

"Hey," she said again.

Rogers awoke with a start, and then began to rub his face and yawn loudly. He blinked as he looked around, confused.

"What time is it?" he asked.

"I have no idea. What day is it?"

Rogers pushed the smaller chair away with his foot and sat up straighter in his armchair. He was wearing jeans and a sweatshirt that she didn't recognize. They didn't fit well.

"How are you feeling?"

West considered the question for a moment. "Groggy. My shoulder hurts. Where's the boy?"

Rogers hesitated, a frown on his face. "You don't remember?"

"Remember what?" A sense of dread filled West's mind. "Is he dead?"

Rogers' face changed. The frown turned to a kind of amused disbelief.

"No. Far from it. He's running around the station telling Lieutenant Langley how to conclude this investigation. No one can shut him up from all accounts."

This time West frowned, struggling to remember. "What happened?"

"You really don't remember?"

Fragments of it were already coming back to West. The crazed way she had worked her arms underwater, freed this time from the drag of pulling Stone's body with her. Ignoring the massive pain in her shoulder. "When you first tried to get out, he only got half way. He stopped in an air pocket." Rogers began, but she knew. She'd swum too fast. She hadn't taken the time to fill her lungs with air. She got inside the cave and felt her muscles begin to seize. Her lungs screaming. She was unable to resist rising to the top, but instead of finding the surface and cool air, there was just the blackness of rock. She fought it till the last, clawing her way forwards - no longer in search of the boy - now just in a desperate last fight to prevent her body sucking in salty water as it shut down. And then the air pocket. The boy's light. His frightened face. And then nothing.

"HE PULLED YOU OUT. God knows how the kid did it. I mean I've been down there. Had a look. It's not *that* far, but Christ. To swim through when it's filled with freezing water. In the dark. Christ. The kid's a god damn hero."

Rogers looked at her seriously.

"And so are you Detective. So are you."

"HOW ABOUT STONE. Did he make it?" West said a few moments later.

"He came out of surgery last night. The bullet somehow managed to miss anything vital. He lost a lot of blood though." Rogers shrugged. "Doc's think he'll make it."

West breathed a few times, the act of it hurting her throat still. "How about her? Emily Franklin?"

"We got her. Langley's with her now."

"I saw her threatening to shoot the boy. She was trying to frame Stone for Curran's murder. Set it up like a murder-suicide."

"We know. The boy's told us everything. There's still a few bits left to piece together, but it looks like she set up the whole relationship with Stone just to cover up killing Curran. Dumb schmuck had no idea what was going on." He raised his eyebrows.

"And what happened before? Billy's twin...?"

"That too. The guy doesn't have too much luck with women does he?"

West frowned.

"Christine Austin left a message on your answer phone. It was pretty confused but she was talking about when Eva Austin was murdered. She claimed responsibility. The Oregon State Police are with her now. And a psychologist who says may have been suffering from postpartum depression. They think her family might have covered up what really happened and blamed it on Stone. To protect their reputation. It seems your visit triggered something."

"No. It wasn't me. It was hearing about her son being alive."

"Well. Who knows. But you were the one that insisted on going to see her. Without that who knows how this would have ended?"

Rogers took his feet down from the chair. He rolled his neck around. Then he turned back to West and spoke a final time.

"IT'S NOT ALL good news. We recovered Olivia Curran's body from the cave." There was a moment of quiet in the room, when the only noises were the soft beep of the ECG, and the city sounds from outside.

78

I 'm sitting in the office of someone really important from the hospital. I'm wearing the clothes the hospital lady gave me. They're a little big for me, and they probably came from a dead person, but they're better than wearing the blue gown I was given first of all, so I don't mind. Detective Rogers is here with me. He let me sit in the big leather chair that swings round. I didn't like Detective Rogers much before because he's like a big bear. But actually, he's OK, although he does ask a lot of questions. That's what we're doing. What we've been doing for hours. Or it feels like hours. I've been telling him everything that happened inside the cave, and earlier, at Emily's house. He writes it all down. I can tell he believes me this time. He's really impressed too. Especially about the part when I swam through the cave entrance. I got stuck halfway in the high part. Then just as I was trying again the other detective got stuck there too so I pulled her out. It was just like when Dad took me surfing and I got pushed underwater by all the waves. I thought Dad was trying to kill me then, because I thought he'd killed Olivia Curran. But he wasn't trying to kill me. He was just trying to save me.

* * *

DETECTIVES ROGERS KEEPS BRINGING me candy and soda from the

machines in the hallway. I've got it all stacked up on the desk in front of me. Detective Rogers tells me that Emily is going to go to prison.

"Why do you think she did it?" I ask him. He stops writing and thinks about this for a while.

"It's early days, kid, but a lot of folk have come forward saying Ms. Franklin has had issues for a while now. Your Dad too, he says she made his life hell when he was dating her in secret. He was trying to break it off with her, but she kept threatening to tell you." He hesitates. "You ever see it yourself? You spent time with her."

I think for a bit. I picture Emily, leaning over my shoulder. Helping me with my science homework, telling me the teachers at school are kind of stupid, and I shouldn't listen to them.

"No," I say.

* * *

"Can I go in the helicopter again?" I say, a moment later. "When we go back to the island? I didn't really get to enjoy it the last time."

Detective Rogers shakes his head in a funny way but doesn't answer me. Then there's a knock on the door. A doctor comes in and tells Detective Rogers that Dad's awake again. He had to have an operation. To remove the bullet. I asked if I could keep it. As a souvenir. But they said the police would need it for evidence.

The doctor talks with Detective Rogers for a while, talking about how Dad's operation went. They both look happy enough.

"Can I see him now?" I say suddenly. The doctor hesitates. He looks at Detective Rogers.

"I don't have an issue with that. But you'll have to keep it short." He looks at Detective Rogers, who shrugs.

"OK by me."

Detective Rogers gets up and holds the door open for me. "Come on kid," he says.

* * *

Dad's lying in a bed. He's connected to lots of tubes and machines which beep every few seconds. He looks really white but he's got lots of stubble. I can see the top of his chest. Below that it's just bandages. Everything smells of antiseptic. When I come in, he turns his head to look at me.

"Hello, Billy," he says.

"Hi, Dad," I reply. Suddenly I feel really worried. I don't know where to look.

Dad looks away too. He glances over at Detective Rogers, and a look passes between them. Then his eyes come back to mine.

"They told me what you did. What Detective West did."

"They said I might get a medal. I might get my picture in the paper. Do you think I might get my picture in the paper? Do you think that might happen?"

"It might." Dad says.

"Is that going to be OK?" I ask. I remember how Dad doesn't like that sort of thing. He looks at Detective Rogers again, who clears his throat, and looks a bit embarrassed.

"All the charges against you have been dropped." Detective Rogers says it in his gruff voice. "Both here and over in Oregon. There's a hell of a mess to sort out still but..." He doesn't finish his sentence, just fades out.

"I guess it's OK then," says Dad.

I don't move.

"Billy. Come here, will you? Give me a hug."

I walk over to him slowly and put my arms around his shoulders. Only gently, but I can feel him flinch anyway.

"Are you OK Dad?" I suddenly feel a bit worried. I didn't really hear what the doctors were saying, I was a bit too excited. "Are you going to die?"

Slowly Dad begins to smile. "I don't think so kiddo."

But I'm worried now. I feel my eyes begin to prickle like when you're about to cry.

"Is everything going to be OK?" I say. I can't help myself now. I'm properly crying.

"Yeah." Dad says. He pulls me closer and holds me tight. It feels good. I cling onto him.

"I think so. I think we're going to be OK."

A SHORT MESSAGE FROM THE AUTHOR

Hello!

Thank you for reading *The Things you find in Rockpools* and I really hope you enjoyed it. I certainly enjoyed writing it, especially the character of Billy. He's my favourite character to date.

If you did enjoy it, I'd be so grateful if you could leave a short review on Amazon (and anywhere else). Reviews make a huge difference to authors in their struggles to gain visibility. It's easy to do, just visit the book's Amazon page and follow the links to leave a review. Thanks!

As I write this note I'm about halfway through my next novel. It's currently called *The Girl on the Burning Boat* (working title - it might change). It's another psychological thriller, this time set around a very wealthy British businessman, his family, and his shady connections to politics and power. This one has a very big twist built in from the start. I'd love to keep you up to date on its progress, and I offer all my new releases at a discount to people on my mailing list. You can sign up by visiting my website www.greggdunnett.co.uk

Thank you again for reading. I really appreciate it. 😊

Gregg Dunnett, Feb 2018

THE WAVE AT HANGING ROCK

Natalie, a young doctor, sees her perfect life shattered when her husband is lost at sea. Everyone believes it's a tragic accident. But a mysterious phone call prompts her to think otherwise. She sets out on a search for the truth.

Jesse, a schoolboy, is moved half way around the world when his father is blown up in a science experiment gone wrong.

Two seemingly unconnected tales. But how they come together will have you turning the pages late into the night. And the twist at the end will leave you reeling.

The Wave at Hanging Rock is the debut novel from British author Gregg Dunnett. With over a quarter of a million downloads it became an Amazon bestseller and was shortlisted for the Chanticleer Award for Best Mystery or Suspense novel of the year. It is now available as an audiobook and has been translated into Russian and Spanish.

Available now on Amazon and in print

THE DESERT RUN

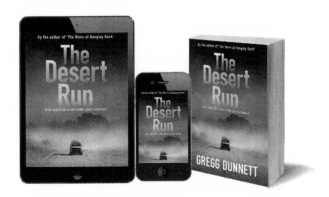

Newly-graduated Jake has a money problem, a job problem, and a girlfriend problem too. But his best friend has the perfect plan to fix all three. It draws upon all they've learnt in their Economics degree: Supply and Demand. With a bit of statistics in there too: The odds of getting caught are vanishingly small. Or should be.

So how does Jake end up about to be arrested with enough dope to put him inside for twenty years? And why, when it finally happens, is this only his second biggest worry?

Can they somehow escape? How exactly did they get there?

And what's really on Jake's mind..?

The Desert Run is a gripping and page-turning thriller with plenty of twists you won't see coming. It celebrates what it's like to be young, to make mistakes, and to feel the call of adventure just a little too strong.

Available now on Amazon and in print.

ACKNOWLEDGMENTS

Before I began writing books I used to read the acknowledgement pages of novels and wonder what all those people actually did. Now I'm a little more experienced I'm beginning to understand. By spending long hours in front of a computer I'm now able to muddle together a place, a cast of characters, and the outlines of a plot, but it takes many long - and probably frustrating discussions with the people closest to me - to help shape that into a finished story. I'm incredibly lucky to have a very supportive partner who puts up with me going on and on about each book. I'm also able to judge just how gripping each story really is by how long she's able to read it before falling asleep. Thanks Maria. :-)

I never really used to know what editors did either. I'm grateful to Marcia Trahan for her work pulling this story into shape, but also my family - especially my brother Jono, who took time out from his expedition around Europe, to deliver 419 comments and suggestions for improvement on the 'finished' manuscript (I counted them). He also drew the map at the beginning, or rather borrowed it from its more familiar place in the Bristol Channel.

It then takes another group to take the finished story, smooth out the final rough edges and hunt down the typos like the vermin they clearly are. I had a fantastic group of beta readers this time around, and it's incredibly valuable, not least as I'm able to put the book out knowing that it's as near to error-free as it can be. Therefore a massive thank you to (in no particular order): Elaine Palmer, Pippa Morgan, Pete Tommo, Leah Finch, Keith Smith, Brad Hogan, Debbie Randolph, Louise LaRocque, Liz Bilcliffe, Jean Ward, Leah Gould, Pamela Sorrels, Lorraine Falconer, Laura Scott, Stephanie Curtis, Caroline Radway, Christine Ryder, Ronald Eden, Lesley Ford, & Chris Toase.

I hope I haven't missed anyone out - If I have I'm very sorry, but I really do appreciate it!

And last but not least, thanks to Grubby the dog, for making me take him out on thinking walks, and keeping my feet warm under the desk.

ABOUT THE AUTHOR

Gregg Dunnett is a British author writing psychological thrillers and stories about travel and adventure, usually with a connection to the coast or to the oceans. Before turning to novels he worked as a journalist for ten years on a windsurfing magazine, briefly owned a sailing school in Egypt, taught English in Thailand, Portugal, Turkey and Italy, taught sailing in Greece and Spain, and also had several rather duller jobs along the way.

His brother is the adventurer Jono Dunnett who in 2015 windsurfed alone and unsupported around the entire coastline of Great Britain, and who is currently windsurfing around the coastline of Europe.

Gregg lives in Bournemouth on the south coast of England with his partner Maria. They have two young children, Alba and Rafa, for whom the phrase "Daddy's working" has absolutely no effect.

Gregg's debut novel was an Amazon top 100 best seller in the UK and was downloaded over a quarter of a million times across the world.

Gregg on why he writes:

"I've always wanted to do two things in life, to write, and to have adventures. When I was a kid I imagined grand affairs. Kayaking across Canada, cycling to Australia. Whole summers in the Arctic. Did it happen? Well, partly.

I've been lucky, I spent some years abroad teaching English. I worked in sailing schools in Greece and Spain. I really lucked out with a job testing windsurfing boards for the magazine I grew up reading. I made a questionable decision (OK, a bad decision) to buy a windsurfing centre on the edge of the Sinai Desert. I've also done my fair share of less exciting jobs. Packing and stacking potatoes on a farm, which got me fitter than I've ever been in my life. A few years in local government which taught me that people really do have meetings that result only in the need for more meetings, and they really do take all afternoon. I spent a pleasant few months in a giant book warehouse, where I would deliberately get lost among the miles of shelves unpacking travel guides and daydreaming. I've done a bit of writing too, at least I learned how to write. *Boards* Magazine isn't well known (it doesn't even exist today) but it did have a reputation for being well written and I shoe-horned articles in my own gonzo journalism style on some topics with the most tenuous of links to windsurfing. But the real adventures never came. Nor did the real writing.

Then, in 2015, my brother announced he was going to become the first person to windsurf alone around Great Britain. I don't know why. Apparently it was something he'd always wanted to do (news to me.). It was a *proper* adventure. It was dangerous, it was exciting. Before he even set off he got on TV, in the papers. Some people thought he was reckless, some thought he was inspirational. Lots of people thought he'd fail.

But he didn't. He made it around. He even sailed solo from Wales to Ireland, the first to make the crossing without the aid of a safety boat. I was lucky enough to be involved in a superficial planning level, and take part in a few training sails, and the last leg of the trip. But he did ninety nine percent of it on his own. One step at a time, just getting on with it. That was quite inspiring.

In a way it inspired me to pull my finger out. I'd been writing novels - or trying to write novels - then for a few years. But it was touch and go as to whether I was going to be one of those 'writers' with a half-finished novel lost on a hard drive somewhere, rather than someone who might actually manage to finish the job.

I've now got two lovely, highly demanding children, so real adventures are hard right now. I still try to get away when I can for nights out in the wilds rough camping, surf trips sleeping in the van, windsurfing when the big storms come. I love adventures with the kids too.

I hope in time to get around to a few real adventures. I want to sail across an ocean. I want to bike across a continent. I definitely want to spend more time surfing empty waves.

But for me, for now at least, the real adventures take place in my mind. In my real life I'm too chained-down with the mortgage to travel the world at the drop of a hat. But when I'm writing I'm totally free. When I write, that's me having an adventure."

For more information:
www.greggdunnett.co.uk
hello@greggdunnett.co.uk

[f]

Made in the USA
Middletown, DE
04 June 2018